PLEASURE ISLAND

The Chronicles of Lidir

PLEASURE ISLAND

A Saga of Erotic Domination

Aran Ashe

Nexus

First published in Great Britain in 1992 by
Nexus
338 Ladbroke Grove
London W10 5AH

Copyright © Aran Ashe 1992

Typeset by TW Typesetting, Plymouth
Printed and bound in Great Britain by
Cox & Wyman Ltd, Reading, Berks.

ISBN 0 352 32817 7

A catalogue record for this title is available
from the British Library

To Sun, Sea, Sand
            (And Slaves)

CONTENTS

[1]

A Shortfall of Doves

It was the kind of late spring day that should have gladdened every heart. The ship was small, but strong. She had braved the storms around the cape and now she raced the whitecaps steadily homeward across the sparkling turquoise sea. Flying high above her, beating steadily like a giant tethered snake, was a magnificent royal banner of heavy red braid adorned with golden sunbursts and flashes of splendent blue. It had withstood the vicious storm winds totally unscathed. That too should have been an omen of good fortune.

But on the quarterdeck, the Prince of Lidir stood unmoving, and below him, every man seemed turned to stone. All eyes were fixed aloft, watching the single tiny figure clamber up into the crow's nest, then shade his eyes and stare out far ahead.

Below deck, in the great cabin, another figure stirred. She was unaware of the tension up above, of the way her destiny was being moulded to the fickleness of fate. Languidly she drew the tousled covers aside, then knelt up on the bed, then stretched her smooth nude soft-skinned body. Silken tongues of copper hair snaked down across her shoulders; spun gold gleamed in her underarms as her scent caressed the air. When she raised her chin, her perfect face was lit by softened light. Fine freckles lay like tiny jewels upon her cheeks. Her eyelids were half closed; she was relaxed.

Then suddenly she turned and looked towards the door, as though an apparition had entered to challenge her very presence on this scene, as though spectres from her past were haunting her. And for a second, her confidence faltered. Her eyes opened wide and dark, like the eyes of a startled doe. Anya trembled, and those old fears overtook her.

Can a slave become a princess? If fate decrees it, it is in her

1

gift, as sure as limpid eyes are windows to the soul, as sure as winsome ways can melt a young girl's heart. But that gift, once promised, can just as surely be rescinded.

Anya knew this. Yet she knew her Prince was true. Her fingertips stroked the sheets where he had lain, traced the line of the folds, touched the smooth dried satin spillage, and now she smiled as she remembered last night – the way she had urged him onward, pursuing her pleasure, torturing him with wanting in the way that lovers do. Then in the end, that second time, she had just held him, not releasing his flesh, but touching him, kissing him with her open belly while the warm milt dripped between her fingers to the silk.

Two decks above her, in the open air, the Prince allowed his gaze to lower. His calm green eyes moved round, taking in the helmsman's iron grip upon the tiller, and beside him, the captain, ashen-faced and intent. The Prince knew it boded ill. Looking forward now, beyond the anxious men, he saw his lieutenant – the only man who moved down there – examining the two small cannon on the foredeck. The Prince's heart sank; they seemed so feeble. Then he stared out again at the ship on the horizon. It seemed to be growing larger – it was swinging round, turning broadside on. He needed no lookout now to tell him. But as the terrible confirmation at last was shouted from above – that one word, striking fear into every heart, even the Prince's, though his eyes would never show it – two things happened at the same time. A row of tiny puffs of smoke arose to cloud the tall ship in the distance, and a hooded figure emerged from below deck and came up the stairs towards him.

'Pirates!' came the heart-stopping cry. It was followed by the sound of rippling, distant cannon thunder.

The figure froze. Her head lifted, and in the second before she turned to see the waterspouts bar the way ahead, the Prince's cool green gaze was melted by the look of terror in that beautiful, innocent face.

'Anya . . .' But before he ran to her to take her in his arms, he whispered quickly to the man beside him. 'Captain – they must not reach us; they must not be allowed to board.'

The captain glanced at the young girl on the stairs, then set his jaw and nodded grimly. He strode forward and placed both hands upon the rail above the maindeck. At the first command of that powerful voice, the ship was transformed. The men of stone suddenly came alive. They were filled with purpose, scurrying across the decks, hauling down the red and gold royal pennon, breaking out cutlasses, pikes, longbows and arrows, then starting to hoist the cannon aft while the helmsman and his mate strained to bring the ship hard round.

But on the stairs, it was the slender figure's turn to stand immobile. The Prince of Lidir placed his arm very gently about her shoulder and led her away from the hubbub and towards the starboard rail. He did not speak, for he could not find the words to say. He could only look into that perfect face – the olive eyes; the pupils, wide and black as night now; long hair of copper fire; the gentle freckling on her cheeks; her lips, so warm and trembling – as her cool slim fingers reached to brush against his cheek and to touch his earlobe gently.

'My lord,' she whispered, 'I am afraid.'

'Shh . . .' He kissed those warm lips softly, repeatedly. He wanted time to stand still for the two of them now, while he held her to his breast and breathed the soft warmth of her skin. 'You must not fear – this ship is fast; she will outrun them.' And yet, as he looked out above her at the ship that had taken up the pursuit, he saw that it now looked even larger. He could see the row of gun ports down one side and the chilling emblem flying from her mast: the horned black goblin on a blood-red base was the flag of a pirate slaver.

Suddenly she turned and saw this image too, then buried her face once more against his chest.

The Prince felt desperation welling up inside him. He gripped the hilt of his sword. But as the minutes ticked away, he felt only more helpless. His ship had earlier moved so fast, but now it seemed so sluggish. What were these sailors doing? They were supposed to be a hand-picked crew. Exasperated, he shouted across the quarterdeck: 'Captain! Why do we make so little headway?'

'But Sire, we are against the wind now, and a fresh wind at that. We have to tack across it – as they do too.'

'Then why are they gaining ground?'

The captain shook his head, then sighed in resignation. He looked steadfastly at the Prince. 'They have the sail, Sire. And to bring her round so quickly, they must have the men. I have but a dozen sailors – and your guard.' At that moment, the harness about the cannon broke and it crashed to the deck. The captain sighed again. 'Good men. Alas, they are not seamen.'

The Prince spoke more softly: 'I was hasty, captain . . . I know you do your best. And I have not forgotten the valiant way you brought about our rescue. I will never forget that.'

He was interrupted by the lieutenant running up the stairs.

'Sire,' he shouted. 'A cracked pulley block, no more – the cannon will be reinstalled. The men are ready.'

The Prince took heart from the resolve in the young man's face. He had seen that look before, when, injured and on the ground, he had watched this man single-handedly beat back three Surdic swordsmen. The Prince slowly clapped the young man on the shoulder and took hold of the captain's hand. 'Lieutenant . . . Captain . . . I could not wish for better men by my side.'

The lieutenant's pale blue eyes narrowed. 'Whatever befalls this day, Sire, they shall not prove us milk-bellies.' Then he glanced uneasily towards the young woman, who had been listening but now had turned to watch the enemy ship approaching. His voice fell to a whisper: 'Sire – the Lady Anya . . . I fear that we must guard against the worst.' The Prince bit his lip, then nodded. The lieutenant turned and gave an instruction to one of the soldiers, who hurried down below.

The Prince returned to comfort his betrothed. The hood of her cape was down now and her long red hair flowed in the breeze. Together they stared out across the sea, at the ship steadily tacking across behind them. It seemed so quiet now, yet somehow even more menacing than when it had fired upon them. The Prince prayed for something – a sea mist, even a storm – anything that might grant them some respite. Faint hope it was, he knew, against that fresh spring day.

At last, she spoke. 'It is as if they were waiting for us.'

'No. They are opportunists – vagabonds of the sea. It is chance that they are here.' Then his gaze was distracted by

4

two seabirds floating down to alight upon the stern rail. His eyebrows knitted in a frown.

She turned and stared at them. The Prince was lost in thought now. Something about the arrival of those birds was troubling him. Her voice became less steady: 'My lord . . .' She looked at him. 'What if the pirates should board this ship?'

'No . . .' But he looked away, at the birds again. It forced her to persist:

'Their ship is large. The captain said that they are many; we are few . . .'

He tried again to reassure her: 'But we carry little coin – no treasure. They are interested only in gold and jewels and . . .' Their eyes met; suddenly, his mind went blank.

'And me?' she whispered faintly.

He put his finger to her lip. 'Shh . . . Do not say it. I will never let it happen.' And then, as he touched the softness of her cheek, he remembered the doves – six white doves, released two days ago, as they rounded the cape. They were ringed with the royal braid – a signal of his homecoming. But this time, the doves had also carried a message: *The Princess of Lidir is coming home.* The blood drained from his face. Could it be? Again he looked at the gulls, taking flight now after their rest, and again the Prince felt helpless, sinewless, caged upon this ship; how he wished he had his feet on solid ground.

'Sire?' The lieutenant stood behind him with a small bundle of clothing. 'Sire – it is better that the Lady Anya goes below now. On deck, there is the chance she could be seen.' He nodded in the direction of the pursuing ship. Then he spoke to the young woman; his voice was subdued and his tone encouraging: 'My lady, please take these; put them on – as a precaution.' As she reached uncertainly to take the cabin boy's suit and cap, the lieutenant looked upon her gentle face, so very pale now, framed by the soft red hair.

The Prince paced the length of the great cabin again, then hesitated at the stern windows and looked out at the ship that had dogged them so relentlessly. But now it seemed to be hanging back, as if toying with them – it could easily have outrun them long ago. Perhaps the pirates were afraid to come within cannon range: they could not know that his ship had but two small guns.

Then he saw a flurry of activity on the deck of the enemy ship. Something was being roped to the mainmast. Wooden beams were being carried and hoisted upright on the port side – it could only mean that a boarding would be tried. But again, something was being fastened to the beams. Was it some weapon – bundles of sacking they might set alight?

'Sire . . .?' The soft voice made him turn and the vision salved the torment in his mind. She was kneeling up on the bed, half turning towards him. Draped limply on her arm was the final linen undergarment she had only just removed. Her body was illuminated in a soft creamy light diffused upwards from the ruffled sheets. The Prince remembered last night – the way she had tantalised him so deliciously with her fingertips, lips and tongue, the way she had pursued her pleasure tirelessly on into the morning. And now she looked at him again with languid eyes.

'Sire . . .?' She placed the linen garment down beside her and took up the dark blue tunic top. Light touches of her hands smoothed the densely woven material; every movement that she made spoke sensuality. Slender fingers slipped into the sleeve, then opened out the jacket, straightened it and caressed the interior, gently brushing, assessing it as if it were a lover's skin. Nervous fingertips tested the ornate brass walnut-shaped buttons, traced the edges of the collar, the tight, silk-lipped pockets – slipping within them – then stroked again across the surface of the lining. And all the while, as Anya examined this uniform, her body moved – smooth lithe movements, so innocent, yet so very sexual. When she reached, and her body rotated forwards as she balanced on her knees, the hollows of her underarms would deepen and her tight full breasts would sway and lift. Her back, narrowing so deliciously from the hips, would form a perfect downsweep furrowed by a backbone supple enough to tempt a tongue to paint it from the shoulderblades to the tip. And the temptation would progress further. Her thighs would tense, the rounded buttocks would rise, then separate slightly as she settled down again upon her upturned feet. Each time she rocked, peeping between those

6

lifted, separating, rounded cheeks, was the gently bulging fleshy pouch – a twin fruit, with a fine infold of potential cleavage to tempt that tongue to make the split and to taste the salt-fruit moistness which was dusted very lightly by the soft bright curls of fire.

'Sire . . .?' Anya reached and rested upon her elbows while she adjusted the belt. Her back arched down until her smooth round belly almost touched the ruffled sheets. And still the Prince of Lidir had not answered. He could not, for he was waiting for the gap to close, for her supple back to bend that little more, like a longbow drawn to its final curve of tension before the arrow is unleashed. He was waiting for the tight skin of her belly to stroke against the heaped-up silken sheet.

'Sire . . .?' Anya sat up again and lifted her hair away from her densely freckled shoulders. The shoulder blades slid smoothly beneath her skin and almost touched. She turned to face him fully. The Prince waited. Anya placed her hands upon her hips and the wing muscles tightened from her shoulders to her breasts. Deep, delicious hollows opened underneath her arms. She raised her head; her elbows moved back and her nipples pointed upwards. They were black. Her breasts were milk white but her nipples were velvet black, and large, with no surround, as if a velvet-coated acorn had been fitted to each tip. She was sitting on her heels again with her slim thighs apart. Below her belly was the bush of soft red curly hair and the curls were slightly parted. The satin lips projected starkly – matt black against the red curls, inky black against the whiteness of the fold of sheet which pressed them to one side. As she breathed, her belly lifted and the pure black gently moved against the sheet.

'Sire? Why do you not answer? Come to me.'

But now, he did answer. He knelt beside the bed, looked up into the dark pools of her eyes and he could smell her scent of almond oil and butter. 'I love you – as I have never loved another,' he said.

Anya took his face in her hands. Her fingertips stroked his hair. She kissed him. He sucked upon her soft lips. Her small tongue pushed into his mouth. His hands moved over the smooth skin-coated shoulderblades and down the warm slim

7

back, and tickled, making the belly curve towards him. He touched her belly; then his fingers slipped between the silken sheet and her open thighs. The black and satin skin felt hot and soft. Her tongue pushed deeper into his mouth, assenting, touching against his own. His fingertips searched out that other tongue between those other lips. She murmured as he gently split its fleshy sheathing. He used his fingertips to kiss that small moist tongue and to milk it very gently. Anya lifted. He slid one hand beneath to touch the skin within the groove, which became deeper and warmer as she edged her thighs apart until his little finger touched the inswirl of her bottom. It felt like very fine twisted velvet. The other hand held her sex lips open, nipped the bud and made it slip.

Still the kiss continued. Her neck craned forward; he could feel her warm breath coming quickly through her nose. His lips closed about her tongue and sucked; her thighs began to move; he could feel her sex lips pressing moistly about his fingertips while he milked her, pumping the tiny tip up hard until it could not be retracted. It remained pushed out like a small hard ball which touched the backs of his fingers as he brushed them up and down the soft skin pouch. Finally, she pulled away from his embrace, but he would not release her. He held her hips while he took the black and fleshy nipple tips to his mouth and sucked them until they hardened and became wet. As he sucked she arched back tighter until he was sucking the undersides of her breasts, then sucking her belly, then tracing the fine line of downy hair below her navel until she was arched back with her shoulders to the bed and her feet still tucked beneath her and the soft fine downy hairs that he kissed were replaced by wiry curls.

His lips moved downwards, teasing the bright red curls upon the soft skin pouch, exposing the warm dark fleshy lips and the hard projecting bud. He breathed warm air upon her, then drank the aroma of her flesh, the strong warm scent of earth and ocean. He brushed his lips against her. The outer skin of her sex lips felt dry, yet smooth and slippy, and swollen. When he brushed those lips to the side, they slowly rolled back, pulsing very slightly, swelling fuller than before. He nuzzled her and pressed his lips against her where her sex lips joined

8

her body. He nipped them gently with his teeth. He dusted his lips with Anya's body scent. He lifted her legs and lowered her hips, then bent her knees, exposing her bottom and rocking her very gently while he stroked it with his thumb. Then he pressed his lips to her sex and pushed. She whimpered as her sex lips split. He tasted earth and ocean. He formed his lips into a tiny collar for the small hot tongue of pleasure to slip between. Then he sucked upon it as Anya, with her knees bent tight enough to touch the sides of her breasts, pressed her hands upon the bed to push her bottom up to meet him. And as her belly tightened to a ball, he held her bud of pleasure locked tightly between his tongue and upper lip and he stroked his thumb across the entrance to her bottom. He used this light stroke of his thumb alone to bring about her pleasure, for each brush, or simply the pressure of the thumbpad in so intimate a place, forced her belly to contract, and his lips to tighten round her bud, until at last she tried to lift her knees and bring her legs together round his head. He sat up quickly, opened her legs, returned her knees to the sides of her breasts and slowly stroked her open moistness with his fingers until the soft gasps gave way to moans of pleasure overdue, whereupon he bent to press his lips against her sex. That first touch tripped her; he breathed upon her gently, drinking her aroma again, as he held her sex lips fully open while she spasmed with delight.

Then he unbuttoned his breeches, allowed his rigid cock-stem to spring forth and, placing his palms beneath her buttocks, lifted her on to his stem and pushed until he would slip no further into the tightness of her warmth, until the underside of his cockhead, deep inside her, had touched against something hard. And, turning with her until they lay upon their sides, with Anya totally nude and himself still dressed, but with his cockstem clothed within her living flesh and her bare body moving against the close wool of his jerkin, he kissed her, pressed her tightly to him, closed his hands around her buttocks once again – one buttock fitting perfectly into each palm and cupped like an individual hard round fruit, while those fruits somehow seemed to knead his cockstem from inside, as Anya's legs began to move alternately, and the fruits independently in his hands. His fingertips sought the groove, touched the open earth, while the hard flesh knot inside her kept plucking against the end of his cock as if trying to spear him – as if the tip of her backbone deep inside was trying to spear his cockhead like a squirming fish that jumped and thrashed within an oily sea. And then he felt it pierce him – though he tensed and held his breath, he could not stop the swelling ball of pressure deep inside, then the bursting and the thick and lumpy milt being drawn out through his spine. But those perfect buttocks just kept undulating smoothly, squeezing independently of his tense, abated breathing and forcing him onwards, pricking him repeatedly with that hard bone deep inside and drawing every drop of fluid from his body, making him die slowly, drown deliciously, enveloped in her warmth, intoxicated by her scent of almonds, earth and ocean.

'Sire – these clothes. You wish that I should put them on now?'

Anya was sitting up beside him. Her words had shaken him completely from the sweet bed of his dreams. She had tried to sound confident, but her voice had been unsteady. Then their gaze met and the Prince of Lidir saw a fleeting vision in her eyes and it pierced him to the quick. It was a spectre of a goblin and a portent of the fate of precious doves.

[2]

Amongst the Pigs and Pickles

'You will be safe here. Open the door to no one – whatever you hear. Trust me. I will return for you – I promise.' Those had been her Prince's parting words before he kissed her for the last time. And now Anya was on her own. But how long would she have to wait here, and what if something were to go wrong and prevent him from returning? She looked down again at the uniform she had been forced to wear and her cabin boy's cap fell off. It had done this twice already. She picked it up and pulled it on again, but with her hair tied up, it would not fit properly. And the tunic was too tight. Her breasts hurt from the way it buttoned so tightly. Then the trousers were the wrong shape for her hips. She knew she must appear foolish in this outfit: nobody would ever take her for a boy.

She looked around to see whether there might be a mirror here. In the half-light filtering through the porthole, she could make out barrels and sacks and boxes. She could smell dried fish and vinegar and cheese, and there was a sweet aroma too, like that of apples. There were sides of bacon hanging from the ceiling. This place must be the pantry. She was about to investigate when, without warning, the ship shook with a jarring thud which made her stumble to her knees, then with a crash which sent her sprawling. Her cap rolled across the floor and was crushed by a falling barrel. Suddenly, all the order in the cabin was gone; there were boxes everywhere, still falling. And there were more thuds, seeming to come through the floor; she could feel them thump against her body. She was sure the ship had struck rocks. A shelf support broke; jugs of vinegar shuffled to the end then crashed down, narrowly missing her feet. She twisted round and covered her

11

head with her arms. A side of meat shook free, fell diagonally across her and lodged against the wall. Then there was a deafening bang very close by and she realised what it was.

The cannonade had begun; the Prince had warned her this might happen. He had told her to stay away from the porthole, but he hadn't prepared her for this. She heard shouting, then screams. Now she was petrified. There was another bang, of bursting planking, and the ceiling shattered; giant splinters angled downwards through the dust cloud and deep into the room. The terrible cries came louder, against a background of moans. There were three more thuds in quick succession, then nothing more seemed to happen. Anya heaved the carcass of the pig aside, crawled over the sacks of peas and through the toppled boxes and managed to reach the door. With her eyes shut tight, she crouched behind it, coughing from the dust, and waited. It began again. This time, she heard the salvo being fired, then two loud splashes in the water, then one direct hit aft, then two others somewhere above her. She curled up tight, with her hands around her ears to try to keep at bay the pitiful sounds of newly splintering wood. Every impact caused the ship to shudder. But why had she heard no cannon fire being returned? All she heard were the cries of dismay, the sounds of running feet and the agonised creaks and groans of slowly yielding timbers high above. The rigging came crashing to the deck and splashed into the water. How long could the ship survive this punishment? Suddenly, the cannonade ceased a second time and all the shouting stopped.

For many minutes, Anya was afraid to move, though the ship now seemed quite steady. She could hear the waves lapping against its timbers. The room was littered with fallen crates, spilled apples, split pigs and pickled cabbage. But Anya was unhurt. Slowly, she got up. Was the danger past? Was her Prince safe? Why had he not come to get her? What if he were injured? She tipped a box of dried fish out of the way and put her ear to the door but she could hear nothing.

She waited – still no sound could be heard – then tried the door. It was stuck. Surely he would never have locked it? Again she tried it, but it would not move. Perhaps the frame had twisted? She tugged the handle of the latch with all her might, but still to no avail. She was trapped in here and her fear was turning to panic. She clambered back over the debris towards the porthole, then stopped in her tracks. There were footfalls and agitated whispers from above, and shouts, but distant shouts; they seemed to come from outside, across the water. She climbed up a stack of tumbled crates and warily peered outside. What she saw there made her gasp.

Beyond the floating wreckage of the topsail, and sweeping silently towards them, was the great ship, so large it overshadowed their own. Her bows were painted to look like the mouth of a vicious saw-toothed sea beast. Flying high above the deck was the sinister black and red emblem. For the first time, Anya could see the detail of the wicked image upon this flag. It was a bristle-haired humpbacked goblin and its eyes glowed evil green – they seemed to stare straight down at Anya, as if the monster could see her hiding place. Between the evil icon's legs was a grotesque black barbed cockstem, sticking upwards and pointed like an arrow. As the flag flapped in the breeze the creature seemed to leer at her and thrust out its lower belly. She would not look at it again. Her gaze lowered and now her heart leapt to her throat. Fastened to the mainmast was a naked woman – not a painting nor a statue but a living woman, bound and gagged. What manner of creatures would do this thing to her? Then she saw another prisoner, and another; the ship was full of slaves. Each mast had a naked woman fastened to it. A fourth woman was slung below the bowsprit. Amid the brightly coloured throng of pirates seething at the rail were other women, secured at intervals to upright wooden beams.

Anya now understood the reason for the lack of retaliation from her own ship. No gun could have been fired without injuring these women. Each mast was protected by an innocent. The women spaced along the rail were there to protect the men – cruel men, to hide behind defenceless, tethered women. It made Anya's heart beat faster; she bowed her head from fear of what such men might do to her if she were caught. She had been a slave; she knew that they would never show her any mercy.

And now, as the great ship drew nearer until it dwarfed

their own, Anya, frightened yet unable to prevent her eyes from bearing witness to this awesome scene, could see the evil glee on those pirates' faces and the terror on the faces of the gagged and tethered women, in fear for their lives. Her heart went out to them; they could not know that her Prince would never allow his men to endanger any women, but would rescue them if he could and then vanquish these cruel beasts – burn their flag and mayhaps sink their ship and bring them back in chains to Lidir – and punish them in the kitchens and the dungeons. Her Prince would have some plan, she was certain. At least, she hoped and prayed he would, for now the ship had almost come alongside.

She could see the women clearly – some were blonde and pale-skinned, others golden or dark, and there was one whose body appeared entirely bound in chains. It made Anya shudder; it made her wonder what might happen to these women after the battle. Would they be shared amongst the men for their pleasure and reward?

When the first grappling irons were flung across and bit into the woodwork and the belly-tightening screams of the attack went up, Anya backed down from the porthole, crouched beneath it and hid her head. She wanted to keep as far away as possible from the door.

The cries came louder. Now she could hear the clash of swords and the screams of pain, then many stampeding feet above. Frightening shrieks were followed by splashing sounds, as of men being tossed into the water. She covered her ears again. The stampeding sound was now below her, in the hold. She knew the defenders were losing. There were doors and hatches banging, as if a frenzied mob was raging through the ship. The footfalls came louder, nearer, on the same level. A door banged in the next room. There were shouts and laughter, the sound of bottles breaking, then muttered curses, thuds and cries. It sounded like several men, their voices coarse and guttural. Anya held her breath. Suddenly, the voices were outside. She could not take her eyes from the doorway. She prayed the door would hold. There seemed to be some argument. The latch moved. She froze. It lifted, then dropped again. There was a grunt as a shoulder was unsuccessfully put

14

to the door. The door was kicked. Her heart was bursting. Then the footsteps and the voices retreated.

Anya covered her face with her hands and tried to breathe steadily. Suddenly there was an abrupt shout which made her jerk with fright and, with a bang like a thunderbolt, the door bulged, then splintered as it was hit a second time. A wooden beam burst through it and jammed. There were grunts from the corridor. She had to will herself to move and find a better hiding place. Shaking uncontrollably, she crawled between two crates in the corner by the porthole, then managed to pull a plank of wood part way across the gap. More grunts signalled that the beam had now been freed; it was slammed against the door repeatedly until the obstacle was finally battered down and the contents of the pantry stood revealed. There were deep-throated chuckles of satisfaction. The voice was coarse:

'There, what did I tell you, lads? – Grub. Just look at it.' Peeping out from her hiding place, Anya saw three men. They all looked evil. Their hearts were black, she knew, despite their bright attire. The pirate who had spoken was a swarthy villain, in a sweat-stained orange shirt and striped blue pantaloons. He had wavy, unkempt black hair. A cutlass was tucked through his thick leather belt. One eye was half closed. His face was gnarled; his right ear looked as if it had been chewed by a dog. In his hand was a short knife. He crouched and, with a quick movement that made the others dive out of the way, the knife stabbed to the floor. It reappeared with an apple impaled on it. The pirate rubbed the apple, then took a bite. 'Mmmm . . .' His thick lips pouted wetly, then his eyes rolled upwards as he munched. His mates – one of whom hadn't stopped scratching since walking through the doorway – watched the look of delectation on his face. 'Here . . .' Now he collected up an armful of apples and handed them round. 'Taste – as fresh as if you'd picked 'em from the tree.' But the others seemed hesitant.

'But what about the captain's orders?' asked the one with the continual itch. 'The girl?' He began scratching the back of his head.

'Girls, lad? You're as bad as Travix. Can't you get it into

your skull . . .?' Anya crouched back as his good eye roved round the room. 'There's no wenches aboard this bucket – a score of our lads have been through her from stem to stern and what's been found? Not so much as a stocking.' Then he stepped across the crates to drape his arm about the one piece of smoked pork still attached to a hook in the ceiling. 'But this lot here is surely prize enough for any man.' His grimy fingertips caressed the meat lovingly; his nostrils dilated wide and drank its fragrance. 'And it'll do you far more good than any girls.' But his companion was unconvinced. 'Cheer up, lad. Look – all that talk of a princess was nought but eyewash to a haddock. Take it from me – I know.' The good eye opened wide and the finger pointed as if to hold the other's itch at bay. 'Now think, lad. Would a princess travel without a gaggle of maids, trunks of finery, a treasure trove of jewels? And what did we find of those?'

The lad, looking downcast, did not reply. His expression told of long lost maids-in-waiting and of the poor consolation in a barrel of apples and a side of salted pork. His hand moved up across his belly; his fingertips began to delve beneath his arm.

The eye now distributed its encouragement more widely, taking in the third pirate, who had not spoken. His face had maintained a fixed frown throughout, as though completely baffled since the start of the proceedings. 'Never mind lads – you'll be heroes on the *Goblin* when you get this lot aboard. Then Travix is sure to find you some little wench to keep you busy.'

He shouted along the corridor; many more pirates appeared and began crowding into the small space at the pantry door.

Anya cringed in terror as they started removing the crates, refilling the barrels, trundling them out and gradually emptying the room. She tucked her feet up tight and tried to make her body very small, knowing that at any second she might be discovered. Yet it seemed to take a very long time for the jumbled mound of provisions to diminish. The men kept stopping for a break. Those times were the worst, for with nothing being moved, the room went very quiet and she was afraid they would hear her breathing. In the confined space, she felt cramped and very hot; there was no air. As she peered at the men through slitted eyes, as they yawned and rubbed their necks or scratched their knotted hair and stared vacantly round the room – perhaps in her direction – she almost became convinced that they were playing games with her, that they knew all along she was in there, and that they were simply waiting to pounce on her when she least expected it and drag her screaming from the room. And when that vision took shape, fed by the passing minutes, the constant grunts and sounds of scratching and the constriction of the airless space, she did begin to panic. She felt an overpowering urge to scream – to fling herself at them, kicking and spitting and tearing their hair out by the roots, so they would not need to scratch at it any more.

When work resumed, she breathed deeply and closed her eyes until a sudden noise reminded her the men were drawing ever nearer. And then the panic rose again to suffocate her.

Finally, deliverance came. As a sack of peas was lifted, some boxes collapsed sideways and the plank of wood that covered her hiding place tilted. She gasped and tried to catch hold of it, but a shout from the corridor made her hand jerk and the plank fell to the floor. She hid her face in her hands. There was a muttered curse. A box was dropped. She cringed. Any second, the crates would be kicked aside and she would be dragged out, screaming for her life. She kept her eyes screwed up tight. But her hands closed into fists now, held before her and squeezed so hard that her forearms shook.

But nothing happened. It had gone very quiet; the only sounds were distant and on deck. Very slowly, her fists uncurled, but she kept her hands in front of her face and looked out through the slits between her fingers. The room was empty of people; the doorway was clear; the floor had scattered broken crates, an upturned barrel and a pulp of cheese and apples matted into the planking. She drew her hands slowly down her cheeks, dropped her head back, rubbed her neck and sighed, but she did not move from the security of the crates. Her heartbeat gradually slowed; she felt tired.

Above her, the hubbub seemed to be subsiding. There were cries, but no screams or clashes of steel, and now there were

17

banging noises on the side of the ship. She wondered what they might mean. Without taking her eyes from the doorway, she got up very cautiously and edged over the remaining litter to the porthole. But before she even had the chance to look outside, the footfalls came again, very rapidly across the deck, then they started down the stairs. There were muffled voices, shouts. She was trapped. It would take them only seconds to cover the distance along the corridor. This time, there was no door to stay them, and nowhere she could hide. Anya had to decide. Should she make a dash for it and try to get past them? But she was too frightened to move towards the doorway. There was nothing else for it.

She looked out of the porthole. High above her were the ropes that linked the ships; pirates were clambering back across to their ship and manoeuvring nets of booty; below was the heavy green swell of water surging up to a narrow ledge around the hull. The downswell made her feel giddy. Then she heard a clank – a rope had snapped and dropped against the hull. She heard a shout. It happened again – the rope dropping – and she realised it had been cut. Then she heard another shout, followed by the skid of feet in the doorway at her back. 'She's here!' But Anya did not stop to listen. She was through the porthole before the intruders had time to step across the threshold.

She hung on by her hands and allowed her body to drop. But the ledge was narrower and further down than she had judged and her arms were almost wrenched out before her toes could reach it. Pressing her fingertips into the coarse seam of the planking, she began edging sternwards as fast as she could – which was all too slowly. She looked up; all the ropes were cut, but there were none she could reach. The topsail and its broken spars floated forward of where she clung. Below, the surge rose almost to touch her feet, then abruptly dropped to leave an empty chasm. She felt sick. And she had been spotted by the pirates at the opposite rail. They jeered and hooted, waiting for her to fall. She could hear other shouts from directly above her. Her legs felt weak and her fingers ached; she was afraid to move; she was unable to look either up or down now for fear of falling.

'Anya!' Her heart stopped altogether. It was *his* voice. 'Hold on!'

She forced herself to turn her head round and looked back along the hull. How could it be? The faces at the pantry porthole were not pirates at all but the Prince and his lieutenant. They looked battle-weary, but unhurt. 'It is safe now,' the Prince cried. 'Do not move. We will come to get you.'

So Anya clung there, trembling, her terror allayed at last by tears of sweet relief. She knew that she had only to hold on until she felt those strong arms round her waist, sweeping her back to safety. She closed her eyes as the ship rolled with the deep swell of the sea.

'Look out!' His cry was almost drowned by the belly-churning grinding noise. Her eyes snapped open; the ships were being pressed together by the swell. They touched in the middle, then began to swing, nose apart, and the point of contact was travelling rapidly towards her. Anya watched in horror as the buffer beam of the larger ship rubbed ever closer at belly height, accompanied by the squealing protests and knocking snaps of slowly tortured timbers. 'Quickly – give me your hand!'

Somehow, she unfroze, but it was too late. She was in the jaws of a giant, ridged vice and it was closing. Her belly would be squashed to a pulp; her body would be cut in two before she reached him.

'Jump! Jump across!' She did not understand. The entreaty was echoed from above, from both ships. The pirates watched with fascination. She twisted her head and stared behind her at the ledge of wood that fast approached. 'Jump!' At the very last second she turned and took a giant upward leap across the space, landed on one knee, almost toppled back again, then grasped the rebate, clawed her way upright and managed to balance, pressing her body hard against the pirate ship's hull. The point of contact reached her, seemed to pause, then very slowly began to pass. Out of the corners of her eyes, she could see the vast expanse of moving hull behind her; she could almost feel it as a pressure against her back, preventing her from breathing. She felt light-headed. She heard the debris of

19

the topmast trap, then splinter between the hulls. She felt the judder of grating friction through her feet. Then suddenly, the danger was past. The cheer went up from both ships.

She balanced awkwardly, waiting for the ships to steady. But they carried on moving apart. The chasm opened up behind her and quickly widened. She turned her head and saw her Prince, immobile at the porthole, his arms outstretched towards her. He could not save her now. Nobody could. Then she heard the weighted rumble of the swell. She gasped and held on for her life as she watched the slow broad wave approach. It rose, freezing, up her legs, then waned, then surged again up her body, up inside her jacket, sucking her breath away with the shocking cold. It kept rising, over her shoulders, over her head, and squirted up her nose. She fought against the urge to cough and the urge to let go, though the water lifted her as if she were weightless, tugged her gently, silently, as the bubbles streamed round her face, then slowly lowered her. Suddenly, she could hear and splutter and cough and breathe, but her body just got heavier and heavier as if it were weighted down with stones. The muscles in her arms screamed out for mercy; the tendons in her wrists felt like burning strands of wire. The sea sucked slowly down her body, then, as her feet found the ledge again, reluctantly released her, leaving the saturated tunic sleeved tightly to her skin and the water cascading down her body to her boots. Her head was pulled back by her copper hair – no longer tied, but drawn down by the weight of the water into a smooth straight fan across her shoulders. There were gasps of delight from the pirates up above.

'Why, it's a girl!' The astonished cry was from a pock-marked pirate at the rail.

'No . . . What say ye, Spragg?' came the quick reply. 'Stuck upon the hull like that, I thought it were a limpet!' The ship erupted in guffaws of laughter – with the speaker bellowing louder than the rest and slapping the spotty one heartily on the back.

Nobody cared about Anya's plight – about the fact that she might easily have drowned. Looking up, she was enveloped by a slowly creeping fear – far more chilling than the sea – as

20

she divined the wicked intent that lurked behind all those sparkling, laughing eyes.

A gaunt, grey-whiskered pirate pointed a crooked finger: 'But look at her – dressed like a cabin squirt. Why?'

'Hmmm . . . I wonder now. She's got to be a valuable one to be set in that disguise.' Anya bit her lip. Then the man suddenly thumped his fist upon the rail and cried: 'Quick, Spragg. Get Travix. And tell the captain.' He nodded towards the other ship, drifting slowly away: riddled with holes and with her topmast gone, she looked a sorry sight. 'We can forget that leaking bucket and her jelly-bellied crew, for it's a mackerel to a maggot that we've got our prize – down here!'

For a second or two, the pirates stared at each other, then stared at Anya. Spragg hadn't moved. Then suddenly one of them lifted his leg astride the rail. 'Forget Travix. This one's *our* prize. Come on, lads – let's give our guest a pirate's welcome. Pipe the girl aboard!'

[3]

A Severed Lip

Rough hands grasped her sleeves and collar, hauled her dripping body up the side of the ship and dragged her over the rail. She was lifted to shoulder height on a forest of strong, eager arms and passed from hand to hand – above the sea of pigtailed, grinning, flap-eared faces with breath that spoke of rancid fish and tainted meat – and deposited, kicking defiantly, in the well below the quarterdeck. They tried to take hold of her flailing arms and feet.

'Get back,' cried she. 'Unhand me!' Brave woman, brave words. She was on her back, hemmed in by a tight double circle of leering pirates. A pool of water welled from her saturated clothes.

'Undress the girl, more like!' came the quip, spurring a renewed attack and more wild kicking. Then someone intervened.

'Now calm down.' He spread his arms and held the others back. 'Don't rush her. Can't you see the girl's upset? Take it gently. She hasn't got to know us yet.'

'Oh then, let me introduce myself . . .' The quipster began undoing his belt.

'Shut up, you witless gawk. Get him out of the way.' But the rescuer's voice turned oily. His hands began to dance and his grimy fingernails clawed the air as he tried to coax: 'Shh . . . Now, my dearie, we're your friends. In those wet things, why, you'll catch your death of cold. Here, let Luggins help you.' The dancing fingers reached for Anya's jacket. She spat on them, then kicked him in the shin, sending him hopping to the howls of laughter.

'It seems she knows you well enough already . . .'

Someone caught her wrist and twisted it and the next time

that she kicked, they were ready. Two of them grabbed her feet, pulled her boots off, dragged her up and held her by the ankles. She took hold of the nearer assailant's leg and bit it at the knee. His breeches tasted musty. He screamed and dropped her. Anya twisted as she fell and her shoulder broke her fall. She tried to drag herself away, but there was no escaping. She was held face down by hands pressing heavily between her shoulders and pinning her to the deck. The pirate's full weight descended; he sat upon her, trapping her upper back between his knees. She could hardly breathe – her ribs were being crushed – but she kept kicking, though she hit no one and her toes kept stubbing against the floor. He wrenched her face to one side and forced her cheek against the planking. Then his face moved closer. Even with her eyes shut, she couldn't get away from this nightmare: her wet things now felt hot and clammy; she could smell the staleness on his breath; her chin was held in an iron grip and a cracked dry thumb was pushing deep into her cheek.

And still she would not give up; she would never give way to these creatures. She pressed her knees into the deck to try to lift the dead weight from her back, to try to throw him. But that only made her more vulnerable. Other hands slipped beneath, around her waist and grasped her tunic bottoms. The hands tugged, the wet waistband clung to her at first, then slipped and dug into her back above her bottom. At her belly, she felt the cloth drawn tight, the stitching beginning to strain, then giving, then loudly ripping. A roaring cheer went up. Her hips gyrated wildly to try to throw the maulers off. Her arms, trapped above the elbows by the pirate's knees, could not move. Her hands waved ineffectually as the ripping continued, accompanied by the cheering, and the breeches were stripped off her buttocks, down her legs and to her ankles. The wet skin of her thighs and buttocks turned to gooseflesh.

And now, against the catcalls and the whistles of the mob, she was defenceless. She could not stop the pirates spreading her legs, still fastened by the rags wrapped round her ankles, then bending her knees outwards, scraping them across the deck – hurting her. But worse than the pain were the tears. She had fought against them from the start and now she had

23

lost. These men, cruel though they were, had not defeated her. They never could. She was defeated by her own tears, which connived with these hardened hearts to deliver them greater satisfaction. They trickled down her face to wet the rough cruel hand that held her yet more tightly through those tears. Her ankles were forced up, to make her bottom lift. Callused fingers rubbed her legs, the backs of her open thighs, the cheeks of her buttocks, then parted them.

'Look out, lads! Travix!' Suddenly, her assailants lost their nerve. The brave attack miraculously melted away at the very mention of that name. The hands released Anya's face, her legs were straightened, the weight was lifted from her back and the cowards edged away.

Anya lay on her front, her body trembling, her tears welling silently. The tunic top was still in place; the remains of the bottoms were tangled round her ankles. Her shoulders ached; she felt as if her ribs were cracked. Her knees throbbed as if her skin was rubbed away and bleeding.

'Turn her over.'

Anya abruptly stopped trembling and her eyes opened wide, for it was a woman's voice she had heard – very clear and strong, decisive, yet not harsh.

A seaboot prised her shoulder from the deck and rolled her limp body over. Immediately, in reflex, she closed her eyes again and crossed her hands to cover the joins of her thighs, for the jacket was very short. She could feel the cool pool of water against the small of her back and the skin hairs prickling as the moisture began to evaporate from the outswell of her belly.

For a while, nothing happened. She listened as she tried to fit a picture to the name she had heard – Travix. Then she heard footfalls, slow deliberate footfalls, close by. Her hands tightened defensively below her belly, for now her mind had formed the picture. She thought she heard a sigh. Then the voice came again and this time it had a cynical edge: the picture had been right. 'Modesty and mettle so delicately balanced . . .' The toe of a different boot – velvet – slipped along her thigh. 'Innocence so sweet to test . . . But will you not open your eyes?'

Anya had to force herself to do it. The ragged crew had moved back. Above her stood three people who looked very different from the pirates – the woman, Travix, in a closely fitting suit of blue, and two men, standing one to each side of her but slightly behind, clad in moleskins and sleeveless leather shirts. The men's arms were folded. Each had the same stance and the slightly glazed, indifferent look of guards. They were young – about as old as Anya – but Travix must have been a few years older. She held her head a little to one side and lifted her chin, so she was forced – or she chose – to look obliquely down at Anya. Her lip appeared drawn up very slightly at the side away from Anya. As Anya waited for her to speak again, Travix's gaze lifted. Her eyes were a clear ice blue. They impaled a short fat crewman who still held one of Anya's boots. Uncertainly, he lowered his body by bending his knees until the boot touched the deck beside Anya's feet. Then he released it, straightened and backed away in tiny shuffling movements. Travix's gaze returned to Anya. The woman seemed to be assessing her from head to toe.

Anya in turn tried to fathom this person. She was tall – or perhaps it only appeared that way, for the crew stood before her with shoulders hunched and eyes downcast. Her hair was shoulder length, blonde, thick and straight, like filaments of pale gold wire, drawn back and tied with a black ribbon. In her left earlobe was a single gold ring. Seeing that earring reminded Anya of her Prince. Beneath Travix's collar was a scarf. Her hands, on her hips, were slim, but the nails were short, like a man's. She had pale eyebrows and her cheeks were weather-reddened. As the woman's head turned, Anya's breath caught. Travix's face was scarred; there was a curving pale red line down her right cheek and a fine furrow across her upper lip. The lip lifted in a faint half-smile, and the woman's eyes narrowed – as though she were mocking Anya's discomfiture at seeing this disfigurement. Her teeth were pure white, and very slightly crooked below the line of the cut.

Anya winced, for though the severed lip was long ago healed, she was imagining it happening – the sword slash cutting across the cheek, the blue steel slitting it, then slipping against the cut flesh of the lip, then grating shrilly against the

25

teeth, before being drawn sharply away. For some reason –
something about Travix's look perhaps – she imagined that
cut being delivered not in the heat of battle but in cold-
blooded punishment. In her mind's eye, she could see the lip
lifting afterwards to a mocking smile, the pure white teeth
flooding red with blood, then the tongue licking out to taste
and test the raw-nerved pulpy slit. It sent a peculiar shiver
through Anya's belly.

Travix had not failed to notice; now she looked down to
where Anya's hands still crossed below her belly. The lip curled
once again to that same disdainful smile. Anya coloured. The
blue eyes flashed at her. Suddenly annoyed, afraid – of the
eyes, of the peculiar feeling that had touched her belly, and
of the premonition of wicked sensuality that now inveigled
her mind – Anya spat the words out:

'Who are you? What do you want of me?'

There were murmurs from the men. Anya bit her lip. She
ought to have bitten her tongue. Travix slowly looked round
at all the faces. She did not look at Anya as she spoke. It was
as if she were intent upon preventing this insubordination from
spreading to the crew.

'Ah – the Princess of Lidir, I presume.' There were uneasy
chuckles from the men. Now Travix did look at Anya and
Anya turned bright red. 'For you see, my dear, I judge you
not by your manners – nor yet by your frippery –' her velvet
booted toe touched the ragged trousers wrapped round Anya's
ankles; the chuckles turned to laughter – 'but by the disquiet
your hasty defection appears to have provoked.' She turned;
the men quickly moved aside as if her gaze had cut a swath
through them. She took several paces towards the rail, then
said slowly, almost to herself, her voice tinged momentarily
with a faint note of uncertainty: 'Even now, your puny ship
would try to follow.' Then she turned sharply on her heel and
strode back to confront Anya. Her lip curled again in a twisted
smile: 'But your pigeons made a tasty pie – as you will too, I
am sure.' Anya's eyes widened in fear as she recalled the doves,
sent to warn of her return.

Travix held her hand out to the man beside her. He placed
in it a whip with eight or ten strands. She snapped it quickly,

making Anya jerk in fright and automatically turn on to her side and draw her knees up sharply. Travix ignored her and raised her voice. 'A tasty pie indeed . . . For what is it we say, lads?' Again she snapped the whip.

'First meat to the captain!' was the quick rejoinder from every man gathered round. Again the pointed toe of the boot rolled Anya over. She kept her knees bent, pressing tightly together. The way the woman looked at her made her shudder.

'Aye. And any man that wants to keep the skin upon his back will do well to remember it in future. Now be off with you. Boatswain – release the slaves; deliver them below decks for the port watch, then set a trim for warmer climes.'

As the crew dispersed, Anya felt more exposed than ever. Travix bent over her. She moved the tightly pressed-together knees down and away from Anya's belly. The rough dry strands of the whip hung down, brushing her bare and tender skin, tickling in the hollow of her navel. Anya's belly shivered. The strands were laid across it; they moulded to the gentle swell. The woman whispered: 'The cat – she is tempted, she would love to kiss you – but she is not for tender skin. For you, Princess, and for that place you love to hide from me, we may choose a more playful little kitten.' She slid the whip strands slowly, so they snaked as they lifted from Anya's skin, then she folded them and turned to her attendants. 'Lift her up.'

Strong arms slipped beneath Anya's shoulders and knees. She was raised between the two men in leather shirts. Her tunic bottoms were pulled from her slender ankles and cast aside, as if they would never again be needed. Travix kicked them away. Anya's bare thighs rested on the dense hair of the men's forearms. She could smell their body scent; they did not smell stale, like the others. 'Open her thighs.' Those words, so calmly delivered, sent a shiver again to Anya's belly.

'No . . .' she whispered. But how could she prevent them doing it, how could she resist, with Travix standing so close by with the whip? She tried to look away, in shame, as Travix approached her, though with the men to either side, holding her firmly with her back upright and their arms locked round her thighs, there was nowhere she could look to for respite.

She closed her eyes. But even then, there was no reprieve. 'Turn her head.' A strong hand gathered her hair and slowly twisted it until her scalp felt tight. When the tightness turned to pain, her head turned. As the twisted hank of hair was drawn down, her chin lifted. 'Open your eyes.' The face was very close – too close; the blue eyes, looking down, were piercing. The skin upon Anya's neck felt hot. 'Princess – you are blushing.'

All Anya could see now was the scar and the deep furrow across the upper lip, as if an invisible thread were drawn tight across it, leaving the right side of the lip contused, swollen like a pale pink berry. A finger touched her cheek and Anya shuddered, for it traced the line, in mirror and on Anya's cheek, of the woman's scar, down to the upper lip. Then the lip was lifted. The finger ran along the line of Anya's perfect teeth. The face moved closer, the lips descending as if to kiss. Anya gasped and pulled away. Then there was a stifled murmur from the mast. From the corner of her eye Anya could see a movement. Suddenly, she remembered – the naked women tied to the masts; one, it seemed, had been left in place and she was gagged.

'Ah, Niri,' Travix said. 'Turn the Princess, let her look.' Travix stepped back. 'Niri does not fear the gag; for her, it is no obstacle to explanation, for she does not speak our tongue.' Anya stared up at the young girl bound to the mast. She had never before seen a person who spoke in ciphers. Niri was small, her body was perfectly proportioned and her skin was golden. She had unusually wide eyes, which were black. 'Niri is my favourite. It is better that she sees.'

But favourite or not, Anya could tell that Niri was being treated very cruelly. Her mouth was gagged with a broad leather band. Her arms were drawn tightly back, and fastened high above her head. Her breasts pushed out strongly. A heavy rope, wound only round the mast and not the girl, pressed into her back above her waist, forcing it to curve. Her belly arched tightly. Her knees were drawn sharply upwards and fastened, exposing the flesh between her thighs. And that flesh had been partly shaved: the outer purse was prominent and bare, but with a flare of carefully manicured short brown hair

28

brushed back from the point of the hood, as if the pressure in her overfull purse had somehow leaked, spraying colour from the tip. As Niri tried and failed to ease the straining tension in her arms, her belly arched more tightly, her breasts moved, her belly rotated, and the purse pulsed softly. With every pulse, the sparse triangle of colour sank, then lifted sharply and appeared to spread, as if it might have sprayed.

'See how she struggles; she is jealous of these small attentions. She does not understand that we must investigate our new-found prize.' Travix's hand reached.

'No . . .' Anya murmured again as the fingers moving down her cheek were now complemented by the other hand. As one set of fingers lay against the thick vein in her neck, the other set quickly forced each large brass jacket button through its eye in the wet material, then opened out the jacket. Anya could feel her heartbeat throbbing faster against the fingertips at her neck. But Travix looked only into Anya's face while she touched her breasts and nipples. 'Lift her arms,' she said. She touched the wet warm hair in Anya's underarms; then her fingers returned to touch the nipples – which were hard. And still the gaze would not release Anya, still those other fingers tasted Anya's heartbeat in her throat. Anya could have tried to struggle, as she'd done against the men; she could have cried out, spat; but she could not deny the hardness of her nipples, nor the effect of the light fingertip pressure upon the heartbeat in her throat. 'Hold her still . . . Push her belly out. It must be pushed out – hard and rounded to the touch.' And now her heart was bursting. A large hand pushed flat against the base of her spine, pushing her bottom forwards, arching her belly, forcing her legs wider apart, offering her sex for those fingers now to touch while the pulse at her neck cried out the feelings that this deliciously tentative touching brought.

The fingertips teased the wet curls aside, unbound the lips; only when each individual curl was lifted, when the warm lips were completely bare, did the fingers open Anya's living flesh, spread it like a warm wet beating heart, and touch within that heartbeat. Only then was Anya permitted to close her eyes. She heard another murmur from the mast. But the fingers at her belly were unhasty. 'Black lips, black nipples . . . You are

29

beautiful, Princess.' Anya heard those words but distantly. She was trapped between the warm round pressure of the hand against her back and the fingers, slipped between her legs, moving gently in her heart. She wanted those fingertips, oiled with her body-wet, to search deeper, very gently against the pressure, while she closed her flesh around them tightly, while she squeezed them to her heart. Travix's voice came very softly, so Anya heard her faintly, above the sea sounds of the warm deck breeze that brushed across her ears:

'There ... Enjoy ... For throughout this voyage into pleasure, my Princess, your wantonness will be evoked. We shall teach you many ways. But your lust will be tempered always with longing, delicious pleasure shall be pricked with pain. Your satisfaction shall be delivered slowly, beautiful one, against the sweetness of your shame.'

The hand slid very gently from Anya's body, then slowly wiped the oily moisture upon her bush of copper curls while the soft distended lips of her sex gradually closed. Anya opened her eyes; her breathing would not steady. Travix smiled, then carefully straightened Anya's jacket, but left it unbuttoned, with the two sides barely touching together down the middle. 'Release her hair,' she said. Now Anya could move her head, but the men still held her thighs locked open and straddled across their arms. And the ordeal was not over. Travix stepped forward again, very close, so she stood between Anya's legs. 'Remember – slowly, beautiful one,' she repeated. Anya felt a slow weight sinking to her belly.

The hem of Travix's tunic brushed the bare skin of Anya's inner thighs. Travix lifted aside the jacket, touched the breasts again, tested the velvet tips. Anya shuddered. The fingertips of two hands followed that shudder down the belly, below the curls, touched the silky outer skin of the soft warm weighted lips, then closed about the purse as if it were a swollen sunwarmed fruit that might split or bruise. Four soft pressure points to each side tested those lips, made their inner surfaces kiss together and slip; alternate movements drew pleasure slowly, to make a pressure sugarsweet like wine until, trapped between the pads of each forefinger was no longer soft flesh, but a small hot round bone sleeved within the slippy silk. And all the while the blue eyes held her. The fingertips coaxed warm nectar into that fruit, lifting it to test its weight within the palm, then returning to rub the sides. The fruit swelled to make the pressure of sweetness an ache, the delicious ache that comes before the soft split of deliverance.

But there was no deliverance, just the very gentle rubbing, drawing the fluid ever down into her flesh until it seemed that flesh could take no more. It was as if Travix would rub and coax it until the fruit burst of its own accord. Was it pleasure? Was it cruel? It was both. Anya gasped as Travix tapped the weighted fruit; she wanted her to draw the skin back fully, search within the pulp and nip the hot round bone. The fingertips gently pressed against her once again where the fruit was joined to her body, then took the bursting fruit and very gently pulled it. Anya moaned. She wanted it to burst; she knew that Travix would never let it happen. The hand closed round her. The fingertips quickly nipped the flesh about her nub of pleasure, then released it. Too late, she tried to thrust her belly to meet that nip. The blue eyes looked on impassively and the back of the hand stroked against the swollen seam of her sex lips. When she pushed again, it pulled away. Travix gave an instruction to the men. Anya's knees were lifted, bent and pressed together. The black-lipped purse pushed out between her thighs like an overripe plum. Like a plum that the small birds had pricked with their beaks and sipped, it slowly seeped. Small droplets of Anya's honeydew swelled from the swollen seam. Travix pressed her fingertips against that fruit once more. The honeyed droplets welled and merged into a continuous seam of syrup. The fingertips touched the thin sleeve of skin that sheltered the hard little bone. Anya tried to thrust again. 'Lower her knees. Press her thighs together – tight!' Anya whimpered as the pressure surged; her pleasure almost came. 'Open her quickly. Keep her legs apart.'

Travix approached very closely again. The jacket brushed against Anya's thighs. The eyes fixed her. It began all over again – the fingertips touching her breasts, closing around the nipples, then the shudder coming and the fingers moving down, touching the curls, moving in, closing very softly about

31

the lips, with the pressure from the fluid filling up her flesh lips unto bursting, yet the bursting not being allowed. It was crueller than before. But was it still pleasure? Yes. She wanted the bursting to come, but if that were to be denied, she did not want the fingertip touch to stop.

'Mister Travix!' The sudden shout freed Anya from the thrall of the woman's gaze, and though she was confused by the strange mode of address, her attention was taken fully now by the figure in red, high above them, behind the quarterdeck rail.

'Captain?' Travix cried.

'You have the prisoner?' With that reference, delivered so casually, all the sweetness of those feelings in Anya's belly was swept away on a new tide of her fears.

'Sir . . .' Travix stepped aside. Anya was turned to face the man in the long red velvet coat and tricorn hat who was walking down the stairs, his left hand behind his back and his right hand slowly gliding down the rail. The men supporting Anya tensed as he approached, and that made her feel more afraid. The captain came to a halt at the foot of the stairs, several feet away. He was very tall – taller by a head than Travix – and much older, yet his dark hair showed no hint of grey. None of his movements seemed hurried. The fingers of his right hand drummed the balustrade. He looked out to sea, then his gaze worked slowly round the ship. A few men had been working close by, but they had disappeared as soon as the captain had shouted. His gaze seemed to pass through Anya as if she were not there and settled instead on Travix. Anya watched him now in profile. He had thick, bushy eyebrows, a large curved nose – long, soft earlobes, Anya noticed – and a prominent chin. His voice was resonant.

'You have set the course that I requested?'

'Aye, Captain. South, sir,' Travix replied, then added after a short delay, 'But they try to follow.' Her voice had carried a hint of criticism. The captain pursed his lips and looked out again to sea. Encouraged now, Travix continued, speaking quickly through her teeth. 'We should have fixed them – flayed them, then burned their ship and let them fry or drown like rats.' Anya was horrified by those words. Her belly

32

tightened to a knot against the memory of what she had allowed a woman such as this to do to her.

But the captain did not need to raise his voice. There was a soft irony in his tone: 'But they are men, Mister Travix.' Travix's look was venom. 'You would not put good men to the torch for fighting for their ship?' He paused. She did not answer. He continued with the measured, resonant castigation. 'And surely you would not be so foolhardy as to kill a Prince?' He did not wait for an answer, but looked at Anya. 'And who is better placed to raise the ransom for his Princess?'

Travix was nettled. Her jaw was set, her eyes were half closed, but to no effect, for the captain would not condescend to look at her. 'Then why did we not take him when we had the chance?' she snapped. 'And claim double ransom?'

He smiled, then turned to face her: 'Or none – should it suit his successors not to pay.'

As Travix fell silent beneath the captain's steady gaze, Anya tried to analyse these words. She knew they boded ill for her. Even the Prince would have great difficulty in raising a ransom for her. She had many enemies in the castle; they had tried repeatedly to forestall her betrothal. And so far they had succeeded, for even yet, she was not in truth the Princess. Probably, she never would be – she could see herself a prisoner here forever aboard this ship, at the merciless whim of Travix and these heartless pirates. And now, still held, her arms pinned back, she could not even wipe away the tears that welled to blind her. They trickled slowly down her cheek, ran along the ridge of her upper lip and seeped into her mouth. Suddenly, the men beside her tensed again. Her head was drawn back sharply. The captain stood before her.

He was looking down into her tearstained face. Anya's lip trembled; with her head pulled back, she could not swallow properly; her vision swam. All she could see were the strong nose, the dark bushy eyebrows and the eyes of bright, liquid green. All she could hear was the deep resonance of his voice. Had he spoken to her? She did not know. But again she felt the large hand at her back, low down, warm against her bare skin, pushing her hips forward, as it had done for Travix, but further forward this time, spreading her thighs until they ached,

33

lifting her until her sex, still swollen hard, was exposed, until she felt the tension across her creases, until the pressure throbbed deeply behind the sticky-sealed fleshy join. But it seemed the captain wanted more. Her knees were crooked up tightly until her bottom was lifted in the air and the cheeks of her buttocks were spread.

Suddenly, he held his left hand up. There was a flash of light. She screamed. It was a hook, a double one, glinting in the sun. Two vicious steel arcs, curving the same way from a stump, almost touched at their points to form a vee. The hook moved; she screamed again. The guard clapped a hand over her mouth but the muffled screams continued through her nose. The captain's expression was unchanged by Anya's terror; he was intent about his purpose, which was now to use the hook to lift the jacket gently aside, to expose each full and black-tipped breast, which trembled as her belly shook, while he placed against her matt black sex lips the long cold fingers of his one good hand. The fingers pressed; she gasped against the hand across her mouth, then shuddered and the warm fruit burst; the shudder grew deep inside her; the fingers opened out the warm moist beating heart. Her flesh was left thus – exposed to his gaze – while he touched the uplifted velvet black mouth of her bottom with his thumb. The shudder came again, much deeper. Though it was not a release from pleasure, it was a deliverance of a kind, for it drew within her belly, drew within her bottom, touched her nubbin from inside.

'Delicious . . .' the captain murmured, as the thumb elicited a second soft contraction of the velvet. Then he turned on his heels.

'Mister Travix – show the Princess to her quarters. Show her no undue favours, but treat her kindly – as you would any guest.'

Then he swung round to Anya so quickly that she thought her heart would burst. She gasped for breath against the hand that gagged her. 'Our ship is humble, Princess. Our rules are few. But like you, we are hostages – to tradition.' He smiled. 'Tonight, I offer you my own hospitality. I request the pleasure of your company in my cabin.'

34

He did not wait for any reply but turned and walked back up the stairs, his left hand behind his back once more, the hook glinting, steel blue.

Travix came near. 'Set her down,' she growled. Her lip was twisted; her look was evil. She lifted her arm and Anya thought she would be hit. But Travix waved the arm impatiently and shouted: 'Ratchitt!' A small man emerged from a hatchway to forward of where she stood. It was the same man who had earlier attempted to make off with Anya's boot. He skidded to a halt in front of Travix.

'Ma'am?'

Travix scowled at him. 'Mister Travix – if you don't mind.' He had very large ears for his size and a small curl was plastered to his forehead. And now he replied, not by speaking, but by looking balefully at her, with the eyes of a punished hound. 'Take the prisoner down. Chain her. I will be down later, to attune her to the captain's . . . particular requirements.' Anya shivered. 'And if any man-jack lays a finger on her, I'll have him hoisted by his ballocks to the masthead – and that goes for you too, Ratchitt. Is that clear?' she snapped.

'Yes ma'a . . . Mister Travix.'

She turned quickly to the men in leather shirts. 'Bring Niri to my cabin.'

Anya's mouth fell open; she looked up again at the young girl, still gagged, and tethered to the mast. But Travix had witnessed Anya's expression. 'Now do not tell me you are jealous?' she said. She tossed her head back and looked at Anya through half-closed eyes. Her top lip curled to a twisted smile. Her tongue licked out and slowly stroked the furrow of the cut. Anya's heart was in her throat. Travix came close but did not speak to Anya. The toe of her velvet boot simply eased Anya's feet apart, one foot then the other. Then Travix took from her pocket a soft, brushed-velvet cloth. She looked into Anya's eyes. With a pounding in her throat and a delicious sinking in her belly, Anya felt her fleshpot being gathered in the cloth, then, through the cool soft velvet, her bare and swelling sex lips being stroked. It was coming again – the feeling. The fingertips tasted the slow pulse through the velvet. Anya watched the blue impassive eyes, the scarred cheek, the

35

full and severed lip. And everything she felt deep in her belly was delicious. She closed her eyes. Travix whispered in her ear: 'Do not be jealous, my Princess, for I shall attune you to my requirements too.' Again she shivered; the fingertips caressed her through the velvet and the soft and severed lip brushed gently against her ear.

[4]

A Punishment by Proxy

'A princess, you say, Ratchitt?' The voice was sneering; the eyes looking down at her were harsh. 'We don't get many princesses down here in the brig.'

Anya was deep in the heart of the ship, below the water line, and she was terrified, for Ratchitt meant to leave her with this man. But she did not want to return the way she had come: even now, she could hear the boisterous laughter directly overhead.

She had been taken down a broad flight of stairs, then a narrower one, with Ratchitt having to coax her all the way, as she kept stopping. At one point, they had passed before a large noisy open area full of hammocks. At the far end of this place were tables and on them she had glimpsed women, their naked bodies disported before a raucous crowd of drunken crewmen. Opposite, Ratchitt had pointed out the captain's cabin, with large panelled doors over which was a carving of the goblin. Dangling from a chain beside the entrance was a cage containing a human skull. It had made her shiver. The walls were covered with other terrifying trophies – cutlasses dripping long-dried, blackened blood; plaits of hair with skin attached and other things that looked like tiny wrinkled human heads. Then he had led her down again and along a narrow lamplit corridor. As they hurried through, the lamps had flickered in the draught and cast giant swaying shadows across the ceiling. Her heart had sunk lower and lower with every step she had been forced to take, until her heart was in her belly. It was as if she could feel the pressure of the sea all around, just waiting to burst in, snuff these feeble lamps, trap her in the cobwebbed rafters and drown her in its freezing murk.

Yet even that might have been better than the fate that she

had seen reflected in the hard, cruel eyes of the man who had met them and looked upon her so unsparingly as her frightened body shook.

They had emerged into a large, almost circular area. Through the centre, the mainmast passed from ceiling to floor. Anya stood with her back to it. On three sides were doors, each embossed with ironwork and studded with nails and bearing a heavy iron bolt. On the fourth side was an embayment furnished after the manner of a small cabin – there was a chair, a table, some drawers, a dishevelled bed and even a small stove. She could smell hot metal and hear the soft sizzle of the coals. The man had walked casually away from them and over to the table, where a mug and a bottle of wine stood and the remains of a chicken rested. It reminded her that she hadn't eaten. He ignored the mug and drank directly from the bottle, then took a bite from the carcass of the chicken. Anya's eyes moved round, beyond the cosy arrangement, to see rings and chains in the wall behind. More frightening still was a heavy post projecting horizontally at waist height for about an armslength from this wall. The surface of the wood was smooth and highly polished. Above the post were two rings. Propped lengthwise against the wall a little further along was an angled table top with fetters attached. And there were whips of many kinds hanging from a rack to the right. She shivered. But none of these things terrified Anya so much as the man spitting out the chicken bone and returning to stand before her.

He was strong – his muscles rippled – and bare to the waist and clad in black leather. He could have lifted Anya easily and carried her under his arm. There were thongs tied round his upper arms and diagonally across his chest. His head was shaved, apart from near the back, where the hair had been allowed to grow very long and was gathered into a heavy plait which hung down between his shoulders. And he had only one ear. When he turned, there was a small hole in the side of his head, as if the ear had been abraded away and the side of the head polished flat. Anya winced to look at it. But the ear hadn't been rubbed away. It had been cut off: it formed a grotesque rounded amulet of flat and wrinkled thick dried skin that hung from a thong round his neck.

'Well – what are the instructions?' he growled, looking straight at Anya. He tucked his thumbs into his belt. That gesture made Anya back away, for tucked there too was a broad black leather strap attached by an iron ring to a short wooden handle. Both the wood and the strap looked shiny – from use, she knew. Then her eyes, downcast now from fear, fell upon a greater terror yet, which she had so far tried to ignore. Below the belt – projecting, threatening, already half erect – was a thick and bulging codpiece; his sex and ballocks were gloved and outlined separately within a tightly moulded pouch.

Ratchitt shuffled his feet. His small round face lifted up as he looked at the man. 'The captain says to treat her kindly, Kasger,' said Ratchitt warily, as the muscles across the shoulders flexed and the heavy fingers closed firmly about the handle of the strap.

Kasger chuckled. His gaze lifted from the downcast form before him and fell instead on Ratchitt. 'Then why did he send her to me?'

Then he stepped forward. Anya could not move away any further; her back was pressed against the mast. Kasger wore cutaway leather gloves which buckled at the wrist but left his fingers free. The fingers lifted Anya's chin and held it, though only lightly. But even so, she knew this man was capable of great cruelty. She could see it as he stared again into her eyes. One by one, his questions set the seal on Anya's fate.

'And did the captain say to treat her any differently from the rest?' From the way he said it, it was clear he knew the answer; he was playing games with Ratchitt, while his eyes continued to search Anya's face minutely and his fingers held her chin.

'No . . .'

'Did he say not to chain her?' He lifted a strand of still-damp hair from Anya's face and placed it behind her ear.

'No, but –'

'And what about the strap?' His gaze worked downwards to where the jacket was slightly open, lifted by her breasts. 'Is the Princess to be punished?' The skin upon her breasts and belly tingled.

39

'Well, er . . . the captain never mentioned that, Kasger, and I wouldn't think –'

'Ratchitt, just tell me – who sent her down here? Was it the master's mate?'

Ratchitt looked away. His answer was a barely visible nod.

'Then that's all I need to know.'

'But Kasger, Travix didn't –'

'Ratchitt . . .' The cruel eyes turned to fix upon him. 'Remind me – and the Princess – of your job aboard this ship.'

Ratchitt looked hurt, to be so demeaned in front of Anya. 'You know that I look after the hens.'

'And who looks after the prisoners and the slaves?'

Ratchitt bit his lip. Kasger waited, still holding Anya's chin while he stared down at the small, round, quaking form beside him. Anya hated him for his cruelty to the one person aboard this ship who had shown her any kindness. Kasger looked again at Anya; Anya looked away. 'You do, Kasger,' Ratchitt finally admitted.

'Then go about your duties, Ratchitt. See to your hens. Leave men's work to the men.'

Ratchitt nervously twisted the single thick stray curl that stood out from the rest and pressed it to his forehead. He opened his mouth as if to speak, then closed it. He looked one last time at Anya, then he left with head hung low, hurrying away – as always. But this time he was not fast enough. Before he even reached the far end of the corridor, the torment rent his ears – the first cruel crack of the strap against that innocent, perfect form. The short legs moved faster and the small round body speeded up. He scuttled up the stairs towards the deck, towards his chickens, towards escape from the iron fist that squeezed around his heart.

'Princess . . .' Now that Ratchitt had gone, the intonation was more mocking. Kasger had stepped back. His hand was at his belt again, at the handle of the strap and Anya was at his mercy. She felt as if an icicle was being drawn slowly down the furrow of her spine. She knew what he would do to her; she knew he had decided in advance. 'We are not at court now – *Princess*.' This time he had spat the last word out. 'Life,

40

you will find, is simple aboard this ship, provided you obey the rules.' He withdrew the strap, stepped back again and cracked it down upon the table. Anya immediately jumped. 'Ah, good – you learn quickly. For that is lesson number one. But there is a second lesson to be learnt – in fact, an association to be made. It may take time. But we have the time.' He smiled; his arms swept out to indicate the various trappings on the walls. 'This is why we are here. I will attempt to demonstrate, then we will see if you – or rather your body, for the association is made by the body rather than the mind – have made the correct connection.'

He looked down at her, at her bare belly, and that belly shuddered, for it understood. He lifted up the strap. 'Turn round, Princess . . . Ah, do not fear. We proceed by stages.' Yet she was afraid. As she turned to face the broad solid curvature of the mast, the shivers came, turning the backs of her thighs and her bare buttocks to gooseflesh, making every skin hair bristle. Before her, spaced wide apart and set into the mast, were four polished thick brass rings attached to staples. Two were above shoulder height; the other two were a few inches above the floor. 'Roll your sleeves back.' Then he showed her what to do. The cold brass slipped over her wrists and, when she lifted her heels slightly, to her elbows. When she bent her arms, her weight was taken and she was hanging from these rings. Yet seemingly, this was not enough. 'Open your legs,' he said very quietly. She could not breathe. She felt the strap – cold smooth flexible leather – against her, directing her to edge her feet apart. The shivers kissed her inner thighs and belly. Then she jumped – for his half-gloved hand had touched her right ankle. He was kneeling; she felt his breath against the back of her knee. He lifted her ankle, carefully bent the foot, pressed the backs of his fingers against the sole and stroked, making her try to lift the foot away. He sighed. Nervously, the foot returned and touched then pressed into the half-gloved palm. And when she did that, Anya felt a soft wave – a peculiar pleasure – travel up her leg and draw within her belly. Under the guidance of his hand, the leg gradually angled, the toes pointed down, the smooth calf muscle trembled. One hand closed over the upper surface of the foot; the other stroked the fine downy hairs upon that trembling calf, then stroked behind the knee, then rubbed the curving sole of the foot very gently. The toes were now directed through the brass ring near the floor until the slender ankle was encircled. The left foot was taken, stroked and similarly installed.

'Grip with your forearms – tight!' She gasped as her body lifted and her belly touched the cold wooden surface of the mast. With her legs so wide apart, she needed to balance on tiptoes. It hurt her to have to do this; it tensed the muscles of her inner thighs; her buttocks shook. She felt Kasger behind her, very close. He opened her jacket, pulling it back beneath her arms. He took each breast and lifted it to the side. Then the jacket fell back against her. 'Grip tighter,' he said. The tight and tender skin of Anya's breasts was pressed against the wood. Kasger stroked the nipples through her jacket, rolling them between the unyielding rough hewn wood and the soft silk of the lining. The nipples became larger. He slid his right hand beneath the jacket and pressed his cupped palm against the warm round of her breast, as if trying to contain it. Though his palm was large, her bosom would not be contained. He pressed the breast against the wood and touched the tip. He laid his fingers underneath her arms, against the dry salt of her curls; his fingertips followed the lines of her ribs, at her back, beneath the jacket, across her skin, then down, cupping the narrow waist between the two palms, containing her. His hands approached each other and pressed; he tried to make them touch and the pressure took her breath away. He took the strap; she felt it stroke the surface of her buttocks, down, then up. She was so afraid. Why did he taunt her, when she knew what he would do? Why did he not just do it?

Her buttocks were lifted; she held her breath; her eyes were wide, for suddenly, she thought he would open her and smack her in her split. 'Keep still, Princess.' Again the cheeks were lifted apart. She gasped. A fingertip touched her, precisely in the centre. It was held there while the cheeks were drawn more tightly apart. Then the fingertip began to rub, back and forth across the mouth of the funnel of silky black flesh. She shuddered and the fingertip withdrew.

'Has the captain examined you?' the voice asked calmly. Anya stopped breathing. 'Answer me . . . Has he examined you here?' The fingertip pressed against the funnel.

'Yes . . .' she whispered, then she closed her eyes and she relived that first deep drawing feeling, as the captain had stood above her, watching her so coolly, while he touched her there. The touch, so brief yet searching, had triggered memories so profound, memories of prolonged submission and of pleasures sweet as warm mulled wine dripped slowly in her throat.

'Did he say anything?'

'No,' she answered quickly, then remembered. He had said something and now the memory made her blush with shame.

'And he expects you in his cabin, tonight?'

'Yes,' she whispered softly to the mast.

'I see.' He took hold of her right leg behind the knee and lifted it, so her foot slipped out of the ring, then he bent the leg and raised the knee to the level of her waist. 'Keep it there.' He left her and began doing something behind her, at the table. Then he returned. 'Keep your leg up.' She was very frightened. The finger again touched the mouth of her bottom. It smeared something on it. A small dollop of something soft and cool – a paste – now filled the small well. She found it very difficult to keep her leg up. Her leg ached. She heard him unhurriedly drying his fingers on a cloth. 'Keep still.' She pressed her hot flushed cheek against the wood and closed her eyes. 'Relax . . .' But that threat only made her buttocks tense. What was it he had put there? She felt his hand pressing against the left cheek of her bottom. The hand held the strap and the leather dangled down and brushed against her thigh. 'Relax it . . .'

It, he had said. Waves of premonition kissed the small and painted mouth. He took the leg that was bent and raised it higher, until her knee lifted her jacket away and brushed against her breast. Then something touched her; something small and round was being slowly turned and pressed against her bottom. The waves of delicious fear came stronger; the cool paste spread against her. The pressure increased. 'Push . . . There . . .' Her bottom opened and the cool paste slipped within. Then the narrow object holding her bottom open

43

slowly turned. The peculiar feeling – deep and drawing inside her, the same one that she had experienced when the captain touched her bottom – came again. But this time it was stronger.

She could hear Kasger's breathing; she could feel this thing that held her body open slowly turning inside her, while her leg was tucked up high, while her belly trembled and her short curls brushed and snagged and twitched against the rough wood of the mast. Her leg was then released, but Anya did not lower it. She kept it pressed against the mast. Kasger stood back and watched her body's gentle shaking cause the leather strap to sway upon its ring and to kiss against the hard tense muscle of her upper thigh.

The handle of the strap was taken out of her. As she was wiped dry with a cloth, she felt her face and neck turning hot. She was overwhelmed with shame at the feelings that this terrible intimacy had provoked. And she was afraid too – of what this man had done, of what he might have put inside her – the paste. Already, she could feel something, a soft warmth there. But most of all, she was frightened by the thought of what these preparations might mean, and of how they might relate to the captain – what he might want to do. Her leg was lowered and carefully replaced within its ring, so the cheeks of her bottom were kept apart. The half-gloved hand patted them. 'You are learning,' he whispered, 'but we are not finished yet.'

The cloth was returned to the table, then the strap was hung on a hook above her head, leaving Kasger with both hands free to explore her. Reaching beneath, he took her fleshpot, still sticky and half swollen from Travix's prolonged touching. The fingertips took the coated, clinging, roughened curls and pulled the lips apart, then the two thumbs slipped within to test their fleshy thickness, and though Anya did not want it so, her tiny tip of pleasure bestirred itself to make a bone. Each lip was squeezed between a finger and thumb; each lip thickened quickly. The thumbs slipped out, then the lips were held together – not squeezed now, but simply held – in the fingers of one hand. The fingers of the other hand, beneath her jacket, stroked the smooth skin in the small of her back.

They found the sensitive downy hair and brushed against it gently while, between her legs, her flesh was held with the small bone of pleasure trapped inside. The fingers slowly moved her flesh lips and her body stayed still and tense; the small bone peeped out from its hood and her body seeped new oil which liquefied that stickiness, wet those curls and soaked into the leather of his glove. She murmured softly, though she did not want it so.

The hands released her sex and stopped stroking her back. They lifted and separated her thighs, to leave her swollen purse exposed between them. Anya gasped, for she felt the buckle of his belt press against her bottom. Something nudged between her open thighs and touched against her at the front. It felt hard but warm and very smooth, covered in a fine soft skin. The cockstem sleeved in soft matt leather stroked her lips, then pressed until its smooth head cleaved her purse apart. It pressed against the entrance, holding the lips open. And with Anya's flesh so tight and swollen, and the cockhead thicker by virtue of its extra skin, the mouth of her sex was distended. The inner surface clung about the leather like a pouted thick-lipped mouth. 'Stay on your toes,' he whispered.

The fingertips pressed her sex lips round the plum, trying to form them into a third skin over it. Yet those lips were too full of fluid; they were far too thick, so when the fingers squeezed them, the pressure was turned into pain. But the pain in so hard and sensitive and sexual a part was partly pleasure. It was not a stabbing pain but a slow pressure of bursting in each flesh lip which Anya could feel not only in her sex but also up into her belly. And when the fingertips pressed upwards to trap the swollen hood, the feeling was sweet. It made her neck arch back and her belly slowly curve to meet the pleasure of distension. The fingers slipped the hood against the bone beneath it, then touched the bone itself and Anya's body stiffened. Kasger grunted; Anya murmured and the fingers carefully explored her. She wanted to close her legs and squeeze. She could not; her feet were captive in the rings; her knees were kept open against the mast; her buttocks were separated. And now, with her sex lips still distended about the

45

soft capped plum, her nubbin was being tortured inchmeal by the slow slip of the swollen hood and the inquisitive tip of an index finger. Yet the feeling was delicious. If that feeling were to continue, her belly would surely burst.

The squeezing now resumed and the pain of pressure became unbearable. Anya tried to push, to bed the thick plum deeper in her body. Kasger would not let her do this; he wanted the entrance to her sex held wide. Moving up again from between her legs, the fingertips concentrated only on the small raw and now fully projecting bone of Anya's nubbin. And to Anya, it felt as if the bone had pierced her sex lips and they were seeping fluid on to the fingers and around that cockhead that so cruelly held her open. Again she tried to push; again that push was thwarted. The fingertips just held the hood back and kept it so while her bottom cheeks were lifted on his hands; the pressure tightened and it was as if everything between her legs would burst. Her feet were almost lifted from the rings. She was breathing faster and faster, pulling herself up by her arms now, trying to pull her body forwards to press her belly to the mast, but the hands against her creases simply held her, cruelly tight, cruelly open, with her nubbin pushed out hard, with her buttocks in the air.

When Kasger was ready, he lowered Anya. The fingers gave one last painful squeeze about her sex lips before the leather cockhead was withdrawn. Her lips, hot and swollen, tried to cleave to it at first, then slowly closed. So sensitised was that flesh now that even their touching together sent a soft wave of pleasure up inside her belly. But it was a pleasure that only added to her wanting. She pressed her head against the mast, for she knew that what she had suffered at this man's hands was a torture – as surely as if the flesh between her legs, instead of being stimulated with this pressure-pleasure, had been systematically whipped with a thin and supple switch.

The voice came. Anya's body jerked, for the voice was Travix's.

'Kasger! I see you have found time to amuse yourself with the Princess.' Kasger coughed and immediately moved away. Travix approached. Out of the corner of her eye, Anya glimpsed the pale blue suit, the lifted hand, the lightly ruffled wrist. She shuddered when the cool hand came to rest upon the patch of warm perspiration in the small of her back. The hand moved down and smoothed across her bottom, making it tremble, triggering the deep feeling inside. The fingers rubbed the surface of the skin, then nipped the flesh tightly, twice, making Anya cry out.

'You have not smacked her yet?' Travix asked.

'No, I thought that you —'

'Quite right . . . Quite right.' The second time she said it, the words were rasped through clenched teeth. The fingers continued downwards. The lower part of Anya's right buttock was taken between a finger and a thumb and pinched very hard indeed, until she screamed, then pinched again, harder. The fingers moved closer to the join of the cheeks. With the collusion of other fingers, not yet warmed by contact with her flesh, the cheeks were opened and again the feeling came. 'The unction has been administered?' Anya's teeth began to chatter. The cooler fingers took hold of the flesh very close to the small puckered mouth. 'But have you forgotten, Kasger? She is a prince's lady . . .' And now the fingers nipped her more wickedly than ever, in that very tender place. 'Keep open, Princess. There . . .' said Travix and she just kept nipping in that one place until the screams had shattered to gasping sobs of supplication and the belly had tried to push itself through the mast in a vain attempt to get away. Both sets of fingers then moved unwaveringly below, between Anya's legs.

'Oh, please. Pp-*please* . . .' she whimpered, '*Ooooh* . . .' The grip, dispassionate, came so firmly that the short nails of the finger and thumb seemed to touch each other through the lips. Anya's fingernails clawed the wood, but the grip was not released. Yet a soft whisper came into Anya's ear. '*I* will teach you pleasure, Princess, and I will teach you pain.' The sex lips were now twisted. Anya screamed continuously as she rose up on her toes; the tears rolled down her cheeks, but Travix was unmoved. The grip was held, the twist increased; the soft wrist ruffle brushed between the shuddering thighs. 'Is that understood, my sweet?' Travix whispered, softer than before.

'Yes . . . *Yeeesss*.' Suddenly the fingers sprang apart. And now the pain was excruciating, as if her sex lips had been bathed in burning oil. Travix moved away to address Kasger.

'And now, the spanking. Lift her from the mast. Bring her over here.' Then Travix held up Anya's tearstained chin and laughed: 'Do not look so downcast, Princess.' Her eyes sparkled; her single earring glinted as she wiped the tears away and watched the deepening frown on Anya's face. 'We have a proxy for this pleasure. A whipping girl to take your punishment – for though we may perhaps be permitted a little nip, we can hardly spank a princess on her first day, can we?' Travix bowed and held her arm out. 'Step forward, little one.'

Anya's jaw fell. 'No, please. You cannot . . .' But Travix had already taken Niri's hand and led her into the middle of the room. She began stroking the girl's dark shining hair. Niri seemed very afraid of Travix and cowered away whenever Travix made any sudden move, as if she expected to be hit. She was small and very beautiful, and also very young – too young and tender to be treated in this way. Her long hair hung straight down between her shoulders. Her skin was smooth and uniformly bronze and her breasts had large brown conical nipples. 'A fair substitute for a Princess, do you feel?' Anya's heart sank even further, for it was certain now what Travix meant to do to this innocent girl. It was clear that Niri knew too, whether she understood the words or not. Her eyes were pleading as Travix turned her to the side, then ran her palm over the rounded surface of her buttocks, then made her turn fully and spread. Travix's hand slipped underneath and the girl lifted slightly. Anya's cheeks coloured. Travix noticed this, for she was looking at Anya while she continued to touch the girl. 'We must dispel her fears, prepare her . . .' she explained as Niri's ankles lifted higher. The smooth thighs moved apart a little, then together, about the hand that held her, making the small round buttocks tighten. Niri murmured softly. At a nod from Travix, Kasger moved Anya's feet apart. Her elbows were pinned behind her back, but otherwise, he did not touch her. Yet Anya felt it – the tightness in her belly, the warmth in her bottom and the slow swelling pressure in that flesh which Travix had nipped. But as she watched what

Travix was doing to Niri, the ache within Anya's sex lips was no longer the ache of pain.

Travix next edged Niri to the mast and slipped the brass rings over her wrists. She stood back. Niri's hair hung straight down her back and brushed against the swell of her bottom. Not content with this arrangement, Travix lifted the hair, gently eased it over Niri's shoulder and under her right arm so it lay against her breast. It made Niri's head turn to the left. It emphasised the smooth curve of her back. And it left her bottom completely exposed. Travix lifted each small slim ankle through a ring. Once the feet were placed, the knees had to remain very slightly bent to accommodate the angle and the spread and the bottom formed two quite separate globes. Travix stroked each globe. She stood to the side while she did this, that Anya might witness her fingers test the separation. Travix looked thoughtful; the fingers gently moved and Niri murmured. When the fingers entered and the legs began to tremble, Travix looked straight at Anya and Anya turned bright red. The fingers then withdrew and gently patted the bottom.

Travix left the girl, came over and sat on the seat beside the table. She bade Kasger release Anya and had Anya stand to her right. 'You would not wish to miss this, I am sure,' she said to Anya, as she poured herself a cup of wine. She wetted her middle finger in the wine, then, watching it circle slowly round the rim of the cup, she said in a low voice, weighing every phrase: 'Use the strap, Kasger. Use it only on her bottom. Then play with her a little. But –' the circling finger stopped; she looked directly at Kasger now – 'do not bring her on. That pleasure is for me.' Niri whimpered, as if she had understood.

Anya looked at the woman beside her, so calm, so cruel. She felt a hard lump rising in her throat. Travix glanced up at Anya and when the cold blue eyes touched hers, Anya shivered. Travix's wine-wet middle finger reached. It stroked slowly down over Anya's trembling belly, then lifted and slipped into Travix's mouth. At intervals, this gesture was repeated. Anya stood with legs apart while the wine trickled down her skin.

The strap was taken from the hook above the girl. Kasger's

leather sheathed cock stood brazenly hard. Anya could not take her eyes from it – until the strap swung back on its pivot ring through the wood. At the sound, the buttocks tensed to two hard balls pressed tight together. The leather swept forward. *Crack!* Anya jumped; the buttocks shook; the girl went rigid. From the corner of her eye, Anya saw Travix remove something from her pocket. It was the brushed velvet cloth. The feeling of fear, of delicious anticipation, came between Anya's parted thighs. 'Spread your legs wider, my Princess . . .' At the second smack, Travix gathered Anya's pulsing sex lips in the soft cool velvet; at the mast, Niri burst into tears. 'Smack her harder,' said Travix. 'I want to see her buttocks jump.' This time the strap swung down and back, then it was delivered in an upward cut that lifted the cheeks and made Niri, in an effort to escape the pain, force her belly against the mast. 'Good,' said Travix. And against this torture, as the smacks kept coming, all Anya could feel was the delicious stroke of velvet pleasure between her open thighs. Kasger changed hands and moved round. Niri's belly was pinned to the mast for this second smacking, but her buttocks remained free to move. Anya felt her sex lips gently nested, softly squeezed, each time the strap smacked home. The stripes of cherry red grew plump upon the pale bronze struggling cheeks.

The smacking stopped. Travix sat back and spread the cloth upon her thigh. There was a small dark patch in the centre. Her fingertips now lay against this dampness, tasting it, as she took a draught of wine. Kasger hung up the strap and began to rub the cheeks that he had punished. His hand moved beneath, searching. Niri's sobs gradually turned to murmurs of uncertainty then, finally, assent. Her knees bent a little more; her body moved fractionally down the mast and her fingers gripped the rings. One of Kasger's hands pressed against the small of Niri's back whilst the other worked beneath. Travix took another drink.

Niri began to gasp and the cup hesitated a fraction of an inch from Travix's lip. Her tongue slipped out and slowly licked the golden rim. The fingers underneath Niri withdrew. She was encouraged up on to her toes. Then the strap was lifted down. Travix put the cup down and carefully moulded the cloth into the hollow of her palm.

'Open your legs,' she murmured. Anya's belly sank; there was a buzzing in her ears. The velvet slowly gathered the thick warm fleshy droplet and very softly moved. Across the room, Niri began to whimper as Kasger stepped to the other side. The strap swung back, licked forward, smacked; the buttocks bounced; the tears flowed freely. Throughout the smacking, as the cheeks, already red, turned even redder, Travix's fingertips milked Anya's fleshpot gently and precisely through the velvet. Anya's belly slowly arched, her legs bowed outwards and she tried to place her flesh more fully into this velvet milking cup. 'Keep still,' Travix whispered. The squeezing stopped and the lips of the sex were simply held while the back of Travix's fingers brushed the tight curve of Anya's belly. Kasger changed sides again. Anya felt as if her belly was melting. At the first smack, the velvet moved, brushing against the smooth bare skin where her flesh lips joined her body. Then each subsequent smack was accompanied by a slowly sucking pull. Anya's body delivered up its honeydew, which seeped into the velvet.

Once again, the smacking stopped. The sobbing gradually abated. The cheeks, striped with bright red horizontal bars, were parted and held wide while Kasger touched the tender flesh about the small dark eye within. He stroked the eye until the legs began to move and the belly tried to thrust against the mast.

'Smack it.' For the first time, Travix's breathing was uneven. 'Smack it, quickly!' Travix's fingers, through the velvet, found the bone of Anya's nubbin.

At the mast, the buttocks moved to try to escape; the small slim ankles even tried to lift out from the rings. But the cheeks were held firmly open with one hand, the strap was held in the middle to make it shorter – easier to direct – and smacked down, as instructed, quickly. The dark eye pulsed. 'Again!' Niri tried to squeeze her buttocks shut. Kasger held her open. The small smack sounded, against the tender eye. 'Lift her!' Kasger's hand thrust up between Niri's legs and spread under her belly. He grunted. Niri's ankles slipped out from the rings and her legs dangled down about his forearm; the cheeks lay widely separated. 'Now!' Kasger lifted the belly even higher and smacked the strap repeatedly against the tender funnel. The back arched down, the legs shook, the small mouth palpitated and the belly wriggled in his hand until Travix cried, 'Enough!' She released Anya's pulsing sex, folded the wetted velvet, placed it in her pocket and pushed Anya carelessly aside. 'Now bring her here.'

The young girl's face was tearstained. Her eyes were puffy. Travix moved her chair a little away from the table. 'Here, my darling . . . On my knee,' she said softly. Kasger, leaning against the wall, his cockstem now subsiding, watched with interest. Anya had no option but to stand there. The girl, being shorter than Anya, was quite small compared to Travix, who made her lie face up across her knee. She began playing with her nipples, lifting and turning them, rubbing them between two fingers and a thumb. Gradually, Niri's thighs relaxed. Suddenly, Anya realised that between those thighs, Niri was bare – not partly shaved, as she had thought, but totally bare: the fine spray of black-brown lines above the smooth pouch was not hair at all but threads and tiny dots of colour somehow painted into Niri's naked skin and patterned to look like hair.

'Did it hurt, my darling?' Travix whispered. 'Let me look. Lift. Bend your knees. Oh . . .' The bright red bands glowed across the uplifted bottom. Travix touched it tentatively and Niri murmured. The murmur became a sigh as Travix fully parted the knees to open out the cheeks. She touched the matt, pale bronze-coloured skin between them, then the dark bronze fleshy eye, until it tightened. The fingers moved to the front, eased the small lips back and Anya gasped. Something bedded between the lips had glinted. The hood was teased back. And what Anya saw beneath it made a tiny tumbling shudder come between her legs, as if her bud were being rubbed with the cold stem of a needle. For pierced through Niri's little nubbin was a tiny gold ring. Travix's short nails tried to lift this ring, then the fingertips rubbed around it. Niri cooed; her belly rippled. Finally, the fingers moved away, leaving the nubbin poked out hard and the tiny ring upstanding. The hood slipped back a little but would no longer close

52

about the ring, which formed a minute lengthwise glinting arc at the junction of the lips. The fingertips were now wetted and applied. Niri had difficulty controlling her breathing as the fingertips massaged the small ringed bud. Next, one set of fingers held the flesh hood back and the other set moved, first to Travix's lips then, glistening, to the nubbin, then down to press against the small eye in the groove. Back and forth went the fingers until the knees jerked, the small eye opened to that touch and for the first time, Niri spoke.

'*Niri*,' she said, which to Anya seemed a very strange thing for her to say. The fingers were wetted more thickly with saliva, which was smeared around the sex lips and the hood. And now the ring was very carefully turned, fed gradually through the nubbin. '*Niri?*' the girl began to whimper urgently as her belly progressively lifted.

'Kasger . . . Our guest. Make her comfortable.' Travix took time to wave an arm in the direction of the wall.

'No . . .' said Anya softly, fearfully, guessing what Travix meant. But Kasger, his cock quite rigid now, lifted her body easily and carried her. With Anya facing into the room, her thighs were held apart above the smooth horizontal pole projecting from the wall. Very slowly, she was lowered. The cold wood touched her thighs and spread them. Her hot lips touched the wood, then curled to the side. Her toes touched the floor. Unsatisfied, Kasger lifted her again. A line of wet was brushed against the polished wood and it glinted in the light. Her purse was straightened; again she was lowered. Her sex lips split about the broad curve of the wood. He grunted. Her arms were fastened behind her to the large rings on the wall, her knees were drawn back and her ankles were roped together across the pole. Kasger supported her trussed-up body while he made sure her thighs were fully opened. Then he checked that the hot wet sex lips still lay apart before allowing her belly to roll forwards until her ankles lifted and her open fleshpot suckered down upon the polished wood. He adjusted the tension in the rope until he felt the pivot point was right and he checked it with his fingers.

'There,' said Travix. 'That should help you, Princess. Niri is quite near now, but for you, my darling, there is still some

53

little way to go.' She held her hand out. Kasger took two items from a drawer below the table and placed them by her wrist. Anya knew what one of them must be. It was in a jar. Though her flesh was numb, she could feel the warmth still, in her bottom. 'Shhh . . .' said Travix when Niri whimpered. 'She is frightened,' Travix explained. 'She thinks that I will put her to the captain.' And that made Anya feel afraid again of the contents of the jar and of what all of this might imply for her.

The fingers, having dipped into the jar, smeared the pale blue ointment into the small dark eye between the open cheeks. Travix wiped her fingers on the cloth that Kasger handed her, then took the second item, which was cylindrical, very heavy and sheathed in blue silk. Travix slipped it from its casing, handling it carefully. 'Good . . . very cold,' she said, wrapping the silk around the base. It appeared to be made of gold. It was thick but with a rounded end, necked an inch or so below the crown. She took no notice of Niri's protests but made the girl arch backwards, so her whole body formed a curve and her long hair spread across the floor, and she kept her knees bent tight. She also kept the lips of Niri's sex held open, with the outer fingers of one hand. The blue ruffled wrist brushed Niri's painted naked lower belly. The middle finger gently stimulated the places where the gold ring pierced the nubbin. And all this while, the hard round golden pressure was applied to the slippery eye, which in due course opened, making Niri gasp against the sudden shock of cold, then grip the tighter about the bulb as it very slowly turned. When the knees tried to close, Travix waited. Niri kept them open. Niri understood. Travix fitted her palm to the roundness of that belly and pressed, and as she did so, gently twisted the cylinder of gold, until Niri murmured, '*Niri* . . .' whereupon Travix bent forward, down, and pushed her tongue out.

Anya watched the tongue snake round the nubbin ring as the cylinder was gently pulled and then Niri's belly burst. Her back arched to a curve so sharp her forehead touched the floor, then pressed against it while the tongue snaked leisurely round the nubbin for three more wriggling turns, then hooked through the small gold ring and lifted. The tongue-tip formed a small pink snake head encircled by the ring. The snake head pushed, withdrew, then pushed again and lifted; Niri's belly burst a second time. The snake shrank back, leaving a small pool of saliva gathered in the tiny fleshy hollow around the bright gold ring. The severed lip pouted and the tongue tubed beneath it to sip from this small clear pool of spittle infused with Niri's heat.

Travix – calm, relaxed – then sat up and watched Niri's body continue to heave and shudder. She waited until the shudders softened, then placed her arm beneath the shoulders – heavy now, a dead weight though the girl was slight – and raised the pliant body. The heavy eyelids opened and the girl looked into her eyes. Travix offered her lips. The girl, reaching up, sucked softly upon the pink contusion once, then again very fully. Her small moist tongue slipped out and touched the line of sever. Anya shuddered; between her legs, though her flesh was numb, she still felt swollen. In her belly was a peculiar tightness. Travix stroked the girl's breasts, touched the hard conical nipples tenderly, then opened the buttocks and very gently removed the gold cylinder against the reluctance of the gripping fleshy ring. At that critical point of distension before the cylinder slipped free, the girl reached up and kissed Travix again. And again the tightness came in Anya's belly.

Travix then laid Niri back across her lap while she took a cord, about as long as her hand, drew the sex lips back and slipped the end of the cord through the tiny ring. Niri murmured as Travix carefully knotted it. She pressed the arrangement back so the ring, the knot and the short loose end disappeared, leaving the rest of the cord hanging. At the free end she tied a small loop. Then without a single glance at Anya, she simply stood, lifted Niri in her arms and began to carry her away.

'Travix!' Kasger called after her. He took Anya by the arm. 'This one – she is wanted by the captain tonight?'

'Chain her,' she called over her shoulder, 'she will be sent for in good time.'

Then Travix hesitated and turned her head again. Her coarse blonde hair moved like a solid mat. She still held Niri in her arms. Niri's knees were tucked up tightly. The knotted string dangled down across the bareness between her thighs. Travix glanced down at Niri. The string moved. It was as if it had caught Travix's attention, fascinated her, as it might a cat. Travix came back. She put one foot on the chair and balanced Niri's lower back on her knee. This freed one of Travix's hands. This hand moved nervously. It began to stroke the string, to rearrange it to one side then the other of the bare sex lips, to stretch it lightly, then to open out the looped end which, dangling down, brushed across the small bronze swollen funnel in the groove. As Travix's fingers now began to touch the sex lips, to press the string against them and very gently squeeze, it seemed at long last she remembered what had made her hesitate.

'Kasger,' she said, as Niri softly cooed, 'she must be pouched.' Anya held her breath. The middle finger slipped through the loop and touched the small bronze funnel. Travix now looked at Anya, her jacket drawn back from her breasts, her thighs spread and her open belly pressed about the beam. Anya waited. Travix did not speak further. But the middle finger tensed. Niri moaned; the funnel opened, swallowed; the tension in the string increased and the small ring slipped out, glinting. Niri's arms reached up and fastened round Travix's neck.

Now Travix spoke again: 'I want the Princess pouched – and tight.' The finger bedded deeper. Niri moaned again and Anya's belly shuddered; the deep drawing feeling came within her bottom. Travix offered her lips to Niri. With the middle finger still implanted and the hand cupped between Niri's legs, impressing the string into her bareness, Niri kissed her. Then she was lifted up once more and carried away.

Kasger waited till they had disappeared beyond the end of the corridor. Then he looked at Anya. Immediately she cast her gaze downwards to the beam. Her breathing had not steadied; it would not. Her thighs ached; her flesh felt numb; but what she had witnessed – Travix's cruelty, Niri's response – left a deep disquiet in her belly. And the pouch that Travix had referred to, what was that? Kasger moved. His iron grip upon her arm relaxed. But now she could see that other thing – his maleness – stir between his legs and again she was afraid. He crouched beside her to unfasten her bonds and she watched the thick shiny plait of hair moving between his shoulder blades as he worked; she watched the muscles rippling on his back and upper arms. She could smell his scent, strong from the effort of the smacking and strong from wanting, too, she knew. What would he do with her now that Travix had gone?

When he lifted her by her shoulders and placed her on the floor, her knees buckled. He caught her and propped her hands against the table. Then she heard him fumbling through the drawers. What looked like a small bundle of leather thongs was thrown on to the table. The jar was placed next to it. When he went over to the mast to retrieve the leather strap, Anya felt as if ice water was being sponged between her legs, for she thought that he meant to use the strap on her there and then, while she was bent across the table. But he tucked it into his belt, collected up the other things and led her, staggering, down the corridor and to a door in the middle of the row. He slid aside the heavy bolt and opened it. It was dark in there. 'Your quarters, Princess.' He pushed her forward; she didn't want to go.

In the faint light through the open door, she could see that the cabin was small. It was warm and she could smell straw. Something glistened on the walls. And now she was more afraid. He pushed her in. There was sawdust on the floor. Almost immediately, her shin bumped against a wooden bed, which he pushed her on to. It was covered in straw. He put the things on a small table by the bed. 'Sit down. Take your coat off.' Her hands were shaking as she did it. He took it from her, rolled it up and put it under his arm. And now, completely naked before this man, she felt more vulnerable than at any time since she had been aboard this ship. She knew he was looking at her in the half-darkness. She tried to keep her breathing steady. Her hands clasped together for reassurance and her fingers searched out her one remaining possession, a turquoise ring upon her middle finger. They turned it, tested it, proved that it was still there, then closed about it tightly, hid it in the dark. Kasger left, taking the jacket with him, then returned without the coat but with a lamp, and placed it on the table. Suddenly, he knelt down.

Behind him, on the walls, she could see now what had

glistened – there were rings, four rings again, like those on the mast. Hanging from the ceiling in the middle of the room were two long chains, with large leather loops at the bottom. The sinking feeling came. She was frightened of what these looped chains might be used for. Then she heard a clink. A chain was drawn across the floor and fastened between her ankles. She almost panicked. She was turned while another chain was secured behind her back, between her wrists. The chains were short, only three or four links each, but they were heavy iron chains. Then something wooden scraped across the floor.

'You wish to use it?' It was a bucket.

'No . . .'

'Suit yourself.' With her heart pounding now, she was lifted fully on to the bed. 'On your side.' She struggled to face the wall. 'Move your legs back.' She heard the sound of a chain again, being pulled through a hole in wood. Then she saw it, a long chain this time, with a hook attached, being drawn lengthwise up the bed, from the panelled footboard, between her chained-together ankles, up her back, then between her arms, to fasten to an iron ring in the headboard. She was turned on to her back. 'Bend your knees. No . . . Open them.' Again the coldness washed between her thighs as Kasger gazed down at her. The heavy plait had fallen forward over his shoulder to hang alongside the talisman of wrinkled skin. The lamplight reflected as a dull orange glow from his polished head and the sockets of his eyes looked black. 'Keep them apart.' She had tried to lift her knees when the half-gloved hand had reached. He waited until her knees were fully opened and the light reflected in the creases of her thighs. Then, as Anya shuddered, as she turned her head away, the hands, two hands now, not one, and expert hands, massaged her, rubbed the feeling back into the numbness in the bridge between her fleshpot and her bottom, rubbed her aching thighs, rubbed in the creases, stirred the bright red curls, then gathered up the softened open matt black lips and gently closed them. Her hips were lifted. The leather cord he had brought was passed around them. Attached to it at the front by three drawstrings, one at the top and two beneath, was a small pod-shaped leather pouch,

58

slightly shorter, slightly narrower than Anya's little finger. He tested the thin skinned pouch by pressing the tip of his little finger into it from the back. The skin was matt and covered with very fine dense hair; it looked like closely shaved fur. It stretched around the pressing finger. Anya could not swallow her heart. As the small bulge of the fingertip slid up and down the pod, the feeling came between her legs, and now it was not cold.

He pushed her knees out until they almost touched the straw. Then his fingertips teased her sex lips, lifting them upright. As he let them fall and they rolled to the side, she felt them swelling. Again they were lifted; again they fell, but more slowly. The thongs were lowered loosely against her belly; the swelling lips were pressed to the side, though now they seemed reluctant to remain there, and the pod was laid casually upon them. He did not attempt to fit it. The strings below dangled across her bottom, tickling, reminding her of Niri; she was imagining the things that Travix might be doing to Niri now, with the leather cord attached so intimately, knotted to the ring pierced through her nubbin. Such thoughts caused a wave of pleasure deep in Anya's belly. Kasger's fingertips had moved up and closed about Anya's nipples; the fingertips were wet and the nipples were gently worked. Anya's hips moved. The chains between her ankles clinked; the thongs, the soft pod, moved against her like living things. The tips of the fingers brushed the soft hair upwards on her belly. Her belly lifted; her sex lips were erect. 'Push . . .' he said. 'Lift . . .' The pod was slipped quickly over her, sheathing only her sex lips, and it was as if all her pleasure was constrained now, contained within this thin-skinned bag. The strings were drawn tight; she was turned while they were fastened at the back. The tightness made her sex lips swell; the leather stretched and the fine soft furry coating bristled.

Kasger unhooked the long chain. He made her kneel with her bottom up and her breasts pressed to the straw while he took that warm hard swelling between his fingers. It was neither fruit nor animal, yet like a fruit, it dangled, and like an animal, it was very warm. He held it while he spread her knees, then spread her cheeks and applied the unction to the small black mouth. Then he held the polished wooden stem of the strap there, between the double string. The round stem slowly twirled; the face buried deeper into the straw. But the small pod continued to swell between his fingers and eventually – though very quickly when it happened – the small mouth opened to the slow, persistent twirl. The protest was there – he heard it murmured – but so was the pleasure, he knew, for each application of the unction progressively sensitised that place. The belly began to tremble and the knees tried to move together to trap the pod more tightly between his fingers. But he kept those knees apart, to stave off any deliverance, while the round stem was carefully turned and the unction was worked, against the protests, deeper into the pouted black-lipped funnel. He then removed the stick, reattached the chain and turned the girl on to her side with her knees tucked up and her breasts upon the straw, then took the lamp, the jar, the strap and left and closed the door.

The cabin turned soot black. Suddenly, it seemed very much smaller than before.

Anya listened. Gradually, her breathing slowed. Above her, she could hear muffled sounds of chairs being moved across the floor, faint sounds of merriment, but there were no other noises. All seemed quiet in the corridor. She tried to make herself more comfortable, but the straw was hard. It tugged her hair and rubbed against her skin whenever she moved. With her hands behind her back, she could not protect her breasts from all the nips and scratches. The chains lay against her buttocks. She opened her thighs, but the swollen feeling there would not recede. In her bottom was a throb of pleasure, as if she were still being touched. And the visions of what she had witnessed conjured themselves up again: Travix – so cruelly calm – and Niri, being smacked on Anya's behalf. Watching that had caused a strange feeling deep in Anya's belly, and when the girl's buttocks had been spread apart and they had smacked her there . . . Anya shivered. She arched her belly; she wanted to be touched now. She tried to squeeze her legs about her bursting fleshpot. The lips felt hot and hard, distended, sheathed in this fine soft leather pouch.

And in the dark, though all was silent, Anya was reliving

Niri's punishment over and over again – the belly lifted on the hand, the whimpers and the rhythmic smack of leather against naked skin. When she pressed her thighs together, it was as if Travix were still there, pressing the soft brushed velvet gently about her flesh lips, coaxing them cruelly to the edge of pleasure while that deep dark tender mouth was smacked.

[5]

The Captain's Table

That evening, when the sun balanced a claw's-breadth above the horizon at the end of an outstretched arm, two men in leather shirts were dispatched. They found the girl – the Princess – chained and asleep, but not still. The straw was matted in her tousled hair; her breathing was staccato, as if she were dreaming, perhaps running in her dreams, for the muscles of her thighs tightened and relaxed and the slender ankles lifted and tried to brush across the straw. Between those thighs, as she faced half downwards with her ankles shackled together and her wrists behind her back, was the long chain, its iron harshness softened by the smooth curve where it draped across her buttock and lay against the bulging leather pouch. The pouch looked thick and swollen; it was moist. The men approached in silence. They took one knee and crooked it so the pouch projected. One of them laid a palm against each inner thigh, which felt hot, while the other squeezed the pouch. She murmured; her thigh muscles tightened against the palms and her buttocks tried to clench about the double thong between them.

When the men unfastened the long chain, she awoke. And though it was not bright in that small cabin, she hunched as if to shade her eyes from the light, though she could not, for her hands were shackled. The deep red locks – like dense ruby soaking up the light – fell away from a visage that was perfect, kissed with freckles, smooth, a soft warm glow upon the cheeks and a long wavy wisp of clear red hair beside the delicate ear. The full lips moved apart; she frowned; the eyes widened in realisation, reflecting the lamplight like two black onyx stones. Yet though her fear was there, she neither murmured nor complained.

They lifted her and made her walk shackled, though they had the keys to free her. One man walked on each side, towering above her. And it seemed, despite the fact that the linkage between her feet was short and her steps were thereby stilted by the chains, she was able to accommodate their inconvenience. And when they took her up into the crew-deck, catching her as she toppled forwards on the stairs, then rearranging her hair, drawing it back, away from her breasts, it seemed that, though she faltered at first, she could walk before them, through that throng, with her shoulders back, her breasts lifted and, between her legs, the pouch quite visible, full, a clear sign of her sexual excitement – not at this treatment perhaps, not at this display, but not lessened by it either. But of course, they were here on the crewdeck for a deeper purpose – to prepare her, 'to make her young blood course through her veins . . . She must hear it, like the roar of the storm wind through the sails.'

This was the captain's first instruction to the leather-shirted men. His eyes had smouldered when he said it. They smouldered now, with the special fire, as he stood on the deck outstaring the setting sun, listening to the sounds of raucous laughter from below. And the girl – the Princess – would be unshackled at the wrists, then resecured with the chain about a hook in the low rafters, high enough to keep her on her toes, small toes, he had seen that afternoon, slim feet, still shackled at the ankles, slender thighs – good muscles – a bright, open bush of red curls, which would be slicked back now, by her own moisture, from the black lips sealed for him within a warm skin pouch, for the sailors to nip and squeeze to their hearts' content, yet to go no further, but within that constraint, to do as they would, approaching from the front, or from the back to touch the soft shaved fur beneath the small mouth, kept very tight from fear, no doubt, while the double thong stretched across its tightness, sensitised with the unction, while the shackled legs were drawn apart, while the attendants stood back, until the slow roar came coursing through her sweet young veins until she could not breathe. The captain closed his eyes; the vision was there still, drawn in perfect detail upon the back of his resting, heavy eyelids. He opened his mouth and breathed the cool late day air. Soon now, they would bathe her and she would be ready. And he would be the first man to taste her body once her flesh had known the special intimacy of the pouch.

Anya stood once more before the large, panelled door, but on the side away from the skull. Its hollow sockets stared at her from behind the wooden bars of its small cage. Her hands hung limply in front of her, touching at the fingertips, fastened at the wrists, which lay against the bareness of her belly. Her ankle chains had been removed. Her skin felt soft and warm. It tingled from the bathing; the hot salt water had left it feeling moist. She had been embarrassed – she still felt embarrassed at the recollection – to be bathed by two men, the leather-shirted guards, while Ratchitt stood by, averting his eyes and holding the towels. When they had untied the pouch, it had clung to her, from the pressure, from the moistness – from the touching she had been made to suffer, chained to the hook in the thick oak ceiling beam while the two men sat back upon the table and drank their mugs of beer. Once the pouch had been removed, her flesh, cool yet swelling still, had felt peculiarly naked before their scrutiny. And as if to make her feel more naked yet, they had made her use the bucket. In a very matter-of-fact way, they had made her kneel up, then had tried to place the bucket between her knees but, discovering that this was not possible with her ankles fastened by the short chain, they had removed this and tried again. Their methods would admit of no refusal. They had sponged her lower back unhurriedly, recharging the cloth in fresh cold water, until the thin trickles, running down the groove and between her legs, had provoked her beyond the point of urgent need, to the sweet release of a warm wet pulsing pressure that, once started, would not stop. But they had continued trickling the water down her until the last hot shivering drops had dripped from her person. And though she had thought that she might die then from shame, the men had continued their preparations for her ablutions as if nothing had befallen that was in any way untoward.

The pouch was carefully wrapped in a soft cloth and put to

one side. Again she felt a wave of shame. But once she was lifted into the giant shallow copper bowl and she felt the soothing warmth of the water on her skin, it was as if an unbearable weight was gradually lifted from her mind. The men had sponged her breasts, her belly and her back and had made her kneel. Then with her eyes tight shut but her knees apart and the warm salt water lapping heavily against her, dripping from her curls, her chained wrists were lifted and she was opened, back and front. Warm ocean flooded inside. Her leaves of flesh were held apart and the inner surfaces stroked; two fingers pushed inside; a third finger, oiled, was slipped into her bottom. 'No – keep your arms up,' one of the men had said. 'Fold your hands across your breasts.' The weight of her forearms, pressed against them, made them push out to the sides. The fingers, moving round inside her, pressed against each other through the inner skin. Warm oil was massaged into her nubbin until it came up very hard. The men made her lean back against the shallow side of the bowl, her hands still across her breasts and the fine golden hairs upon her forearms touching the enhanced tightness of those breasts, which to Anya now felt overfull and heavy, while the men looked at her nubbin, while each of them touched it.

In time, they had lifted her out and made her sit astride a simple padded stool on which the towels had now been placed. Throughout the drying, her nubbin had remained erect. They had checked it at intervals, not touching it directly, but expressing approval each time the hood was slipped back and the nubbin was seen to be poking out hard. They had pushed her belly forward until it touched the padding and then had examined her bottom, touching the soft, sensitised skin very lightly, debating whether it should be fully oiled, then at last deciding against it, but fingering that skin repeatedly, while beneath, her rigid nubbin was pressed into the soft damp of the towels. They had brushed her hair until it hung straight and heavy and shining, then had refitted the leather pouch – dark golden with her moisture – about her sex lips. They had simply made her kneel and rubbed those lips very gently with the backs of their fingers. As the flesh lips swelled, they were captured in the pouch and sealed skin to skin against the

65

leather. Finally, her legs were fitted into thick, bright yellow woollen stockings which, even with their tops turned over, extended nearly to the tops of her thighs. But at no point in these preparations had they unlocked the chains that held her wrists.

And now, Anya stood at the captain's door, afraid of what might befall her at his hands, yet unable to dispel the memory of the gentle stimulation she had experienced with the two young men. It had been so different from the cruel kind of stimulation she had been forced to suffer; it had made the pouch soften again, swell warm; it had left her feeling very aroused.

Ratchitt knocked. He waited, his head bowed, his eyes looking up at Anya then, as he listened, ticking slowly from side to side. On the third tick, a muffled sound was heard. Ratchitt lifted the latch; the heavy door opened smoothly. Anya was ushered in and Ratchitt retreated, quietly closing the door.

The first thing she noticed was the heavy sweet scent of ripened fruit; the second was the evening sky, deep red and capped with purple clouds, framed within the great bow window above the low divan bed. That second vision vanished as the furled, deep orange curtains were drawn together, secured with a sash and the stooped form of an ancient steward lumbered round, lighting extra lamps and drawing them up towards the ceiling, until the room swelled with a light which swept the darkest recesses clean. The walls were dressed with trophies in gold and silver; in the alcoves, jewel-encrusted treasures caught the light. At first, as her eyes had nervously danced about the room, Anya hadn't seen that there were two figures, because one had remained still. She had seen the ornate oak carvings, pillars and fretwork and the inlaid painted panels showing blue seas, ships in full-bellied sail and sunlit shores bedecked with naked bronze-skinned dark-eyed women. And below these panels, to her right, she had seen the table – a great black oak table, laden with mouth-watering roasts and sweetmeats, fruits on golden platters and clear crystal jugs of wine. Behind the table, in the centre, was an enormous chair, so large it would have taken four men to lift it. Like the table, it was made of oak, but it was thickly upholstered in deep orange, so little of the wood was visible. The armrests were as wide as Anya's waist.

Then the second figure moved. She stood. She was nude; her form was sylphlike. Around her waist was a plaited flat green twine. Anya's eyes followed her as she walked over to the great chair and sat upon the armrest casually, as if to assert a claim, then lifted her delicately furrowed chin and looked sidelong at Anya. Finally, to make her position quite clear, she picked up a small green fruit from one of the platters before her, nipped the skin open with her small teeth, spread it and sipped. She did not look at Anya again, but seemed to be engrossed in the detail, or the display, of eating this fruit. Her eyes would close; the lashes would flutter – they were perfectly curved and black, like her eyebrows, dense black – yet her skin was pale and her hair blonde. Anya did not understand this dissonance. And her lips were red, as if they had been painted, yet they had not. As her head tilted and her hair fell back, finely twined as if repeatedly twisted round the finger and combed by the wind, her lips pouted and her tongue emerged to collect the heavy green-droplets squeezed out from the fruit. Anya looked to the steward, who had almost finished moving round, but he too ignored her and began adjusting the deep orange cushions on the soft cream sheets of the bed.

The door opened again behind Anya. From the corner of her left eye, she saw the deep red coat, the dark hair, then the blue-grey glint of steel. Every muscle in her limbs locked; her eyes turned forwards, very slowly. The captain passed, turned, looked down at her. She averted her gaze by turning her eyes very gradually to the right. She could feel the power of those green strong eyes still, though she stared at the table. In that first glance, Anya had noticed that under his good arm he carried a rolled-up chart. And now all she could hear was the parchment creaking. The girl on the chair moved. She put the half-eaten fruit carefully aside and got up slowly. The steward stopped what he was doing and stood by the end of the table; for the first time he looked in Anya's direction, but now that extra pair of eyes upon her only added to her plight.

Having hesitated, as though he might have been surprised

at Anya's presence, but without acknowledging this fact – indeed, without acknowledging anybody's presence – the captain then walked round the table and the steward to the chair, cleared a space in front of it, placed the chart on the table, unbuckled his sword with one hand, hung it over the back of the chair and sat down.

He unrolled the chart and pinned it open with the back of the double hook. The fingers of his right hand drummed upon the surface of the parchment. It was now the only sound in the room. The steward, his arms folded across his breast, waited. The girl stood to the captain's left and a little behind him. Her hand stretched across the back of the chair, stroking the dense orange cloth. She looked at Anya. The steward looked at Anya. But the captain still pored over his parchment. To Anya, the air in the room felt very warm. The girl's hand gradually advanced; it dangled forwards from the back of the chair; it touched and stroked the thick black hair, then moved round. The fingertips settled around the long soft earlobe and began to play with it, gently pulling, lightly squeezing. The chart was now propped open between a jug of wine and a bowl. The captain sat back, resting his head against one of the soft heavy wings of the chair. His right hand came round and touched the girl's belly. Encouraged, she sat sideways on the armrest, with the captain's hand upon her belly, above the plaited twine, testing the well of her navel and touching the soft pale hair below it. Behind the girl was the captain's left arm and curving round now and fitted to the underside of her breast was the double hook of steel.

Anya could feel the moisture forming under her arms. The yellow woollen stockings tickled her where they clung against her thighs. The pouch was biting; the drawstrings nipped her flesh lips. The drawstrings were unyielding; the passage of blood into her flesh was one way and the more her flesh swelled, the more the pouch bit, the more it made her flesh lips fill with blood until, standing as she was now, with her thighs together, she could feel it like a soft leather creature pressed against the ticklish skin at the tops of her inner thighs. It made her think of the way Travix had touched her between the legs and the way the two men who had bathed her had wanted to prolong that bathing, keeping her in the water, recharging it when it turned cold, opening her flesh repeatedly to the flood of warmth and playing gently with her nubbin.

And now, the girl's leg was slowly lifted astride the dense round armrest. Her bottom eased forwards and her head moved back. Her blonde hair, with its thin strands, lay beside the captain's dense black mane. Her soft complexion pressed against the bushy eyebrows, lay skin to skin against the wrinkled cheek. Between her thighs, the pale blonde curls had separated and the lips had opened to a bright red eye. The bottom edged forwards again; below the bright eye was a smaller tight one, its eyelids squeezed shut, brown. And now it was the brown eye that the captain's fingertips sought to taste, while the girl's own hands descended over her belly and slipped beneath the plaited green twine. With the twine appearing as a bond about her wrists, her fingers held her body open, touched the lips, then squeezed the upper corner of the open eye, to develop the small red swelling bud while lower down, the captain's finger and thumb continued to stroke towards each other across the small, raised, wrinkled, tight-shut, swelling brownness. And all the time, the girl – red-lipped, open-sexed, nipples pink and belly round – stared blue-eyed at Anya.

The captain lifted his hand, snapped his fingers, pointed and the girl's expression suddenly changed to one of pique. She slipped off the armrest and strode sullenly across the room to a thickly cushioned low square stool next to which was a small stand with multicoloured lengths of twine attached to its top. She turned half away from Anya and began rapidly plaiting this twine with exaggerated movements clearly designed to draw the captain's attention and to indicate her annoyance. But seemingly the captain did not care to have his attention diverted by a sulky girl. He leaned forward in the chair, placed his left elbow on the table, so the hook was raised – poised, it seemed to Anya, as if about to fall. The distilled light of every lamp was somehow captured between the twin cusps of that glinting double claw. She could not take her eyes away from it. It was as if there were no one else in the room but she and the captain and no other item but the hook. Beyond it, she could see his craggy face, the jutting, deeply lined forehead, the strong curved nose and above all, the eyes, which glittered like the jewels embedded in the burnished trophies all around the room. The right hand lifted; the finger crooked and Anya began to shake. She did not move; if she were to have tried to move she would never have been able to lift her legs and she would have collapsed in a heap on the floor. She glanced across to the attendant, who stared incuriously straight ahead; then she looked towards the girl, who now seemed interested. She was still plaiting, but more slowly and looking at Anya instead of at her work.

Very slowly and with the weight of the world upon her shoulders, Anya did move; her leaden feet lifted. A slow smile began spreading across the girl's face. She released the plait and drew her blonde strands back and tucked them behind her ears. Again, the finger at the table beckoned. Anya edged towards it. The captain waited until she had reached the opposite side of the table. Then the bushy eyebrows frowned and the hook twisted, glinting, indicating that she should come round. She felt like crying. Once again, her legs could hardly move. The chains between her wrists tightened as she twisted them in anguish. Very haltingly, she obeyed, walking the length of the table, round the attendant, then back again until she stood beside the chair, which now seemed immense, and the figure dressed in red, seen in profile, with black hair down to his shoulders and eyes staring intently now at the hook in front of him, as if Anya's presence had been temporarily forgotten again and the hook, having mesmerised him too, would suddenly swing down of its own accord and embed itself into the table.

'He is following you, Princess . . .' The voice, though deep, trailed away to hollowness. Anya's head made a quarter turn to right, then left; each time, the pupils of her eyes moved down and to the side. The captain's gaze remained fixed on the hook. 'He is persistent.' Then she realised. Suddenly, she knew. Immediately, she turned and looked towards the heavy orange curtains. The captain, awake now, turned and sighed: 'Go on. Draw the curtains. Look.' She ran across, then hesitated at the bed which barred her way. She looked over her shoulder. The captain nodded. She climbed upon the bed. He smiled wistfully as her knees and elbows sank into the softness of the sheets, their creaminess so stark a contrast to the iron chains about her wrists. She reached the opposite side and drew aside the heavy drapes and stared against the deep magenta skyline, thickening beneath the blue-black clouds of swiftly sweeping night.

Now the captain stood to Anya's left, at the head of the bed, watching not the view but her face in profile, illuminated with a deep glow from the last rays of the sun – the red hair burning, the full breasts gently rising and falling and the delicate fingers pressed against the thick glass, tracing a fine line of tender supplication. He saw the eyes suddenly widen and light up, the full lips open, the breathing quicken and the fingertips stretch and press very lightly to that glass again as if to kiss it. And the captain was pleased, because he knew from her expression that he had stirred the girl to a need much deeper than that of the flesh. The sight of that ship had moved her to the heart pangs of wanting. Soon those pangs would become inseparably merged with the pleasures that he would force upon her and in due course – in retrospect perhaps, as she lay in the silence of her cell – would add an extra depth to her shame. Then later, that very shame could be used again to force a pleasure that was overwhelming. And so it would continue.

'Close the curtains.' The muted voice was beside her. Anya hadn't even known he was there. Then he returned to his chair. 'Come here,' he said and again she was afraid. His eyes had become staring. His appearance was harsh and the hook forbidding. 'There are things we must discuss, Princess. Step closer.' He waited until she had done so. 'This man – the Prince – he does not give up easily.'

'No . . .' She lowered her eyes. She watched the right hand dig into the armrest.

'The constant shadowing makes the men uneasy. Some of them agree with Travix – that we should have dispatched them straight away.' Anya looked up pleadingly; she felt the colour draining from her face. He leaned towards her and his eyes seemed to glow. The lines deepened on his craggy forehead.

The lips moved slowly, so each word was clear and biting: 'If your Prince persists –' the lips hesitated – 'I will destroy him.' The hook dropped; with a sickening thud it stuck itself into the table.

Anya jumped. Her hands lifted to try to hide her face. 'No, please. I beg you . . .' she whispered through her fingers. As her hands gradually lowered from her chin, her upper lip began to tremble. The hook pulled out and reached. Anya shied away. 'Stand still!' The green eyes flashed maliciously. And now she could not stop the tears. Though she did not move a muscle and her hands hung limply, chained together, her vision swam and the tears rolled silently down her cheeks. And it seemed her tears were a potion to this hard-hearted man. His breathing slowed and became deeper, as if a calming drug now surged through his veins. 'Stand still,' he said again, but this time it was a whisper. 'And you may in time convince me that he should be spared.'

The attendant was dismissed. The blonde girl on her stool turned and sat cross-legged. Her fingers plaited quickly as, by rapid alternation, she watched the work, then the two immobile figures at the table.

The captain looked at the hunched and trembling form beside him, with her red hair hanging down but pushed aside by the swollen breasts, tipped with perfect blackness. Gazing down, he saw the wrists chained across the belly and the yellow stockings working up to cup against the buttocks. He decided that he wished this woman round – curved, in the way that he had envisioned her on the crewdeck, with her wrists fastened above her head, her back arching forwards, her toes – for the heels of her feet would certainly never have touched the floor – wide apart, gripping precariously on the rough and sawdusted floor. Though she was slim, he wished her curves to be emphasised, with a rounded, pressured weight distending every protrusile part.

He made her stand with legs open, and on her toes, though he could not see the toes buried in the thickness of the yellow woollen stockings. But now he could see the pouch, gripped about her flesh lips, swollen and round. He made her raise her wrists and place her hands upon her head. And now, above

72

the bellying breasts and to the sides, the hollows appeared, deep rounded hollows filled with moist dark copper curls. He savoured those wet curls with his fingers. Then he touched the roundness of her breasts, the warm tips. Though she tried to edge away, though the tears rolled freer still, he touched them with the blue steel, pressed the converging double curve of coldness about them, like two smoothly rounded fingers not quite touching at their tips, and lifted, slid the steel across her skin until the nipple was necked between the shiny metal cusps. And in turn, each nipple swelled polished black until the hook had to be eased back before the nipple would squeeze between the prongs and slip free. Then he made her arch her belly until the thong about her waist was tight and the thong that descended along the line of faint curls, through the thick curls and to the pouch, was even tighter. The point of the hook had now to impress against the tight skin first, then slide beneath this second thong while he carefully folded the stocking tops down to leave two fingers' width of bare tight skin before the crease. He twisted the hook, which tightened the pouch until the skin upon it stretched and assumed the appearance of a hard carapace rather than fur. He did not touch it yet, but removed the hook and made her turn to the side, facing the table, though a little way from it, and open her thighs and bend fully down.

As her hands dropped, the chain between her wrists fell against the floor and now her body was doubled. He pushed the flat of the hook against her lower back to encourage it in its curvature, until even from the side, he could see both belly and pouch pushed between her open thighs. He touched the pouch, feeling its extent, measuring its girth between fingers and thumb, pressing to test its resilience, then urging her backbone to a deeper hollow to make the pouch stand out even more. He drew the outer lips away from it, held them back with thumb and little finger, to keep this part of her – the inner lips, closely clad with warm damp fur – completely isolated while the middle three fingers explored and kneaded it. And he listened for the breathing, pausing at times to roll the stockings perhaps further down and to touch the newly bare inner thigh, or to roll them up again until the woollen lip lay against the crease and nothing of her legs was visible, just her buttocks and her pouch, which then stood out harder by contrast – dark wet brown against the sunflower yellow of the stockings. The captain's gaze would at times return to the double thong that lay within the groove, to watch it lifted slightly by the small black mouth which pushed and pulsed against it as the belly between the open thighs writhed, as his hand diverted to touch that soft belly skin, warm pink between the yellow, before returning to flick or sometimes pull against the pouch.

Anya felt the pressure of the cord suddenly burst from round her belly. 'Keep still,' he said. He eased her legs apart. The thongs, unknotted at her back, dropped and swung to the front, hung across her belly and touched her upturned breasts. But the pouch still gripped about her bursting flesh lips. The loose cords between her buttocks were lifted. She heard the captain call to the girl. Slim feet appeared beside her. Slim hands touched the cheeks of her bottom, then held them open. A heavy finger pressed against the mouth, which tightened. The large hand moved down, stroking her belly as if to soothe it. When it withdrew, she tightened. The slim hands held her, encouraged her. She heard a loud metallic click. Then she felt something, round-tipped, thick and firm and cold but smooth, like a naturally oily animal skin, pressing assertively against the small mouth while the slim fingers brushed against the inner cheeks until the soft cold smoothness gained a purchase and her tender inner skin at last submitted and opened to form a gently kissing cup.

'Lift up. On your toes.' The cool-skinned firmness kept coming; her bottom was distended until it was filled. The coldness lay heavily inside her whilst the cords were gently pulled. The pouch began to peel away. She murmured, her bottom squeezed about the unyielding thing inside her while her sex lips slowly burst free from their extra skin. And those lips felt very swollen, soft and moist. They wanted to be touched. Then the thing inside her bottom moved. Though she tightened hard, it made no difference. Like a snake, it shed its supple skin. She felt the coolness sliding while the oily skin covering was left in place until the thing slipped free and the

74

muscle of her bottom necked about the skin. The remaining short projection of the sheath was moulded into a soft fur cup that mirrored the tighter black cup beneath it. Anya was made to stand.

She averted her eyes from the blonde girl standing beside her. On the table, she saw the chart, coloured pale blue with, in the centre, a small elongate patch of yellow with a fine ink line drawn round it. To the left of the chart was a cockstem, intricately worked, life size, complete with ballocks and fashioned from polished iron. She knew that this was the thing that had been inside her. But as the captain drew back his left arm, she realised that his hook now lay detached on the table and it was instead the cockstem that was attached at its base to the stump of his wrist. And suddenly, a horrible fear played across her mind – that to the captain, this thing might be to his manhood as his hook was to his hand. She shivered. She was pushed forward; her buttocks were parted and the soft skin cup was touched.

There was a knock and the door opened. Anya was facing it as Travix entered. Though Anya tried to back away, wanting to hide herself, she was pushed forward deliberately until her elbows came to rest on the table and her hands, still chained, spread out on the parchment. The blonde girl, no longer confident in Travix's presence, edged away from Anya.

'What is it?' asked the captain coldly.

'Sir – I have come for the chart.' Travix had spoken through her teeth. Anya's hands tried to lift. The captain stood up but he held her pinned down with his right hand. Anya watched his left arm lift with the polished iron thing attached. Her heart was beating wildly. He stroked her hair back. 'Lift your chin,' he whispered. She did not want to be made to do it. But the fingers rasping beneath her chin demanded that it lift. She wanted to close her eyes. Travix stood across from her in her pale blue suit, her face drained, her gaze as fixed as if she were chiselled from marble stone, with the line across her cheek picked out in narrow shadow as if reincised. She did not appear to breath. Travix's gaze did not falter as, with Anya's chin lifted but her belly touching the table top, the funnel-mouthed sleeve was spread back and the rounded iron was pressed against it. But Anya gasped; the iron slipped and the sleeve within her body was filled out quickly with its rigid coolness. The iron bulbs lay coolly against her throbbing sex lips, yet Anya burned with shame. And there was no sound other than Anya's breathing for many long seconds until the captain spoke.

'She is beautiful, Mister Travix – do you not think so?'

Anya closed her eyes. Travix did not answer. Anya felt a tug inside her, then heard the loud metallic click. The captain, his left hand now only a stump, lifted Anya aside. The iron stem was still inside her. Its ballocks rested on the table where she lay, her belly pressed down against its surface and her legs drawn together, hiding her disgrace. She heard a second click and, peeping, saw the hook attached now, moving the bowl aside while the right hand rolled the chart then threw it. Travix caught it with one hand. 'Will that be all, Mister Travix?' Travix threw an icy stare at Anya, who looked away but could feel that freezing stare still washing over her until she heard Travix turn and go, slamming the door behind her. Then she felt the iron stem being slowly withdrawn, the fur skin cup being shaped against her and she heard soft grunts of approval from behind. She did not move but lay upon the table, afraid now of what Travix would do to her when she got the chance and afraid of the feelings in her belly. For when the captain had slipped the cockstem fully home, he had touched her between the legs; she had squeezed hard against the cockstem, she had tried to push her hot wet flesh against his finger, taking pleasure from that touch. Travix had witnessed it, Anya was sure. And the captain had felt that signal too.

He sat down now to his meal, took the Princess on his lap, with her body half curled in his arms, her head upon his left shoulder and his right hand free to play with her while the blonde girl brought him food, though he required but a light repast. The young girl's pleasure was food enough for him. Sometimes he would lift her nipples on his fingers, pulling them gently outwards, then turning them up and, with the tip of his little finger, stroking the nipple's underside. At other times, his hand would venture further, splitting the dark moist fruit between her legs and applying that fingertip touch within. And any welling oily droplet would be caught – upon a fingertip or a titbit or a small fruit, perhaps – and tasted. Small tufts of bread – the inner part of the bread rolled into small soft white balls – would be wiped upon her female lips, outside and within, until the pure white darkened with collected moisture, then he would deliver it, spiced with her saltings, quickly into his mouth. And the air would gradually strengthen with the smell of yeasted female heat.

And at such times as he judged fit, he would lift the young girl's upper leg, take the iron stem in his hand this time and bed the tip against the sleeve and the iron would slip freely in. Having done this, he would make her close her yellow-stockinged legs and perhaps he would rearrange her hair, which lay so deliciously heavily upon her shoulders or her breasts and reflected the light in narrow snakes of copper, bronze and gold. He would lift the chain between her wrists to expose her underarms. He would make her hold her wrists up while he brushed the curls that nested in the hollows. And it seemed to him his fingertips could almost taste the aroma there. But his fingertips were always anxious to be on the move, to explore her every intimacy, to get to know her body very fully by touch, that even when she was gone, the skin of his fingers would remain imbued with her taste and he would need simply to close his eyes and he would see her again. So once her flesh had become adjusted to the presence of the sheathed iron stem inside her, he would slip it out and form the sleeve into a cup. His thumb would rest within this cup whilst his fingers held her sex lips wide. And then he would want to hold her nubble with his claw.

He would make her sit astride the padded arm of the chair. The claw, curving down, would be used to lift the hood and to press against the nubble, which, like a soft wet pip, would squeeze between the polished points that he might touch it with his finger. And he would always make her lean back when he did this, in order to make her belly arch. He would brush back the wet hairs from the vicinity of her sex, which would appear as an open black-lipped pouch with the nubble trapped between the blue steel pincers at the very tip. Then

77

he would proceed to rub this small pink nubble slowly with a wetted finger until her belly pulsed and bulged, her breathing became strained and her sweet thighs tried to grip about the armrest. At such a point, he would instruct her to open her thighs and to remain very still while the nubble was wetted and the rubbing resumed, that he might watch her belly gradually distend against the force of swelling pleasure. It would make him want to kiss its perfect rounded pushed-out form. It would make him want to kiss her at the moment of her pleasure, to feel the warmth and tightness of that skin against his lips and to taste her sweet round trembling shudders when she came. But instead, he would return her to his knee to touch her and proceed with the repast.

In due course the attendant returned with a covered dish, placing it purposefully on the table by the captain, then retreating. The captain called the blonde girl over. She knelt beside the chair, at Anya's feet, while Anya lay across the captain's lap, her naked body warmly cradled in the rich red coat, her legs enveloped to the creases in bright yellow wool. The girl lifted up the heavy iron stem from the table. 'Not yet,' said the captain. He nodded towards the covered dish and Anya was afraid. The girl lifted the lid and immediately the air was pervaded by the scent of fish, not a strong scent, but a warm and sweet one. She offered the bowl. When it tilted, Anya heard the sound of soft shells sliding. The captain reached inside and what he pulled out made Anya shrink away. It was a large dead insect, as big as Anya's thumb, with a long pointed head with feelers, a tightly curved body and tail, and many legs beneath its belly. Yet this insect was not black but pink. He held it in his right hand, slipped the upturned double claw behind its head and pulled. The head came off and dropped into the bowl. Then he held the body in the claw and pulled the legs off. Finally the skin was peeled back, shed and he held up a soft curved tapering white sliver, criss-crossed by pale red veins. He lifted it, as if to eat it, then instead offered it to Anya. She sealed her lips tightly and twisted her head away. He shrugged and offered it to the girl.

And it was as if he offered the most delicious sweetmeat in the world. She threw her head back and closed her eyes. Her blonde hair dangled down in finger-thick wavy snakes as if it had been worked repeatedly about a finger until it was smooth. Her eyebrows seemed so strange – dense black – with the long curved black eyelashes below. The full lips opened and closed about the sliver, which was taken in and slowly chewed. Then the eyes opened in a heavy-lidded smile; the lips pouted again. The captain peeled another morsel, then a third and fed them to the girl. The smell of sweet warm fish was appetising. When he offered one to Anya again, she turned her head away more slowly: now that she had seen the girl's reaction, she half wanted to take it. It had brushed against her lips. It was warm; the taste on her lips was sweet and salty; it was fish – but a tastier kind of fish than she had known. The captain replaced the peeled fish in the bowl. Very gently, he turned her head back. He lifted aside her hair, touched her earlobe. And perhaps it was the way that he did that – touching reverently, as you would touch a perfect creature – perhaps it was something in the clearness of his eyes, but at that point, something happened in Anya's belly. It was as if a weight which had been slowly building up there suddenly melted, as if warm oil flowed inside her body. And she took the titbit that he offered on the claw. She closed her eyes and took it on her tongue and folded her tongue around it until her tongue touched metal. And when she felt him touch her belly, she spread her legs wide – not caring that the girl was there – for him to touch her. When the fingertips took her nubbin, she squeezed the fish flesh between her teeth, gently at first, but ever tighter, until it burst, while her own flesh was held open, the nubbin gently turned and touched until it swelled like the tightly doubled warm and rubbery fish that again was pushed into her mouth, this time by the girl. It was the girl who fed her – slim fingertips pushing between Anya's willing lips – while the captain continued to fondle her between the legs until she moaned. And it seemed this was the signal.

Her eyes stayed shut but between her legs, she felt the lips being parted, this time by the slim fingers, and she did not resist. She felt the fingertips explore inside her, then retreat. Then she heard the fish being peeled, close between her yellow-clad thighs, and she felt its skin being placed upon her

79

naked belly. Again the lips were parted. She could not breathe; she felt the fish – thick like a thumb, but softer and warmer – being slipped between the lips, which then were closed about its bulging curve. The tail of the fish was slipped beneath the hood; it pressed against her nubbin. The arrangement was smoothed down; the sex lips, warm and thin now, were wetted with a finger. Thick saliva coated them, rendered them shiny black and sealed them round the bulge of pink. Her legs were tucked up and the pink pushed through; it was resealed. The iron cock was lifted, the projecting cup of furry skin was spread back, the cock was fitted, the bottom opened, the belly arched and the cock slipped smoothly in to fill the inner sleeve. The pink pushed through again; it was resealed. Two slim fingers were thickly wetted with saliva. Pushing downwards, they entered the sex without disturbing the pink. Inside they could feel the warmth and the cooler iron against the thin flexible wall. They turned, cupped forwards, reaching up behind the nubbin and massaged; the pinkness bulged again. A small tongue pressed against it to hold it down and the nubbin was trapped between the fingers massaging from behind and the rubbery pinkness pressed against it by the tongue.

Anya's head began to move from side to side, as if she were in fever. In her belly, the weight had formed again and it was pushing forwards, down. Her thighs began to tremble. The tongue lifted away. The captain's hand moved down. Gradually and alternately her stocking tops were unfurled. The bareness of her inner thighs was rubbed, with the two slim fingers still inside her and the cockstem in her bottom. It was as if his fingers were tasting her thighs. They rubbed gently, slowly back and forth, then moved up to touch her where the fingers entered and where the cockstem held her bottom open, then up again to lie against the roundness of her belly. They remained there, held it, rubbed it, only the rounded skin, so swollen up with the nearness of pleasure, while the tongue returned to press the pink. When Anya groaned and pushed her belly into the hand and squeezed her bottom around the sheathed iron and her sex around the fingers, the tongue quickly slipped beneath the fish, lifted it away and the fingers

80

slid out. Then she felt the girl's lips above her face. She could smell the fish; their lips touched and the fish was pushed into her mouth. It filled her throat, then suddenly slipped down it. The girl's tongue pushed deep into her mouth, as if trying to follow, until Anya could not breathe. But the kiss continued while Anya felt the captain's hand between her legs, and first the cock and then its sleeve being drawn out from the tightness of her bottom. The girl lifted away. Anya opened her eyes. She saw the blonde hair, the dense black eyebrows, the wide bright eyes and on the upper lip a very faint pale down, which brushed against her as she was kissed again, and the girl's fingertips touched the soft down on her jawline. In Anya's belly, beneath the pressure of the captain's hand, the weight inside remelted.

She was carried to the bed then fastened in the middle of it by a single chain which looped round the chain between her wrists and was drawn and fastened under the end of the bed above her head. By this means, her body was free to rotate about this single axis, that she might be made to lie on her back, or on her front or side, as necessity dictated and her legs, clad in the long bright yellow stockings, might be completely free to move – to be opened or closed, or to be doubled up perhaps, if she were on her back, or on her front and kneeling.

Standing by the bed, the captain watched the beginnings of this scene. The Princess was outstretched, her full breasts pressed into the soft relief of his damask sheets, black-brown swollen tips pressed into the cream. Her legs were moulded separately in the yellow stockings which had to be rolled up again to bed into the creases of her thighs, to flare out and to cup her buttocks – slightly separated – while the blonde girl, half kneeling, half sitting, thighs apart, blonde fleece against the cream, leisurely fitted the iron cockstem into its fur skin glove before resting it against the groove between the open cheeks. Then she took from the bowl beside her another prawn, peeled it, placed it lengthwise between two fingers and slipped it underneath. While she worked the sleeved stem gradually into the spreading black cup, her fingertips slowly rubbed the prawn against the open bud beneath. The captain then left, accompanied solely by delicious visions such as these.

81

He stood on deck in the still night air, a solemn watchmate to the silent steersman beneath an inky, star-pranked sky. When he returned two hours later, the Princess, still chained, was on her back. The girl was kneeling across her, sucking one nipple, touching her between the legs.

'Has she . . .?' the captain asked.

The girl shook her head slowly without removing the nipple.

But whether the Princess had or had not, her sex was overflowing between the blonde girl's fingers and there was a damp patch on the damask cream. And the insides of the tops of her stockings were cut by two crescents of deeper yellow as a consequence of her wetness. Beside her was a bowl of heads and legs and carapaces, the iron stem, unsleeved now and probably recently withdrawn, and a narrow hard roll-shaped cushion covered in prickly fur. 'You have done well,' the captain nodded slowly. 'You may continue.' The girl lifted this roll and drew it horizontally up the Princess's belly, to her breasts. The Princess moaned. The girl rolled the stockings back and stroked it over the insides of the thighs. The Princess whimpered. And the captain was moved. Between his legs, his cockstem stood erect. It was time, he knew, for otherwise this young woman's pleasure would very soon spill. He called for his steward and dispatched him. The man returned a few minutes later with a bucket of cold water drawn from the sea. By that time, the captain had disrobed and the Princess lay on her belly with her open thighs spread upon the roll of prickly fur, which was turned so its pile swept upwards. While the iron stem was dropped into the freezing bucket, the captain began his pleasure with the Princess. He separated her thighs more fully. He spread her sex lips wide about the fur. He withdrew the sleeve from the small black puckered mouth and he stroked that mouth. Then he anointed it with unction, pressed the cap of his very rigid stem against the tight but slippery mouth and pushed. It slipped smoothly in and up through the tight rim into the freer ground, until his ballocks rolled against her buttocks and rubbed against the fur, which tortured her tender skin with a thousand little points pricking into it. And on the forward push, his cock sank deeper into

82

the warmth, the unction bathed his plum with pleasure. On the pull, the girl's fleshy hood was drawn back and the long spines of the fur slipped beneath to prick into her nubble.

But even this constant pricking would not stay the girl forever, for each forward thrust was up-pile – smooth wet rubbing – and would threaten to bring the pleasure on. So at such times as her moans became too deep, too urgent, he would lift her on his cock to break her contact with the fur. As the imminence waned, he would lower her again, separating the lips about the fur and pushing up inside until he felt her first contraction, before pulling until her flesh was pricked, then lifting her again, until the slightest touch of flesh against the pricking fur made her bottom tighten until his cockstem hurt. He knew then to turn her on her side with her bottom still impaled and to allow the girl to take command.

He watched the blonde girl's face – the sudden awareness in it that he waited. She glanced at him and she melted him with that glance. The dense dark eyebrows furrowed to total blackness, then she calmly took control. The beautiful strands of sunsnaked hair were lifted from her cheek and placed behind her ear. She dipped her arm into the bucket. Her full lips parted as she drew breath quickly and the fine hairs on her upper arm bristled with the cold. She dried the cockstem on a towel and placed it, cradled in the towel, beside the girl's hips. She lay alongside her and stared into the soft eyes, the pupils of which were like pools of perfect night. She stroked the belly, with the cold hand, once. It shivered. Working by touch while she watched the eyes, she held the fleshpot open with her warm hand, held the hood back, kept it back and inserted the freezing iron stem very quickly – bare iron to warm bare inner flesh – and still, she had to force it against the strength of the contraction.

Slipping up, the iron formed a freezing line of pressure through the inner wall and against the captain's stem as it swept up the underside to bed beneath the plum. She took his bag in her fingers and quickly moulded it to the freezing iron ballocks and his pleasure came in long thick spurts which were reluctant to desist. She could feel it pumping past her fingertips pressing underneath him. But her other hand still held the girl's flesh back through the tight contractions, keeping the nubbin isolated and exposed, preventing her deliverance, yet nevertheless delivering pleasure of a kind as the limpid eyes before her widened and the soft lips moved as if to speak, to beg – to try to kiss the bristling downy forearm that had administered such bittersweet pangs of pleasure and distress. The blonde girl pressed her own lips against those pleading lips very gently, very lightly. But she kept a small circle of free space around that nubbin until any danger of release was long past, until the captain's cock had squeezed out weakly and he had turned and was asleep. Then she washed the Princess between the cheeks, turned her on her front with the cock still inside her and the iron balls between her thighs, weighing her to the bed, and she lay beside her, stroking her through the night.

[6]

The Key

The sun was streaming through a gap in the curtains, but it was the noise of the cabin door banging that had woken Anya. She was still chained. There was no captain, but the girl was beside her on the pillow, staring into her eyes. The twisted blonde tresses curled across and touched her cheek. The girl smiled. Anya felt very tired. When the girl climbed over her and began to stroke her back, Anya fell asleep again. The second time she awoke, she was still chained between the wrists but no longer fastened to the bed. The iron stem had been removed. The girl was gone, but now there was something round Anya's neck. She looked down and saw it was a necklace of flat plaited twine. Anya curled up with her arms about her breasts and with her chin on her wrists. She was thinking of the girl. Where had she gone, or been taken? And why was Anya left alone? Suddenly, seeing the shaft of sunlight again, she remembered. She jumped up quickly, drew the curtains aside and squinted against the bright light as she scanned the horizon, looking for the ship.

'What are you doing up there?'

Anya gasped. She turned to see Travix in front of the bed. Beside her was a leather-shirted guard, holding a pair of shackles. The door stood ajar. But Travix didn't wait for a reply.

'Get up, Princess. There's work to do.' She walked over to the table, evidently looking for something. The guard took Anya by the arm, pulled her stockings off, lifted her down and fitted the shackles to her ankles. Travix returned with the pouch, which had lain where the captain had left it on the back of the chair. 'Put your hands on the bed.' Travix opened Anya's legs and touched between them, squeezing and flicking the lips to make them swell. Then she fitted the pouch quickly, expertly, very tightly, and the wanting that overnight had ebbed away came flooding back again.

Anya was taken up on deck, into the sunshine. A few sailors worked nearby, sewing a sail. Others were splicing a rope. A few more were aloft in the rigging. Today, they seemed to take little notice of a Princess, but last night, on the crewdeck, it had been very different. She bit her lip and looked out to sea.

A large empty bucket on a long rope was brought. In it was a scrubbing brush. 'Get on with it,' said Travix, 'scrub the deck.' Then, 'Wait!' she shouted when Anya stooped to pick up the bucket. 'What's that?' Her hand went to the plaited twine round Anya's neck. Travix looked at it. Then her jaw set and with a sudden pull she tried to wrench the necklace free. Anya was dragged to the deck, for the twine was strong and well fastened. Travix cut it with her knife and cast it over the rail to the sea. Then she and the guard walked away, leaving Anya on her knees. And had she stayed thus, the bucket would surely have filled with her tears. But she struggled back to her feet, tried to block those tears and took the brush out, walked to the rail, wrapped the rope around her wrist and flung the bucket over the side. It hit the water but would not sink until the current had dragged it back. Then it was so heavy that she could hardly lift it. A third of the way up the side of the ship, she could no longer hold it and the bucket dropped back in. But at the third attempt, she managed to lift it over the side and staggered across the deck.

She started in the corner by a hatch. She didn't mind the work, but the sun was hot and the water quickly soaked into the wood. The bucket was soon used. She went back to get another and then she saw, far away, just at the horizon, three double flecks of white – the sails. Her heart leapt. She just stood there looking out, hoping against reason that she would be seen, that he would know that she was alive. She didn't hear them approach; they must have been watching her and waiting for an excuse.

'Idling . . .' Quickly, Anya dropped the bucket over the side, but it was too late. Her upper lip was already trembling at seeing this woman so soon after her callousness over the necklace. Travix looked cruel. She said, 'Give her something to remind her what she is about.' The man in the leather shirt took the rope from Anya, wound it round the rail, then took her by her wrist chain and held it up. He pulled the strap from his belt. 'No . . .' said Anya, trying to back away. Travix stepped forward and whispered to the man. Anya's hands were dragged back above her and forced behind her head. Her legs were parted as far as the short chain would permit. She began to plead. Her breath was wasted. A shiver touched her belly as he took her pouch in the fingers of one hand and held it. Then he smacked her with her legs apart, holding that leather pouch, making her keep still while the strap smacked across the backs of her legs – only in that place, four smacks below the buttocks, across her upper thighs, while her small tight pouch was held and Travix looked on, her thin lips smiling, her fingers gently pulling at the earlobe with the ring. Then he and Travix walked away, leaving Anya with her hands upon her neck still, the backs of her legs scalded with the smacks and her sex lips throbbing, swelling tight inside the pouch. And she was frightened, for that kind of smacking, though not across her bottom, reminded her of things that had been done to her in the forest. At those memories, her throat tightened until she could hardly breathe.

Later that day, as Anya was kneeling on the deck, still scrubbing, Travix came again and found some excuse to scold her, shouting at her till Anya felt a lump in her throat, for she knew well what was coming. And this time, though it was still the man who smacked Anya, it was Travix who held the hard round pouch, with Anya's legs parted, angled outwards and bent at the knees, her hands upon her head and her elbows out, so her breasts were pushed forwards, while the scalding smacks turned the tender skin bright red at the backs of Anya's thighs and Travix's face dissolved into a blur with two hard eyes and a grotesquely twisted mouth above a swath of blue. At that point, the smacking was stopped, the face reappeared and a small white kerchief took the tears. 'Keep your legs apart,' whispered Travix and her fingertips stripped down the moistened pouch firmly, as if it were a thick rubbery teat

87

which she was milking. 'What is the feeling? Tell me.' The action was repeated six times. Each time, Travix whispered, 'Tell me . . .' But Anya could not answer, though the feelings were very clear. The feeling between Anya's legs was pleasure, very strong and near, the feeling at the backs of her legs was burning and, at the sixth slide of the fingers, which slipped like soap now, the feeling in her throat was inability to breathe. And she knew that if Travix herself were ever to smack her, she would die. Her heart would burst right through her breast. Did Travix know it too?

That evening, Anya was returned to the small cell down below. Her knees were raw and she was very tired. Despite her chains, she turned on her back and fell asleep.

Suddenly, her eyes snapped open. She was on her side again, with her head pressed to the wall. She had heard a sound, a door being opened, but it wasn't her door. Light streamed through the wall beside the bed: there was a hole in the woodwork, where somebody had picked at it and broken it away. It was a small hole, not large enough to get a hand through, but certainly large enough to see through. Anya edged across as far as her chains would permit.

In the room was the girl with blonde hair and the plaited twine about her waist. Why had she been sent down here? She was sitting up on the bed and rubbing her eyes. One of the men in leather helped her, for she moved as if in a dream as the man now led her to the middle of the small room, to where the two long chains hung, as in Anya's room. The chains were not designed to take her wrists, for they hung to the level of her waist. The large looped leather straps attached to their ends formed two rings. As he took hold of her behind her thighs and began to lift her, she tried to shy away, kicking out her feet. She did not wish to step into this thing. But he made her. He threatened her and she acquiesced. Her sylphlike body was lifted and her slim ankles were threaded easily through the loops, which slipped up to her knees.

'No. She must face the other way.'

Anya gasped. The voice was Travix's. She must be in the room. Anya tried to peer to the side but still she could not see her. The man grunted, pulled the girl's legs out from the loops again, lifted her round and reinserted them with her facing now away from Anya. The girl tried to keep her legs horizontal but the man pushed her forwards, lifted her and made her point her feet down. The leather loops – or collars, each about two inches wide – slipped up the backs of her legs and bedded at the tops of her thighs, against the base of her buttocks. The girl's toes, though stretching downwards, were still a good six inches above the floor. Her body and her legs shook as she tried to balance. Her hands reached up to grasp the chains, but much as she tried, she could not keep steady. The man retreated.

Travix appeared and Anya's heart began to thump. She still wore the velvet boots and the blue suit with the ruffled sleeves. Her coarse blonde hair was still tied back with a black ribbon. It seemed so stark a contrast to the free and silken snakelike tresses of the girl. Travix stood calmly now, beyond the girl and facing her, intent only on her. Slowly she unfastened the plaited twine, which fell away from the belly. Travix then examined this belt. 'You have acquired a new friend, I hear, kitling,' she said, rubbing the girl's belly with the flat of her palm. Anya moved her head back from the spyhole; she felt a sudden chill of fear. The girl trembled but did not answer Travix. Her buttocks moved uncomfortably in the leather slings, which sank gradually deeper into the creases of her thighs. 'Ah – my kitling is impatient,' Travix said, then whispered something to the girl. The thighs opened and the toes now pointed out and down. Travix's right hand moved down but her left hand moved up to lift the blonde strands out of the way and lie against the girl's neck, against the thick and thumping vein. 'Open, my precious,' she said. 'Wider – for Travix. There . . .' Travix's fingers had surely eased the small soft lips aside and slipped inside that body, for now the hips moved in the slings, the legs arched and the toes formed perfect points. And between the open thighs, Anya could see the wrist writhing gently as the buried fingers sought submission. 'Move . . . move against my hand.' The girl moaned. Her buttocks began to tighten and relax. The fingers lay against the girl's throat, tasting her heartbeat. The hips careened, the arms strained and the legs, still arched, began to move together. 'No, do not close. Keep open. There . . . Let it press against my thumb.' The girl's breath snagged. Travix emitted a soft deep grunt and Anya held her breath. 'Kitling . . .' Travix whispered softly. The girl's head moved back. The hand still lay against her neck and she was panting, moaning. Travix, her wrist scarcely moving now, watched in fascination. The head lolled forwards and down.

She looked over the girl's bowed head and nodded to the man in the leather shirt. He held something which seemed a cross between a switch and a strap. It had a short handle but a thin and supple stem of tightly twisted cord which fanned out at the tip to a thick leaf of leather. Anya felt a wave of icy prickles across her belly and up the front of her body, turning her nipples hard. Between her legs, where the pouch gripped – where Travix had held her wet-sheathed sex and milked her like a cow – she felt a pulse which should have shamed her.

'Shh . . .' whispered Travix again. The girl had become very tense. Travix did not move. She stood before the girl, looking calmly into her face, with one hand still at her neck, the other hidden in her belly. The scar was visible as a fine deep purple line on Travix's face. Against the cool paleness of Travix's cheeks, the colour of this scar seemed to have deepened. When the hips began to twist, slowly at first and then more definitely, the hand at the girl's throat moved down to play with her breasts then to join the hand that bedded in her belly. The two hands worked in unison. The girl began to moan and to push against them. Travix's wrist movements slowed. The girl's head arched back again and Travix nodded to the man. 'Quickly, she is near . . .' He spread the bottom cheeks and held them. The girl gasped. Her legs angled diagonally down; her feet pointed as straight as if drawn out and pinned to the floor by invisible twine. 'Keep her open,' Travix told him. 'Smack her in the crease.' He used the leaf of leather, whipped upwards quickly. The first smack made her whimper. 'Shh, kitling, shhhh . . .' murmured Travix. They waited until the trembles had subdued. Then he smacked again, downwards, directly in the centre of the crease. 'So slippery. Let me hold it . . .' The girl was sobbing. 'There . . .' Travix's wrist began to move and the sobbing turned to grunts. 'Now, keep very still. Again . . .' The smack came, upwards. The girl bucked. 'Shh . . .' Three fingers slipped through the girl's legs from the front to smear a shiny wet slick within the groove. Then Travix took her upper body, bent it forward and supported it with one hand under her arms and the other still between her legs, yet not moving. 'Now smack it wet,' she said. 'Keep smacking. No – keep it open. Smack it . . .' The pad of leather cracked down upon the small wet mouth four times, then the girl's body turned rigid. She began to moan continuously.

Travix acted quickly. She had the man hold the girl horizontally. She took from the table a pouch, wrapped the thong around the girl's waist and fitted the pouch between her legs. She worked efficiently and dispassionately, while the man held the body face down and the girl emitted sobbing moans. The straps of the pouch were drawn tight. Travix then stood behind the girl and between her legs. She held up something small, elongate and white, before it disappeared between the girl's legs and into the pouch. Travix's wrist – the wrist that held this white thing by the end – moved very slowly. The girl's moaning gave way to gasps and the wrist moved slower and slower until it hardly moved at all. Then suddenly, the girl's legs kicked; her belly bucked, yet the man held her. 'Shh . . . Too soon. Keep her still,' said Travix. 'Play with her nipples; wet them; milk her.' Anya shuddered. As the man pulled the wetted nipples on the breasts that dangled down, Travix's wrist gently twisted and the belly bucked again. 'Lift her up; her belly must not move. The key must take her slowly.' Travix stepped back. She no longer held the white thing. The girl, still moaning, was lifted upright. Her arms were quickly fastened up to the chains. Her legs were doubled up and her ankles trussed behind her to the loops. Her body rolled slightly forwards, leaving her belly arched. Clearly seen between her legs now was the pouch. Projecting down from it and twitching, was the tip of the small white thing that was bedded inside. Travix stepped round the girl and stood in front. She lifted the hair aside again. Her fingertips pressed against the neck. Her other hand pressed against the rounded belly and the small white projection moved. 'Shhh . . .' said

Travix, against the murmurs. Between the legs now, the finger and thumb were holding the pouch and squeezing. Then moving back, they closed around the white projection. The wrist movement was very slight, a scarcely perceptible roll, but the girl's breathing came deeper, louder, turning to gasps and little screams until she cried out through her teeth and the trussed and doubled knees jerked open thrice as if the belly would keep pumping pressure into the pouch that the white thing snagged within and would release that sweet entanglement by bursting. The cry of tortured pleasure came again; the body spasmed. But Travix's wrist continued to twist the small white instrument back and forth inside the pouch at the same slow precise rate until the knees no longer tried to kick, until the belly ceased to shudder, until the whole tight body turned limp.

The slim white object reappeared. Travix carefully wiped it on the silk strand tresses then left the room. The man lifted the girl from the loops and placed her on the bed.

Anya felt hot; she was sweating. Between her legs, her sex was weeping. The pouch was soaking wet. The pressure of her swelling there had forced the seepage through. She turned on to her back. The long chain lay pressed against her buttocks. Suddenly, the door opened and light flooded in. Travix swept in closely after it and before Anya could turn away, Travix was upon her, kneeling on the bed. Immediately, she noticed the shaft of light from the next room, but she smiled. 'And did you enjoy our little display?' She must have been aware all along that Anya had been watching. Anya, her heart in her throat, turned her head away. 'No? But let us see.' Travix separated Anya's knees. 'Oh yes, yes indeed . . .' she murmured. She touched the hard wet pouch and gently squeezed until it slipped. Anya gasped, for the pleasure was sweet. Travix turned Anya's chin and stared into her eyes. 'But are you ready, Princess? For this is why I have come to you, why I arranged that little game – to prepare your body.' Anya could not breathe. The fingers came to rest against her neck. Anya could feel her pulse bursting. 'Oh yes, you are ready.'

Travix pushed Anya's feet as close up to her bottom as the short chain between her ankles would permit, then opened her thighs so wide her knees almost touched the straw. She made her curve her belly upwards, hard.

And now as Travix looked upon her in the lamplight, all that she could see were curves – curves of breast, crowned by tight black cherries; curve of belly, almond curve of shadow in the well; curving thigh muscles, open; re-entrant curves of creases; and the most delicious curve of all, a hard pod – shiny, slick with sweated seepage. She knelt between those thighs, upon the straw and took another curve – the small, carved precisely shaped and polished bone that in a sense was part of Niri's dowry. It had been acquired – together with Niri, several other trinkets, many golden promises and a chart – a week ago in part disposal for a merchantmaster's life. Travix had discovered how to use it; Niri hadn't seemed to know, but Travix had quickly taught her. And now she would teach this girl. 'The key to your heart, my Princess . . .' Travix whispered.

One end of the bone was shaped into a small pad that fitted perfectly between the finger and thumb. The other was carved and polished to a minute round arrowed tongue. The body of the bone was a smooth curve, like a bent twig but flatter in section than a twig would be.

Holding the instrument with the curve uppermost, the same way as the curve of the pod she would use it to investigate, she slipped the arrow into the entrance to the girl's sex by way of the narrow gap below the slippery pouch. She pushed until only the fingerpad was exposed. The belly tightened. The girl gasped as Travix applied a lifting pressure to the pad; in the tight confines of the leather pouch the narrow curve of bone hesitated, vied for space, then suddenly slipped up between the pressed-together lips. And now it burrowed like a small worm, just below the surface of the leather, slowly upwards, twisting very slightly as Travix's fingers worked it like a locksmith testing a key, until the small round arrowhead, in that gentle twisting, sought out, pressed against, then slipped beneath the hood to bed against the soft bone of the nubbin.

The girl groaned as her belly jerked. Travix released the key, which stayed rigidly in place, held by the tension of the bursting lips against the thin leather skin, while she shaped her palms and moved them very lightly over the surface of the belly, brushing the fine upstanding hairs, sensing the warmth of the skin, and instructing the girl to keep her thighs very widely open, to keep the tightness concentrated there, and to rock her thighs, thereby to impart the pressure of the small bone intruder in her pouch as a pulsebeat against her nub. 'There . . . Arch your belly. Keep it tight,' she whispered and lightly touched the handle of the bone to instigate a moan. Then as the knees rocked up and down, Travix settled down to watch the pod tighten and relax, the outline of the bone show through, the belly turn hard, then harder, the creases show polished, then matt and the fringe of black and wetted curls beyond the pod soak very slowly out to subdue the tight red springy bristles with softness and with wet. And Travix wanted to take her ribbon out and let her hair cascade across that belly, to make it shudder and to nip her teeth around that hard black pod and make it burst warm oil into her mouth, then to slip her tongue into its broken sheath and press the small bone arrowhead against that nubbin to bring it on. Yet she could not, for the girl's pleasure must be delivered very slowly, by degrees.

But Travix helped her. She lay beside her, pushing the fingers of her right hand – steeped in honey from her sweet blonde kitling – deep into this girl's mouth, while stimulating the stub of the bone, then offering her lips to be kissed while her fingertips drank the wet upon the soft black curls. Then she wetted her middle finger – though it did not need it – and very slowly pushed it up the seeping well below the hard black pouch, and when the base of her finger touched the pad of the bone, the pressure was transmitted through the small round arrowhead to the nub, and even with the ankles chained the belly lifted from the straw. Travix turned the small key very gently and pushed it deeper beneath the hood, twisting until the shudders came again. Then she unfastened the girl, turned her on her front and, guiding the key very deftly, with the cheeks of the girl's buttocks spread and a fingertip within, brought her to the point again. She stayed with her throughout the evening, removing the key, kissing her breasts, her lips and her belly then reinserting, slowly and precisely twisting, holding her on the point of pleasure, then touching the hard round belly, the shiny creases, stretching the skin back, tightening the pod, then sometimes taking out the key and beginning again, sometimes pressing on, lightly twisting it, bone to bone against the rigid nubbin, until the pleasure came. She wanted the girl to experience that kind of pleasure – pleasure against which she was defenceless, pleasure concentrated entirely within the confines of the hard tight pouch and extracted by the smooth intruder – many times that night. And even when the girl was exhausted, Travix would continue, lying beside her, taking control, pressing the bone, feeling the arrowhead through the pouch and against the tip of her finger, and eventually it would happen again – the longer that it seemed to take, the stronger it came – with Travix sometimes sucking the nipples, sometimes sucking the tongue, sometimes being forced to pin those knees down hard to stop them lifting from the straw.

For the next four days, on Travix's orders, Anya had to scrub the decks. In all that time, she never saw her Prince's ship. Each morning, Travix would find some pretext to have her smacked. One of the men would do it. Travix would hold her sheathed-together sex lips while the backs of her thighs were smacked. When her duties were done, she would be returned to that small room with nothing but a lamp for company. And for many hours, at night she guessed, even that was taken away. Other than to work, she was taken out only to witness the punishments and pleasures of the other women at the mast, across Kasger's table or at the pole. Usually Travix would be there to supervise, to touch Anya and to stimulate her flesh in various ways, until the torment became unbearable. When Travix was not there, Anya would be fettered, pouched and made to sit astride a chair and watch. Afterwards, she would be returned to her cell with nothing to occupy her mind other than the cruel pleasures she had witnessed and the all-encompassing wanting in her belly.

Sometimes, in the cell, she would be chained, at other times left free to sit on the small bed with her head in her hands, sobbing. And at those times when her heart was heaviest, when despair would well inside, a knock would come at her door – a knock, it seemed so strange – then the heavy bolt would slide back and a small round smiling face crowned by a thick stray curl would appear. It would be Ratchitt. He would bring her food – not the stale bread, gruel and pickled cabbage served to the crew, but titbits from the captain's table – perhaps a leg of chicken, strange sweet yellow fruits with very sticky juice, or sometimes raisins, nuts and apple cake, or honeycomb and cheese. And for a short time she would set aside her sadness and her plight.

Ratchitt would sit quietly on the end of the bed and wait until Anya had finished. Whenever Anya looked at him, Ratchitt would always look away. He never attempted to touch her. He never seemed to say anything, even when the last of the food had gone and Anya lifted the tray from her lap and thanked him. He would smile, then nervously twist the dark brown curl, then take the tray and go.

On the evening of the fourth day, she took her time with the food, offering him some, though he refused, and tried to get him talking.

'You have many chickens to look after?' she asked him.

He looked surprised. 'Not many hens now – just seventeen, and two cocks. We've eaten most of them.' Then his eyes lit up. 'But I can get you eggs – would you like some?'

'Mm,' Anya said, then raised her eyebrows. 'If it won't get you into trouble?' He shook his head and smiled. Anya hesitated, then asked: 'But how long will your chickens last?'

He pursed his lips. 'When they're down to six, I have to keep them for the captain. But they say we might make landfall soon.'

'Landfall? Where?'

'Don't know. Some new place. They never tell me. Something to do with the girl, though – the one that Travix keeps in her cabin.'

'Niri?'

Ratchitt nodded.

'She's very beautiful . . .'

'Not as lovely as you, ma'am,' he whispered, then glanced away.

'Ratchitt – what will happen to me?'

He looked at her with sad, gentle eyes, opened his mouth to speak, then Kasger walked in. 'Haven't you finished yet?' Ratchitt quickly collected up the things, glanced once at Anya, smiled sadly and left.

On the morning of the fifth day, Anya saw her Prince's ship. Even before that, she knew it was there. Travix and the captain stood together on the deck above her with a chart, scanning the horizon then turning, looking back and pointing. Soon afterwards, the ship changed tack. It was as if they were not entirely sure of their bearings and at the same time, worried about still being followed. Then Travix spotted Anya looking at them. Too late, Anya buried her head in her work.

'Get up!' Anya was not quick enough. Travix, with the chart screwed up in one hand, grabbed her, screaming, and dragged her by the hair then kicked her when she tripped. She hurled her down, then dragged her up again and pushed her against the rail. 'Look!' But Anya was afraid. The crewmen were beginning to gather round. Travix turned her, pushing her belly to the rail. Far below was the water, bottomless and crystal blue. Her head was pulled back. 'There. Is that what you're looking for – what you've been looking at all these days?' Travix's voice was cruel. Anya could scarcely see anything through her tears, but far out, near the horizon, was the ship – small, but unmistakable, with her topmast gone. Immediately, her heart leapt – to know that he was still out there, a thorn in the side of this evil woman.

'Mister Travix – over here!' cried the boatswain.

Anya was frogmarched across the deck to the other side. And far away, ahead, there was land, beautiful, matt green against the blue and rising to dark, mist-shrouded hills. The boatswain came up and stood beside them, gazing across the water.

'That is it?' he asked. 'The island?'

Travix nodded slowly, her eyes half closed. 'It seems our merchant friend was faithworthy after all. Have Kasger prepare the slave-decks for cargo and the captain's coffers for gold.' She stared at the chart. 'We must approach from the south.'

The boatswain pointed his thumb over his shoulder. 'But what of them? What good your secret chart? They know now where it is.'

Travix chuckled. 'Then let them dare to follow.' The boatswain frowned. 'Let them brave the reef – without the chart,' said Travix calmly. And as the boatswain smiled slyly, Anya's brief exhilaration rapidly ebbed away. She turned towards the other ship, but now she could no longer see it. She turned back. Travix was watching her and Travix's look was no longer cruel. Anya's tears had dried, in the soft warm wind, but now her face was burning. Travix looked upon her – looked into those liquid eyes, still brimming with the last salt wet. She lifted back her hair. She raised her chin. She stroked her finger across the upper lip, full red – very warm. Now Anya wanted to look away, but could not. 'I will have you for my own,' Travix whispered. And Anya, looking up into that face – the scar, the earring, the deep incision through the lip – was frightened by the feeling in her belly, and below, within the soft skin pouch that sealed the purse of her desire. 'I will be your Prince,' murmured Travix. 'And I will train you to my ways.'

'No!' cried Anya, not forcefully enough, adding: 'Never,' very weakly.

'We shall see.'

And that afternoon on deck, Anya's punishment was very severe and no reason for it was given. Her pouch was taken away. Kasger's broad hand pinned her belly to the mizzenmast while the backs of her thighs were smacked. Then she was made to open her knees, press her thighs tightly to the mast, with her arms about its enormous girth and her breasts pushed to the sides, while her bottom was smacked. Travix, standing to the side, watched the tears roll down her face. No pleasure was bestowed. Afterwards Anya fell, dizzy, to her knees and Travix walked away.

That same night, her wrists were chained above her head and fastened to the headboard, but her feet were left free. Then she was pouched. It made her frightened, for she knew this was a preparation and that eventually, that night or in the early hours, Travix would come to her. Later, Kasger returned and she was suddenly afraid that he would smack her. But he massaged her arms, then opened her thighs, tightened the pouch and left again. Soon afterwards, she heard noises next door. When she turned on her side and wriggled down the bed, she could see. The man was there again with the blonde girl. Both were nude. Travix, fully clothed, sat on the bed, with the girl half reclining against her. She pinned the girl's arms back with one hand. With the other, she played with her breasts, nervously plucking at the nipples. The girl's knees were tightly bent. Her ankles were held apart and pinned against her bottom by the man. His face moved slowly between her open thighs. She could not move, with Travix holding her arms and the man's hands tight about her ankles. And Travix's fingers moved from one nipple to the other, steadily plucking, as the girl's hair lay draped in snaking golden strands across the pale blue suit and the man's lips and tongue worked between her thighs, wetting the soft blonde curls, then moving down to suck upon the entrance to her bottom. When the girl's first shudder came and her belly tightened, Travix drew her head back, drew the hair back from her dense dark eyebrows and her delicate ears and held her tightly as the eyes closed, as the full lips opened to a softened moan, and touched those lips with the tip of her tongue. Each touch triggered the surge of pleasure between the wide-open thighs. Travix held her while the man's tongue laved her sex and bottom until he too was satisfied, having drunk his fill of her liquid warmth and burning sexuality. Then Travix lifted the slim yet suddenly very heavy body, chained her with her legs apart, face down on the straw and bade the man watch her while she attended to the girl next door.

When Travix entered, Anya's pouch was wet indeed. Travix drank the scent from Anya's underarms, brushed it with her lips but did not lick, while those arms were tightly stretched, held by the chains, while those underarms were quite defence-less against that soft-lip brushing. And having charged her lips with the warm musk of wanting, Travix brushed her fingers through that hair, then touched the nipples, which were hard. Then she lifted the ankles, bent the knees, lifted the hips, pushed until the back was vertical, and beyond, until the knees had tumbled over with the feet against the elbows, leaving the wet tight pouch exposed. She fitted the small bone key within that sweet warm fleshy lock and turned. The small pouch tightened. Very carefully she split the double thong that bedded in the groove and held it open so the entrance to the bottom was accessible and the tension was increased within the pouch. And then she smacked – two fingers, wetted and pressed together, she smacked within the groove, against the tightness of the mouth; she smacked once, twice, rewetted, then thrice and the pleasure was triggered. Travix leaned her weight against the thighs to stop the feet from lifting while she pressed her hand against the belly and slowly turned the key. Then she stripped the pouch completely from the sex and held the lips open with her fingers while she massaged the small round arrowhead back and forth across the nubbin, with the knees still tucked tight, the bottom in the air, until the pleasure came again, delivered by the smooth bone key.

'Yes, Princess,' she whispered, 'I will train you to my ways,' and she stretched the girl out, secured her ankles together and turned her face down with her tight full breasts pressed deep into the straw.

[7]

Abaata

Next morning, the long chain was unfastened and the lamp was filled, but Anya was not taken up on deck that day. She kept dozing. Eventually she was woken by a sound as of a giant hand pounding on the hull. The ship was rolling strongly, groaning, and every few seconds it would shudder beneath this terrible slam. She could hear a distant low howl, like the wind, and occasionally, faint shouts, she was sure. She looked through the hole in the wall but the cabin on the other side was in blackness. When she called through, there was no reply. She got up, ambled to the door, dragging the chains between her feet, nearly falling as the floor kept swaying whenever she put a foot down, then fell against the door and listened. There were no human sounds, only the pounding and, up above, the noise of chairs sliding and objects falling to the floor. The chains that hung from the ceiling were intertwined and swinging in a large erratic circle. Suddenly, the ship pitched steeply and she fell to the floor. And now it was like a giant hammer slamming against the hull. The reef, she thought, the rocks; the ship is banging on the rocks. She had been afraid from the beginning but now she was terrified. She buried her head in her hands. But she kept looking up, watching the hull, expecting it to cave in at any moment.

Then all at once, the pounding stopped and gradually the ship steadied. The wind seemed to have got fainter – she couldn't hear it. Anya waited, then got up and stood there, listening. For a long time, there were no sounds other than occasional creaks. She moved back to the bed and sat down warily. Gradually, her breathing slowed. Then there were footsteps along the corridor, voices, some laughter and sounds of doors being opened. Her door opened.

101

'Get up, Princess. She wants you up on deck.' It was Kasger. He wore a cape and it was saturated.

'What is it? The ship is leaking?'

He chuckled. 'No – some big waves, though, through the reef. But it's quiet now. You'll be safe.'

He unfastened Anya's chains, then took her out, up a flight of stairs, past a landing with a heap of chains to one side, then up twice more and through a hatchway which opened below the foredeck. The sudden blast of fresh air made Anya shiver but the scene was beautiful. Beyond the prow, she could see green mountains lit by the sun, but the ship itself lay in the shadow of bronze-grey clouds raging silently above her. The deck was wet. At her back was a continuous roar. She turned and they picked their way along the deck, through snaking coils of rope and fragments of timber spars. Halfway along was a longboat tipped on its side. High above were sailors, drenched to the skin, struggling to stow a tattered sail. Anya's face and hair were already wet; her naked body was rapidly coating with a film of spray.

Travix stood with the captain on the quarterdeck. She was illuminated by the low, bright golden light. Her suit was wet and for the first time, her coarse blonde hair had fallen free across her shoulders. It was weighted by the rain. The single earring glistened with reflected light. Her lips curled in a smile of cruel satisfaction.

'Come up, Princess – there is something you might wish to see.' She turned and looked over her shoulder towards the thick clouds and the roar.

Anya was afraid to move. Travix strode impatiently up and down, then stopped and waited with her hands on her hips. Finally, Kasger had to take hold of Anya and push her up the steps. Travix caught her and held her head up. 'There – the fate of fools,' she said.

Anya's hands went to her cheeks. 'No . . . *Please no*,' she begged, 'Oh please, it cannot be.' Her liquid eyes beseeched the waves, her trembling lips whispered forlorn prayers, then she stared in paralysed horror at that scene.

The small ship – her Prince's ship, closer than she had seen it – floundered in the mouth of the channel with her mainmast

102

gone. She was pinned against the reef and being tossed by giant waves. Her plight was hopeless. Any minute now her back would break. Anya turned to Travix and the captain, looking for help. Vain hope that was. The captain's expression was impenetrable. 'You said that you would spare them!' she cried, as though he had decreed this fate. He would not look at her tearstained face; he stared out in blank impotence at the ship in its death throes on the reef.

But Travix was laughing. Anya's lips clenched, her teeth clenched, then her hands. 'No!' she screamed. 'You tricked them. It was you!' But Travix caught the small hard fist before it landed home.

'You are free now, Princess.' She reached, almost tenderly, to cup the tears that overflowed so freely down the cheek already wet with spray, but the cheek was jerked away. Then she caught the second fist. Anya spat. Travix, her face cold, her lips stitched together by that gob of spit, yet her eyes savagely intent, took charge. She pinned Anya's wrists together, then kicked the feet from under her and whipped her hand across that face again and again until Anya, terrified now, cowered down coughing, choking, then finally, as the vicious swipes assuaged, whimpering, her nose dripping, her burning cheeks bedaubed with snot, bespattered with her tears.

'The Princess will be taught her place,' said Travix coldly. 'Get the cat.'

Anya, her eyes wide with terror, wrenched her hands away before Travix had realised what had happened, then struggled up, half running, half falling down the steps and scurried back across the deck, dodging round the astonished men who tried to grab her when Travix screamed: 'Get her. Don't let her go!' Yet her arms were wet and she was too slippery to hold. She reached the hatch and ran down the stairs but hesitated at the second landing.

She could hear voices below. If she carried on she would be cornered. How could she escape? Frantically looking round, she saw again the heap of chains. She crouched behind it then threw herself flat to the floor when she heard her pursuers clattering down the stairs. They ran past, down towards the crewdeck and the cells. Anya waited, trying to keep her breathing under control. Another group passed. Then she heard slow footsteps. Travix was walking down the stairs. Anya briefly saw her face, which had that same intent look, and her fist, now clenched about the cat. Anya squeezed her eyes tight shut, held her breath and tried to press her body through the floor, but she could not quiet her heartbeat. Yet Travix somehow passed without noticing her.

In time the excitement seemed to calm. Crewmen still moved up and down the stairs, but no longer appeared to be searching. Anya knew it was only a matter of time before she would be found. It was a mistake for her to stay down here – the space was too confined. But wherever she went on this ship, she would never be safe from Travix. She looked up the stairs. Her only hope lay there: she must escape from the ship completely. She would hide on deck amid the debris, then in the morning try to swim ashore; the land had not appeared too far and the ship must be getting closer all the time. She might be seen, but she would have to take that chance. Clenching her fists, she stood up, started up the stairs and froze – for a pair of legs had appeared at the top of the flight. Her courage immediately drained. She panicked and turned to run the other way.

'Princess!'

Anya stopped and looked over her shoulder. 'Ratchitt!' Her eyes widened, then her legs were suddenly too weak to support her. She slumped against the wall and sank down, burying her face in her hands. 'Oh, Ratchitt – she is after me.' And it was clear, from his fidgeting and the nervous glances he kept casting up and down the stairs, that Ratchitt already knew. The whole ship must have known by now, she realised. Fighting back the tears, she looked up at the rotund pink face that was turning longer and paler by the minute and said: 'She will kill me if she finds me. What am I to do?' At the mention of murder, the cheeks above began to quake, the bottom lip was bitten. The ears moved independently. 'Ratchitt – what am I to *do*?' Her voice had softened to an urgent, plaintive lamentation that surely could not be denied. The feet in front of Anya shuffled back and forth. The tiny eyes above her darted about, the bottom lip was plucked, then the small brown curl that

104

crowned the forehead was twisted into a corkscrew. But Ratchitt didn't speak until the sounds of running footsteps echoed from below.

'Quickly! Come with me!' He turned and scuttled up the stairs so fast that Anya could scarcely keep pace, then he stopped at the final landing before the deck and pointed to the darkness of a narrow corridor on the forward side of the stairs. 'This leads to the prow,' he said. 'Hide in here. I'll come for you when it's safe.'

The passage was so low that she had to crawl. The smell was musty. It was very dark – what little light there was, her body blocked. After twelve feet or so, the area widened and the ceiling lifted. The space was still enclosed but she could feel a breeze. Before her was blackness and to the right was a wide ledge with many empty sacks. She drew the sacks around her, for she was cold now as well as wet, and sat in the corner, listening to the breeze funnelling from below and the water lapping against the hull. After a while, she realised there was light, a faint horizontal rectangle to the right, several feet above her head. She stood up. Behind her and above her shoulders was a ledge. Gaining footholds in the corner, she climbed up and banged her head on the ceiling. The space up here was extensive, but low, only three feet from floor to ceiling. But she crawled across to the light, which was only a few inches deep. And now she could see the mountains, black against the dark blue of the twilight sky. The ship was moving steadily parallel to the shore. She felt safer here, in this hiding place. She moved some sacks up, made a bed, but did not sleep: wrapped in sacks, she watched the mountains sliding slowly past. She had much to think about in the quietness – the reef, the wreck; the ship was broken, but what about the men who sailed her? Could her lover have survived? And this place, it seemed a vast land – it looked empty. It gave her hope. She could lose herself in a land such as this, if she could but reach it.

There was a sudden splash followed by a continuous grinding sound through the fabric of the ship. Anya gave a start and bumped her head on the ceiling. But now her hiding place was filled with daylight. She peered warily over the ledge. Below the second ledge, a large hole funnelled downwards and a great rope hawser stretched tightly down its middle and disappeared through an opening about two feet wide in the side of the ship. The rope shuddered and came to a stop. The ship had anchored. Anya crawled across and looked through the narrow light. The sun was to her left, still ahead of the ship, so they must have sailed round the island in the night. And what she had felt yesterday was true – this place was beautiful.

It was early morning, but the landscape already had a warmth; a thin haze hung about the shoulders of the hills, which stood back, much more distant than they had appeared last night and less precipitous from this side. The ship stood in a small bay. The water was clear blue and beyond it was a band of bright yellow sand which, to the right, formed a curving bank extending into the bay. Behind the sand was the green of the forest, open at first then denser in the distance and lush, pervasive green, but with small islands of intense colour – many reds and yellows of flower-clad trees extending up the hillslopes. Even the tops of the mountains were clothed in green. But the place seemed silent and deserted.

Anya looked at that view for a long time. Then she heard banging sounds on the side. A longboat appeared, bearing eight men rowing briskly for the shore. How she wished she were aboard it. She watched it reach the sand and the men drag it ashore, then head towards the trees. It had not taken long for the boat to cover the distance and the water was calm. She ought to be able to swim to shore. She left her vantage point again and slipped to the ledge below. Looking up, she saw that the hawser disappeared into darkness. Below was the well with sloping sides draining to the hole that the rope passed through. She could easily fit through that hole. But the drop to it frightened her; she would have to lean too far out in order to reach the rope. She could jump across to it, but then what would happen on the other side of the hull, with the drop into the water? If it were too far, she would have burned her boats and never be able to reach the ledge again, even if she managed to climb back up the rope. Either she would have to wait for Ratchitt or she would have to find another way.

She crept back along the low passageway and waited near the entrance. At first it was quiet. She was about to leave the safety of the darkness when she heard voices down below, then squealing sounds as if an animal was being strangled. Then she saw them heading up the stairs. Travix had Ratchitt by the ear. 'But I don't know where she is,' he wailed. 'I haven't seen her anywhere.'

'Don't lie to me, Ratchitt. Kasger told me what you said, so we'll just keep checking each of your little hidey-holes until we find her. And when we do . . .' There was another squeal.

Anya banged her head in her wild rush back down the corridor. At the ledge, she only just managed to stop herself falling head first into the drop. The rope was her only escape; it seemed a very long way out and it angled away from her and down. She stood up fully, balancing giddily on the edge. When she stretched up on her toes, the rope seemed closer, but still too far and she felt even more unsteady when she reached. She lost her nerve and backed away, knowing she would have to jump. She kept advancing, but quailing when the rope retreated each time she neared the edge, then backing away again and wringing her hands in defeat. Wild horses could not have driven her to make that jump. Yet the echo of a woman's voice in the tunnel behind her was more than enough propulsion. Anya drew a deep breath, ran three steps and flung herself into the void.

She caught the rope in her hands but missed it with her feet and, on the back swing, with the sudden pull of her body weight, she couldn't hold on. Her fingers slipped and she plummeted into the pit. Her body bounced then jammed beneath the rope. Her right ankle had twisted underneath her and her shoulder had slammed against the sloping wall. But there was no time to think about hurts. The voices were very close. She pushed her feet through the portal, trying to feel for the rope on the outside, but her feet couldn't touch it. In desperation she turned, slid through and hung. The anchor rope was in front of her as she faced the ship; it angled sharply underneath. As she reached for it with her feet, her hands gave way and she fell backwards, arms outstretched, and the water hit her with a vicious smack. Bright shapes all around her scattered and she was enveloped, drifting downwards, in a heavy opalescent world of shimmering, bubble-filled dusty turquoise. The bright shapes slowed and became fish about the anchor rope. The water was warm. Yellow patches slowly danced across the sand ripples on the sea floor. She drifted up beneath the overhang and held on to the rope. She was sure her ribs were broken. But she was exhilarated. She had escaped.

Anya waited until she had regained her breath, then swam until she could see along the side of the ship. There was no sign of any activity, but she was too low down to be able to see anyone who might be at the rail. And if she were spotted swimming ashore, they would only need to send another boat, or alert the men on shore. She decided to risk it; there was nothing to lose. But she set off forwards along the line of the prow, hoping that in this direction, there would be less chance of being seen. The ship receded quickly at first. When she tired, she floated – the water was calm – then set off again, gradually veering shorewards. Nobody followed. Perhaps everyone's attention was still taken by the search. She smiled to herself – the first smile for a long time – and drifted. Sometimes, she would drift face down and watch the fish darting beneath her above the yellow sand, which rose ever nearer as the water shallowed. Once, in the distance, she saw a dark fin stretched like a lateen sail sweeping gracefully above the water, though she never saw the fish attached to this fin. She wondered if it might be a flying fish; she had heard that such fish existed.

As Anya floated to the shore, she heard cries. She turned and looked towards the ship, but could see nobody. The cries came again, to her right, from where the boat had landed. It must be the men shouting to each other but she could not see them. She found her feet and waded ashore, keeping low, creeping across the wet sand and hiding in a hollow at the margin of the bushes. The sand here was not like river sand. It felt very warm and dry; it was a strange substance indeed, made of tiny coloured grains, but flowing like liquid through her fingers and sticking like dust to her calves and feet. Yet it was not a dust that would leave you muddy when you wiped it free. And once your leg was dry it would not stick but would flow across it and tickle. There were bits of shell in it. When Anya squeezed the sand, it suddenly locked hard and squeaked. The last of the water on her skin had collected into oily salted droplets. She sat back and allowed her eyes to close while the warm air currents drifted heavily in the well of sand to caress her body and make the tiny oily droplets disappear.

This place was truly beautiful. She had never imagined such a place could have existed. Trees with curving slender trunks bellied out above the sand; their long leaves rustled lazily in the breeze. She listened to the waves breaking gently on the shore, then sizzling as they swelled on to the hot dry sand. Behind her, she could hear many different bird calls as if the treetops were alive. And she could smell the rich and varied perfumes of the flowers mingling with the warm breeze from the sea. Now that her skin was dry, it felt tight. Small white crystals spangled in the fine hairs of her arms; the sand flowed through her toes. When she dug her hand into it, it felt cool below the surface. Then her fingers touched something hard. She brushed the sand away and saw that the surface she had touched was wood – the grain was clear – but it was cut and shaped wood. She cleared a larger area. The wood curved everywhere just below the surface of the sand and it was dished. Then she realised it was the remains of a small boat. Its upper planks had been worn away, leaving only the belly of the hull embedded in the sand to form the hollow in which she lay. She found a rowlock, then her hand touched something soft. Part of a coat projected from the sand. She shivered when she saw the buttons. The cloth had a dark stain – was it blood? Afraid to dig any deeper, Anya backed away, half crawling out of the hollow and moving towards the trees.

Then she caught a glimpse of movement. She hid. Four sailors ran down the beach, short of breath, shouting, racing for the boat. One of them stumbled and let out a belly-churning scream as if terrified he might be left behind as the boat was pushed into the waves. His companions did not wait, but he managed to reach the water's edge and fling himself headlong into the surf. He was dragged, clinging on to the side, until they had made some distance from the shore. Only then did the boat slow while his crewmates drew the man aboard.

There had been eight men on the boat originally, Anya was sure. Where were the other four? Why had their mates been in such a hurry? What did the half-buried boat mean? Did it contain a body?

Though the smells and the sounds were still the same and the sand was still warm beneath her hands and feet as she crouched down even further, though the bush she hid behind was decked with lush red flowers, suddenly this place did not seem quite so attractive as before. Her eyes were fixed on the point ahead where the men had emerged from the trees. Then she heard a cry. Someone was leaping through the bushes, but parallel with the beach and heading straight for her. There was no time to get out of the way as the young sailor, his eyes wild with fear, jumped over her crouched form then rolled, picked himself up and carried on running. His bare foot had touched her shoulder, yet so intent was he on getting away from whatever was chasing him that it was as if he had not seen her. There were more crashing sounds through the bushes, sharp whistles, soft cries – signals between his pursuers, Anya knew. They would never ignore her. She jumped to her feet and began running as fast as she possibly could in the direction the man had taken. She saw a shape behind her, flowing swiftly, before something lashed round her left ankle and she toppled to the sand.

She pulled, but it was no good; her foot was held fast by the tendril of a whip. A knee pressed into her back and pinned her belly to the sand. Her arms were quickly pulled behind her and bound at the wrists. She heard the handle of the whip being knocked into the sand. Then she was turned over. Above her stood a woman, bronzed and lissom, completely nude apart from a thin skin belt around her middle and a rope-work thong sheathed in gold wire which was knotted about her upper arm. Anya's eyes widened, but her captor seemed astonished, for she gasped and momentarily backed away, then stood there looking by turns anxiously over her shoulder then frowning at Anya and muttering or singing something under her breath. Anya did not understand her words, if they were words, for she might have been humming a tune. There was a low bird-whistle and another woman appeared. She too seemed very surprised indeed. It was as if they had never seen another woman and now were afraid to approach. They murmured to each other without ever taking their eyes from Anya. The new arrival, presumably deciding that Anya, however unexpected, was not a threat, replaced her knife in her belt. But Anya was not untied. She lay on her back looking up at the two. They had no belly hair and the skin between their thighs was painted in a pattern of lines and dots.

'Niri . . .' whispered Anya, for even apart from these markings, they were very like Niri – dark-haired and dark-eyed, though much longer limbed and with their hair tied back in a tail. At the mention of the name, the two women immediately stopped talking. Their mouths fell open; they understood. Perhaps they knew Niri. 'Niri,' Anya said again, more loudly, though her voice was shaking. The women looked at each other, then one began to giggle. The other tried to speak to Anya but couldn't complete what she was saying without laughing. Then she tried to whistle – there must be others about, Anya realised – but again, the whistle failed and erupted as a giggle as the smooth bronze belly shuddered uncontrollably. Anya now recalled the strange circumstances in which Niri had been made to cry her name and suddenly she turned crimson with embarrassment. What had she allowed herself to say?

As they helped her to a sitting position, two more women appeared from the direction Anya had been running towards. They had the young sailor, his head was bowed and he looked beaten. But when the women stopped to look at Anya, the sailor tried to break away. Though neither woman took a step in pursuit, one whip lashed out and caught him round the ankle and a second wrapped around his wrist. He was tugged to the ground and the handle of each whip was driven into the sand. He could have unleashed himself easily with his free hand, yet it seemed that, with all four women now standing over him, he was disinclined to try. He lay on his back shaking,

111

his eyes darting from one woman to the other. The leading woman drew her knife, which had a thick spatulate double-edged blade. She twirled it through the air and caught it. The man began to plead. She shouted at him in her own tongue. He shut up. Then she knelt beside him, placed the blade beneath the neckline of his shirt and slit it down the front. He swallowed; the apple in his throat bobbed up and down. She slit the sleeves, which fell away, leaving his upper body bare. The women began to chatter excitedly. They descended on him, touching the curls on his chest and making small appreciative cries. The leading woman spoke again; she must have instructed them to stand back, for they moved away and fell silent while she continued the operation on his trousers. Anya watched the fascination in the faces of those beautiful bronzed forms as they stood, hips angled, slim thighs moving gently, toes kneading the sand and thumbs tucked into each fur-skin belt. She watched the fingertips then reaching to the lips, or behind the neck, to stretch across a smooth-skinned shoulder blade while perhaps the head was tilted and a lifted foot began to scratch behind a knee.

On the ground, against the faint pleas, the trouser legs were slit to the waistline, the belt was unbuckled and the prisoner's sex lay revealed, surrounded by a thick dark bush of hair. Next, his legs were parted fully. His cockstem lolled. The leading woman then moved so rapidly that the man cried out from fear. She lifted back the cockstem and placed the blade flat against the bag. He gasped when the cold threat touched him. She gritted her teeth and cried, '*Abaata!*' He did not understand her, but his eyes were wide with fear. '*Abaata!*' she screamed again and pressed the knifeblade harder. One downswipe of a blade such as this would surely have severed his ballocks from his body, and he knew it. His breathing came in sobbing gulps; his cheeks became wet with tears, but the woman would show no mercy. She screamed the word again. The knife was taken away and his bag was gathered in the woman's hand; then the blade returned to press against him more threateningly than ever. '*Abaata!*' the woman cried again, though clearly her patience now was running low, as the man's sobs welled ever freer.

112

Then all at once it happened. Perhaps it was the way the knife pressed against him; perhaps it was the attention, so closely directed there; perhaps it was the way that anxiety had gripped him in its thrall. But whatever the driving pressure, the cockstem suddenly began to swell. Though no one touched it, it rolled across his lower belly, sufflated strongly and lifted. The women looked at each other, murmured softly, '*Abaata . . .*' and nodded knowingly. The leader released the bag and stood up, pointing the knife at the man. '*Abaata,*' she said firmly, and the man understood. His cock, curving very stiffly up above his belly, had pulsed when she had pointed. She tucked her knife away and folded her arms. For a while all the women watched the cockstem throbbing gently on the otherwise immobile frightened body on the ground.

They made the man kneel up while they tied his wrists behind him, then the youngest of the women knelt before him, spread his knees apart and touched his stem and bag. But her fingertips kept returning to stroke his curls as if they held a special fascination. The others watched her and advised. Each time one of them spoke, she would look up at her and listen carefully, then touch him in some way that she had evidently instructed. There were many nips in places on the underside of the stem and beneath, in places Anya could not fully see. But it was not clear whether she did it to hurt him or to cause him pleasure. The young woman then closed her hand around the dangling bag as if it were a fruit on a twig and she would pick this fruit by cupping it and twisting. The man groaned gently with what Anya assumed must be pain. But the women nodded sagely as the cockstem stood up harder than before. And Anya was stirred inside by witnessing these women take a man like this and use him in such ways, as if he were their plaything.

When the whip was produced again, he tried to back away on his knees until the leader threatened him again. He was made to lean back on his elbows with his cock pushed in the air while the bag was gathered up with it and the end of the whip was wrapped for three times round the entire collection. A leather collar was tied round his neck. Attached to this collar was a length of twine which, once he was lifted to his knees, dangled down his back to the level of his waist. The twine was wrapped once around the cord between his wrists. At the end of the twine was a small loop. He was made to stand while the whip was drawn back between his legs, up between his buttocks and was threaded through the loop at his waist. Now the handle was tightly pulled until his head was forced back sharply, the whip strands bedded deeply between the cheeks of his buttocks and his cockstem, drawn down by the tension, stood straight out from his body. The women seemed satisfied with this arrangement. The leader then came over to Anya, still pinned by her ankle, with her hands tied behind her. The woman pushed her back on to the sand and Anya's fear welled up to choke her as she read the woman's lips before the word was uttered.

'*Abaata*,' said the woman firmly as her hand went to the knife. And at that word, Anya felt the fear sinking back down again, very deep inside her, pushing out hard as she spread her thighs. The woman reached; she stroked the bright red curls between the legs and touched the sun-warmed flesh; she lifted back the swollen lips and deep delicious fear pushed out – a small hard ball of excited shame, for all to see. '*Abaata*,' the woman murmured, nodding gently as the others crowded round to look at it and Anya's cheeks flushed crimson.

And though Anya was not trussed in the way the man was, with one of the women behind him, controlling the traction in the thong between his legs, keeping him hard and bobbing, still she remained in that state as they were driven before the women, who would not leave her be but kept stroking her curls and touching her in that one place even as they hurried her onwards through the open bushes. When one woman left her side, another would take over. Momentarily, they would stop. '*Abaata*,' the new woman would say. Anya, her breathing now deliciously shallow, would feel her legs slowly bowing outwards as the hard bud swelled again to meet the specific predilections of these new and urgent fingers.

They would touch her in ways she had not known; there would be things – small polished objects – held between their fingers when they touched and soft things pressed against her. While the fingers or the objects touched her, she would be

114

watching the tethered cock throb gently beneath the stroking fingers of the youngest as the other two women waited, seemingly indifferent to the young man's murmurs, and advised the young girl how to edge his pleasure forwards. As the cockstem swelled up harder, as its colour deepened, as the throbbing turned to thrusts, the leather would be tightened, the man would moan, he would be rubbed, then the plum would be held between two cupped palms, then rubbed again and all this while the small polished thing would be investigating Anya between the legs, or the fingertips would be taking the measure of her ever swelling bud. When it was judged the man could take no more, he woud be driven onwards once again, his head back, his cockstem stiff and throbbing purple, tethered, drawn down to make it project horizontally and sleeved intermittently in a slim bronze hand until it was decided that a halt should once again be called while the young girl was instructed further.

They came upon a clearing fringed by bushes full of lush red berries. The women stopped and began to pick and eat them. The man was made to kneel while he was stimulated. The handle of the whip was introduced between his buttocks. Still tied, he was made to lean back on his elbows with his belly in the air, so his cock stuck straight up. The women clustered round his arched, defenceless form, sweeping in, touching, working him quickly, treating his tortured flesh roughly, nipping his belly, squeezing his tethered ballocks, tightening their hands around his plum, then suddenly releasing when he moaned, until they appeared to Anya like she-wolves – circling, feinting they would come in for the kill then retreating, only to return. As the movements came quicker, the women seemed more excited. A thick twig was taken from a bush, stripped of its bark and used to whip the underside of his stem. Then he was worked and whipped again until he pleaded for respite. '*Abaata*,' the women told him as the whip thong was tightened once more about his cockstem and his bag and the youngest one took command of him again.

And the woman guarding Anya, the one who had captured her, whispered that word too. She was so beautiful, this woman, so relaxed; her eyelids were heavy as she bit into the lush red fruit. Anya felt a warm tingling sensation washing up her inner thighs as this woman opened them; she felt the warmth bathing her swollen sex lips; she felt her nubbin pushing out hard, wanting to be measured by those fingers. She heard the moan and turned to look at the man. She watched the girl's fingers touching and stroking the tip of his stem while further down, other hands pressed a small round pebble against the base, on the underside, trapping the tube where it fed into the bag. Then she watched a thin skin strip being slowly bandaged round the pebble and pulled very tight, forming a tourniquet around the base of the stem until the pebble was pressed so deeply into the thick tube that its shape could not be seen. But before the bandage had even been wrapped around him for three full turns, his pleasure spasmed as the young girl's fingertips rubbed beneath his tip. It was as if that pleasure had been dragged from very deep within him, yet not a drop of milt came out. The cockstem pumped in quick convulsions, each convulsion echoed in a word, shouted in unison by the women, but a different word each time. Anya realised that the women were counting.

As the count of each failed emission continued, Anya turned and looked at the woman before her. The woman's full lips kissed the fruit; her teeth bit into it again and her fingers squeezed the pulp. '*Abaata*,' the woman murmured and Anya opened her legs wider, planted her feet deep into the liquid sand but closed her eyes when the soft pulp touched her and the gentle fingers squeezed. The smooth unyielding pip inside the fruit touched her like a stone. It pressed against the underside of her nubbin. Again the fingers squeezed. She shivered very gently when the warm thick juice divided down her open flesh lips and trickled down her legs.

[8]

The Village

The women seemed untiring as they led their captives onward through the bush. They moved with a smooth loping stride which Anya found impossible to match. She stumbled many times in the soft sand underfoot, but they never scolded her. Each time she fell, she would be lifted up again and one of them would wait until she had regained her breath. But they were much harsher with the man. He was made to run collared and erect, with the cord of the whip secured around him. When he fell, he would be punished: they would turn him on his side, and fold his knees up whilst the youngest girl whipped the underside of his cockstem with a thin resilient stick then threatened him with the bandage and the stone.

They appeared to be following a line parallel to the shore; at times Anya could glimpse the sea to her right. But she could see no path underfoot. Eventually, they came to a ridge of black jagged rock sparsely clad with trees and began to climb it. There were many footholds and Anya found the going much easier than on the sand. When the ground began to level, the women stopped. Two sat down and Anya followed their example, but the man was tethered to a tree. The women standing next to Anya had turned to look back, shading their eyes. As they spoke to each other, the two who had been sitting stood up and joined them. Anya looked out above the trees and in the direction they pointed. The air was misty with the heat of day, which softened the colours in the distance, but even so, the wide sweep of the bay was visible ahead and to the left as a thin yellow line between green and blue. To the right were the mountains – very tall but showing no bare stone; they seemed so different from the mountains of her homeland, which were craggy and covered in snow. One of

117

the women shouted and pointed to the sea. Then Anya saw the pirate ship; she hadn't noticed it until now because it appeared so small. When she realised it was moving away from the shore, she glanced at the man. He had seen it too; his look, already sad, was now forlorn. There was no possibility of escape from here for either of them now.

Anya stared out into the distance, looking for the reef with the ship dashed upon it, even though she knew the wreckage must be far away on the other side of the island. She looked again to the mountains. She thought of her Prince again, pictured his face, focused it into her mind. Last night she had seen the waves; she had seen his ship broken, in its death throes; she had seen the wide expanse of raging water between the reef and the dry land, so why did she not accept that her Prince was surely drowned? Because she could see his face too clearly.

A hand touched her shoulder. As Anya looked up at the slim bronze figure of the beautiful woman beside her – the woman who had caught her, had touched her so deliciously – a tear escaped and trickled down her cheek. The hand squeezed her shoulder gently. The expression in those dark eyes was one of concern. The woman helped her up. She stood taller than Anya by a hand's-breadth. The fingers touched Anya's red hair, straggly from the dried salt water. The dark eyes searched her own. 'Ikahiti,' said the woman. Anya's eyes, a little apprehensive, looked to the side, then back again. The woman stepped back. Her hand lifted then swept gracefully down in front of her body, then pointed to her heart. 'Ikahiti,' the woman repeated.

Anya's chin lifted. Her lips parted. 'Anya,' she replied tentatively.

'An-i-ya,' said the woman, nodding gently.

'Ika-hiti,' whispered Anya and Ikahiti smiled. She took off her gold sheathed ropework thong and knotted it about Anya's upper arm.

Once they had crossed the summit of the ridge, they could see below them a village of wicker huts clustered in three or four main groups and nestled in a clearing floored by sand.

118

On the inland side of this clearing was a large cave in yellow rock. Bronze-skinned people moved in and out of this cave and across the sand to the water's edge. To the right, the ridge that Anya stood on became lower and less craggy but extended out into the sea like a giant arm sweeping around the blue water to capture it in a clear lagoon. Drawn up on the shore were long narrow boats. There were people bathing. Anya could hear their laughter. Behind the huts was a place where it appeared that trees had been felled and left on the ground. As the party began to pick a route down the steep slope towards the village, and people by the water's edge, noticing them, began to wave and shout, Anya was secretly excited at the prospect of this meeting. She felt she had a friend in Ikahiti.

Even before they reached the level sand, the women of the village were crowding in on them. The man, tied as he was, exposed and still very much erect, seemed very frightened, but the women seemed to take the man for granted; they were far more interested in Anya. It was as if they had never before seen a woman who was not of their own kind. Their dark eyes flashed as they studied her and their fingers moved quickly, agilely, through the air as they spoke in a very rapid chatter to the ones who had captured her. Everyone wanted to look at her. They smiled at her and touched her hair; they became very excited when they saw the bush of red curls between her thighs. And Anya realised why: she noticed that these women, like her captors, were bare-bellied, but the flesh between their legs was decorated with inks or paints which made it appear to be covered in finely combed hair. These women were more decorated than the others; when they turned, Anya could see fine radiating coloured patterns on their lower hips, above their buttocks. They wore necklaces and earrings and belts of polished shell and bone. One or two women wore gold. Everyone had similar features – small noses, large deep brown eyes and very dark brown hair; their breasts were small and tight and pear shaped; their hips were narrow and their limbs athletic – flexible, slim and strong. Some of the younger ones would stand with their heads to one side and their fingertips intertwined so their hands formed an arch in the air as they listened to the others talking. Their eyes would be watching Anya, washing up and down her body, as Anya listened for some clue in the intonation of the voices which might indicate how she would be received here and what might happen to her next.

When the crowd eventually parted and allowed them to proceed up the beach, Anya realised she had seen no men here. All the people of this village seemed to be women. Where were the men? She looked out into the lagoon. A number of the long boats, drawn by the excitement, were coming in to shore. But the people paddling them were once again women. It seemed very strange that there were no men.

About fifty yards further on, the women stopped and made the man kneel as they looked expectantly towards the cave. Anya watched too. Some young girls came running out and formed two lines. It seemed to be a signal, for the whipcord was now removed from the prisoner's tethered parts and his hands were untied. Ikahiti took hold of the loop of the cord attached to his collar. He was then pushed forwards on to his hands and knees and driven up the sand towards the entrance to the cave. He was made to crawl like an animal. When he tried to raise his head, Ikahiti pushed her foot down hard on to the cord against the side of his neck and his face was forced into the sand. Anya was allowed to walk unshackled, but she could not understand why these women – especially Ikahiti, who had shown her such consideration – would want to be so cruel to this man when all he had done was to set foot on their island.

The way swung to the right before they reached the cave and it overlooked the cleared hollow that Anya had seen from the ridge. There were many felled tree trunks and lengths of pole, some of them secured together to make framework structures which could have been the skeletons of huts. Small groups of women were working around these structures. Suddenly, Anya caught a glimpse of someone hard against one of these frames and reaching up as if climbing it, except that he wasn't moving – for it was a man, and a pale-skinned man at that. She knew he could only have come from the ship; the other three from aboard the rowing boat must have been captured too. But why was he there in the clearing and what were the women doing? The man in front of Anya had noticed; his frightened eyes were redirected forwards by Ikahiti taking him by the hair. Anya's eyes, darting round for one last time before the view was lost, saw other men, again not moving, against or even within these frames and she was sure she saw more than three. Then she heard the unmistakable sound of smacking before the women pushed her onwards to the cave.

Though the entrance itself was large, the space within the cave seemed vast. The air was fresh and pleasantly warm. Again, the floor was golden sand. The walls of yellow stone bellied out and up to form an enormous many-ribbed arched roof, like the bones of a gigantic creature. It was as if the skin of this creature had stretched and broken over the years: large holes were present in the roof. Through the ones high up near the centre, pillars of yellow sunlight shafted down to turn the floor to glowing pools of sand. Other openings threw diffuse shades of blue or forest green. Tendrils hung down from them like necklaces of multicoloured flowers; in places the walls were clad with broad-leaved vines bearing succulent fruit. To the left was a large lake. Its crystal waters appeared lit from below as if it was connected beneath the rock to the open air. Far ahead, towards the back of the cave, was a tall cascade of thin water which tumbled to a milky mist. The right-hand wall of the cave was terraced; steps cut into the stone ran between the various levels. Smaller cave entrances fed on to these terraces. On some of the terraces were small gardens. There were women descending the steps towards the cave floor, congregating to see the new arrivals.

The man was driven forwards to a place, facing the lake, where a large plinth had been cut into the stone and was surmounted by a great chair embellished with ornaments of polished shell and intricately fashioned ropework gold, which wound round the arms of the chair in snakelike tendrils. The back of the chair was decorated with the shapes of fishes – pearl-eyed, finned with polished nacreous shell and scaled with beaten gold. Again, the man was made to kneel, with head bowed. But his head kept moving as he glanced round him, trying to absorb his surroundings. Anya was very aware of the

121

man's uneasy movements and of the way it seemed to annoy the women and disturb the silence that had fallen. She was more aware still of the broad flat sticks carried by the women waiting to greet them and now advancing towards the man. Anya, standing with Ikahiti behind her, remained as still as she could.

The younger girls, gathered in a circle behind the new arrivals, suddenly bowed and a small procession emerged one by one from an archway to the right of the chair.

Anya's head was bowed but her eyes were lifted; from the shelter of her eyebrows she studied the group as it approached sedately. There were four women and all of them were remarkable in appearance. One wore an animal skin; two, who were taller than the others, were nude although their bodies were painted; and the last and youngest of the four had hair that was lighter by several shades than that of any other island woman Anya had seen. She was very heavily decorated in jewellery of shell and gold and, unlike anybody else, wore a kind of short, tasselled cape in red and gold. This cape appeared out of place amongst these people, who otherwise seemed to wear nothing but necklaces and skins; it was the kind of thing that would be worn by a noble in Lidir. The woman – or girl, Anya saw now – had the same small chin, full lips and childlike, wide-eyed expression as Niri, but her hair was this pale golden brown and her skin was not so bronzed as the others. Bending forward, Ikahiti whispered in Anya's ear, 'Kal-isha', and Anya wondered, as the young girl took up her place on the chair, whether Kalisha was her name or her title, for despite her youth and stature, her disposition was that of someone of great importance.

The two tallest women stood to her left, leaving the fourth woman to the right. Unlike the girl, her skin was deeply bronzed and also wrinkled, for she was much older – or appeared to be, from her thin limbs and from what little Anya could see of her face. She too wore a cape but it was an animal skin, a little like a giant cat's. The creature had been skinned in one piece, so the skin extended as a head-dress which hung down the cat-woman's back. Her appearance was fearsome – it seemed she had an extra pair of eye sockets on the top of her head. When she bowed, the jewelled blood-red eyes sewn into the skin seemed to stare at Anya; when the woman raised her head, her own eyes smouldered deep within their hollow sockets in her wrinkled dark bronze skin. Around her neck was a string of teeth and in her hand was a small wooden ball on a stick. The surface of the ball had many holes in it, and it rattled when she shook it.

The golden-haired girl whispered something to one of the women beside her, who then shouted a command. Immediately, the man on the floor was pushed forwards and his collar was drawn tight. Not knowing what to do, Anya stood her ground. The girl got up and was followed by her retinue down the three steps on to the sand. As the group walked past the man, whose head was bowed as he knelt up straight, still breathing heavily, though his sex was relaxed now, lolling to the side, it seemed that their eyes were not attuned to the man at all, but were fixed on Anya, who stood slightly behind him, shaking. They came to a halt in front of her. Kalisha – a Princess, Anya knew this girl must be, from the respect which the others, even the cat-woman, showed her – glanced briefly at the young man on the ground, then spoke to the two women guarding him. One of them then took him by the shoulders and pulled them back. The Princess pointed to the thick stem resting softly against his thigh, then whispered to one of the two women with her. These women were completely nude. They wore no necklaces or bracelets, but their bodies were entirely clothed in fine flowing patterns of lines in black and brown and gold, which swirled around their bellies, down their thighs and snaked up to their breasts. Each nipple was pierced by a ring. Between each pair of legs, Anya could see what appeared to be a small gold pouch; it seemed to clothe each flesh lip separately so the line of contact was clearly visible. She wondered how this double pouch could be held in place when it lacked any visible cords. Then she saw something tiny and white catch the light at the upper junction of the gold-sleeved lips. Seeing that made her shudder; again she wondered how it was attached.

When Anya looked up, all four people in front of her were staring at her. Ikahiti, standing behind her, edged Anya's legs apart and nudged her. Again she whispered the name 'Kalisha', and nudged Anya more urgently. Anya suddenly understood. As the Princess stepped forward, Anya whispered, 'Kalisha,' then averted her eyes for a second. A faint smile crossed the Princess's face. When Anya returned that smile, the Princess's glance broke away, then suddenly stabbed back, making Anya flinch. Though a young girl, she had the confidence of a mature woman. She touched Anya's long red hair, her skin, her nipples. The nipples gathered to that touch. The Princess's gaze came to rest upon the knotted golden thong. She glanced at Ikahiti, then looked again at Anya and her eyes glittered; her lips, slightly parted, were like soft brown luscious fruits.

The pale bronze fingers touched the belly, then the hair below, bright red and wiry from the salt evaporations; they touched the lips, sticky black, cloyed with the red juice smeared about them, but they did not retreat from this sweet-stickiness; like small brown bees, they tasted it, then they found the small pink stud. It was painfully hard now while the soft bronze bees murmured round it and the Princess's gentle voice spoke, not to Anya, but to the women. She seemed to be questioning them. Anya heard her name being mentioned. 'Aniya . . .' the Princess repeated softly. While the conversation continued – faintly to Anya's ears, behind the thrumming of murmurous bees – the young man beside Anya was made to atone for his disgrace.

The women with the broad flat sticks took charge. They stood him up and turned him towards the Princess, that she might witness it, though it seemed the Princess was more concerned with Anya, who did not know which way to look now – whether at the Princess and the older woman beside her, whose eyes stared at Anya from their hollow sockets with an expression of intense disdain, or at the young man about to be punished. One woman stood to each side of him and slightly behind. His legs were moved apart and prevented from moving back together by a foot locked against the inside of each of his; then his elbows were pinned behind him. The first woman raised her paddle-shaped stick. The man's chest heaved as he gulped for breath. The paddle smacked across one buttock. His breath was sucked in quickly, but his belly had arched out too late to mitigate the blow. The second woman touched the tip of his lolling stem to realign it. It pulsed. She raised her paddle and smacked the other buttock hard. The cockstem pulsed again. There was no more touching with the fingers now; no more touching was needed. The smacks alternated quickly across the separated buttocks and each smack pumped the cockstem up until it swelled to make a curve which touched his belly.

But the Princess was interested only intermittently in the man. Her eyes kept drawing Anya's while her hand explored. It kept returning to Anya's curls, as if those curls held a fascination, while Anya listened to the smacks. It seemed to Anya that each smack searched through her to her belly, each murmured groan evoked a soft tremble between her thighs. She was thinking of those times that Travix had had her smacked with her legs apart – the shocking, sharp, stinging coldness of the smack, that feeling like no other, which somehow caused a wave of tingles underneath her chin, and the giving way of that coldness to warmth, and then the slow, passionless yet so delicious milking of her pulp, sealed within its seeping pouch, the massaging of her body-milk to butter. The Princess's hand moved up to touch her breasts. She was made to lift her arms while the fingertips examined her underarm skin, unwound the tight wet curls there and touched that wetness to her nipples.

When she opened her eyes again, the smacking had stopped. The hard, purple stem had been fitted through a polished loop of wood on a long stick and the man was kneeling. One of the women was sliding this loop slowly up and down the stem. The second woman was forcing the man's shoulders back, which made his belly curve and seemed to push the stem out further. The stick was pushed until the loop slipped down to press against the bag and the plum swelled deeper purple. The next time the loop was withdrawn it locked against the plum. The man was whimpering as this tight wooden band was forced up a fraction further against the resistance of his distended plum. Then it was massaged against it, very slightly back and forth, so the skin was drawn with it. The Princess, now mildly interested again, issued a command and the

125

woman's foot pressed against the belly. The toes expanded, dug into the flesh and the foot pushed. Accompanied by a groan, the wooden ring came free. But the respite was short. The man was lifted, pushed forwards on all fours and the ring was now refitted from behind, between his legs, so the stick could be used to pull the ring until it slipped past the resistance of the plum then quickly slid down again and jammed against the base, leaving the skin about the cock drawn very taut indeed. The stick, when pulled and lifted, pressed between and separated the ballocks and the cockstem pointed down. The man was turned sideways, that the Princess might now see the dense, tight, purple plum perform.

While one woman reined it back within its skin, the other smacked the buttocks and the victim sobbed into his folded arms; he tried to bury his face in the sand, but each time his hips rotated forwards and away from the smacks, the tightness of the pulled-back skin made him cry out with the pain. When he gasped on the verge of cruel deliverance by this means, the Princess shouted something to the women and immediately, they desisted. The ring was unsweated from his stem and a small support was brought. He was made to bend across this while the Princess examined him. She touched him only briefly, pressing her hands against the angry red bands across his bottom and closing her fingers round the bright red stem, with its ballocks clinging to it tightly, seeming small now against its thickness. To the man, the Princess said but one word, 'Abaata,' and nodded with satisfaction at this lesson learnt well as she tried again to make her fingertips close around his turgid stem.

The woman with the catskin cape was looking at Anya, who, already pale in the face of such cruelty, had paled further beneath this gaze. The woman stepped towards her, raised the ball on its stick and shook it in her face, enveloping her in a cloud of pungent spice. Anya cried out and tripped as she shied away. With her eyes watering, she was hauled up and pinned by the women, who were shouting at her, making her cry for real now as Ikahiti tried to calm her and the woman advanced again. The Princess, turning, held her hand up. The women released Anya and the cat-woman reluctantly stepped

126

aside as the Princess returned. An argument now ensued between Ikahiti and the cat-woman. The Princess held her hand up again. She pointed to Ikahiti, whose cheeks turned deeper bronze, then she pointed to the entrance to the cave. The cat-woman folded her arms in satisfaction. Ikahiti, downcast, was forced to leave in disgrace before the weight of all the eyes and the muttered disapprovals. But as she passed Anya, her hand brushed tenderly down Anya's side and their eyes met briefly. Ikahiti shook her head and though Ikahiti had tried to smile at Anya, Anya's heart sank at that shake of head and the foreboding in those eyes.

The captured man was given over to the dozen or more young girls already armed with sticks and paddles. They began by making him stand while a thin skin belt was wrapped for two turns around the plum of his cock and pulled tightly. One girl held each end of the belt taut while two others smacked his buttocks with the paddle until his milt was ejected in three thick arcs on to the sand. Then he was made to kneel while the handle of the paddle was introduced into his body to render him hard again. Finally he was driven out by the delighted horde of nubile bodies to join the others in the clearing where the framework structures were kept. Throughout that long afternoon and even into the evening, Anya could hear many cries of delight, many sounds of punishment, interruptions of pleasure with pain. Yet these noises were but brief interludes of distraction from her own protracted torments as the rites of her initiation were begun.

[9]

Initiation

Were she to have looked down between her feet now, Anya
would have seen the narrow cylindrical pool which appeared
cut into the rock floor of this part of the cave. The water
welled over the lip and felt cool against her toes, not cold
enough to make her shiver, yet she shivered all the same. In
the depths of this small pool was an eerie glow. When she had
first stepped up to its edge, she had seen something down
there, swirling round, a dark living garland, a predatorial
turbulence in the water. The women had had to hold her to
prevent her running away. The second time she had looked,
with her heart in her throat now, she had seen nothing but
the dappled glow of pale green light and a faint disturbance,
as of a distant landscape seen through shimmering heat. Once
her hands had been tied to a thick ropy tendril that was slung
over the wooden frame above her head and she knew for
certain what would happen, she would not look again. She
stared across to the lake until that vision disappeared too,
behind the young girls crowding round, and her apprehension
drew sustenance from the expressions – each bright young face
at once excited and vicariously afraid. For though Anya did
not know it, the things being done to her were part of the
ritual of the island, done to every island woman. Yet without
this foreknowledge, she was as unprotected as if she were being
drawn blindfold through an endless passage with many bumps
and turns, by a guide who was oblivious of her state.

The cat-woman walked as far round Anya as she could,
showering her breasts, her underarms, her squeezed-together
buttocks and thighs with the spice. A young girl pushed a
wreath of bright red flowers out into the pool. With a shudder,
Anya watched it sink. Then the women, one to each side of

the frame, wound the handle click by click and Anya's body stretched until her breasts were lifted high, her belly tautened and her legs seemed very long indeed as her toes gripped fecklessly at the smooth wet stone where countless antecedent toes had surely gripped in vain before. Once those toes were finally lifted from the floor and the body, seen from behind, formed a perfect streamlined shape – hands pinned wrist to wrist; fingers pressed together as if in supplication; hair straight down the shoulders and smoothed by brushing to a shining tongue with a pointed tip; delicious swell of hips, smoothness of bottom, delicate split; and a tapering flow from thighs to calves to feet that formed twin arrows pointing downwards – the frame on its hard wooden rollers was trundled over the pool and that perfect nubile pendulum swung. It was steadied by sure hands, positioned above the centre of the pool and lowered smoothly, so it cut then slid into the water, which took it like a slowly slipping glove.

Anya was too frightened to move; she was too afraid even to lift her knees and press them to her belly for protection. But she squeezed her thighs together hard enough to make them behave as one. As the water touched her coldly then began sliding up her legs, she bit her lip and looked up at the human ceiling closing in above her – arched forms capped by enthralled faces – and then she closed her eyes. Trapped bubbles tickled up her legs; the water wet her curly bush and seeped between her buttocks. When it touched her belly, she began to shudder with the cold. When it began to lap beneath her breasts and the clicking wheel stopped – jammed perhaps, for the women above had begun to mutter urgently – she suddenly became very aware of this separation; her lower body was below the water and vulnerable and it somehow made it worse than if she had been totally submerged. She began to panic silently, inside. It was as if she were drowning, yet her head was far above the water. She was trying not to move her body, trying hardly to breathe, yet her body needed giant gulps of air in order to survive.

Suddenly, the rope jerked and she began to slide again. And now she thought she would truly drown, for the sliding did not stop even when her chin was lifted high, with her head held back and her hair floating and the water lapping round her ears. She took one last gulp as she was lowered into the blackness – for she kept her eyes shut tight. Then she felt it touch her. Something smooth slid like a snake around her legs. She bucked. The snake moved up, curled round and began to search blindly against her belly. The head of this thing was round and tapered. It had lips; she felt them pull against the fine hairs on the skin of her belly, reach into her navel and press against her like a sucker. Then it tightened round her like a belt, making her thrash her body, shake her head and cry out under water, gulping and gasping. Suddenly she was breathing air, the creature fell away from her and she was racked up from the pool. The water streamed down her body; her hair was heavy and wrapped around her face like a spider's web. The bubbles in her ears burst and she could hear the excited chatter all around her. The frame was rolled slowly across and the tendril was lowered until her feet rested on the floor.

Now the cat-woman lifted the weight of clinging hair away from Anya's face. She studied that face closely, then looked down at the heaving bosom traversed by rivulets of water. Assessing her, she turned her round, then back again, then nodded slowly to the women. A heavy stick with a loop at each end was brought. It was laid at Anya's feet. 'No . . . Oh, no. Please . . .' she begged. And though they did not know her language, it seemed they understood her, for one of the women touched Anya's cheek, trying to calm her while others shackled her feet apart. Next, a wooden comb was used to draw the curls back from her fleshy lips, which were then nipped until they plumped up hard. A bowl was brought containing a paste, which was stirred. It smelled strongly of overripe meat. It was smeared thickly about her nipples. Between her legs, the lips were separated and it was smeared about the nubbin, then down the edges of the lips. The cheeks of her buttocks were separated fully and the paste was buttered against the mouth. Prepared and terrified further, she was wound up into the air and the frame was again dragged over the pool. She made the mistake of looking down. The water boiled with swarming, coiling shapes, drawn by the previous bait – her body. She tried to move her legs together but her feet were shackled apart. The rope was lowered very quickly. Her right foot touched the lip of the pool and held, but the wheel kept clicking; her body tipped, then splashed into the water. Her left foot jarred against the stone and the feeling came again, the crushing tightness in her chest and now the terrible open feeling, the open bareness of her belly and the split cheeks of her buttocks and the tender tops of her thighs. The clicking wheel stopped when the water reached her neck and her uplifted terror-stricken face began to gulp for air. But this time the wheel had not jammed; it had been locked by means of wooden pegs. And now the women gathered closely round to watch the shadowy shapes spiralling slowly upwards round the slender body struggling so ineffectually in the pale green light.

The muscles of Anya's upper thighs were cramping as she kept trying to bring her legs together. The snakes swirled between her thighs; they wrapped around her waist; soft cool slithering scales caressed the warm reluctance of a skin which tried to crawl away from the horror of this intimacy. Her breasts, lifted by the water, floating upwards, proffered tight projecting sustenance coated thickly with the paste. Thick soft lips suckered coldly about them, sucking awful, shivering pleasure from deep within, drawing their terror-haunted tips to bellied bulbils, then gorging on those glutted teats while the pale green bodies, gently pumping, flailed softly in the water like willow branchlets tugged by a sluggish stream. Then the cold soft lips began searching between her open legs, nipping the hairs by suction, then sliding along her sex lips. A gelatinous slipping clamp moved up them, extracting every trace of paste, then drawing again – a horrible drawing feeling as her sex lips swelled with blood – while a second sucker searched inside, its soft head pressing against her until she opened, then bedding until its suction pulled deep within. And while this head was bedded in her body, the other sucker, edging up, had found the hard tip of her nubbin and closed upon it, sucking very deeply. The head emerged from Anya's sex, moved back and found the entrance to her bottom.

The women on the poolside waited. Anya's mouth, fishlike

too now, opening and closing with no sound emerging, finally closed completely. Deep shuddering breaths were suddenly taken through her nose. Thereafter, her mouth opened only intermittently, for little gasps, soft moans, but her eyes told all of what was happening beneath the wavelets, which became more subdued too as the five snakes settled to their soft rhythmic suction, green garlands wafting gently, feeding, pumping the velvet feeling into the nipples, the nubbin, the bottom, the base of the spine, then drawing the rich red blood back out.

Anya felt so warm, so heavy-lidded now. Each breath she took was a cooling, heavy blanket lying upon her, then dissolving, its weight soaking deep into her body. Only the places that the fish sucked seemed alive with a softly pulsing pleasure. Her nipples had swelled to fit precisely to each mouth, her nubbin pushed to feed and an ice-cold vein of pleasure threaded her spine. The entrance to her bottom throbbed, sending a deep swelling sensation within her. She drifted, barely awake, with these pleasure points pulsing softly. Between her legs, it was as if a lover were sucking her, keeping her swollen, on the brink; the pleasure surged, then waned. Each wave left her feeling more deliciously weak, until she felt her body would dissolve completely and merge with the very water that lapped between the bronze-skinned toes that crowded round.

When she was lifted, the creatures fell away from her, yet Anya hardly knew; the drowsiness had overtaken her. Her limp body was laid in the centre of a large soft white cloth which then was wrapped around her legs and beneath her arms and she was carried up some steps and into a small room. The women's feet made rustling sounds, for the floor was strewn with leaves. She was placed upon the only furnishing in this room, a raised and cushioned stone altar with four narrow pedestals spaced round it. While she was left alone, her awareness gradually returned. Her hands moved nervously over the cloth that wrapped around her; it formed a soft cocoon of protection as she stared up at the ceiling, adorned in strong relief with garishly coloured carvings of depraved and twisted grinning faces with bright orange tongues pushed out and curling repellently down in her direction. She knew then that her ordeal could not be over.

The heavy curtain at the door was drawn aside and the painted women – the Princess's attendants – entered, though the Princess did not follow. Anya's fingertips froze about the fold of cloth above her belly. She looked up at the women standing one to each side of the altar where she lay; they were beautiful but strange. She could see only the upper half of their bodies, yet only their faces were free of the swirling painted lines and patterns which licked up their arms and bellies, round their breasts and up to their necks. Beneath the cheeks, each chin was framed as if by hands. A brown and purple snake slid round the belly of the woman to the right; its tongue curled round her ringed and painted nipple as if to pluck it like a fruit. Anya could not see below their bellies, yet she knew those bellies to be bare; she shivered when she remembered what she had seen there – the tightly woven double pouch of gold and the small white projection that looked like polished bone.

One of the women moved round the altar, carrying a tiny cage in which a light flickered; she used it to light the four small lamps which stood on the pedestals. These lamps flared strongly at first, then guttered as they were opened again and sprinkled with a powder. A heavy acrid smoke billowed out and across the surface of the altar, making the back of Anya's throat tighten. She had to gasp to be able to breathe and with each gasp she inhaled more smoke. The women, standing above the level of the cloud, watched her. The smoke gradually dispersed and Anya then felt a cool numbness moving through her body, through her limbs and to her toes. Her fingertips no longer gripped the cloth. Her whole body felt soft; it seemed to sink into the cushioned surface, which supported her as if she were still floating in the water. Around the bed the small lamps burned more gently with the fragrance of the spice. Anya breathed it more freely now; it did not smell so pungent as before. The numbness in her flesh had turned to awareness; her skin tingled and the places that the fish had sucked throbbed with an itchy pleasure.

The painted women now attended to Anya herself. They

133

dried her hair, sprinkled it with aromatic oils and combed it out until it shone. When they unwrapped the cloth and removed it, her body felt dry and cool. But she saw that the whiteness of the cloth was besmirched here and there with red. And again she felt a twinge of anxiety at the thought of what the fish might have done. The women placed the cloth carefully aside and examined her body. Each place that the fish had sucked upon had a small welling drop of blood.

Those places were quickly treated with a cool clear lotion which stemmed the flow but did not take away the swelling itching feeling. When they touched her nipples and rubbed the lotion into her skin, the feeling tickled to her throat; the nipples stayed soft and thick and pliant to their touch but to Anya they felt as hard and painfully pleasured as if those fingers were demanding lips which had drawn each nipple to a bursting ball, necked by the lips sealed round it, while a rasping tongue stroked back and forth over the skin of that hard ball on its stalk. As one woman continued to treat her nipples, she was turned on to her side and her leg was lifted. The place at the tip of her spine was wiped and stroked and it seemed her spine was turned to a tingling thread which the fingertip, as it rubbed the ticklish skin upon that itching knob of pleasure, was slowly clawing from her body. And with that tickling in her spine, her breasts, lying heavily, their weight swaying forwards, pushed pressure to the tips which the other fingers smeared with lotion and gently kneaded, though in vain, if they meant to take the itch away.

The fingertip at Anya's spine was replaced now by a stroking thumb while the forefinger itself examined the puckered ring about the entrance to her bottom, which had been sucked in many places as the fish had searched. Each time one of these tiny points of suction was touched, Anya tried to move away, for the softer that the finger was applied, the more unbearable the itch became, but the finger persevered, wiping each tiny lesion, stroking it and coating with the lotion before moving to the front. The edges of her flesh lips were found to be chapleted with ruby droplets of crystallised blood. Anya felt tiny pricks as the tips of the fingernails, pinched together, picked those jewelled spangles one by one. She whimpered

134

with the torture of that itchy pricklishness; she wanted to bring her legs together as the slowly tweaking pick proceeded, the twitch-inducing ticklish pick of ruby blisters from those lips, as the fingertips worked systematically closer to their joining before massaging them with a generous measure of lotion, rendering them supple indeed and turning that itch delicious, so Anya's tongue slid against the back of her tightly clenched teeth in a sure sign of arousal. To Anya, once again, her flesh down there felt hard, yet to the fingers that tasted, the lips felt like wedges of soft warm dough sealed within very thin rubber, unlike the painted women's own flesh lips which were individually sealed within precisely sewn threads of gold.

A fingernail slipped beneath the hooded flesh and Anya felt it catch against the carapace of dried blood around her nubbin and peel it very gently away, then smear the lotion underneath to make that nubflesh, already yearning, quite irretrievably erect.

She was turned on to her back and she felt something being done to her between the legs, something very intimate indeed. Something cold and metallic and very small had touched her and she squirmed, afraid of that small intruder which was lifting her fleshy hood and touching against her nubbin. She tried to lift her head to see what was being done. One of the women pushed her shoulders down while the other climbed up and knelt astride her, pinning her body and preventing it from jerking while they worked. She faced away from Anya with her knees about Anya's belly and her feet pressed into the hollows beneath her arms. Then Anya felt the hands spread and hold open her inner thighs. When the standing woman moved round between Anya's legs, disappearing from sight altogether behind the woman kneeling over her, Anya was completely defenceless. Her head turned sideways; her wide eyes looked askance. As the small sharp piece of metal touched her and her belly tried to lift yet one woman held her pinned down at the creases and the other opened her flesh and worked this thing beneath her hood, then took it out again, Anya had to lie there imagining terrible things and watch the open hips above her gently rocking as the painted woman held her and whispered to her friend. And despite her fear and the sensation between her legs – whether pain or pleasure she did not know – as the metal was tested against her, then taken away again, she watched in fascination the changing shapes on that slowly rocking form. Apart from the soles of her feet, this woman's whole body was covered in patterned inks, depicting trees and flowers, fruit and fish and curling abstract shapes. Anya shuddered; the metal had been slipped beneath her hood again and this time it held.

The first woman returned to Anya's side. She bent her head and kissed her. The woman's lips felt very soft. Then she stood back and placed one hand upon the back of the one who knelt astride Anya while the other hand explored the patterns on the woman's leg. Around each leg and curled in opposing directions was a snake; the one around the right leg was figured sliding over the cheek of her buttocks. Its head could not be seen. As she moved, the painted scales of its skin appeared to ripple and it seemed to bed itself deeper into the crease. And Anya saw again the pouch, each lip sleeved in glinting threads of gold. The skin around the sex was bare and now there could be no doubt – the edge of each lip had been hemmed, pierced repeatedly by a needle and sewn with the gold thread, but sewn so closely, thread to thread, that for the full depth of the lip none of the skin was visible. Her sex lips formed a small split shield of woven gold. But between them, at their joining, was a small projecting bone, like a cockstem, only as long as the first joint of Anya's little finger, but shaped like a cockstem nonetheless. And like a cockstem, it was now erect as the woman's fingers touched Anya between the legs. When Anya murmured, she saw the cockstem move, pushing out a tiny fraction from between the gold-sleeved lips and she realised for the first time that this woman was excited by what she did to Anya. And though Anya still did not know quite what it was the woman did, she found that this visible signal of the woman's state excited her too.

The other woman was intent upon her kneeling companion. She opened the cheeks and touched the place where the painted snake's head buried, then she touched the gold. Each gold-hemmed lip was lifted and gently squeezed; when the lip was released it remained moulded to the curve to which the fingertips had shaped it. The golden lips now formed an open purse which the forefinger freely slipped within then came out moist. This moistened finger stroked the small bone stem, then tapped it, then gently pulled it. The woman murmured softly and the mouth of her bottom pulsed. The moistened finger moved there, stroked it too, then the small polished bone was rubbed; it somehow pushed out harder from beneath its hood. The flexible gold lips were closed about it, to seal it in its pushed-out state. This tiny artificial cockstem poked out and downwards from the hood while the fingernail kept lifting it and picking at it as if it were an itching thorn in the swollen ball of flesh beneath, but the picking was insufficient to pluck that thorn out; it could only disturb its bedding in her flesh, stimulate the irritation and make it throb up harder. And Anya felt a strangeness in her belly to witness this – that these women would have these tiny thorns of pleasure somehow bedded in their nubbins, and constantly projecting, available to be touched, to be stimulated, twisted, plucked and pulled until their flesh was driven to distraction. The woman who did the touching left the other with her belly arching down and this small bone cock projecting betwixt her sealed-together lips and took up a position between Anya's feet, to arouse her too and to keep her erect with the metal device, a tiny saddle-shaped polished instrument of gold, and also now with a small flat polished stick that had a straight edge like a knife.

The hair was brushed back from the lips once more, the hood of flesh was lifted and the saddle, its shape having been modified yet again, was once more slipped beneath. This time the fit was good; the painted woman could tell so by the depth of the pale girl's murmur. The nubbin was sheathed no longer by its living hood but by the less yielding underfold in the gold, and the upper surface of this saddle was moulded to the sensitive flesh that formed the underside of the hood. These two delicate surfaces – the nubbin and the hood – were precisely separated by this rigid interleaf of gold, which therefore made its presence felt in duplicate while the lips were smeared with lotion; then with the knife edge of the stick, the paste was scraped away from the creases and towards the lips, gathering up the wax secretion from the pores and leaving them soft and fresh and sensitised. The small pulling movements of the flesh, accompanied by light tappings at the hood, kept the gold-sheathed peeping nubbin both stiff and under control. Each time the nubbin swelled harder, the tip of the stick was used to press the saddle a little further beneath the hood. The lotion was reapplied and scraped away until every skin pore could be seen and everything about that flesh was hard – the lips themselves, like projecting open fins of rubber, the hood stretched astride its saddle and the swollen bud of pleasure that was captured by the gold. So clean, so fresh was the outer skin of those lips that it would cling to the finger when it was touched. Once this freshness and this state of pure erection had been achieved, then the ceremony of the piercing could begin. This was accomplished with the saddle still in place, for the saddle had on each side of it a small opposing hole.

The women moved aside and the cat-woman entered. Anya was afraid, for the woman's expression was cruel. She turned her quickly on her side, one knee crooked and her breasts pressed to the cushion so that she would not see. But Anya could imagine; she could feel the long bony fingers touching her between the legs, pulling back the thickened lips, searching out the gold-sleeved nubbin and squeezing very hard, so it was nipped. She caught her breath with the sudden pain, but tried not to cry out. When she tried to lift her hips away from that hand, the woman growled at her and in that brief moment, she thought it was indeed the growl of a giant cat. She lay half crouched now, afraid to move at all but knowing that something dreadful would be done. She looked towards the painted women but they stood like statues, watching. The tears welled down her cheeks while the fingers nipped her, pushed inside her body, explored her tenderness freely while her belly quavered as if it had been slit then filled with ice. She felt the bony fingers lift her sex up from inside, so her bottom lifted in the air; she tried to close her legs but the woman forced them open as Anya knelt with her bottom in the air and her breasts pressed against the cushions. She was too afraid to close her thighs though they trembled uncontrollably as the fingers, like hard, angled twigs, penetrated her

138

sex, upturned as it was, pushed out behind her, its hair brushed back, its lips bare and swollen and defenceless. While this hand remained inside her, its nails scraping, the bony fingers of the other hand pushed the hood back until the sleeve of gold was exposed. The first hand withdrew and the long nails closed about the sleeve and pulled. Anya's knees jerked. The cat-woman waited, still holding that gold sleeve, until Anya drew her knees back, until she angled them forward so far they touched the sides of her breasts, then the woman grunted and slowly tugged again. Anya felt that tugging up into her belly. When the gold began to move against the flesh that clung to it, she experienced the sliding feeling to her throat, for it felt as if the sleeve were attached to her and in that pulling, a thin ribbon of her inner flesh would follow.

The gold sleeve came free and Anya's nubbin swelled. The woman prised the sleeve slightly open, slid it back again, pushed it deeply home then nipped until Anya cried out with the pain. She felt her hood being sleeved fully back; she heard the grunt; then she felt a sudden prick of pain against the side of her nubbin. The bony wrist twisted as the fingers searched, while the pain intensified. When the thin and piercing pain stabbed deeper, Anya screamed. But the pin continued searching, amid her whimpers, for the small hole on the other side. It found it; the woman grunted, the bony fingers pushed, the scream came again and the nubbin was pinned within its sleeve of gold. But it seemed this alone was insufficient torture.

Her legs were now doubled up tighter, exposing her belly very fully for the woman to grip the flesh there with the hard tips of her fingers, which nipped until her belly flesh was bruised. But Anya knew not what was wanted of her; her flesh was pierced; her flesh was bleeding, she was sure. Was that not cruelty enough? The woman screamed at her; she began to sob, pushing her belly back between her legs to try to meet the woman, so her sex was pushed up in the air. The twiglike fingers entered her again, pushing down to the front, so her impaled nubbin was pushed out hard. She felt the long fingernails beneath the hood again, holding it back; then she felt her nubbin being squeezed, then the stabbing pain withdrew and the numbness seeped until she felt something like burning wire being drawn through that living bud of flesh. And now the full horror of what had been done to her was overpowering.

The cat-woman, having performed her duty as thoroughly as she was able, left. But Anya did not move; she remained with her head down and her bottom in the air. She felt defiled – and broken, too – more cruelly used and broken than when her husband had taken her and torn her inner flesh so callously, so unlovingly, all that time ago. He had used her body, then had pushed her aside, and left her bed – without even covering her defilement – to let her cry herself to sleep. That was his wedding gift to Anya, the only gift that despicable man had ever bestowed upon the woman he had taken – for she had never had any say in it – without passion, without love, without a trace of human kindness.

So to Anya, that piercing and the fitting with the gold split ring did not appear in quite the light in which these people saw it – as a gift, a window to a world of pleasure through one brief stab of pain, and as a symbol of her freedom, once her apprenticeship was served, to take her pleasure whensoever and howsoever she might choose.

When the painted women returned to her side, Anya collapsed, sobbing tears of hopelessness. They stroked her hair, spoke tender words of reassurance which she could not understand; they wiped the moisture from her sweat-drenched body and brought her food – boiled grain and fish garnished with nuts and small pieces of succulent fruit – but she refused it, accepting only the bowl of milknut liquid served freshly from its shell. This she drank greedily. They knew then that she had retained the will to live – 'Abaata', as they termed it – and would in time recover from her ordeal. On the Princess's instruction, she was therefore given over to the tender cares of Miriri, a woman renowned for her warmth and kindness, for a period of seven days.

[10]

Miriri

Miriri's hut was the closest one to the lagoon; this was what Anya liked best about it. In the morning she could watch from the doorway as the women went down to the boats and she could watch the younger girls sitting out on the sand, carving jewellery and threading necklaces of shells. There were jobs to do around the hut – Miriri saw to that – pigs to feed in a small compound, pots that needed cleaning and sometimes, fruit to be picked on short forays into the bush. But in the afternoon, Miriri would allow Anya to stretch out on the beach in the sun. Ikahiti, the young woman who had befriended her on that first day, would sometimes come to lie beside Anya and teach her some of their words; sand – *arini*, sun – *otei*, the sea – *uliwi*, and men – *rinyi*, but it was never fully clear what Ikahiti actually meant by *rinyi* – whether men or captives. When, on the second day, Anya pointed to herself and asked: '*Rin?*' Ikahiti simply shook her head.

'*Shiniki*,' she said.

'*Shiniki?*' repeated Anya, mystified, for she had not heard that word before. Then she pointed to Ikahiti. '*Shiniki?*' she asked hopefully. But Ikahiti shook her head again and smiled and Anya found that smile exasperating. She was doubly mystified now. She still knew nothing about the native men – there had to be some – and now she wasn't even sure about herself, because the word for a woman was *liwin*. Whenever Anya tried to ask about the island men, Ikahiti either couldn't or wouldn't understand, and though happy to instruct Anya in her own tongue, she seemed to have no interest in learning anything in return.

When Anya, frowning, gave up once again, Ikahiti laughed then reached to stroke the cord around Anya's belly, making

Anya freeze in fear, then begin to tremble like a frightened fawn, for the cord had been fitted to her after her initiation and it passed down between her legs and was fastened through the ring that pierced her nubbin. Ikahiti moved slowly, studying Anya carefully while Anya continued to shake. To Anya, the feeling – any movement which stirred the metal ring inside the tender unhealed skin – was appalling. The cord seemed to pull through her no matter where it was touched, stirring too the memory of the cruelty of that piercing and making her cheeks turn very pale. But Ikahiti did not stop what she was doing; Anya's very faintness seemed to spur her on. It was as if Ikahiti, kind though she otherwise was, gained satisfaction – or at least a calmness – from touching Anya when she was afraid. With Anya's breathing very shallow now, she was turned on her side, in plain view of the women strolling past them across the beach, and Ikahiti, languishing above her, toyed with cord and ring and bead while Anya quavered on the verge of passing out. In that brief time, a conversation to all appearances between equal friends had transformed into a tableau in which one woman, according to the vagaries of whim, would dominate and the other, scarcely conscious, would submit.

The cord, a single loop around Anya's waist and through the ring at her nubbin, had a sliding wooden bead attached to it. When the cord was first fitted, it was slipped through the gold ring and drawn up to make a pair of parallel strands. The ends of these strands were pushed through twin holes in the bead, which was next threaded all the way down until it touched the ring. Then the loose ends of the cord were fastened behind her, at her waist. When the bead was pushed up towards her waistline, the cord tightened, the ring was pulled upwards and the feeling made her squirm. The bead had not been adjusted in the two days since, but Ikahiti adjusted it now, with Anya on her side and without any warning. Her fingers lay against the cord, a fingertip toying with the bead while the lightly pulling feeling surged then ebbed away in Anya's nubbin and the ring, as it was lifted, softly pressed against the hood. Anya's mouth was open, but she did not breathe. The fingers tugged, the bead moved up and she felt a wave of nausea. Ikahiti's hand encompassed Anya's belly, pressing lightly against the cord and held her, rubbing gently, very slightly, until amidst the murmurs, the awful sickly feeling turned to a swelling arousal. She turned her on her back and kept her open-legged and kissed her while she held the cord – wrapped her fingers round it now – and Anya, belly bowed and nubbin ringed, could hardly breathe. She lay there with her swelling bud of pleasure tethered to this woman's hand, while the woman kissed her open-mouthed and she trembled in submission. It was a feeling that was both profound and delicious. Ikahiti turned Anya on her side again and tickled her nipples with a fine stream of sand. As her breathing gradually returned to normal, Anya's body glowed with an inner warmth as if velvet pleasure had seeped into her veins. It was the kind of feeling she experienced sometimes after her pleasure had come; but this time, the afterglow was there without the peak itself. In her belly was the echo of the trembling fear and in her throat, the honeysweet aftertaste of submission.

Ikahiti's fingers, now tiring of the sand game, slipped and snaked about the sunwarmed nipples, plumping them up to firmness.

When at length Anya opened her eyes, she saw a captive man, his cockstem bobbing hard, being chased up the beach by a woman with a stick. This sight was still at that time strange to Anya. When she sat up, Ikahiti smiled, apparently amused by the disquiet as Anya watched the punishment, then she drew her down again and continued touching her skin.

Over the next few days, Anya witnessed many such incidents. There were many pale-skinned men about this village, far more than the four that Anya had known about from the start. They must have been taken from other boats, such as the one she had found buried in the sand, perhaps, to be held by these women as slaves. But the women had been very selective, for all the men were young and there were none of the ugly unkempt creatures that stood starkly even now in Anya's recollection of that contemptible pirate crew. The men here were made to fetch and carry and were frequently beaten with the flat wooden sticks, often for no reason that Anya could determine other than to keep them hard. Every time she had seen one of these men kneeling up and waiting, hands behind head and knees apart, while the woman measured the swing and destination of the stroke, his cockstem had been upstanding and the spanking had seemed only to make his condition burgeon. Anya wondered if this was because of the way the men were tied. Like Anya, most of them had a cord around the waist, but in the case of the men, this cord had been drawn down at the front and looped around the flesh between their thighs. Once, she had seen the woman tighten this loop in preparation for the spanking. To Anya's mind, it was this similarity – the presence of the cord around the waist and the association between such intimate cords and slavery – that most of all made her doubt that she was indeed free to come and go as she pleased. She was never left on her own; there was always someone nearby, working perhaps, gutting fish or shelling clams or weaving leaves, but nevertheless, keeping an eye on her.

The women appeared to use these captured men as they thought fit. Though Anya saw their treatment as nothing less than cruel, she soon gained the impression that to the women, the degradations imposed upon the men were simply allowable amusements. Frequently, when Ikahiti came to visit, she would have one of the men with her and it was always the same man. His skin, though paler than Ikahiti's, was very sun-bronzed. His hair was long and untidy, though his body was very clean. Anya found him attractive, but very docile. When she tried to speak to him in her own tongue, it was apparent that he understood her well, but his answers were vague and faltering and his accent was strange. She asked him how long he had been there.

'I . . .' He looked very worriedly at Ikahiti. When she didn't speak, he continued. 'Many days . . . Many. Our ship . . .' his voice trailed away, as if it were a strain to talk and he was unsure. He kept looking sidelong at Ikahiti, who seemed very annoyed that he had even attempted to answer Anya and who glared across at her when she persisted.

'Days?' said Anya, admiring the uniform sun-bronze of his skin. 'But surely you have been here much longer? What land

144

are you from?' Ikahiti muttered something sharply to the man and now he was afraid to speak at all. Anya became convinced that Ikahiti's vexation stemmed from the likelihood that she had understood not a single word of what had been said.

The man got up slowly, his eyes downcast, and began to walk away. Ikahiti, still annoyed, shouted something after him then watched him disappear into the trees. Anya, aware that she had been the cause of the upset, but feeling none the wiser after this exchange, had just settled down on the sand and was gazing out into the lagoon to watch the women diving from the boats when the man returned. Anya saw the expression on Ikahiti's face – no longer kind, or even simply annoyed, but harsh. Her chin jutted strongly. Anya turned and saw that the man carried a fruit. He offered it to Ikahiti, who took it. But Anya soon realised that though this was a peace offering of a sort, Ikahiti did not mean to eat it. The fruit was long and smoothly skinned and purple, and she meant to use it on the man. She had turned him round and made him kneel.

But it was the way the man behaved that amazed Anya. He showed no resistance. His forehead pressed against the sand. His stem, already partially erect, curved down between his thighs. Its pale bronzed skin looked marked and reddened on the underside, as if it had recently been abused, and the bag was tight against the base. Ikahiti unfastened the cord from his waist, but only to double it and form it into a slip loop which collared both stem and ballocks together. She drew the slip loop tight until he groaned and his back arched down and his buttocks lifted. Despite the pain, he had let her do this without attempting to get away. Ikahiti grunted and he now remained still, his sex and ballocks tightly tethered. Anya could see the double cord cutting so deeply into the flesh below the bag that it appeared almost as a painted double line across the surface of the skin. Ikahiti's fingertips now tested that line for smoothness before gliding gently over the pale coarse hairs on the smoothly upcurved flesh leading back into the groove, to reach the mouth, which looked contused and tender. Anya knew then that he must have suffered this treatment many times before. She looked at Ikahiti's face – an intentness, a

145

kind of cold love burned there as she kept him in this position of subjection.

Ikahiti touched that mouth very tenderly at first, then nipped it. When he murmured, she kept nipping it until he acquiesced. But even that nipping had made the cock stand harder. Then she took a thick ring fashioned from bone. It looked too large to fit upon a finger. She slipped it over the end of his cock and managed to push it past the rim, but it would go no further and he began murmuring more urgently. She pulled the ring off again and placed it in her mouth. It came out shiny with spittle. After forcing his legs apart and drawing the cockstem down and back until it almost touched the sand, she pushed the ring over the cap then used the fingers of two hands to push it back until the skin was forced back with it and the ring formed a tight immovable constriction at the widest part. Then she made him spread his cheeks apart while she gradually introduced the fruit into his bottom. Women moving across the beach stopped to watch and to comment on its progress. While Ikahiti held the fruit in one hand, the fingers of the other worked him. The cock pointed down; Ikahiti's finger and thumb closed around the plum and the cap immediately below the ring; the fingers curled to seal the plum tip in a cup and milk it until the first shudder came. Ikahiti then slowed her wrist movement, but kept pushing the fruit inside him until most of it was buried. Then she shouted, '*Tika!*' and he became very still and tight. She let go of him completely.

Anya looked at the throbbing purple stem so wickedly constricted by the ring. There was that same calm intentness in Ikahiti's face as she knelt beside him, waiting. Involuntary spasms moved the end of the fruit between the cheeks. In time, they slowed. Ikahiti sat back on her heels and sighed. There was now a look of satisfaction on her face – as of a job well done, a training of her slave advanced. '*Chiri,*' she said to him and immediately, he turned, still crouching and laid his head on her lap. Ikahiti stroked him, touched the fruit and the ring about his stem. She smiled when his body again became still and tense. He was fighting against the pressure which must have been welling deep inside him. Ikahiti

146

continued to touch, closing her hand by alternation around the stem below the ring and then above it until Ikahiti's palm became slick with oily weepings.

'*Niri* . . .?' whimpered the man and Anya's cheeks, already red on his behalf, glowed even hotter.

'*Tika,*' whispered Ikahiti, then took out her knife and pressed the smooth round wooden handle very firmly across the place where the cockstem fed into the ballocks. '*Tika,*' said Ikahiti very softly, '*tika,*' while he groaned. But the smooth round wooden handle pressed, rotating slightly, and the pleasure was provoked: the fruit bobbed rapidly; narrow streams of very thin milt pulsed through the ring constriction to disappear quickly into the heat of the sand. '*Tika – shirula,*' said Ikahiti and at that second word, he tried to bury his face against her belly. Ikahiti reprimanded him and turned his face away, but Anya saw again that Ikahiti smiled. She began to understand then that there must be a peculiar bond between these two; it seemed that Ikahiti would force these degradations on her man, who would freely acquiesce, but Ikahiti would accept no pleasure from him in return. It was as if even the suggestion that he might have desired her and wanted to touch her was sufficient. To Anya, it seemed peculiarly one-sided and not based on love at all. But Ikahiti laid her man down on the sand, carefully and lovingly removed the fruit that had bedded within him and sat above him stroking his back and belly for a long while afterwards.

During this time, Anya became less and less certain of what she had witnessed – was it a punishment the man had suffered or a peculiar act of love? She wondered if Ikahiti and the other women ever took pleasure directly with the men or preferred to take their pleasure only by abusing them. As Anya lay there in the sun, with the warm air washing over her belly, constrained beneath the delicious cord which held her flesh erect, she realised that the customs of this island were very strange indeed.

Whereas Anya had these last few days been very unsure of Ikahiti – what she really wanted from Anya – she had found solace with Miriri. She took comfort from her warmth, for Miriri pampered Anya almost as if she were a child. On that first evening, after Anya's flesh had been so cruelly pierced, Miriri had cradled Anya in the softness of her arms – for Miriri was a big woman, big in heart as well as big in body – and had rocked her till she cried herself to sleep. When Anya had awoken later, she found herself, still enfolded in those arms, looking up into Miriri's face and basking in the tender warmth of her deep brown eyes. Miriri reminded Anya very much of the woman who had looked after her in the castle and had shielded her from the pain and shame of all those cruel hurts. But now she had received a hurt more wickedly cutting than any she had received in the castle: now she was permanently scarred. But this woman seemed to understand her anguish. She placed Anya on a bed prepared from the softest leaves, then covered her with a skin and sat beside her through the rest of the night, stroking her hair and smoothing her fingers over the hot flushed cheeks until long after Anya had fallen asleep.

Each subsequent night, before Anya was put to bed, Miriri would hold her in her arms and rock her before the examination was performed. That closeness stilled but did not fully take away Anya's apprehension. Miriri would glance at Anya, then briefly stroke a thick soft fingertip against her lips, to indicate that she should not murmur, and Anya would feel the slow surge of fear deep in her belly as her shoulders were laid upon the leaves but her hips lay cupped in the pillow-soft bowl of Miriri's lap while her thighs were gently opened. Miriri would look upon that flesh, blue-black, moist and puffy from sympathy with the speared and tortured pip, a tiny pink pearl still nestled within its living oyster, yet threaded on a loop of gold. She would loosen the wooden bead and the cord would slacken and lie in gentle curves upon the red curls of the belly, which would be squirming before she even touched it. She would open the lips, which would try to retreat. With the tips of her thumbs she would lift the hood. The fine gold ring, large enough to slip over the tip of a finger, would fall back under the hood and Anya would murmur – not with the pain, but with the more awful, more intimate feeling that this small rotation bestowed, for the gold thread would be turning deep inside her healing flesh. Where it entered, to

148

each side, would be two tiny flecks of blackened red. Miriri would catch these under the pointed tip of her fingernail and gently pull, then purse her lips and blow a very thin stream of air. The flecks would blow away. On the first two nights, the blood welled again to fill the two tiny craters round the gold but on the third night, the flesh stayed open and pink. Thereafter, Miriri applied a healing lotion then carefully fed the ring through its sleeve of pink while the open thighs before her gently shook. The first time Miriri attempted this, Anya was sick on the floor. Subsequently, though her cheeks would always turn deathly pale, she was able to bear the horror of this feeling – the sliding through her flesh – as long as it did not continue for very long.

When she had finished, Miriri would push the bead up Anya's belly to tighten the cord until the ring impressed across the hood again, and with that pressure, Anya would begin to feel aroused. The awful sensation would be forgotten, only to be replaced by a need which had not been fulfilled for many days now. Each application of the lotion, each renewed pressure there, made the need more compelling.

On the fourth evening, when the treatment was finished and Miriri held Anya in her arms and Miriri's warm aroma – like milknut – descended all about her and Miriri's very thick nipple lay pressed to Anya's cheek, Anya wanted to ask Miriri to bring her pleasure on. She knew what to say – for she had heard the man say it that afternoon, when, despite herself, she had been so aroused to witness his pleasuring in that way – but she was afraid to say it, to ask outright. Anya pressed her cheek against the nipple and turned her cheek so the thick dark rubbery warmth tickled her ear then, rubbing back again, brushed against her lips. Miriri murmured. Anya wet her lips and pushed them about that teat and sucked, then felt afraid at her boldness. The nipple slipped out wet across her cheek. Miriri lifted it and pushed it in again. Beneath her, Anya felt the woman's belly shiver as she sucked. She took the nipple very fully, pressed it to the roof of her mouth and nipped below it with her tongue. The nipple swelled up harder. Miriri's hand brushed Anya's belly and began to play with her curls. Anya, her heart in her throat, opened her thighs. She

149

felt the woman's hand beneath her back, lifting her hips, lifting her bottom in the air. She heard the hand move in the bowl of lotion. She trembled, sucked the breast more strongly, lifted up her thighs. And now she felt the lotion being worked inside her, the fingers stroking deep inside the lips, soothing, coating them and penetrating ever deeper, making her feel more aroused. Her lower back was lifted and supported by one broad hand while the other stroked the lotion deep inside, making her fleshpot grip those slipping fingers. Then when the fingers slipped out quickly and touched her nubbin once, squeezing so the flesh tip bit against the·gold ring, her pleasure came, with her bottom in the air, her mouth sealed tight about the nipple and the fingertips re-entered her against the strength of her contraction. After that, Miriri washed her and put her to bed. She slept soundly until she heard a noise in the night and was aware that the lamp still flickered.

Peeping out from under her covers, Anya thought that she was dreaming. Miriri lay naked on her back. Her full and very heavy breasts lay pointed to the sides and a face lay pressed between them: lying atop her was the sailor who had been captured with Anya a few days ago. Miriri held his head tightly against her. But his body was not still, though he himself did not move it. Miriri's thighs lay open and her belly lifted him slowly, then suddenly dropped and the cycle then repeated. Each time he dropped against her, he let out a sobbing groan and Miriri gave a grunt of pleasure. The movement was rhythmic, the slow uplift as he drew breath deeply, followed by the sudden drop. The young man seemed powerless to stop it. Now the giant thighs locked about him and squeezed until his back was arched down by the pressure above his buttocks. And though he cried out loud for mercy, it seemed that Miriri would take her time. The thighs unlocked, the hands released his head, but only to move down over his back, then over his buttocks, spreading them and searching the tight unwilling opening within, probing until it yielded to two, then three thick fingers. Then the slow movement began again, the lift and then the drop, until the man was truly gasping on the verge of cruelly penetrated release. Miriri held him steadily – very still now – while the fingers worked within and her other hand investigated the contents of the bag beneath, lifting up each ballock individually and rubbing it until it slipped. The fingers withdrew and both hands slid beneath his hips and lifted. Miriri herself lay quite still. Anya could see the slick stem gleaming as it slipped from between the sucking thighs, then, controlled by the lifting action of Miriri's hands, slid back in again. And with a catch of breath, Anya saw that the man's flesh, the stem and dangling bag, were bare of any curls. How could it be, when he had been so thickly curled the other day? She watched it lift again, naked, smooth and shiny, then sink inside the woman's body. She heard the suddenly indrawn breath, deeply sobbing this time, as he was held in the air, unmoving, with only the cap of his stem being sucked by Miriri's fleshpot. Her thighs flexed more strongly and he whimpered. She squeezed again; he gasped. She pulled him out completely. 'Tika,' whispered Miriri very firmly. He swallowed, then shuddered as she held him in the air. 'Tika . . .' She lowered him again. Her thick soft sex lips reached to take his tip and suck upon it while the tight and intermittent whimpers unfolded to a continuous mellow moan and Anya felt the peculiar feeling in her belly as she realised that, tortured and powerless though he was, the feeling that he moaned against was pleasure. The heels of the broad hands pressed against his belly to lift him, the large moist sex lips sucked; the fingertips reached to touch his bare bag as it dangled. His breath caught; Miriri pulled him out, too quickly, for the cockstem spurted once before he regained control. And now it pulsed above her gently, a thick drip poised at its very tip.

Carefully, Miriri lifted him down and placed him on his side. He faced towards Anya, who was trying to appear asleep as she watched through half-closed eyes. Miriri took the wetness that had escaped on to her belly and wiped it over his stem, which stood out horizontally, hard and bulging, angry red. She placed a pillow of leaves beneath his head, then lay behind him, keeping his thighs pressed together, which pushed his bare ballocks forward and seemed to force his cockstem further out. She lay for some while, just rubbing his belly gently, causing the stem to sway, then at intervals, sliding her fingers up and down the smoothness of his stem, for the miltings she had spread upon it had very soon dried and the skin had now acquired a silkiness. Then she rolled him over until his upper knee touched the floor. She angled this knee a little, reached between his legs, cupped the hanging bag in her fingers and stroked the back of it with her thumb. Whilst maintaining this tender action with her right hand, she lifted across the bowl of lotion, poured a little into the crease of his buttocks, which caused him to jerk with the shock – though not too far, for her fingers still cupped his bag – then her wetted fingers followed swiftly, slipping freely up inside him while his belly tensed, his back arched down and Miriri's right hand maintained the smoothing rhythm up and down the back of the bare skin bag. When Miriri turned him on his side and he faced Anya again, her fingers were still inside him, searching gently as his belly at intervals jerked and the heavy plum of his cockstem bobbed and sometimes throbbed as if it would spill. But Miriri's right hand, coming round to the front, closed again around his ballocks to squeeze at times and to slow these periodic bobbings of the stem. On rare occasions, she would release the bag and stroke the cockstem downwards, almost to the point of spillage, then wipe the leakage over it and grip the bag again, allowing his distributed milt to dry upon him while the fingertip explorations of her left hand continued deep within.

This it seemed was how this person, so tender, so gentle with Anya, preferred to seek amusement with her man, who somehow, in those few short days, had been conditioned into accepting that his pleasure should thus be measured and controlled. And having to stay awake throughout that night to witness this prolonged torment, awaiting its resolution, though such resolution never came, was the reason that in the morning, when she watched the man being ushered out with his cockstem still iron hard but extraordinarily silky, Anya felt simultaneously exhausted and aroused.

[11]

The Playground

There was a very marked air of excitement about the village next morning. There was no fishing or diving, none of the routine work seemed to be being done, and there were none of the slaves to be seen anywhere, yet everyone appeared to be very busy. Groups of women were decorating each other's bodies with intricate shell jewellery, with paints applied with the finger and inks which would be pricked into the skin using pointed fish bones, and they were fitting each other with headdresses made from the plumage of richly coloured birds. Miriri tried to explain to Anya. '*Achira!*' she said, laughing, placing her hands at the sides of her head, pointing her fingers upwards and dancing with surprisingly delicate footfalls in a circle while her heavy breasts stretched rhythmically and elastically up and down. Then she took Anya's hand and led her down the beach. Again, Anya was struck by this woman's open-heartedness and she wondered if what she had witnessed last night could have been a dream.

'*Otei,*' Miriri said, pointing to the hazy mid-morning sun hanging high above the ridge. Anya didn't see anything unusual about that; the sun appeared there every morning. Then the woman turned her round and pointed the other way, far along the beach to where a second ridge completed the enclosure of the bay beyond the lagoon. This ridge was much sharper than the first and close to its end was a curious hole just below the upper edge, where the waves had caused the rock to break away. Through this hole, the sky was visible. Miriri lifted her finger and drew an arc across the sky from the present position of the sun to the site of the hole in the ridge. Then she threw her arms wide and with her fingers gripping at the air and her eyes staring wildly from side to side, she advanced, grunting, towards Anya. Anya thought she understood now, apart from this last display – she would watch for the sunset through this gap tonight – though she still did not see what the fuss was about. She was more interested in these preparations and in the form the celebrations might take.

'Aniya!'

Looking up the beach, Anya saw Ikahiti coming towards them. Ikahiti's face was painted; her eyebrows looked thicker and darker; her cheeks were streaked with orange and yellow and she wore a bright red plume at the back of a band around her head. But she still wore the single narrow skin belt angled across her belly, so slim above the smoothly flowing muscles of her thighs. And between them was this curious contradiction to the dense dark hair of her head and the bushy black of her underarms – the very youthful, bare yet ink-pricked shield around her sex. It made her look so vulnerable, yet she was far from being that. When Anya's gaze returned to Ikahiti's face, she saw that she was smiling at her; she looked fresh and beautiful and happy and her eyes had that glint – wild, untameable and free. She greeted Miriri and began explaining something to her, while Miriri first nodded, then her eyebrows lifted.

'Irin-ta-shakahini,' said Ikahiti, pointing back towards the cave and making Anya feel mildly apprehensive. 'Shakahini-ta Kalisha.' She must mean to take her to the Princess, Anya thought. Now she felt afraid; her expression must have showed it, for Ikahiti laughed. 'Shi-shinula,' she whispered warmly, and took Anya by the wrist; her slim bronze fingers touched the knotted ropework armband that she had given Anya, then stroked back and forth across Anya's palm, tickling. Anya's hand closed about those fingers and squeezed them gently. Then Ikahiti led her up the beach and into the cave.

They passed the pool in which Anya had been submerged; the winding frame still stood beside it and Anya gave this a very wide berth. Beyond it were women bathing in the lake. She shivered when they came upon the place where the cruel rite of piercing had been performed, but Ikahiti carried on until they passed through a large archway and into a second series of caves – or rooms, perhaps, for the walls and ceilings were so well adorned with tapestries woven with bright feathers that it was unclear which parts of these chambers were wood and which were living rock. Here were several of the women whose naked bodies were entirely covered in patterned inks. They watched Anya with interest; Ikahiti squeezed Anya's hand and returned their gaze with open smiles; it was evident she was proud to be accompanying Anya and this gave Anya reassurance and also food for thought.

In one of the rooms was a pale-skinned man, young and quite handsome. He lay naked on a very large bed – a true bed rather than a bed of leaves and the first such bed that Anya had seen here – and he was being caressed by three of the painted women, who appeared to be working oil into his skin. Ikahiti stopped. Anya watched until she was distracted by a shout and they were ushered into the next room, where the Princess waited.

Anya and Ikahiti bowed before the Princess, who remained standing, despite the presence of several chairs. Once again, Anya was struck by the comparative paleness of this young woman's complexion and the honey-coloured hair, much lighter than anyone else's. The peculiar combination of strength and innocence was still there in her gaze. In place of the red and gold cape, she now wore an extraordinarily elaborate and beautiful high-collared flowing cloak, closely woven with vivid green, blue and yellow feathers, which, when she strode majestically about, almost gave her the appearance of an exotic bird. But round her neck was a jewelled golden amulet shaped like a sword. Its blade was studded with blood-red ruby and its hilt with minute pearls. Anya stared at it because it seemed so different from the usual decoration that the island women wore, which was fashioned mainly from shell and shaped in the form of animals, birds or fish. Perhaps it had been taken from one of the captive sailors, though the owner of an amulet so lavish as this would certainly have been no ordinary sailor.

At first, the Princess seemed pleased to see Anya. 'Aniya – si shiniki,' Ikahiti said. The Princess gave a very slight nod of her head and suddenly Anya was afraid of something she had seen momentarily in that glance – the way the eyelids had half closed. The Princess advanced and Anya looked down, aware that she was being studied closely. She closed her eyes, expecting something to happen. She heard them talking – about her, she knew – then she heard the heavy rustle of the quilted feather cloak. The small fingers touched her skin. She quaked in fear as she felt them take the cord and tease it out, turning it into a shivering line, then trace it down between her legs, hesitating at the hood, touching its drawn back inner skin, then investigating the gold ring. When she heard voices behind her, she automatically tried to pull away. '*Tika, shiniki,*' said the Princess. Anya opened her eyes; she swallowed. The Princess's face was close. The eyes seemed so wide and innocent as the fingertip, pressing now against the underside of the nub, rotated very gently. Then it withdrew and the tip of a small tongue slipped out deliberately to wet the tip of that finger, which returned to that same place, to rotate beneath the nubbin as it swelled. The Princess's calm and innocent gaze moved down; she watched the pale legs begin to tremble; she instructed that they be moved apart; Ikahiti opened them. And she kept rewetting and reapplying her fingertip to that one spot, the underside of the nub, which she could feel engorging, swallowing by degrees the ring that pierced it, while her slave was delivered from the next room and prepared by having a gold chain fastened through the rather heavier ring that pierced the underside of his cockstem at the place where it joined his bag.

When the trembles in the thighs extended upwards through the belly to the breasts, the Princess took away her fingertip and looked into the girl's now pleading eyes while the trembles in the outbowed thighs continued unabated. Then she pointed the finger at Ikahiti and delivered this one instruction, '*Nisha!*' – meaning 'denial' – with the force of a decree. Ikahiti nodded gravely though Anya, not having encountered the word before, understood the weight of its delivery but could not know its meaning. Neither could she know that the Princess had offered the word from spite – to a girl with skin paler yet and hair more brightly golden than her own, for even her favourite slave was eyeing this girl with a desire that was plain to see. She therefore added to the pointing finger another, wetted both quite liberally and applied them this time to the slave, only at the place where the cockstem joined the bag, that is, at the place where the thick tube below his fully erect stem finally disappeared into his person. She did it with the heavy ring turned downwards, rather than up, as it had been upon the girl, so that it pressed against the delicate twin tubes in the bag and made the balls protrude below, through brightly polished skin. The two wet fingertips massaged through to the part of the ring that was inside him, looped through the thin layer of skin, rubbing the ring against the soft undertube which would, after long stimulation throughout that day, finally be permitted to carry his ripened and copious miltings upwards and deliver them on to the Princess's tongue that night, in the privacy of her chamber.

For the Princess felt very powerful womanly desires for men – particularly pale-skinned men, despite the fact that these were the very men who kept coming in their giant boats to take the island women. One of her own forebears had been pale-skinned; he too had come from far away, but it was said that he was very different. Strong and true and kind, he had won a princess's heart. And that princess had been her mother's mother's mother. Such men then, were few and far between. Her own sister had been carried away and she had never seen her since. Kalisha had therefore been forced to decree that pale-skinned men, whenever they were taken, whatever their apparent worth, must unceasingly be punished. Pleasure could be delivered to them only as an adjunct to pain. As regards pale-skinned women, whom she had never seen before, her feelings were unresolved. But if they were all as beautiful as this one, they could certainly prove a threat to her self-esteem.

'*Achira*,' declared the Princess. A heavy curtain was drawn aside to reveal the outdoors and the forest green. With her slave closely tethered on his gold chain and her painted attendants following, the Princess then walked out. Ikahiti quickly took Anya's hand and they followed at a deferential distance.

Anya soon realised that this was the place she had noticed on the first day, the clearing with its timber frameworks and poles. There was much more activity today. She could hear shouting and laughter. Congregating there were all the women, their bodies decorated with feathers and paints; some of them even wore masks. Dozens of men were being chivvied into the clearing. Anya watched carefully to see if there might be any native, bronze-skinned men, but, without exception, these men had skin almost as pale as her own. The area into which they were being driven was a hollow, filled with complicated and curious-looking timber and rope framework devices and cages of differing sizes. There were poles arranged singly and in groups at a variety of angles, and ladders, swings and wheels; some of these things made her shudder, for they resembled the frame that had been used to dangle her over the snake pool. There were also many fetters and harnesses attached to the surrounding trees. Lying about on the ground were whips and sticks, which some of the women were collecting up as others began to attach the men to the various instruments of abuse. At this point, Anya became very afraid indeed – and not only for the men, for she was reminded by Ikahiti's constant presence and the Princess's close attention, that she too was a captive in this land.

Very soon, there were sounds of whipping and smacking, then sudden gasps between the spanks. As they approached the scene more closely, it became clear that the punishments were being prolonged and made crueller by the use of pleasure. The men would be pleasured for a while, then whipped, sometimes in the very places that had only just been pleasured. They would be collared around their intimate parts, often very tightly indeed, and would then be thrashed. Polished sticks would be introduced into their persons while they were played with, smacked or whipped. The women seemed to be vying with one another to stimulate their slaves in ever more degrading ways. Anya did not want to witness it; the men had surely done nothing so wicked as to deserve such cruel treatment.

Near the centre of the clearing, the Princess stopped to watch. One of the men had been led to a point where a wooden bar was supported about three feet above his head. He was strung up unceremoniously by his wrists, so his feet, kicking down, hung above the floor. One of the women standing behind him drew his ankles back and apart, then snapped them shut again, which forced his erect stem and his ballocks out in front of him from between his squeezed-together thighs. A second woman now tied his knees together but left his ankles free to wave helplessly above the sand while a young girl lifted a short-handled flat stick and the women collected a sturdy wooden beam, the centre of which had been carved and shaped into what looked like a small heart-shaped shield or cup containing an oval hole near its top. With one woman at each end, the beam was lifted and tilted, the women angling until the cap of his stem was captured through the hole. Then the beam was pushed back and down against his weight until his stem was forced completely through this constriction, the arms of the beam pressed across his lower belly and the heart-shaped cup of the shield formed an envelope round his bag. With the skin thus drawn back, the cock swelled harder. Pushing the beam back until his body was supported at an angle, the women held him while the girl, standing on a block, smacked him. No stimulation was given other than the smacking across his bottom, with his cock jammed tightly through this narrow oval hole. The girl was forced to use two hands to lift the stick – so large was it – and she smacked it across his buttocks as hard as she was worth. Each smack induced a jerk which bedded the cockstem deeper.

The Princess now stood closely beside her slave. She allowed his gold chain to dangle to the ground and gloved his cockstem with her bare hand, simply holding it close to the base, with her third finger slipped through the ring. She whispered to him and he uneasily edged his legs apart. Then Anya was distracted as the stick above cracked down again, then again, smacking the buttocks cruelly, propelling the base of the cockstem hard into the narrow hole in the beam, making the veins stand out, making it throb and jerk, making the ankles sway wildly below the secured-together knees. While this was taking place, the Princess's fingers, attending to her own slave in a rather gentler fashion, urged the skin down against the base of his stem. However, the ringed finger controlled his progress more cruelly by lifting, pressing and rotating, while splitting his bag into two distinct and slowly moving bulging parts.

The smacking now grew louder, harder, ascending to a crescendo; the girl was frenzied in her efforts to make the pleasure spill. Suddenly, the victim screamed and tried to thrust his cockstem through the hole; the girl waited. The Princess waited, holding her slave quite steady; then the fingers of her free hand slipped behind him and into the groove. She nodded. While the Princess's fingers now performed this deep massage, the girl delivered a powerful upwards smack to the man whose belly was pressed against the beam and the pleasure seemed to shoot as if propelled. The girl quickly threw the stick to the ground, walked round, stretched her small and delicate fingers out and bathed them in the spurts of milt, which kept coming while the women rocked the bar rhythmically against his belly. The girl then held out her fingers, dripping white. The Princess approved. The beam was pulled away but the man was left suspended, his body shuddering as the last drops of this very full pleasure continued to be expelled. Then the Princess took her slave by his chain and the entourage moved on. Anya was obliged to follow.

After passing one or two scenes of a similar disport, they came to a place where the punishment appeared to attract the Princess's interest again. She stood and watched, her right hand keeping her slave's chain taut while her left hand once more pinched and stroked the point of its attachment above the bag. His stem still stood hard – as it had remained since Anya had seen him first, on the bed with the Princess's attendants – but he was struggling to hold back the pleasure from the probings that the Princess's impish fingertips kept bestowing. Anya remembered the way the Princess had touched her there; even the single wetted fingertip had been stimulating – wicked. When the slave murmured, and Anya looked again at that fingertip and thumbtip now searching in the soft flesh of the bag, nipping at his tubes, she felt aroused. A quaver came in her belly and a tiny contraction pulsed between her legs where the gold ring, held by the cord, stood up, keeping her flesh hood back, exposing her distending nubbin as a signal, to anyone who might care to look, of the state of her excitement. And she was sure that very soon, somebody would look at her and touch her. Yet at that thought, the sweet pulse came again.

Anya stared around at the instances of pleasure that surrounded her – intimate tetherings, rapid fingertip movements, quiet hand clasps, silent penetrations – then she looked at Ikahiti. Ikahiti's hand came round and rested against Anya's thigh, rubbing it very gently, then it slipped round the cord and gently pulled, making Anya close her eyes. She could hardly breathe with the delicious pulling sensation there, coming so sharply on the fear and the sights that she was witnessing. Then Ikahiti stepped behind Anya. She put her arms around her, beneath her breasts, supporting them and pressing her belly against Anya's buttocks. The Princess saw but did not object – she threw her head back, then turned again to watch the punishment that so entranced her. Anya watched it too, of course, but she was far more interested in the feel of the thin skin belt against her, tickling the top of the outswell of her bottom, and the smooth naked skin of Ikahiti's hips urging gently against her from behind. Anya opened her legs and slid her feet across the sand – it felt delicious, doing that. Ikahiti's hand dropped down over Anya's bare belly, rubbing its pushed-out roundness as Anya looked first at the crowd, then at the Princess and her slave, with his thin gold chain being wrapped around his bag, then stared again at the peculiar sight before them.

A young woman was kneeling before a blank expanse of animal skin stretched between two poles and she appeared to be pressing her lips against it near its middle. Looking up, Anya could see a pair of wrists fastened to the poles behind the skin; looking down, she could see the corresponding feet, also fastened; she noticed that the toes attached to them were writhing. She looked again at the girl, whose head was moving. It lifted to reveal a pair of ballocks, wet with spittle, and a stem which glistened as the lips withdrew to form a seal round the cap. She heard murmurs as the girl fed spittle through her lips and on to the stem, then the lips followed it, pushing the wetness ahead of them in a curtain to the base. Each dripping

161

ballock was taken between finger and thumb and squeezed. The toes dug into the sand. The Princess copied this last action with her slave, who softly whimpered. The girl's mouth moved back up the stem. A cord was tied round the base of the cock and the tip was sucked while the fingers worked firmly up and down the intervening length. When the murmur came again, a very narrow, short smooth stick was inserted under the cord, so it pressed lengthwise near the base of the cock to separate the ballocks and to press against the soft thick tube lying just beneath the skin. At this point, the Princess showed very great interest, approaching closely and making some request or enquiry to the girl. The cord was tightened. The skin of the underside of the stem was pinched an inch below the tip and held. The girl sat back. Very slowly, the cock began to move, trying to push against the fingertips that held it by the scruff. The girl's other hand simply held the now separated ballocks cupped as the movements hastened and the murmurs became groans. On advice from the girl, the party then moved round to the back of the poles, when all became clear.

The man's body formed a cross, with his hips pushed against the leather skin. Every muscle of his legs and thighs was cramped. A second girl stood beside him, kneading the tight muscles of his back, but she used only one hand for this operation. Yet the hand was thorough, slowly massaging his sweat-soaked upper back and beneath his outspread arms before moving down towards the split cheeks of his buttocks, where the other hand, massaging from within, imparted so intimate an urgency that he was lifted on his toes. Then the upper hand pressed against his lower back while the deep hand was withdrawn. The slender fingers came out slick. The girl waited with one hand still pressed against his back while the other hung down, dripping. Yet the protestations of pleasure rose again. Now the girl leaned her weight against him. He gasped; she waited until his breathing had eased and the girl on the other side presumably had stopped whatever she was doing. Then she dipped her free hand into a bowl on the ground between the man's legs, lifted up a leaking handful of clear, gelatinous paste, spread the cheeks and began working it into him. She pressed her fingers together and formed her hand into a narrow pointed shape like a swan's head. The beak, then the head, wormed into him. He groaned when it reached the eye; but the girl pushed and the head slipped in until his body gripped the narrow swan-neck of her forearm, which gently twisted as the swan searched deeper, rubbing its beak inside him.

Once again, the Princess became completely absorbed in this scene. The bowl was brought to her. She ordered her slave to move his legs apart. The girl was brought round from the front. She knelt before the slave now, pulling his chain down but holding his cockstem up and flat against his belly while her pouted lips sucked at the point of attachment of the ring and the Princess wetted her fingers in the paste. While the girl continued to suck in that one place, the fingers were inserted. Anya wanted to get away. The Princess was intent only on cruelty. Why did these women not simply take their pleasure with the men? It seemed that they were really no better than the pirates they had taken. She tugged at Ikahiti's arm. Ikahiti smiled, glanced across at the Princess, whispered to one of her guards, then took Anya by the hand.

They ran up the slope, not stopping until they reached the top, where Anya pretended to trip and fell to the sand. She felt excited now, and safer away from the Princess. Ikahiti collapsed beside her and began to brush the tips of her fingers over Anya's knee. When Anya looked up, she saw two of the women, an older and a younger one, beneath a tree. They were stroking each other's skin and whispering, then embracing, kissing very deeply. Anya watched; the feeling she experienced was a mixture of warmth and envy. The girl was very young; her golden body was much smoother than the woman's and her breasts were small and rounded, not fully developed but dominated by the nipples, which the woman would roll between her fingers as they kissed. Gradually, the girl leaned back against the tree. One of the woman's hands moved downwards while the other played with the nipples alternately. The girl's thighs opened; between them, she was bare, not even painted, the lips forming a small double tight rounded ridge, which the woman opened to reveal a small white bone projection protruding from between them. The woman developed this projection with her finger and thumb while the girl, heavy lidded now, looked across at Anya. Anya felt the weighted feeling in her belly. Ikahiti's fingers, still brushing lightly, moved leisurely upwards from her knee. Very slowly the girl's body sank down the tree trunk as her knees bowed apart. The woman now knelt; her lips pouted out to take the small projection and to suck upon it gently while the girl, sighing softly, cradled the woman's head and gently ruffled her hair. And it was the open abandon which excited Anya – the way these people did these things so freely and unashamedly. The girl, breathing shallowly yet with her mouth wide open, gradually arched back until her shoulders pressed against the tree. Her feet moved crabwise over the sand until her toes pointed outwards. The woman sucked, then sat back on her heels and watched the girl's fingers stretch down over her bare belly, reach the small rounded lips and tease them open wider, so the small white bone pushed out again. The tip of the woman's tongue arched out to touch the underside of this small trembling bone while the girl's fingertips gently kneaded.

Ikahiti moved closer to Anya, who was shaking. Her whole body trembled. In the background she could hear the smacking. She watched the tongue begin to wash the bare lips and then the upper thighs, until the girl murmured, when the woman sat back again and gently pulled the bone with the tips of her fingers. Ikahiti's hand now rested on Anya's hips. When Ikahiti turned Anya and the smooth bronze skin of Ikahiti's belly touched Anya's and Ikahiti's soft brown eyes caressed her own, Anya knew that she would do anything that this woman wanted of her – she wished it were she and Ikahiti under that tree. Her belly shuddered at the deliciousness of that thought. Then Ikahiti moved aside and lay behind Anya, holding her as she watched.

The girl was now facing the tree. She was bent at the waist, so her back was horizontal. Her legs, stood bowed apart, trembled while the woman knelt between them holding a short pointed stick which she was using to prick the exposed flesh lips. The girl murmured and began to lift up on her toes as if to edge her flesh away from this pricking, but the woman

164

continued, pressing one hand upwards underneath the belly while the other moved the stick over each lip with a rapid jabbing action. Then she plucked a large soft leaf from a twig of the tree, folded it, squeezed it, then rubbed the expressed blue juice against the lips that she had pricked.

Ikahiti lifted Anya until she was kneeling up, with Ikahiti still behind her, whispering in her ear, 'Tika . . . Tika, shirula,' so very softly that Anya, looking down and seeing Ikahiti's hands, so smooth and brown upon her, cupping her breast, brushing her belly, again felt a wave of wanting for Ikahiti. It started from the pit of her belly; it shivered through her open thighs, her swollen sex, the lips so proud, and her nubbin, pushed against the ring. The hand moved round to her bottom and even before it touched, Anya fell forwards on to her hands, so her breasts hung down, their weight pulling to the teats. A cool drawing sensation came in her bottom – the premonition of a contraction that she withheld, for she kept the mouth of her bottom open for Ikahiti's fingertips now to examine. And it was to Anya so delicious, keeping her knees apart, her back arched down, her sex and bottom jutted out behind her while this woman touched her bottom's soft submissive mouth. 'Shi-shirula . . .' Ikahiti murmured and Anya felt the velvet pleasure – like the afterpleasure of submission, when pleasure itself has been controlled and deliverance has been denied, but the attention is ever present, ever intimate, ever sweet. It was the prolongation of these tiny intimacies of pleasure which Anya found delicious.

She felt the finger against her again, and it was wet; it licked her like a tongue; it wetted the mouth of her bottom until it was cool and spittle-slick and suddenly, she collapsed to her elbows and her forehead touched the sand. Her thighs stayed tense and very open while the finger pushed deep into her bottom. She tried to turn her toes out to the sides to keep her buttocks open; she tried to push her bulging sex between her open legs. Ikahiti touched it very gently, pursing the moistened lips then, laying her hand against the belly beneath, pressing the cord which pulled against the nub and, as Anya gasped, drawing the finger out very slowly from the mouth that tried to keep relaxed. When Anya fell to the sand, Ikahiti turned

165

her round and kissed her. '*Shirula,*' she said again and when Anya, filled with the urgency of wanting, repeated that word very nervously to Ikahiti, Ikahiti smiled, turned her round, gently opened her buttocks again, and touched the warmth within her.

Across from them, the girl had stood up and turned. Her newly pricked sex lips now looked blue. Evidently prepared, she was given a whip and taken down into the throng. Ikahiti, still tickling Anya in the crease then slipping her finger up inside her, watched them disappear, then sighed and lifted her reluctant charge up, took her by the hand and led her after them.

As they descended, Anya could see the pale pink bodies writhing and she could hear the smacking. When they reached the edge of the clearing, she could smell the heat of their exertions – the sweat and the milt. There were men tied to upright poles while they were whipped; others were kneeling on the ground, bent over bars, or spread astride them with their legs forced apart; collared men were being driven back and forth on hands and knees by women astride their backs and there were men enmeshed in intricate devices of wooden beams and ropes. Others, more fortunate, lay on the ground, being toyed with by groups of girls, who kept them in a state of stiff excitement using whip-licks, finger-kisses and intimate penetrations.

Anya was moved on to where a man was kneeling across a tree stump about two feet high while the underside of his cock was smacked with a stick. The whole of the undersurface was red and the plum was angry purple. The woman lifted the ballocks out of the way while the thin stick swished down and smacked across the undertube very near its base, then these intermittent, very quick swipes worked down until the level of the plum was reached, where the smacking was continued until he milted. The welling liquid, caught in a cupped palm, was smeared back up the stem, to coat the bright red punished skin completely. Then the whipping began again to keep the cockstem hard.

Anya heard an anguished cry from behind her and above. She turned to see a man suspended high in the air lengthwise between two horizontal bars. A woman was above him. Thick white streaks of milt arced through the air and lay in elongate globules on the sand. She turned to the right. A young man stood as his buttocks were thrashed with a thick leather belt and a young girl rubbed his cock until he milted. Beyond him, there were others who were simply hanging from branches by their wrists while their cocks were tied with thong or bandaged completely with lengths of thin material.

Many of the girls carried bags containing small instruments of pleasure and torture – carved and polished pieces of bone for rubbing beneath the stem, single and double rings for fitting over it, smooth flexible narrow sticks for pushing down the tube and small leather cups with cords which would sheath only the cap and leave the rest of the stem exposed. The men, often untethered, would be fitted with one or more of these instruments and placed in a ring of girls who would smack or whip them. Some of the girls had designed leafy bowers in which they would lie with the men and amuse themselves by testing out these toys. In one such place, where there were many women gathered, Ikahiti pushed between them in order that Anya might get a better view, and Anya, though she shivered, was enthralled. The men were being pierced, as the Princess's slave had been pierced, though in more varied ways. No ceremony was involved here, as it had been with Anya; the piercing and the attachment of rings of varying sizes and lengths of polished bone, and the insertion of small, shaped beads beneath the loose skin, was performed while the victims whimpered on their knees and their cockstems rested on the block. The places of attachment or insertion were in the loose skin of the underside of the stem – at any point, it seemed, between the base and the tip – though most commonly in the region of the plum, and the usual procedure was the attach-ment of a large ring, which once inserted could be swung up and the head of the cock pulled through it so it thereby formed a collaring stricture round the cap, a tight narrow band of gold biting into the flesh below the rim. In some cases, as soon as the ring was fitted and the cap forced through, the mere pressure of the bedded ring would precipitate an emission.

Ikahiti watched for a long while and Anya, though she

pretended to look away, found her gaze frequently returning. Ikahiti glanced at her, then moved round behind her, pressing her hand to Anya's belly and gently lifting her ring, moving it only very slightly, yet making Anya's knees begin to buckle slowly as she listened to the groans. She touched Anya's flesh itself where it was pierced by the ring, squeezing it and gently nipping, while on the block, the cockstem that had just been treated was sucked with its newly installed ring in place. The lips withdrew but the tongue snaked out in time to capture the flow of milt. The woman then led her man away. He was soon replaced by another.

The most intimate procedure involved the cutting of a small nick in the skin below the plum, followed by the progressive insertion of round beads or one or more polished oval stones. The cut was kept very small and the larger stones were inserted with difficulty by stretching the skin. The nick was then resealed with a stitch and the cockstem was left with this small bag of stones at the end of the plum. When the slave was made to stand, the weight of stones pulled the end down a little even when the stem was quite erect, and the stones were visible as small irregular bumps beneath the skin. Anya wondered at the function of these stones, but on hearing a shout, Ikahiti, seemingly bored now, led her away.

The call had signalled the arrival of food. The women sat round in a ring and bowls were passed round, each containing a different delicacy: chicken, fish pieces, shellfish – though those that Anya recognised as oysters, she would not touch, for they were raw, and even cooked, she knew oysters to be awful – but more temptingly, there were nuts and many kinds of succulent aromatic fruit. She felt quite hungry. There was also a pleasant drink; sweeter than the nutmilk, it tasted almost like wine and it made her feel warm inside. When she had finished, Anya lay down with Ikahiti by her side. There was much activity around them still. When Anya turned, that Ikahiti might stroke her back, she saw again the Princess and she sat up, disturbed and anxious. She could not understand how this woman – who was these women's leader and was supposed to set an example – could be so cruel to her man and perform these abuses with such coolness.

He lay face down on a horizontal tree trunk two feet above the ground. His stem, now very shiny and slick, had somehow been forced to stretch out behind him along the top of the trunk which his feet were tucked beneath. The Princess had discarded her feathered cloak and sat astride him, facing backwards with her thighs gripped about his waist. Leaning over, rocking gently, she dripped spittle down upon his cock, then smoothed it carefully into the plum. Then looking up, she noticed Anya and called to Ikahiti to bring her over. Anya was very scared to be made to kneel on the sand so close to the Princess. She could see the intentness in her gaze now as she worked upon the man, squeezing him between her thighs, pressing her patterned naked flesh into the furrow in his back, then adjusting his chain, which had been drawn taut and inserted deep between the open cheeks of his buttocks, then tasting the weight of his nearness to pleasure through the wet pads of her fingers as they applied the pressure rhythmically to the underside of his stem. The saliva was dripped again; he murmured when the globule touched, then spread across his skin. The Princess rubbed a finger-sized smoothly curving length of bone into this spittle, then slipped it through the ring and held it pressed against the tube. The cockstem weeped. She encouraged this weeping; she opened her thighs, then opened her sex above his back and something long and slender and golden dangled from between her legs to touch his backbone. It lay against him when she lowered, then it disappeared when she hunched forward to massage the curved bone finger against the base of the tube as she slowly licked the plum, which suffered tiny tremors and a clear and steady leak. Then she sat up, removed the bone finger and carefully pulled the chain until it was withdrawn. A piece of thick and twisted root was inserted in its place. Then he was allowed to stand and the Princess donned her cloak but played with him for some minutes more before leading him away with his sex burgeoning heavily and the root still bedded securely between his cheeks. At no time that day had Anya seen his pleasure fully spilled.

She turned to see Ikahiti staring at her, then pointing to the cord about her waist. Ikahiti's fingers interlaced, then drew apart. Anya's heart was in her mouth, for Ikahiti meant to remove the cord and free the captive ring. Ikahiti made her stand, then she touched the cord, lifting it, causing delicious pressure against the swelling hood, drawing the ring tight, teasing out her nubbin. Anya felt the sliding bead being released, then the cord being unfastened and taken away, leaving her feeling deliciously naked. Ikahiti's fingertips tickled down that naked belly and through the hairs and found the small gold ring, which had remained uplifted, impressed against the hood and held fast by the swelling pressure in her nubbin. Ikahiti gently rotated it down and Anya's knees began to buckle. Her softened sex lips were carefully closed about it, as if to seal the ring within, yet they opened at the top again to form a tiny gape, for the ring had been threaded through her from side to side; it could never be hidden completely but instead pushed out and glistened in the light.

As Ikahiti continued to touch Anya and to make these small adjustments to the ring, the feelings as it moved were so intense, so awful, yet so delicious too and strange – the pleasure and the fright and the harrowing sensitivity as the gold thread turned inside her – that she knew not what would happen next, whether she would faint from such a dissonance of feelings or disgrace herself completely by doing something worse. But Ikahiti moved those shuddering legs apart and slipped the cord, which had cooled now, between them. Using one hand at the front and the other at the back, she drew the cord from side to side across the lips which, as the knees bowed wider, continued to moisten and swell. Then while Anya stood there, Ikahiti wetted her fingertips and played with the ring until Anya almost died; she collapsed against Ikahiti, who gently lowered her to the ground and moved closer, until her face filled Anya's vision.

'*Abaata* . . .' Ikahiti whispered and Anya pushed her belly out and opened her thighs until they ached. The deep brown eyes held her while the smooth bronze fingertips tasted the taut and tender skin and Anya's honeydew leaked from the warm soft lips around the gold ring standing hard now, at one with the pinned bud sleeved around it. It wanted to be touched, to be moved, to be kneaded. But Ikahiti merely

170

brushed the skin of Anya's thighs and kissed her nipples and breathed her body scent while Anya's belly slowly tightened and Anya's sex lips leaked.

The afternoon advanced; Ikahiti lay with Anya, stroking her body, her belly, then turning her and brushing her fingertips down her back, but not touching Anya more intimately than this; around them, the activities became less frenzied, the pace more leisurely, the punishments less acute and eventually the crowd broke up into small groups, sometimes of women only, but frequently with several women to one or two men, and these groups retreated from the clearing and into the surrounding leafiness.

Ikahiti had been tickling the base of Anya's spine and Anya had her eyes closed. Between her legs she felt warm and swollen; she liked that feeling now – the pressure and the constant wanting, and the gentle arousal that the tickling caused. Ikahiti turned her on her back, opened out her legs and examined her. Suddenly she spread the lips, slipped two fingers into Anya and Anya almost came. '*Tika!*' Ikahiti warned, looking over her shoulder then, as Anya squirmed on the verge of pleasure, she looked at Anya lovingly and whispered under her breath, '*Nisha, Kalisha . . .*' then more loudly, '*Shi-shirula, shi . . .*' And Ikahiti wetted and gently rubbed the nubbin ring.

A young girl, the same one that they had seen with the woman under the tree, appeared above them. The lips of her sex were still swollen and marked with the bright blue dye. She stood watching for a while, as Anya's mouth opened and Anya drew breath deeply each time that Ikahiti's fingers penetrated wetly, deeper, and Anya moaned and her knees opened wider until they touched the ground. Then the girl knelt beside Anya and her small fingers began to touch the ring in place of Ikahiti and Anya's pleasure came on so strongly that she thought that she had wet herelf; her belly turned hard and tried to lift but Ikahiti held her, pushed deeper and touched the mouth of Anya's womb while the young girl gently turned the wetted ring. Anya's sex contracted hard about Ikahiti's fingers and the pleasure came again. Ikahiti then removed her fingers and sucked them while the girl took the narrow skin

171

band that had fastened her hair and slipped it through the ring. The soft thin leather, looped through the ring, lay loosely against Anya's belly; its presence there made Anya feel aroused again. Then the girl lifted it over to make it trail against the open wetness of her sex; it became coated in her honey as the girl continued to play with it and press it into her, then tease it out again.

Eventually, she was helped to her feet and led, with the leather skin band sticking to her at first, then hanging down and touching its wet warmth against the tops of her thighs, to a bower in the leafy bushes where two people were already installed: a man – Ikahiti's slave – and a woman, the same one who had prepared the girl. The slave was already groaning with pleasure, though as the woman was above him as he lay belly down with his face turned to the side, it was unclear what she was doing. Ikahiti settled down with Anya on a pile of leaves and the young girl joined the woman.

There were various bowls and sticks and straps scattered about and also several of the long fruits, of the kind that Anya had seen used on the man the other day. They ranged from narrow to thick and from small to large. When the woman climbed off the slave, she turned him over. '*Tika*,' she said when he tried to move away as she touched his erect stem. The expression on Ikahiti's face was one of interest; she watched what the woman did, but without any visible sign of jealousy. She seemed quite happy to allow this other woman to use her man, just as she had allowed the girl to touch Anya and to precipitate her pleasure. There appeared no jealousy at all between these women and Anya then recalled that the only sign of it that she had seen was when Anya had spoken to the man in the Lidiran tongue and that had caused Ikahiti to become very angry indeed and to punish him.

Then Anya gasped at what she saw – the stem was lifted back and its underside was bulging; there was a pebble beneath the surface of the plum. His skin had been opened and filled; a small stitch could be seen and a spot of blackened blood. Ikahiti now became very interested indeed; her eyes widened, but still she did not move from Anya's side. Almost absentmindedly, she played with Anya's nipples, rolling the tips then

172

lifting them and rubbing the undersides. The man turned very pale as the woman placed one hand behind the head of his stem and with the fingers of the other, began to move the pebble around inside him. The oval bump moved below the surface, then stood out progressively further as the skin tightened from the unwanted pleasure of the movement against the sensitive inner core, and the cockstem pumped up until the veins stood out. While the woman held it near the base and pulled the skin down, the young girl, kneeling over his prostrate form, sucked the underside of the plum. When her head lifted, the pebble formed a shiny bump. The flat of her tongue now pushed against this stone to move it in a circle, then her lips formed a sucker which once more drew it to a bulge, the shape of which was clearly visible through the skin.

The girl moved up his body and began to nip and play with the area on and around his nipples. The woman took a double loop of cord and drew it tightly round his bag, so each ballock stood out shiny and separated from its mate. She gradually inserted a thin short rod into his stem and slowly turned it whilst her thumb massaged the stone beneath the skin and the girl continued working the nipples, tugging at them until they and their surrounds had engorged almost to the size of her own small teats. Then she began to bite them and to pull them with her teeth. Between the man's legs, the short rod had almost disappeared and the woman's lips descended to close round the cap. The man groaned. When her head lifted, her tongue was still protruding but the rod was gone. She sat back. The girl moved up the body and held the man's head very firmly by the hair. She kissed him with her small bare sex; the blue lips spread about his own; the bone projection pressed against his nose. The woman gently rubbed his stem and the short slick rod slipped slowly out, forced by the gentle pumping. Bending forwards, the woman thrust out her tongue and pushed the rod back in again while the young girl held him firmly with her thighs against his cheeks.

While this was happening, Ikahiti was merely rubbing Anya's nipples, which by now were very sensitive and standing very hard. When the hand stopped rubbing and moved down her belly, Anya tensed. Ikahiti began toying with the wet skin ribbon, lifting it and placing it against Anya's thigh, fitting it to the crease beside the sex lips on one side then the other, then opening the lips and laying the ribbon between them before pursing them around it. Then she closed her hand around the sex, which throbbed very gently in her palm, and with her middle finger, tickled the end of the ribbon that projected. Anya, turning, pressed her back against Ikahiti's belly and felt the warm bare skin and the band of Ikahiti's belt against her bottom and the rounded breasts pressed against her back. And again she felt the fingertips teasing her pleasure-tortured nipples while the hand enclosed the flesh between her thighs. She felt Ikahiti's breath against the side of her neck. She wanted this woman to take her.

The girl had dismounted from the man and he had been turned on his side. She was sucking and playing with the stone, slipping it around inside his plum. She would take the cockstem fully in her mouth at times and suck, while the man stayed completely motionless and the woman, lying behind him, rubbed the flesh beneath his bag, pressing with her knuckles, kneading, then wetting her fingertips and rubbing the spittle in until it dried. But the fingertips were now replaced by the long purple fruit, rubbed back and forth under his bag while the young girl sucked until he tried to push, when her pouted lips retreated and hovered at a distance of an inch. Then the short rod, held in the young girl's mouth now, pushed out through her teeth and entered him and he was held threaded on this rod while the long fruit, rubbing back and forth, progressively slipped towards the groove. The tongue pushed the short rod fully within, the lips enveloped him and held him, squeezed tight around him and sucked while the long fruit, pushing against the tight resistance, slowly entered. Yet his body did not move as his pleasure came; the lips retreated without the rod; the woman's fingertips held him collared round the base. The fruit slid in and it was as if that impulsion pushed the milt out smoothly, in a sliding stream which forced the stop out and rapidly flowed into the girl's cupped palm to form a small viscid pool in which the short rod floated. She removed the rod and quickly lifted her palm and drank and only then did the pleasure come on fully, with

174

a shudder. She cupped her palm again, but the powerful pumping, somehow withheld until this point made him overshoot and most of the yield of this second spasm ran down her wrist and dribbled to the ground.

Anya felt the hand around her sex lift away; then the skin ribbon was raised, which peeled her sex lips open. She felt the ribbon sliding through the ring. The pleasure almost came. She turned on to her back. Ikahiti was above her. She opened her thighs and Ikahiti slid between them. Anya felt the narrow hips between her legs, the bare bronze belly touching her own, the soft skin belt against her and the bare sex moving, urgently searching. She gasped as the tight firm sex lips separated her own. Something hard pressed against her; it felt like a ball; it was a ball attached to Ikahiti's nubbin. The ball searched, rubbed and pressed until it found her nubbin too, then it rolled against her and the feeling was delicious, the gentle rolling pressure there while Ikahiti's hips lifted and careened, while Ikahiti's sex lips sought within, sucked upon her inner moisture and Ikahiti's small hard nipples stroked against her own. When Anya thought her belly would burst, Ikahiti's hips slowed, but did not stop for they were searching still. The soft brown eyes held her; Anya did not move; she tried to concentrate the swelling pressure there between her legs; then she felt the small ball touch, then lock into the ring and she was sealed to Ikahiti, nub to nub. Now Ikahiti's movements were minute; each movement evoked a whimper of delight. 'Ah,' said Anya, 'Ah! Oh, please . . .?'

'*Tika, tika-i*,' Ikahiti whispered, but her voice was faltering too. There were tiny beads of perspiration on her upper lip. Anya lifted them on her tongue. '*Shirula*,' Ikahiti whispered, gasping, '*Shirula* – ah.' Anya's tongue pushed out again. Ikahiti caught that tongue and sucked it and nipped it with her teeth. The tiny movements still continued. Anya was drowning in those feelings, the pulling, the small ball pressed against her nub, soft sucking sensations between her legs, Ikahiti's wetness leaking, and the awful delicious feeling that a thread, knotted at her navel, passed through her nub and was anchored deep within Ikahiti. And that thread was being stretched to breaking. She lifted her legs and closed them down about Ikahiti's

175

hips and brushed Ikahiti's bottom with her feet. She closed her arms about the back, and her fingers nipped the skin of those sweet bronzed shoulders. She held Ikahiti about the head and kissed her very deeply. And the pleasure came; it spread through Anya's body like a wave; it was as if her body were turned to honey inside, as if her body had split deliciously and she had swallowed Ikahiti up and enveloped her in that sweet warm heavy syrup. She wrapped her arms and legs and lips and sex about her very tightly.

They lay for a long while intertwined. Ikahiti's hand reached down between them and Anya felt a tiny stab of pain and they were separated. The woman and the girl had gone. So had the man. Ikahiti sat up. She looked anxious. It was the first time Anya had seen her that way. Anya felt very uneasy. The sun was low, a golden pillar of light striking through the long shadows of the trees. Then there came noises, low whoops and cries and higher pitched squeals and sounds of something crashing through the bushes. 'Chiriri! Rinyi!' Ikahiti hissed, her eyes now wide with terror, for sweeping swiftly towards them were many bronze-skinned men.

[12]

Taboo

Ikahiti ran but Anya, not quick enough in pursuit, was tackled and brought to the ground. Her captor fell on top of her and they ploughed into the sand. She screamed and kicked his legs but the bronzed arms held her tightly, confidently about the waist. She could hear the screams of other women and from the corner of her eye, she could see Ikahiti, half crouched and backing away with her broad knife drawn. Anya shouted for help. No help was forthcoming; Ikahiti turned again and ran as other men appeared and gathered round. And once again it was clear, from the murmurs of surprise, that these people had never seen a woman like her. The man let go of her and crouched back on his haunches. Anya lay on her side, her dishevelled red hair flecked with yellow sand, her freckled black-tipped bosom swelling with her rapid breathing, while her captors murmured and stared. Hardly daring to look up at the figures towering above her, her frightened eyes darted round from one pair of legs to the next, waiting for someone to make a move. But as the conversation continued above her head, her eyes timorously moved up.

The men were completely naked: they wore no jewellery or shells; they did not even carry a knife. She was struck not only by the bronzeness of their skin, but by the slimness of their bodies, and not all of them were young. Some had grey hair – on their heads – for, like the women, they had no belly hair. Her gaze drifted across the bareness between their legs and to the thick bronze fleshy stems that nestled against large round heavy-looking equally naked ballocks. As the men talked and shifted their stance, these fleshy appendages would move, expanding slightly or retracting and despite her fear, or perhaps because of it, her attention was constantly drawn. She began to imagine things – there seemed so many of these men. What might they make her do? What would it be like to be made to take these very large bare ballocks between her open thighs?

One of the older men bent over her and stroked her ankle. She tugged it away, but the hand moved quickly and caught it easily. 'No!' she cried, 'Let go!' and again there was surprise, at her tongue.

'*Tirishu, sahu-lata?*' said the man. '*Sahu-lata, shirin otei?*'

Not knowing what he was saying only made her anxiety worse. 'Let go of me!' she cried again. But each time she tried to pull her foot away, his naked cockstem stirred. He drew up the captive foot and touched its sole against him. When Anya felt the warm clinging skin of those naked ballocks touch her, she screamed and broke away and tried to escape across the sand. Laughing now, the man caught her again around the waist and began to rub his hand against her belly. Then he murmured in surprise. His hand moved down; she tried to close her thighs. '*Tika, shin –*' he whispered, then turned to his friends. '*Shiniki!*' They crowded round. '*Shiniki,*' they concurred as her legs were opened. Anya tensed. His fingertip brushed the black lips, then touched the ring; again she squirmed and tried to pull away. '*Shiniki,*' said the man softly, almost reverently and with Anya's leg uplifted and her ankle collared by his hand, he touched the ring again. And at that light touch, while she watched his bare stem lifting and throbbing between his legs, her belly overturned. The man stood up. Before she knew what had happened, he had swept her up in his arms and slung her effortlessly over his shoulder.

'*Tika, shirin,*' he reprimanded when she kicked at first, then he held her with one arm locked firmly round the backs of her knees and the other resting over his shoulder and on her lower back. Then they were off, running quickly through the trees, with her knees against his taut belly, her bare breasts bobbing against the smooth bronze back and his short grey bristly hair rubbing against her side. And all that she could see as she looked down were the tight muscular buttocks tensing as the slim legs carried her across the sand then around an inlet and away from the village.

She was taken, along with perhaps eight or ten other girls who had been captured, through the arched gap in the far ridge that Miriri had pointed out that morning. Beyond it, the failing sun illuminated a cluster of huts which appeared to float in the middle of a lake or lagoon. But they could be reached on foot across a kind of floating bridge. When the party arrived, the women were distributed. There was much argument about Anya. In the end, the man who had carried her took her into a large hut which seemed to be subdivided into at least two rooms. In the centre of the first one was a bright fire and though the hut must have been built on a wooden platform, the visible floor was sand. He pointed to a heap of leaves beyond the fire. '*Lakita*,' he said, but she knew well that it was bed without him telling her and she would not sit upon it, nor even move in its direction. She stood firm. She refused. When she stared at him defiantly, his eyes sparkled and he stood before her with arms folded and head tilted to the side, then he shrugged at her and left.

On her own now, she knew not what to do. She looked askance at the curtained outer doorway. Should she try to leave? She glanced around the room. Unlike Miriri's hut, this place was bare of any decoration; there were only the fire and the bed, some pots and some spears standing against the wall. She walked over to these spears and picked one up to examine it. Perhaps she could use it – to threaten them at least – when they returned? Then she remembered that they had carried no weapons during their raid, and she thought that rather strange. Clutching the spear, she advanced through the gap in the reed partition and into the inner room. It was dark, but it too was almost empty apart from a bed of leaves, and there was no other exit that she could see.

She was still standing at the entrance to this inner room when the grey-haired man came back. Automatically and defensively, she turned and her hand still held the spear. 'Keep away!' She held it up, setting her jaw and jabbing the spear towards him. He said nothing in reply, but drew his shoulders back, which made his chest expand. Anya became more worried still as he stepped forwards, causing the point of the spear to press against the bare unwrinkled skin in the centre of his chest. His eyes were unflinching; hers were not. Her arm, very stiff now from fear, moved involuntarily in a tiny nervous jerk. She gasped and her mouth stayed open – she had not the strength to close it when she saw what she had done. From the indentation at the point of the spear, a thick droplet of blood welled and trickled down the centre line of his chest, towards his belly. The spear was so sharp that that one small movement had pierced him. He glanced down at the spearpoint and the welling line of blood, then again fixed her with his gaze. But he did not move back. Her arm, so stiff before, felt suddenly boneless as she stared into those dark and penetrating eyes. She had wounded him and he had let her do it, without retaliation. The spear dropped to the ground and Anya almost followed it as the blood continued welling. Her eyes alone – wide, liquefying into two thick teardrops that refused to break and run – begged for forgiveness; she could not otherwise move.

His eyes expanded to engulf her. His lips moved: 'Aniya,' he said and his fingers lifted and touched the long red strand of her hair that lay across the upper arm that had held the spear. How did he know her name? 'Aniya,' he said again and the fingers touched the skin upon the muscle of that same arm that had now gone very limp indeed. 'Shanam,' he said and pointed to himself and smiled. But his fingertips, where they had touched his breast, were smeared with blood. He smiled again and shrugged, but she could not smile back at a man she had only just stabbled, not when she couldn't even find the strength to apologise to him.

Then another man came in, much younger, also slim but slightly taller, with matt black hair. 'Ranil,' said Shanam. Anya looked from one completely naked body to the other and watched Shanam point out, seemingly with pride, the dark red runnel down his middle. As Shanam pronounced again that word, 'Shiniki,' in a hesitant whisper which seemed to bear such considerable meaning, though Anya did not understand it, she watched the other's eyes drink her in and the thick stem thicken between his legs and she had to will her body to breathe. Her breathing was slowing to a pace where it could not keep up with her heartbeat and she felt as if her

180

belly was turning over. Yet she did not move. She just stood there until Shanam pointed to the bed again. That brought her to her senses. He tried to take her hand.

'*Tika!* No . . .' she said and stretching both hands out, fingers spread, backed away. Shanam smiled disarmingly and Anya became afraid that the word she had shouted might have been wrong or incorrectly applied in this context.

'*Lak –*' he began.

'Keep away! No!' she snapped, trusting her grasp of native words no more. The younger one folded his arms. Shanam took another step towards her and she backed through the doorway of the partition and stood shaking in the half-darkness. She could hear voices outside the hut now, laughter – women's laughter, not screams of terror or pain – and that only added to her consternation. Why were they laughing, when the men had attacked the camp and when Ikahiti had run away in such a state of fear? When Anya glared at Shanam, he shrugged again and turned, tapped his companion on the shoulder and both men went away, murmuring to each other.

And now she felt quite terrible. The spear had been so sharp – she could have killed him. Yet she felt certain they would return; it seemed to be a game to them. Again she wondered how he had known her name. It could only have been gleaned from the other women, she decided; they had probably told him all about her. But why were the women laughing when Ikahiti had been so afraid? Anya wished she had paid more attention to what Miriri had been trying to explain that morning – had she known the men would come? Anyway, game or no, Anya would not acquiesce in what Shanam and his friend wanted. She marched to the curtain in the main doorway, flinging it aside, expecting to see the camp fires and people dancing round. But all she saw was a heavy wooden batter blocking the way. It would not move. She was a prisoner after all. She retreated into the smaller room, sat on the pile of leaves, then got up again, retrieved the spear and hid it behind the doorway. Why the spear should reassure her, she did not know, because she could never use it now that she had seen what it could do. She felt exhausted; her eyes smarted;

she needed sleep, but she could not risk letting her eyelids close.

It was much later when they did return and Anya already felt very hungry. As soon as she heard the obstacle being moved aside, she was standing by the inner doorway with one hand round the shaft of the spear, waiting. Shanam glanced in her direction, but neither man approached her; they now had another guest who had commandeered their attention.

The village girl looked small beside Ranil; her wide eyes stared around the hut as if she found its meagre contents totally absorbing. Her eyes met Anya's for a second, then slid away as if she found her less interesting than the patterns of the reeds matted into the wall. Shanam placed sticks upon the fire and the smoke billowed up through the narrow vent in the middle of the roof; she seemed to find that simple action quite intriguing too, commenting to him, presumably about it, raising her head as she stood above him and drawing her shoulders back until her small round breasts pushed out between the crosswise necklaces of shells. And from behind, Ranil also watched her. She looked over her shoulder, addressing him now, then raised herself on tiptoes, so her bottom pushed out roundly and the bronze skin on one side reflected the firelight, then she overbalanced and Ranil caught her – or she fell into his arms. They laughed and began to kiss.

Anya looked towards Shanam, who continued to tend the fire. She gripped the spear tightly, for he was looking at her, she was sure: though his head was down, she could see his eyes glinting, as if he were waiting to make a move. Then he sat up on his haunches, looking at the couple above him and there was something about his posture, his bearing and his looks – he was attractive; Anya found him so; she admitted this to herself. There was a confidence in his slimly muscled body, a calmness in his gaze and a memory in her mind – of the way he had looked at her when that accident had happened, of the way he had touched her hair. He had not forced himself upon her. He looked at her now; she saw again the cut on his chest. Again she began to tremble; she wanted to heal this cut; she wanted him to hold her. She knew that she would not refuse him again. And that thought – that she would give herself willingly, that she would hold this person in her arms and take his flesh inside her body – made her shudder. Her hand released the spear. He was coming over to her, closer and closer, while she could not blink now, could not lift her arms. But he took them – each of her hands – so tenderly and held them while he stared into her eyes. She moved her head back slightly, parted her trembling lips and closed her eyes. Her breasts and belly tingled with delicious anticipation. 'Aniya . . .' he whispered. In reply, she pressed her cheek against his breast. He had not kissed her. She kissed the place that she had wounded. Then she opened her eyes. '*Shirin – sitika, tika-sin,*' he murmured and again he touched her hair.

Lifting her, he carried her and placed her on the bed of leaves. Languorously, she stretched. He turned her on her side, to face the wall; she felt the backs of his fingers brushing against her lower back. She curled her head down and wrapped her arms about her breast. Her heart was thumping slowly, holding itself in reserve, waiting to quicken when he took her. He whispered to her, '*Tika,*' over and over; her heart slowed; she was soothed. The tickling became gentler; she could hear the sounds of lovemaking next door; they stirred her in her belly. Encouraging him now, her upper leg crooked and lifted up the bed and across the soft leaves. The fingertips stroked down her newly exposed inner thigh, crept beneath and touched the ring with a lightness that was delicious, then moved back to brush more faintly still, upwards on her back. She heard another murmur – her own, though she did not know it – then everything dissolved in blackness and the fingertips were gone.

When she opened her eyes again, all was silent; when nothing happened, she turned over to find the room empty. She must have dozed. Then the sounds came again from beyond the partition. Slowly, Anya lay down again and waited, and thought about it – had he wanted her to sleep? – and listened to the soft low musical sounds of pleasure, but listened now with an analytical ear, dissecting every composite note for the number of musicians. Eventually, she could bear it no more and crept to the doorway, then stood like a statue watching the figures bathed in the continuous glow of the remaining fire and illuminated by occasional flickers as the half-burnt logs flared anew.

The movements were smooth and slow, almost dreamlike, for the bodies were heavy with pleasure – the men kneeling, their slimness counterweighted by the curving thickness of their stems; the girl, beneath them and between them, on her side, her breasts looking fuller now, the nipples looking thicker, the belly pushed out harder. Ranil, at her head, was lifting her breasts, cradling them and gently playing with her nipples. They were wet, as was his stem, which her fingers continued to touch; a band of shiny slickness coated its underside and had spread across his ballocks. Shanam touched the hard white bone projection between her open legs, which at one point moved involuntarily as he petted. He turned to stroking the insides of her thighs. When they had steadied, he lifted her upper ankle to make her turn on to her back then, placing both of her feet down flat, he pushed her ankles back until her knees were bent so tightly that her belly formed an arch above the bed. Again he massaged the bone; it now pushed out rather further from beneath its fleshy hood, which, like her nipples and the paint-pricked naked flesh lips flaring out and down to either side, shone with a wetness as of oil. But Anya knew the wetness was not oil. Shanam rolled the bone very slowly between thumb and finger, then waited, holding it still, and watched the pushed-out belly swell as if the girl were with child then wane again as she regained control and her breathing steadied and slowed.

Her heavy necklaces lay by Anya's feet; they had been dropped on the floor where Shanam had joined Ranil and the men had finally stripped her before lifting her in their arms and carrying her to the bed of leaves where she lay now, bare-sex naked apart from that small piece of polished bone secured by a thread of wire through her nubbin. And Shanam, a look of concentration on his face, touched this bone again; the fingers rubbed it as if it were a cock and the girl responded as if the rubbing of that cock would make her come. So Shanam now desisted and cupped his palm upon the surface

184

of the belly that had pushed again until it looked as if it were pregnant and, slipping his other hand beneath her bottom, turned her on to her other side. Ranil moved round and her small hand closed around his stem again near its base. Shanam turned his attentions to her back. His fingertips moved in a circle on the smoothness near the base of her spine – the small flat place where Anya loved to be tickled – so Anya could almost feel that tickling too, and she could feel the wanting very much more surely. Still they had not seen her; she dared not move lest she should interrupt them, but she could smell their body scents – the girl's and much more strongly, the men's – she had smelled the milt when first she had stepped into the room and now that the girl had been turned, she could see its slickness on her belly. For how long had this been going on while Anya was asleep? She looked again at the large full bag between Shanam's legs as he climbed behind the girl. The girl's free hand reached back, searched down his belly, slipped under his cock and took this full bag lovingly, weighed it in her small cupped palm and squeezed it, making Anya shudder. She stayed very still and watched.

Shanam's hand came up between the girl's legs from behind and her upper leg was lifted. His fingertips opened out the small decorated lips to form a deeply cupped flower, then took each lip and squeezed it, nipping step by step along the patterned edge towards the hood, then taking the small white cock again and rolling it very slowly. When she began to murmur, she was again turned on to her back, where she lay as she had been put, with her legs uplifted, balanced above her, crooked in the air. Her bottom was raised on to Shanam's knees and his upper thighs formed a ramp below her, pressed against her lower back. The back of her head lay flat to the leaves. Ranil knelt open legged above her, then bent forwards, so his thick curved stem and heavy ballocks hovered above her nose. Shanam took hold of her upraised feet and pressed them outwards, so her bottom lifted and rocked. Her mound pushed out; the lips were open and the tiny white cock stood hard. The younger man rubbed his palm over her uplifted belly while Shanam held her feet, edging them wider. The rubbing movement transmitted to her sex and the bone projection moved as Ranil's hand moved, slowly pushing out from beneath the hood when the hand moved up the belly, then drawing back again. The girl's neck began to arch and her head moved back and the cock tip touched then pushed between her pouted lips. And now it was Ranil who gasped: he was forced to release her belly and arch his back while the cap of his cock was held captive in those moistly sucking lips and Shanam played with the girl, placing one hand under her back and lifting while the fingers of the other were wetted and slowly rubbed the hood up and down about the projecting stem. When the girl shuddered once, the tiny cock was plucked, then rolled, then held very still, so the only movements were the hand beneath her – which was kept pressed against her lower back and, in its lifting, moved her body by minute fractions against that single pinned and stimulated fleshy point to which the bone was fixed – and her lips which sucked upon the living cock as if it were the very air and she were drowning.

Anya listened to her guttural groans of pleasure, watched her belly shake, watched the ballocks between Ranil's legs lifting and the thick stem pumping milt into her mouth while Shanam gently held her balanced on his hand and carefully twisted the tiny bone projection between his forefinger and thumb. And the calmness of his gaze upon the girl – his control – made Anya's legs, already very weak, turn to jelly. She drew breath deeply – deliberately so – and he turned and saw her. But though Ranil, pumping still, was yet able to make some exclamation on the matter, Shanam showed no surprise. Getting up slowly, he left the other two lovers on the leaves, came over and stood before Anya with his cock still standing hard, she was aware, though now she would not look at it, despite the fact that she had up to this point looked upon it willingly, longingly in fact, from afar. His hand reached out and touched her breasts – he took each one and weighed its fullness, touched the nipple, then the hand moved down and the backs of his fingers rubbed up and down her belly. She felt the ring between her legs moving and her nubbin came erect; the weight of the small ring readjusting was a feeling quite delicious. His fingers rubbed until the soft hairs on her belly bristled. A sweet sickly tightness filled her throat; she could not swallow properly; her mouth was filling with oily spittle. There was a thumping in her heart and neck and head and she felt queasy. But these were feelings that she loved. She loved the awakening, the wanting, the sinking, suffocating need giving way so slowly to the inevitability of a pleasure that could drown.

He went into the small room behind her, gathered up an armful of leaves and, bringing them through, deposited them by the fire. In three such journeys he had brought the bed. '*Lakita . . .*' Anya whispered when he pointed to it, and this time she obeyed. She lay down upon it, stretched herself and smiled. She felt him snuggle up behind her, turn her on her belly, touch the freckles on her shoulders and tickle her skin. When his hand edged down, she moved her legs apart. The tips of his fingers smoothed into the crease of her buttocks. She could feel his thick stem resting silky warm against her leg, the soft naked skin of his bag moulding to the back of her thigh as the heavy round weights inside it rolled. She wanted to feel them between her legs; she wanted him inside her, from behind, and her sex distended by his smooth brown plum. She turned to kiss him, but he turned her back again and continued touching. He seemed fascinated by her skin – the freckles, her underarm curls and the soft fine hair at the base of her spine, the palest hair sweeping softly down into the deep dark crease between her buttocks. While Anya turned her head to the side, lay on her cheek and watched the lovers, the round tip of a finger repeatedly followed the smoothness into the groove; as she crooked her knee, the round tip found the small warm thin-skinned mouth; her body tensed but her knee moved higher up the bed. The fingertip smoothly tested; the sensitivity increased until she wanted to pull away. However, she did not pull away, but pushed her belly down into the leaves, distending it in the way she had seen the girl do, which caused her spine to arch down like the bent branch of a willow and the cheeks of her bottom to lift and separate and the small mouth to form a definite pouting cup. Then she closed her eyes, waiting for the fingertip to enter her against this tender plea. But her action, in emphasising her perfectly

187

curving shapes, only caused the fingertip to lift and both hands, enticed by the vision of these separated globes, to try to fit precisely to each and to taste its smoothness while the thumbs rubbed the velvet inner faces of the cheeks and the dark eyes watched the small mouth gently pouting.

Her legs tried to move higher; the single fingertip returned and continued to stroke, pulling shivers down her spine. Her eyes opened. The girl's body was draped belly uppermost across Ranil's knee. Her breasts, pointing out and back as her neck arched and her head rested against the floor, were being stimulated with wetted fingers. The cone around each nipple looked very swollen, as the fingertips by alternation pinched and slapped; this was the noise that Anya had heard. Yet the girl did not seem afraid. A stone pot was drawn across the floor beside Ranil. Then he called to Shanam, who grunted in reply, then knelt up. But before he left Anya in that state of ungratified arousal, with her legs so wide apart now and her belly pushing down into the softness of the leaves, he fastened something round each leg. They felt like narrow skin belts – skin belts solely, without any fur – which were fastened high against the creases of her thighs and drawn very tightly. He hadn't fastened her legs to anything, but had merely stretched and tied these thin skin belts tightly round their tops.

So now, even while he was gone, the feeling was there – the tightness against that sensitive place – and it did not go away. And the sensations it induced were contradictory – she felt as if she were tied, yet her legs could freely move. When she drew them together across the leaves, the soft knots and loose loops of the skin belts were trapped against her swollen flesh lips, making her shudder; when she opened her legs, the tension around the tight bands seemed increased and made her sex lips gently throb. As Anya lay there, tied yet free, with the narrow lines of encircling pressure round her upper thighs, the sweet sickly taste came in her mouth and the queasy pleasure came in her belly very much stronger than before. Yet her lover had so far scarcely begun to touch her. What further pleasures would be in store? She bathed in the anticipation. She lay on her front quite wantonly with her thighs open and her breasts and belly pressed into the leaves, wanting to be touched again, wanting to be urged to pleasure, to be penetrated, taken while her lover's thumbs pushed up through the outsides of the tight skin belts to keep the bands of pressure hard against her inner thighs until her pleasure came. But now both men were with the girl.

Ranil held her thighs apart while the older man worked between them. Each whimper that the girl uttered made Anya's belly squirm, for Shanam's fingertips were picking at the small bone prong again, trying to extract it. The lips were opened and the hood was lifted back; the prong was drawn out fully and the fingernail picked at the gold thread of its mounting, while the girl emitted tiny cries – whether of pleasure or fear or squeamish pain, Anya could not tell – yet it was as if Anya could feel it too, between her legs, a pulling picking feeling round the gold ring of her nub. Anya's thighs now closed defensively, yet the girl's of course could not, for hers were held wide to keep her mound accessible and her sex projecting while the small gold snag was painstakingly worked undone and the white bone prong pulled free. Shanam held it up, then wetted his fingertips and worked the spittle into the nub while the girl protested freely with short quick spasms of her belly. Now, more fully naked than she had ever been, she was lifted on to the older man's lap while the pot was drawn near. Water splashed from it on to the floor, making Anya shiver. The girl's legs were balanced in the air. Shanam dipped his hand into the pot and drew from it a large grey gnarled shell. Anya shivered again, for it was an oyster – the same awful creature she had been offered that afternoon, when the women had expected her to eat it – but she was aghast to see it here, in such a circumstance. The young man handed Shanam a small knife and Anya then emitted a cry. Shanam looked at her and pursed his lips, then he whispered to Ranil, who got up and came to her.

She was apprehensive. He lay beside her, unfastened the belts at the tops of her thighs, then retightened them and turned her on her back, but turned her head away. It seemed they did not wish her to witness what was being done to the girl; she could only hear the sounds now – as she watched Ranil but strained her ears to pick up every hint – of the girl's

189

breathing, her murmurs, small adjustments to the position of her limbs, whispers from Shanam, a protest in return, a moan, rather deeper now, a sigh from him, then a cracking sound, a hollow sound, sounds of oyster sinews splitting, wet sounds and a knife scraping back and forth within a shell, then silence. Anya attempted to turn her head to see. The young man would not let her. He took one nipple between his wetted fingers; his other hand gently opened her thighs and closed around her sex and held it. The fingers did not enter her; they were not permitted so to do. The symbol was clear – she wore the ring.

Anya listened; she could hear every tiny crackle of the fire, every shuffle. Her eyes widened as she heard another whisper, then a soft gasp, whispers of reassurance, rapid breathing, panting now and soft wet sounds, of sucking Anya knew. The hand around her squeezed her swollen sex lips while the fingertips rolled her nipple. The panting waned; the sucking stopped and the hand at Anya's sex lifted. Her knees were pushed wide open and the hand began to rub beside the lips, which slowly split, then to touch the ring, feeding it very slowly through the nubbin, causing the awful pulling feeling deep inside her. He placed one hand beneath her lower back and lifted, which pushed her belly out and kept her flesh wide open while he continued to touch the ring, which stood out hard about the nubbin that pushed out from the shelter of its hood. But his fingers did not enter.

More cracking sounds were heard, then shuffling, then tiny whimpers as the sucking sounds began again. The girl began to beg, whispering one word – '*Nin*' – over and over but the soft wet sounds continued long, while Anya lay unmoving, bowed out, the swollen flesh about the ring between her legs being thoroughly yet minutely stroked. In due course, the girl's pleasure was extracted against the strength of sobbing shudders and at this point, the ring was simply held until the gasps had sufficiently waned. Then the ring was pressed, then turned a fraction, then pulled and held, drawn out to make a fleshy cusp, while the tip of the little finger tasted the freshly disclosed half circular furrow around the top of the denuded nub – for this was certainly permitted – and Anya's pleasure balanced on the point of coming until Shanam was quite finished with the girl, at which time Anya was released and allowed to turn, though not to close her legs. She saw that the girl now lay on her side with her back turned, curving, moving slightly as she breathed. Shanam was tracing with his fingertips the smooth bronze curvature. She might have been asleep. Fastened round her upper thighs were the tight skin straps. Trickling down the back of one thigh was wetness. On the ground beside her were the plundered shells.

As Anya lay on her front, her sex, seen from behind, framed by the tight skin bands, pulsed softly above the compressed leaves of the bed, overlaying their faint aroma with the heavy smell of heat. The ring stood out, a sweet temptation for those fingertips that had only just released her to take up once again. And above the pulsing sex and bedded in the groove was the circular well of blackness. Edging forwards, Ranil pressed the warm polished head of his cock – which had stayed erect since first he touched her nipples with his fingers – against the hot velvet well, which immediately contracted and took the clear droplet of liquid that the cocktip proffered. He teased it, pushing harder. The velvet skin turned slippery with his escaped liquid; the girl turned rigid; she did not want it this way. She was strange – wanting it at the front, where she should not, but not in the one place that it was allowed. He drew his cock away and laid it against her leg and instead, tickled the small and now wet mouth with his finger. Though her body stayed tense, the mouth gradually relaxed until he allowed his cock to touch it once again. Again she turned rigid, and murmured some word he did not understand. He pushed her knees apart and rubbed the small black shiny mouth with his thumb while he gently played with the ring, which was wetted now with her inner moisture seeping down to form a droplet. Suddenly, he heard a stifled gasp, the mouth contracted about the tip of his thumb, the thighs shuddered and he felt a rapid tiny pulsing through the ring, as if her body was trying repeatedly to pull it from his fingers. He held the ring against that pulling and her body slowly steadied.

Anya's pleasure had come when the thumb had momentarily stopped stroking her but the pad remained against her and the tips of his fingers, holding the ring, had slowed to tiny movements. She could feel the thick bare stem against the back of her knee; when it had touched her there, she had imagined being made to take it in her mouth – as the girl had done, while Shanam played with her between her legs – and at that thought, her legs had moved slightly more open, she had felt the tightness squeezing the tops of her thighs and then her breathing had brought her on. The pleasure had been quick, but sweet against his fingertips and now she wanted another. She wanted both men loving her together; she wanted their bare hot silky stems rubbed over her body – over her breasts and back and face and in her hair and down her throat and up inside her sex but not inside her bottom – for that was where she would like to feel their tongues. She would like to be sucked at the back and at the front together. She knew she would find the lewdness of such pleasure quite delicious.

And Anya got her wish, and more – she made them break the taboo of the ring – but not that night. The fire ebbed, more leaves were brought from outside, the main bed was enlarged and Anya was laid to sleep beside the girl, whose small bone prong was reinstated for her pleasure, which occurred at intervals during the night – Anya heard them wake her – while Anya herself was always turned the other way. In this manner Anya was made to feel welcome in their bed whilst not being unduly taxed by their attentions. If, as happened sometimes, one or other of the men was not fully engaged with the girl and found Anya restless, he would tickle or stroke her back, the skin bands would perhaps be released and then retightened, and on occasion, her knees would be bent while she lay on her side, that the ring – the symbol of that uncompanionable and already very strained embargo on fully penetrative love – might be touched and tickled and rendered slippy with spittle until she fell asleep, which in her state of permanent excitement from the sounds of pleasure and the smells of premature and sometimes deliberate emissions evaporating from the warmth of the young girl's skin, was a process slow indeed. But the men had patience; they would not rush this new girl.

When Anya awoke the second time, she turned, pretending

to be asleep and watched through slitted eyes. Ranil was on his back with the girl on top of him, also on her back. Her legs had been lifted and the narrow bare buttocks spread so wide that the gulf between them seemed disproportionately wide, enhanced as it was by the thick wet bole of his cockstem pushed between them. An inch at the base was visible; the rest of the tube was buried inside her bottom. Her hand, reaching round from below, cupped his ballocks as tenderly as if they were the eggs of a rare and delicate bird. Her sex, held open by Shanam's fingers and thumb, was being penetrated by the forefinger and second finger of his other hand and was trying to close, though the fingers and thumb held her open. The two fingers withdrew, dipped into a bowl and reapplied the oily paste inside her. Then a short green cylindrical fruit was carefully inserted, her thighs were closed around it and the fingertips rubbed round the small nubbin bone projection until she came, which caused her to lift her pressed-together legs, which in turn stirred the ballocks underneath her as the cock began to pump against the flesh ring squeezing round it near its base. Then Anya was spotted; she was turned to face the wall again and to consider at her leisure what she had seen.

On her second night, after a day spent mainly sleeping on the floating platform, listening to the lapping water and soaking up the sun, the skin belts were fastened round the tops of her thighs and she was left in the quiet of the inner sanctum once again, for by then, word that she was taboo had circulated. But again, she became restless, despite repeated visits in which the men would stroke her and touch her and tighten the belts. In the end they relented, lifted her up and carried her to the bed, but allowed her to rest at first while they attended to the girl.

When Anya was allowed to turn, once the last murmurs had subsided, she saw the smoothly curved back of the body beside her, the black hair being stroked by one man while the feet were tickled by the other, and she saw both stems still erect and one of them shiny wet; she saw again the wetness at the back of the girl's thigh; she could smell the milt. And she felt the ache of wanting so deep inside that it sucked upon her womb until it hurt. She felt the sinking in her belly when a pot of oysters was brought and the two men moved to her side.

That night, Anya acquired a taste for oysters, which hitherto she had hated and would not even look upon in their jellied, open state, let alone touch. But now, she had the juice of oysters dripped into her mouth, and more deliciously, dripped upon her nubbin and sucked, and more deliciously still, she fed oyster flesh to the men from the soft-shelled cup of her open sex. Her hips would be lifted on Shanam's thighs; she would be open – her thighs, with the tight bands clinging wet; the lips of her sex, held open with Ranil's thumbs pressing to either side; and her mouth too – reaching for those large round ballocks dangling up above her. She would hear the cracking as the shell was opened, the scraping of the knife and then her lifted belly would shudder with the first freezing drips that splashed upon her sex lips and within – cold trickling stings upon the soft warm inner pinkness. The roughness of the shell would touch as it was tipped and momentarily, she would turn to stone, frightened of a sharpness that might cut. She would feel the flood of cold liquid, then the cold wet weight, soft coldness slipping in its sea of salty juice, then Shanam's tongue slipping underneath it, lifting, scooping and the juice overflowing, wetting the skin bands, wetting her belly, making her belly arch to feed that tongue, her neck arch, her tongue slip out in lewdness to press into the divide between those ballocks up above her and to lick a wet line up and down the curving soft-tubed undersurface of the salted stem – to feel it shudder in its turn, as she had shuddered last night.

Each time she tried to take the cap of the cockstem in her mouth, it retreated, as if afraid to enter and spill its thickness over her tongue. She knew he was very near; she could feel the trembling and she could feel his thumbtips shaking as they opened her between her thighs, for the oyster to drop and make her shiver as her lips were sealed about it and it moved against the warmth inside her, slipping deep within the neck of the cup while the ocean liquid spilled to wet the gold ring through her nubbin, to wet her curly hairs and to soak into the thin skin belts that squeezed the tops of her legs. And with the oyster deep inside her, she was played with and lifted higher, that her bottom might be touched. The oyster warmed and the liquid continued to trickle out and down the groove. From above, her wetted fleshy lips were rubbed; the ring was teased out and gently turned until her pleasure welled; the lips were opened, then sealed again. She felt warm breath against her; she was sucked. And now she could not bear the deliciousness of the feeling. Her tongue arched up again, licking between the open legs above her, lifting the ballocks. Even as she whimpered with that first deep drawing feeling as she felt one tongue-tip press through the ring from above and lift, a second tongue began the slow licking journey upwards from the tip of her backbone to the mouth of her uplifted bottom, collecting every drop of liquid that had spilled into the groove. Her nipples turn rigidly hard. She felt the nearness of the pleasure of the person up above her and she touched those heavy ballocks with her fingers, splitting them, lifting them to the sides that her moistened tongue might continue to follow that smooth but shuddering centre line from the plum, down the undertube, pushing between the spread-apart ballocks and on and back towards the smooth hard curve of flesh that descended into his groove. And when Anya licked that curving bridge of smoothness, back and forth between his legs, keeping it wet and slippery, she felt his tongue-tip shiver in the ring that pierced her nubbin; she felt his ballocks tighten; then she felt him start to pump. Her tongue, broad now, flat against this bridging curve, felt the milt flow through the tightly tubed polished skin; she felt him coming though she touched his cockstem not at all, with any part of her body; she simply held the ballocks drawn apart, maintaining that line of tightness with her broad warm tongue pressed against the rounded bridge that led up to his bottom. When the first splash of milt fell upon her breast, she shuddered; when the second enveloped her nipple in a warm wet gluey coat, her own tongue hardened to a rigid point; when the tongue that licked her bottom entered her, she came. The milt continued pumping, the point of her tongue moved up and pressed into the base of the soft undertube, to feel that pulse, to try to trap it and to make the owner wriggle. Her nubbin was nipped; she screamed; her fleshpot squeezed and the oyster was delivered on to the waiting tongue below.

They never entered her body or her mouth with any part other than their tongues. She was allowed to play with their cockstems or to cup a plum between her thighs and to press it to her moistened flesh lips, which would form a sucker to the underside of the plum. She would seal the join with spittle and press two fingers down upon the top surface and rub it to make it come. Sometimes she would press the mouth of the cock against the gold ring and the spurting would precipitate her pleasure. The sticky milt would be rubbed into the creases of her thighs, or cupped and rubbed into her nipples; then she would be massaged until she dried or until a further batch of milt was spilled. In ways such as this, her second night passed much more quickly beneath the repeated attentions of these two men.

In the late morning, Anya stepped from the hut to find even the outdoor air heavy and humid. The lake and the sea beyond were silent and blanketed in a pure white mist which formed a wispy wall at a stone's throw from the platform's edge. As soon as she was clear of the hut, a voice called from the end of the causeway. Anya recognised the voice and, staring hard, made out the slim form of Ikahiti, afraid to come any closer but beckoning to her through the mist. Anya glanced over her shoulder to make sure that none of the men had noticed, then she crept over. But she was not sure that she wanted to leave yet: she had come to realise the pleasure that such constant close solicitude can bring – not simply sexual pleasure, real though that was, but also the much more enduring tenderness and warmth. She was surer now than ever that the kinds of things that the Princess and Ikahiti did to the men that they had captured was cruel; they took pleasure from it in a way that Anya never could. But even so, she had really missed her friend.

Ikahiti stared at Anya and Anya, suddenly recalling the way that Ikahiti had run away and left her, knowing how afraid Anya had been, did not greet Ikahiti by taking her hand as she had intended to do but looked away, towards the sea, enveloped in its mist. Anya continued walking on, beyond the camp and round the lake, examining her feet now, watching them press into the soft dry sand. Ikahiti continued by her side without speaking. Then she stopped, faced Anya and planted her feet apart. She held something up. Ikahiti did not look at it herself but, frowning deeply, watched Anya's eyes moving down and focusing, then growing wider and wider with excitement and disbelief.

'He lives . . .?' she stared at Ikahiti and she knew it, though Ikahiti did not speak. 'He lives?' Anya then repeated. Between Ikahiti's shaking fingertips was a thick gold ring; it bore the Sword of Lidir – the Prince's signet. Anya's knees felt weak. She reached to take it but Ikahiti snatched it away. 'The Prince!' Anya cried it out this time, her eyes growing wider and more shining, filling with tears. 'But Ikahiti, is he here? Where is he?' Ikahiti turned away. 'Please – is he safe? Is he in the village?' And then she thought of him taken captive, and was suddenly afraid. 'Is he all right? You have not hurt him? Ikahiti – Please?' But Ikahiti continued stone-facedly ignoring her and trying to walk onwards while Anya tried to hold her back and plead. Finally, Ikahiti flung the ring into the sand and Anya grovelled after it.

'*I-rin-asiirt!*' Ikahiti cried. '*Shiri-ne!*' And she pointed back the way they had come, '*Ta-lata rin asiirt!*' heaping abuse on Anya, kicking the sand up and storming off in the opposite direction. Anya found the ring, though she could hardly see it for her tears. She ran, stumbling, back past the bridge to the men's camp, not stopping though people shouted in surprise. Across the rocks she hurried then up the face and through the hole and down again across the rocky ridges of the small inlet and finally back on to sand. But she did not see the tracks. Something snaked across the sand in front of her and she tripped over it, falling forward into the sand. Before she could scramble to her knees she was grabbed and pinned. These were not the villagers – even through her tears she knew that. She saw the ragged clothing, heard the guttural chuckles, then looking up, saw pushing through the group the creature that she dreaded most. She was released but cowered on her knees. The voice was very quiet:

'Why, Princess – can it be? – and why in such a hurry?'
But even the shore party, tough as this group were, winced
at the smack across the face that knocked the poor girl back
to the ground before Travix dragged her by the hair to the
water's edge and threw her in with the other nubile captives
cringing in the bilges of the boat.

[13]

Loving Retribution

She had had one real chance: on the beach, she could have screamed and fought with the men who held her; it would surely have drawn someone's attention. But in an instant, terror had sucked the very breath from her throat; those cruel, evil eyes and the vision of that severed lip had made her freeze. Once Travix had laid her hands on Anya, it was too late. She turned limp; Travix wound Anya's hair round her hand and would not let it go. 'For fear you should vanish yet again,' said Travix – and like a she-wolf with her teeth into her sapless prey, she dragged her trophy back to her lair.

On deck, the captive girls were distributed thus – two for the captain, three for Kasger on the slave deck, leaving one remaining, the runaway. Travix asked the captain what should be done with her. The captain pursed his lips. He looked at Anya, forced to her knees now, her open belly splayed, with Travix above her, one hand in the middle of her back, forcing it downwards, the other pulling and cruelly twisting the hank of hair. Then he turned to the pair of young girls standing in wide-eyed terror to his right. He studied their smooth bronze naked skin before he spoke. He looked upon their rounded, pear-shaped breasts and their perky little nipples. He noticed that between her legs, one of them wore a gold ring, the other wore a tiny bone. He wondered: why this difference?

'I'm sorry, Mister Travix – what?' he eventually replied.

'The runaway, sir – the one that jumped ship . . .?'

'Ah yes . . . As you think appropriate, Mister Travix; as you deem fit. But be sure it is a punishment she will cherish and not forget.' He watched the slim, full-breasted body shudder at these words. He looked at the pleading eyes, caressing them from a distance with his own. As the gentle lips began to

199

tremble, to beseech with silent words, he nodded. 'Yes, be sure it is a punishment that will bite,' he whispered, then he sighed. Would that he were there to witness it. But a captain must of necessity retain that element of detachment from his crew. He would taste her body later; and he would get her to explain. Again, the captain sighed and looked upon her once more before departing with his prizes.

The boat was again dispatched. The few crewmen remaining on deck retreated to a safe distance, for the expression on the face of the master's mate was at once arrogance, cold hate and evil satisfaction. Anya was terrified and naked, at this woman's mercy. Without letting go of her hair, Travix moved round to her front, so Anya's head was twisted back and to one side.

'And now, Princess,' said Travix, enunciating very precisely, 'where was it that we were?'

'Please . . .?' Anya whispered. She could see the woman only from the corner of one eye; her neck ached; her back was breaking; the muscles of her thighs were cramping.

'No,' said Travix. 'Let us take time to recall. I believe you were attempting to explain exactly what you thought of me. You may do so now. Go ahead.'

'Oh, please,' Anya could only repeat, more plaintively yet, but Travix would not let up.

'Tell me,' she insisted. Anya's fingers writhed, curling tight in anguish then stretching out again in hopeless desperation. Travix spoke through gritted teeth. 'Yes – use your fists again if you prefer.'

'Nooo . . .' she whined, disowning her own hands now, placing them back behind her. '*Please*, I . . . I beg of you, please?' she added very softly, and at those words a shudder came in Anya's belly and the hand that held her hair so tightly suddenly relaxed.

The sun had pierced the mist. It enveloped the deck in warmth, but Anya was shaking. Travix stood back. She called to the men in leather shirts. Anya, her hands still kept behind her and moving only when she shook, began to cry. Her shoulders hunched to protect her breasts, so full, so defencelessly exposed. Then her hair fell forwards to cover her face;

heavy tears rolled down the cheeks that now lay hidden behind their curtain of copper strands. But Travix saw those luscious droplets splash upon the deck – and she felt an inner warmth, more sweetly warm than wine. It was this gift that Anya gave her that would in time secure her full forgiveness. Many times that day, her perfect body would yield this sweet redress. Travix would savour it, drip by drip – now, when she was punished – smacked breathless through the ship, then delivered to the men and later, and most delectable of all, in Travix's bed, when her tears would well freely and again to wet the clean fresh sheets and to mix with the warmth of her emissions. Travix looked upon the breasts now – full, like her own, and suddenly the urge was upon her – to see their freckled fullness fuller yet.

'Lie down on your front – on the deck. No! Keep your hands behind your back.' And she watched the distraught innocent bowing her belly forwards, not knowing how to make the manoeuvre yet struggling to comply. 'Keep your knees apart – wide. Put your shoulders back. Tighter. Fold your arms behind your back.' And now the full breasts lifted, swelled and pointed out and to the sides. Travix moved round to see their bulging shapes in profile. 'Now lie down, as I told you. Do it slowly.' She watched the soles curving, the toes curling in desperation on the upturned feet, the knees gradually edging apart, the supple backbone flexing, unflexing, then flexing hard again. The buttocks opened, the sex projected underneath – and then she saw it, the glint of gold against the black. 'Wait!' she cried. 'Stay still.' The girl trembled. Travix approached quite deliberately from behind, that the girl would not see and would not know until she was actually touched. Travix's left hand slid, palm upwards, along the deck. The middle finger lifted and touched metal bedded between moist and clinging skin. The girl jumped, but it was true – she was pierced. The finger withdrew and Travix stood up and moved back. 'Move over – to the side a little. Keep your hips to the floor.' The girl, open-thighed, inched crabwise over the deck until her bottom balanced above a seam in the planking. 'Stop,' said Travix. Seen from behind now, the perfect bottom bulged, bisected by the deep incision of the groove which, to

Travix's eye, appeared continuous with the split in the flesh lips and below them, with the line of separation in the woodwork. 'Now continue. I want to see those thighs spread wider. Your lips of lust must touch the floor.' The girl shuddered yet she obeyed; her buttocks moved in a slow gyration, bedding downwards; Travix watched the flesh lips brush the wood. The hips lifted slightly. 'Down, I said,' and the flesh lips pressed against then slipped into the groove between the planks. 'Good,' whispered Travix. She strode round to the girl's front. It appeared to Travix that the expression on that face had changed and that behind the pleading in her liquid eyes was a smouldering sensual need. 'Keep your shoulders back.' The breasts lifted again. How Travix wanted to smack them now – with bare hands wetted to the ruffled wrists in clear cool water – but in love, in Travix's kind of courtship, the first punishment must never be hurried. It must enmesh with the sweet tears of submission and the burning warmth of arousal. Then the greater the punishment, the crueller the abuse, the more soft and luscious, the more open and loving would be that body afterwards to punishments of a more intimate kind. A courtship must be conducted properly if love is to be enduring.

'If you defy me once more after today, you shall be secured, in the position you now assume, with the trinket you display so lewdly pinned down to the floor, while your breasts are birched and your bottom is whipped to bleeding point through the application of the cat. Keep still!' she screamed. 'Now do you understand?' The body shook; the shoulders hunched even more; the tears began to well again. 'Then lie down – slowly. I am waiting.'

Travix moved to the side again. 'Keep those arms folded behind you.' Slowly, the knees moved out, the hips broadened, the back arched in a smooth tight curve and the belly bowed. It kissed the woodwork, then the breasts touched, separating, as Travix had intended and pushed out, hard and full, to each side. That vision was exquisite. 'Now put your arms down on the deck – flat. Spread them. Move your knees out – keep them on the deck.' Travix walked round the body that was stretched out, pressed like an open flower to the timbers, then she halted by the girl's right side. She looked at the face turned to the side, the tearstained cheeks, the freckled shoulders and the perfect hollow beneath the arm – with its nestled, dark red curls – which fed out to the sumptuous swelling of the breast and the polished black nipple pushed out horizontally an inch above the grain. She touched this nipple with the soft wet toe of her velvet boot, wet from the girl's faint struggles in the water as Travix had dragged her backwards to the boat. She used this moistened toe to press the nipple to the wood and to roll it back and forth while the girl trembled. Yet still there was a weak resistance to her shame; her fingertips tried to claw clandestinely against the wood. 'Keep still,' Travix ordered very softly and the girl obeyed; the ineffectual fingertips stopped. What Travix really wanted was to take her boot off and to taste the sunwarmed roundness of the breast with the soft skin of her instep, curved until it cramped to match the roundness of that teat, and to tickle the curls beneath the armpit with her toes. But she contented herself with this gentle rolling of the nipple beneath the cool moist tip of velvet.

'Princess . . .' she whispered lazily, 'you must be punished.'

Anya shivered. With her cheek still pressed against the planking, she looked up. Travix held a soft brown pouch. Its long cords dangled down and Travix's thumb was already moving up and down inside the pod to shape it. Looped round Travix's right wrist was a strap.

Running wild, she called it, breathless running, running with her lover through the ship, with the instrument of punishment always available, fastened tightly to her wrist, yet her hands always free to touch her lover's skin, to squeeze her bulbous breasts and milk her full wet pouch and to search into the deep crease of her buttocks. For this tender touching was so necessary to love and the smacking was so integral to pleasure.

Travix therefore smacked her prodigal lover across the deck, she smacked her down the stairs. On the first landing, she held the cord of the pouch and twisted it and smacked her hard again. She smacked her so the tears kept coming, so the cheeks upon that face stayed wet, so the backs of her lover's legs glowed angry red and her buttocks felt hot to the touch. When she drove her down again, the girl collapsed forwards on all fours, head down on the steep stairs, gasping, her breasts swelling down to brush across the step and her bottom high in the air. Travix grasped the waist cord yet again and smacked. 'Open your legs,' she cried and smacked her buttocks, smacked between them, smacked the dark fleeced outer lips of that sweet pouched sex, which forced the encapsulated inner lips to bulge even harder. Then she smacked until the bottom lifted up so far that the girl overbalanced and Travix had to hold those hips to prevent her tumbling down the stairs while she smacked that sex again.

Then having smacked her lover numb between the legs, she ran her on to the crewdeck and there she smacked her breasts; amid the wild activity and the music, a small circle formed and grew as the girl was made to kneel up, push her tongue out and hold her breasts up for this smacking, which soon gave way to touching, warm caresses – the hand of a blue-clad wrist beneath the armpit, feeling the dampness there, then on the breasts themselves, the smoothing of the fingertips over heat of the bulging skin, the gentle nipping of the polished round black bulbils of the nipples and the smacking of the downswell underneath. Then the breasts were gathered from behind in a forearm and one hand and held up, pressed together and caressed again while the strap smacked down repeatedly between the open legs. And to make that pleasure more delicious, Travix made the girl lift her belly and push it out to greet those very smacks; then she made her kneel up and hold the outer lips apart to expose the pouched lips for the milking. The pouch felt hard and wet, but the wet was thick and the fingers slipped up and down it easily. When the pleasure was on the verge of yielding, Travix dragged the girl up and sat her on the edge of the table and smacked her sex again to take the urgency away.

In a kind of intermission, the girl – the lover, rather – was hung from the hook in the rafters by means of a cuffed short leather shackle which permitted only the very tips of her toes to reach the floor. She could have been smacked immediately, but Travix preferred to look at her – her breasts and buttocks an even red, the skin blood-warmed beneath, the sweet dark curls of her underarms glistening, her hair tangled, her cheeks tearstained, the legs pointed straight to the floor and, pressed between them, the dark brown pouch which sealed only her inner lips, only those lips that lovers love to kiss, held them tight, so tight and swollen that the impress of the gold ring could be seen pushing up and out, driven by the stiff erection of her nubbin. And at this sight, Travix's bosom swelled until she could hardly breathe. If this was not love that she felt for the girl, then she did not know what was.

She looked about her, at the scenes of sweet debauchery – naked girls, girls being shared, bodies being touched and tasted, young heads being cradled in ancient laps, slim legs locked round the back of a chair. Beside her was a girl lying back on a bench, holding her sex lips open to form a trembling cup that reached to kiss a bulbous cockhead spilling milt, whilst across the way a girl was being taken on the table.

Travix liked the crewdeck; she liked to watch these gentle juxtapositions of the flesh. She liked to watch the old men too – craggy, shrunken, salt-dried bodies, withered fingers, dappled with age, exploring the tender rounded warmth of young fresh flawless skin. Watching a young girl deliver her pleasure into an old man's hand was nectar to her mind.

She therefore had her lover spread her legs in the air and smacked – her belly and inner thighs, but did not smack her sex lips; these she rubbed, then kissed and licked and gently nipped them with her teeth – then, having had her lover taken down and spread upon the table, she called an old man over. She removed the pouch herself, then watched. It took many sweet minutes, for the lover was reluctant at first to acquiesce. Travix stood, deaf to the music, blind to the other activities all around her, just watching her lover's breathing rising and falling, her body becoming heavy with a deliciousness Travix could almost feel, her thighs lying open, tense at first, innocent and frightened to be thus addressed by the gaunt, withered fingers, then in the end, soft and wide and shameless as the old brown hand, steeped first in olive oil to soften its ancient edge, worked liquid smoothness into that living open sex until the small ringed bud was the only hardness in a delicious pastel pink black-fringed sea and the pleasure came flooding in powerful pulses. But when the eyes were fully opened, that same pleasure was followed by a wave of perfect shame which seemed to suffuse the whole of her neck and face with warmth and could be atoned for only by the refitting of the pouch and a renewal of the smacking until the imprint of the ring could once again be seen quite clearly through the leather skin. Travix then kissed her lover and delivered her up into the sunshine of that bright warm day to be dealt with further by the leather-shirted men, using straps at first and then a rather keener instrument of sexual torture, Travix's 'kitten', which was a thin and very supple greenstick crop.

Anya lay on the deck again, though she could see it not, for the stinging tears which burst again though the punishment had ceased. Between her legs, her sex lips bulged within the narrow confines of the pouch. The backs of her legs burned; her buttocks were striped with overlapping inch-wide weals; the mouth of her bottom throbbed; the creases at the top of her inner thighs were scalded from the whipping with the kitten. Not an inch of skin without the pouch had been spared from these depredations. She had been forced against the mast and bent across the rail. But now at last the men had stood aside. Travix's voice came in her ear:

'My precious . . .' Anya shuddered. 'I have to do these things to you. You understand?' Anya did not understand; she did not understand at all. Travix was kneeling beside her now – crouching on the deck, speaking softly, looking into Anya's eyes. The ruffled blue sleeve lay close to Anya's cheek. The slender fingers reached and stroked; though not soft, they felt cool against her hot flushed skin. 'I love you – you understand me?' And at the first three of those words, Anya's eyes widened. The face was very close now. Anya watched the lips moving, not hearing what they said for they were whispering so softly. Her eyes were fixed upon the small swollen distortion beside the line of the sever incised into the upper lip. The fingertips brushed against her neck, then found the heartbeat there. The lips approached, the small contusion went out of focus, then it disappeared, then she felt it touching – smooth

206

coolness against her own rough dry lips, hot from the dried tears, while the fingertips touched her pulsebeat, until Anya took that small contusion voluntarily between her own lips and she sucked it. Her eyes closed and she touched it with the tip of her tongue. The feeling in her belly, still pressed against the deck, was sweet. She wanted Travix to take her in her arms, so the soft loving skin of Anya's breasts could press against the smoothness of that pale blue suit.

But Travix drew away, that she might look upon that face, its freckles ripened by the sun, its lips so warm and sweet and that she might cup her palm against the breast and press it to the woodwork and thereby feel its fullness tighten to her palm. She looked upon that so-delicious red-streaked bottom and the swollen purple mouth that she had ordered not to be spared the lash and she touched it with the coolly moistened tip of her middle finger. She watched the cheeks try to edge apart in submission, though they were wide already, and deep within her belly, Travix felt true warmth for this girl although she did not fully understand her. When she bent down, she could see the outline of the ring still protruding through the skin of the pouch. She touched the pouch – it was hard and hot; when she squeezed it, it yielded up a silky wet that tasted of ripe buttered honey. 'Turn over,' Travix whispered and the girl obeyed. Travix kissed her. 'I will whip you with the kitten . . . Shhhh,' said she when the girl murmured, 'do not open your eyes. Savour it upon the soft skin where this belly meets these thighs.' She opened the thighs, she took the greenstick switch from the man and, holding the pouched lips to the side, she whipped it down – not upon the pouch itself, for that would be quite pointless – but on the living, bare, stretched skin to the side, between the sex lips and the crease. Three times did she whip on one side then, folding the pouch across the other way, twice upon the other. The third stroke was not delivered. In its stead, she wetted her fingertip and painted the wet along the line the crop would have taken, and the belly bucked more strongly than if it had been cut again with the lash. Then she squeezed the pouch again and it extruded honey more freely than before.

Travix appeared above Anya's face. 'I love you,' Travix

murmured and Anya felt her belly melting as Travix stroked her brow. Then Travix stood up and instructed the two men: 'Smack the insides of her thighs. Use your bare hands; wet them first. Be gentle with her nipples.'

Travix's love was evil – and she knew it. She loved whipping her girls and tasting their bodies afterwards. She loved pleasure frustrated, innocence besmirched, true hearts helplessly enslaved. She had broken every woman aboard this ship. And now she would break another. This woman now before her should surely hate her – but before this day was out, she would love her more profoundly than she had loved anyone, and Travix would be satisfied. Then she would cast her aside, and Travix's joy would be secure.

But love is not rendered shallow by reason of its evil, nor is it sapped by witnessing a lover used. Travix watched her lover lifted on to the broad surface of the hatch. She stood by the mast, distancing herself, finding such distancing coolly appropriate, while the bucket was raised and brought. She watched the girl's head being cradled in one lap, the thighs being held open at the knees – by the girl's own hands – then the wetting of one man's hands, and she listened to the harsh cracking smacks, which made the water droplets sparkle through the air, and the gasps against the hot shivering sheets of pain. Then she watched the nipples being carefully stroked. And to Travix, it was the contrast in this scene that was so spellbinding – the tenderness in one lap, where the head was cradled, and the cruelty perpetrated so blatantly in the other. The long red hair was smoothed, the tears were collected up on tender fingertips and the breasts and nipples brushed and teased, while other hands lashed down, rewetted and lashed again upon that tender skin until both inner thighs were ruby red and dripping, yet the nipples stood out like velvet-coated beads.

Travix approached and the smacking stopped. Her lover's hands were limp now; they no longer held her knees apart, but her knees lay as widely open as if invisible hands were pressing them to the surface of the hatch. Her breathing was rapid and shallow. A dark stain, like a heart, was in the wood, for the water had run down her thighs and into the hollow between the cheeks. But apart from a few stray droplets, her thighs themselves were dry; the water had now evaporated, driven to flight by the deep red glow of blood beneath the skin. The pouch was wet – dark brown – though the water had not touched it; there were two pale untouched bands at the creases, then close beside the pouched lips were the distinctive fine purple welts from the crop, the claw lines from the kitten. Travix lifted the kitten again; her lover gasped, but her belly stayed open. The belly was offered freely to the whipping, delivered so precisely on those parallel claw lines that framed the sex so perfectly to either side of the pouch. The salt-sweet tears of love were silent as they trickled down the freckled cheeks. 'Peg her,' said Travix. 'Make her bottom burn.'

The wicked instrument to which she had referred was fitted towards one side of the hatch. The women were placed against or, more cruelly, upon it, for punishment. It was about a foot long, stout and angled, the end few inches were polished from use, and it had an egg-shaped bulge half way down.

The men hauled Anya to her knees. Then the taller one spoke. 'Remove your pouch,' he said. 'Pull it down.' Her heart was sinking endlessly, like a heavy slug of salted honey sliding down her throat. He lifted her chin. She saw eyes that were wide and black as wanting. She looked to the other; he was oiling the cruel stick; and her heart continued sinking, down into her belly. And behind the two men, she saw Travix. Anya looked down at her bare belly, at the pouch. It was wet; her sex was wet because Travix had made it so. And Travix had forced her tears; time and again that day, she had done it. With the strap and the greenstick switch, she had squeezed those tears from Anya's eyes and she had squeezed that honeydew from her belly. The ghost of wicked, perverse, honeysweet pleasure was disinterred. Anya would give her belly freely again, as she had just done, to be smacked or whipped, if only Travix would kiss her and caress her and make her pleasure come. 'The pouch,' said the man again, then he whispered: 'How are we to peg you else?' She could not breathe. She felt as if a cool blue-wristed hand had cupped her sex and squeezed. Her knees turned weaker, turning to jelly. Her hands were shaking as they went to the back; her fingertips could not cope with the knot. Her head lifted up – as a person drowning, yet her lips were not wide open, gulping air, but trembling, as her fingertips trembled too and could not grip.

The slim arms tensed, the breasts, thrown forwards, shook in perfect roundness – overfull, with thick black cherry tips, and hollows in the underarms begging to be licked. The knot came free; her belly bulged; she looked at Travix. Then her fingers clasped round the cord at the front and deliberately pulled it down, straight down, for it would not come away on its own. It peeled from her wetness. The cords and the sticky pouch lay angled across her thigh and knee. She was lifted and the pouch dropped to her ankles. Then, open-kneed, she was pushed forwards against this peg until her sex lips touched the bulge and the rounded tip was level with her navel. Her arms were pinned behind her; her ankles lay tethered by the twisted leather. The men waited. Travix nodded. 'Make it burn; make it kiss; make her know it happens.'

Anya knew that it happened; the men were not put off by sobs or pleas or broad red marks or sweet wet tears. They smacked her bottom with the broad strap, taking turns to make her belly jerk, to make her sex lips kiss against the bulge in the wood. They smacked until her sex lips felt hot and thick and damp to the touch and her nubbin, nipped by the ring, felt fully distended. Then they smacked again until her belly jerks came on so strongly that her swollen sex lips burst about the bulge and suckered to the smoothly polished wood. Then she was lifted, her sex was opened and she was fitted to the wood. She had to bow her belly forwards to accommodate its slope. It slipped up until her sex lips gloved about it to the bulge.

While the men took off their clothes, Travix approached again. She knelt on the hatch in front of Anya, looking at her, then she stood. She forced her lover's knees apart using the toes of her boots, not stopping until Anya cried out with the pain of penetration. Then she walked round her and pulled her hair back sharply. Travix stared down from above. Her lover was softly whimpering, her body strongly curved back, impaled on this wooden peg. Holding the hair quite firmly, Travix now touched the cheeks that had just been smacked. They were hot and the earlier lashes were still visible under the skin. She pinched the newer welts to make them redder, to make the blood flow freely into these rivulets beneath her lover's bottom skin, to keep it slowly burning and constantly on the move. She spread the cheeks; the dark fleshy ring was pushed out and the bridging skin beneath was shiny, distended from the peg inside. She touched the fleshy ring, moistened it and slipped her finger in. At the same time, she touched her lover at the front. She could feel the peg pushing out the lower belly, making it hard, and she could rub her finger against it from within. She held that hard round flesh about the sex; her lover moaned. She touched the warm bare sex lips, squeezed the ring. She rubbed gently, smoothed wetness there, teased the ring, wetted the belly with water from the bucket, made her lover move her flesh while Travix held the ring, then when her lover was ready, fully ready – close – Travix rolled her sleeve up, then dipped her hand into the bucket, and the girl was breast-smacked, wet. Then Travix left her to the men and went below to collect the body sling.

When she returned, she found the girl – her lover, that is – on her back. Her head was pillowed on a coat. Her legs were open and in the air. The cock deep in her throat withdrew but her belly began to pulse and writhe as the sides of her mound were sucked and bitten, the mouth of her bottom was licked, then finger-smacked, then penetrated with a cock. Her lips reached towards the cock above her. A hand rubbed between her legs. Her neck began to arch and her mouth opened wide. The man above her placed both hands under her neck and lifted, so her head tilted fully back. When the stem pushed deep this time, it reached to the ballocks and her body was bowed between the cock pushed down her throat and the cock pushed up her bottom. And the hand between her legs kept rubbing. Suddenly she jerked, tried to close her arms around the thighs of the man above her and tried to close her legs above the other's waist. But both cocks withdrew and their milt spilled, full and thick. When Travix massaged it into the breasts and into the thighs, she saw that there were two large violet love bruises, flecked with red, in the sensitive rounded flesh of the mound, close beside each crease. They pleased her. She pressed her thumbs into them till the colour drained, then watched it seep back in. Then she took up the kitten, opened the legs quite fully and whipped the belly and touched the girl – touching and whipping alternately – until the pleasure almost came. Then she fitted the sling.

It looked a little like a small hammock, though, once the girl was installed, it was perhaps more like an article of clothing in its intimacy, made as it was from a single piece of the thinnest, finest, softest leather which when held up to the light was a pale translucent yellow. It was shaped to fit a woman. It felt cool and oily to the touch – when it touched the sides of the breasts, stretched across the belly and gloved the space between the legs, the intimacy was apparent. When the pulley ropes were fastened to the hooks, and the drawing began, the leather stretched and this intimacy was enhanced. With the upper body bent from the waist, the breasts could then be drawn by the nipples through the restrictive holes. When the ropes were tightened yet again, the body came up on tiptoes, wavering while the breasts were eased more fully through to form two tight resilient bulges which could be moved independently. When they were pressed together, their resilience pushed them back apart. The outline of the navel could be seen through the sling, but the hairs, pressed down, could not, so the mound appeared as a large rounded split fruit between the legs that now lightly lifted from the floor as the toes clawed the air in vain. When the girl was raised so her body hung a little above waist height and formed a tight round downbow with the twin bulbs of her breasts pointing down at an angle, but partly hidden by her arms, Travix fastened her wrists to the rope, so now her breasts were quite free and unobstructed for Travix to admire. She admired breasts that were as tight and full and swollen as her own. And she admired sex lips that were swollen too, distended by pleasure. She therefore slipped her fingers through the slit in the leather and extracted, in turn, each of the oily lips, drawing it through the narrow constriction, extracting the whole of each lip, including the hood and attempting to fold the flesh back against the outside of the leather, though as the lips were already quite distended, they had acquired almost the resilience of the breasts and therefore would not stay in place, but projected down beneath the smooth surface of the leather, with the gold ring glinting between them.

The whole of this action had been performed with the legs half apart and dangling down. Travix now required the legs out of the way, as the arms were, so that the smooth downcurve of leather-covered belly would be broken only by the projecting bare flesh of the breasts and of the sex lips. Whilst requiring this emphasis on breasts and sex, she also needed the buttocks open, so she had the two men, one on each side, hold the feet lifted and pushed up, so the knees bent in a horizontal plane, and thus the buttocks stayed open for the smacking, which was then administered by one man, while the other held the sex lips nipped, after the girl was gagged with a twisted cloth between her lips, that she might have something on which to bite and that the image might be complete.

Travix leaned casually against the mast and watched for a short while. 'Do not stop until I tell you,' she said. She walked to the side and looked out across the sea – she did not need to watch the whole time, for after the first few smacks, the image was secure within her mind and she could hear the smacks and more importantly, the gasping whimpers through the gag. In fact, she closed her eyes and listened and she could picture the scene – each smack, whipped down upon one or other buttock, making the breasts shake, the belly try to burst down through the leather and the gold ring glint at the sudden downjerk of the hips.

After twenty smacks or so, she returned. 'Do not stop,' she said. 'Bend her knees more tightly – do not lower them. Push her feet up. Good . . .' For the separation now was perfect, two perfect bulging haunches deeply incised by the centre line. She stood beside her lover, stroking her hair and touching her nipples, wetting her fingers first, then watching the strap smack down upon the bright red cheeks. 'Smack her in the split,' she said and, when the girl whimpered, Travix held her head and pressed the girl's cheek against her pale blue thigh. 'Enough,' she said. 'Tie her ankles here. Leave her. Stand back.' The ankles were crossed below the sling and fastened to the rope. The split between the cheeks of her buttocks lay open. Travix touched it at her leisure. She expressed her love by touching the distended mouth, which felt hot to Travix's cool fingers, by listening to the sobbing sounds, by reaching beneath and pulling the ring, then feeling the swollen lips that lay trapped in the slit in the leather, nipping them, flicking them gently, painting them with their wetness and leaving them to dry. While they dried, she kneaded the knotted muscles of the arms and shoulders, the back, the buttocks and legs. Then she took a thin cloth ribbon, about as long as her hand and, crouching down, fed it through the gold ring so it made two equal lengths which she knotted at the ring then twisted to make a short rope which she knotted again at the end. It hung down, curling slightly, for it was as yet dry. She wetted the sex lips once more with their seepage, applying a tiny droplet to this ribbon rope. Immediately, it was absorbed. She called to the men. She laid her hand across her lover about half way down her buttocks. 'Smack between here,' she said, 'and here,' and she laid her other hand in turn across the middle of the back of each thigh. 'And do not forget here.' And she opened the cheeks to indicate the precise place. 'When you are finished, sling her beneath the bowsprit. I will attend to her later.'

'How many lashes?' asked one of the men.

'You see this?' she drew her fingers down the short twisted cloth rope. 'Smack until this is wet to the very tip.'

Travix bent down and stroked her lover's sweat-drenched brow, then kissed her, licking the tip of her tongue along the hot dry lips so sweetly separated by the gag, to wet them. She closed her teeth about the upper lip and bit it till it yielded blood. Then she pressed the breasts together until the nipples touched. 'Do not smack these,' she warned him. 'These baubles are for me.'

When the first canoes passed beneath her and nudged up to the hull of the ship, Anya, gagged and unable to move, was

214

unseen. Even had she been seen, she might well have remained unrecognised as a living creature. With her breasts poking out, glowing in the evening light, she had assumed the likeness of an exotic, exquisitely carved, life-size figurehead.

[14]

Chickens to the Rescue

Travix quietly closed her cabin door, then walked across to the bed. Niri lay belly down beneath the covers, her cheek upon the pillow, breathing gently in her sleep. The blonde girl was awake. Her eyes – so clear and bright – had followed Travix from the moment she had entered; those eyes, so impish, seemed to know no fear. Travix looked upon them now; she looked upon the pouted lips – so red – the eyebrows, matt black as starless night, and the curling twisted strands of sunstreaked blonde hair that lay with such sweet abandon on the pillow. Gently, Travix drew the covers back and watched the pair of smooth bodies, the fair-skinned belly beside the small tight bronze-skinned buttocks. Below their feet and lying where they had been kicked away, were a plaited belt and the effigy of an erect cockstem fashioned from polished bone. Travix lifted the cockstem by the ballocks and pushed it safely beneath Niri's pillow. Then, looking at the blonde girl, she brushed her fingertip all the way down Niri's deeply recessed and very flexible spine, to the very tip. The legs automatically moved apart, though Niri was asleep. The fingertip slipped into the groove, gliding back and forth across the bronze-purple mouth which felt like brushed satin. Travix tickled this place, not taking her eyes from the blonde girl's face, until the blonde girl's cheek moved back across the pillow, her neck arched to make a curve as smooth as alabaster, her eyes half closed and her tongue pushed out through lips that formed an 'o' – by which time, Travix felt a desire so deeply in her belly that it hurt, and Niri was awake.

Travix lifted Niri easily – she was light. And though Niri protested faintly to be used so soon again in that way, Travix carried her across to the large circular mirror, but did not put

216

her down. While Niri's toes writhed and reached and sometimes touched the glass itself as she struggled to keep her legs
wide open and her sex agape, Travix held her round the waist
and in reflection, watched her fingers caress the small bare
painted lips and moisten them and slip inside the gape.

Without releasing the girl, Travix lifted a small cushion on
to the dressing-table top. She placed Niri's back upon this
cushion. Her feet, upraised, lay pressed against the glass, so it
now appeared that two Niris touched each other, toe to toe.
Niri's head fell back; her hair hung down from the edge and
touched the floor. From the drawer to the right, Travix
removed the heavy gold cylinder and unsheathed it from its
blue silk glove. The cylinder was flat at one end and necked
to form a bulb at the other. Niri's belly became tight. Travix
whispered but Niri knew to open her legs – her small toes
crawled up and out across the surface of the glass. Travix
worked in reflection; she applied the blue ointment to the
small brown-purple mouth, then she pressed the bulbed end
against it, rolling it like a ball, not wishing to rush it, for the
bulb was large, and Niri of course was small. But her patience
was rewarded; Niri opened and took it to the neck. Travix
rocked the cylinder, which rolled the bulb in Niri's body; then
she slipped it deeper, past the neck and Niri, though she
murmured, distended quite sufficiently to take it. Then Travix
pushed Niri, on her cushion, closer to the mirror, until the flat
end of the cylinder touched it. And now it appeared that the
two Niris were joined together by a single cylinder of gold.
With Niri in this precariously balanced position, Travix traced
her fingertips over the delicate patterns inked into the smooth
lips of that sex, until she heard a murmur from behind her.

Looking across, she saw the blonde girl lying on her side.
She was waiting, her small oval belly pushed out, her
pink-tipped nipples brushing against the sheet and her hand
caressing the ballocks of the bone cockstem which she kept
teasing from beneath the pillow next to her. When the cap
emerged, she released the ballocks and looked at Travix with
wanton eyes; then her body wriggled like a snake across the
surface of the sheet until the cap was captured in her mouth
and her pouted lips slowly began to swallow.

Travix left Niri and walked back to the bed. She watched the perfect body – wrists clasped together behind her back – arching diagonally across the sheet, with the white stem now buried to the ballocks between those impudent full red lips. Bending forwards, Travix touched the strands of twisted hair that lay across the cheek, then raised them to her lips and kissed them. They felt cool and silky. She could smell the scent of Niri on the ballocks of the stem. It excited her. This blonde girl excited her far more. She wanted her on the sheepskin, with its smooth slippy curls against the girl's breasts and belly and naked thighs, for the girl was shaved now and Travix had found she preferred her that way. She swept the coverlet away and spread the sheepskin on the bed. The girl rolled aside, then back again, face down, one leg drawn up in readiness. Travix stood up, slowly unbuttoned her tunic top, then removed it quickly. Her large tight breasts protruded proudly above her very narrow waist.

Then Travix heard a sound – a splash to starboard. It seemed out of place. She went to the window and drew aside the curtain. Night was fast approaching. The water seemed calm and the mist had lifted. She could see the entrance to the lagoon that they had sailed past that first day without ever noticing in their haste. A whole village, they had missed. But tomorrow they would take it. Tomorrow, the slave deck would be filled and Travix would be busy. Tonight, she could relax. She thought again of the Princess. Then she looked across and saw the blonde girl sitting up, reflected above Niri in the mirror of her dressing table, and again the feeling came so strongly in her belly that it hurt.

Suddenly Travix was beside the bed. The girl, kneeling now, tensed, then realising, pushed her belly outwards for Travix to kiss. She held her arms up, exposing herself fully for Travix's lips to explore the skin of her belly and breasts and underarms. She pushed her belly down, spreading her thighs, so the soft waxy curls of the sheepskin kissed the sex that Travix had shaved to make it so sensitive to the kissing and to the touch of Travix's nipples. The creamy yellow curls brushed coolly against her bare sex lips. Travix stroked the skin that she had shaved. She pressed her thumbs to the sides of those lips to

218

split them open and to allow the creamy curls inside. She left the girl in that position of delicious wantonness, with her legs splayed and her open pink lips bedecked and tickled with yellow waxy curlicues, while she picked up the cockstem and gradually smoothed spittle round the plum. She eased the girl's hips up, placed the plum between the soft bare lips, pushed back, then up and in, then held it with her fingers cupped beneath the ballocks. She turned the girl then watched through the gap beneath the pink cheeks of the buttocks as her fingertips slowly lifted and the fleshpot steadily swallowed the pure white stem. And she held the cheeks open, that she might watch the small pink mouth gently gulping in sympathy with the sex lips until they had sunk down and spread about the top of the bag. Then she lowered the hips until the ballocks rested on the sheepskin. She pushed the girl forwards until her bottom lifted and she rubbed her hand from side to side across it. It caused the ballocks to appear to sway and the cock itself gradually to slip while the wet lips tried to squeeze to keep it in. Each squeeze resulted in a tight contraction of the small pink mouth, which Travix then would stroke to force another contraction. When she looked underneath, she could see that where the lips were split about the stem, the tiny bud projected red from the shelter of its hood.

With the cockstem bedded fully home, Travix laid the girl on her back. She crossed her ankles and forced a pillow under her hips to raise the belly and allow the legs to open wider. The twin eggs of the ballocks lay cupped between the pink lips of the naked mound. Travix tasted every inch of shaved skin with her fingers, then her tongue. She laved the whole mound until it was shining wet. Then she took her kitten crop and whipped it – the sides and then the lips that squeezed around the balls. And while she kitten-whipped the lips, she held the hood back and she touched the nubbin with her fingertip. The girl, of course, was whimpering; wet lines traversed her hot flushed cheeks, yet her nubbin was a boiling ball of hardness. Travix whipped again; she held the hood more firmly back and whipped only in the creases and, sure enough, the pleasure was delivered by that means; the contractions induced by the whip strokes on that bare and sensitive skin brought it on. When it came, Travix rubbed the thin and flexible end of the crop against the hot slippery ball and the pleasure continued long; for as long as Travix rubbed, the belly jerked. She carefully withdrew the cockstem and laid it on the bed. Then she wrapped her arms around the girl's waist and placed her head against the belly and rested, her full breasts rubbing between the thighs, while the oily inner warmth continued seeping out of the girl, over Travix's breasts and tickling her nipples. When Travix was quite rested, she turned the girl, penetrated her bottom with her tongue and with her fingers cupped her sex. The tongue pushed deep and the girl began to writhe. Travix spread the legs, spread the sex lips to the sheepskin, spread the cheeks of the bottom wide, removed her tongue and whipped the crop down into the groove. When the fleshy ring stood out contused, she licked it very gently and slipped the crop between the legs and swept it back and forth again across the nubbin until the pleasure came. Then Travix bit the girl's bottom, sucked it, turned her over, bit her belly, bit her breasts and neck and having thus branded her with her teethmarks, covered her with the sheepskin, offered her severed lip for the girl to kiss, then held her, whispering words of tenderness, until the girl fell asleep.

Travix put on her tunic top. It was time to attend to Niri. She removed her from the dressing-table. And though Niri murmured, knowing what was going to happen, still Travix was kind to her. She caressed her first – there was a faint spark of that first love there yet for Niri – then she made her kneel on the carpet. She tied her wrists to the leg of the bed; she pressed her forehead to the floor. She tucked her knees up until her sex pushed out behind her, then she pushed the gold cylinder steadily into her until it had disappeared. When she slid her fingers beneath and into Niri's sex, she could feel it, weighted down inside her; she could lift it on her fingertips, then feel it sink back down. She withdrew her fingers, teased the ring out and whipped the sex lips with the greenstick crop. And she knew how much to whip – she whipped until the lips had puffed up to the extent that the ring could not be seen. Then she whispered to Niri that she loved her and she sealed that love by drawing the ring out again and passing through it a long pure gold rod, perfectly straight, which pressed across the backs of Niri's thighs yet, secured as it was through the ring, prevented Niri from straightening her legs to withdraw her flesh from between them. Her sex would be forced to remain pushed out for as long as Travix might choose to leave her tied. It was cruel to Niri, for sure, to leave her tethered for the rest of the evening; but it brought a kind of satisfaction to Travix to use her in this way. And later, she would play with Niri in this position – wet her sex, probably penetrate her, bring her pleasure on in some way, then release her, and Niri would be grateful.

Travix left her for the present, tucked the cockstem in her belt and stepped out of the cabin. She hesitated at the foot of the stairs. Her face, illuminated in the flickering lamplight, looked intent yet peculiarly beautiful. She was thinking of her lovers; they were thinking of her, she knew. But she was unaware of the silent swarm of women who, at that very moment, were creeping like spiders up the side of the ship and sweeping out across the deck to parcel up the watch like dozing flies. And because she set off up the stairs, she was also unavailable to receive the Prince of Lidir when, some minutes later, he and Ikahiti broke into her room, only to be greeted by a blonde girl spitting fire at them – especially at him – and to find the long-lost Aka-lisha tied up on the floor.

Anya opened her eyes; somehow, she had fallen asleep, but the low whistling sounds had woken her. There were people running on the deck behind her, but she could not move; it hurt to turn her head. She thought at first that it was dawn and she had slept all night, but she could only have dozed, for though the sun hung low, it was evening. Her breasts ached, her wrists and feet were numb and searing pains stabbed through her shoulders. She stared down at the water far below. The fish were there, the ones she had seen on that first day. But they seemed larger and more sinister in the failing light; their bodies formed dark streamlined shapes below the water and there were three of them at least; she saw now that they had but one wing on their backs and it seemed small in

221

proportion to their bodies. They seemed to slink through the water in interlacing sinuous patterns, as if searching for something that eluded them. For the first time, she felt afraid of the water that she had come to think of as her friend. She wanted to cry out – to plead to be released and stand again on solid ground – but she was gagged.

Then she saw three boats to seaward, like tiny slivers of gold in the evening light. Two more appeared to landward, not fifty feet away, and she knew then what the sounds on deck must be. Other boats must have passed beneath her while she was asleep. Her heart surged – the islanders were attacking; the great ship was beset. Over the next few minutes, wave upon wave of these boats appeared, moving very quickly. Yet nobody had seen her; the boats slid past and Anya could do nothing. But if they had not seen her from below, how would they ever see her at all? Slung below the bowsprit, she would never be noticed by anyone from above. She hung there, listening as the noise appeared to spread to below deck; then there were cries above her, from the men; they sounded as though they were up in the rigging. And there was laughter – women's voices amid the cries – the attackers must be winning.

With a yell, one man fell past her into the water, then another. They floundered and shouted down below – perhaps they could not swim? Then suddenly, it mattered not whether they could swim or not: there was a swift movement – the dark shapes swept across beneath the surface and both men were gone. It was as if they had never existed. She blinked and now the fish were nowhere to be seen. Anya's fear had turned to terror. How had they moved so fast? How had they known the men were in the water? The ship lifted very slightly on the swell, the ropes that fastened her to the bowsprit creaked and the fine hairs stood up on the back of Anya's neck. Then she heard sounds of a scuffle behind her; the bowsprit began to vibrate and the hairs on Anya's neck stood even stiffer. There was a clash of metal, a thud, a scream then a voice, crying: 'Stand back!' then a chopping sound as of a sword biting into wood, then the voice again, harassed yet defiant. 'Stand back – or I feed your precious Princess to the sharks!'

And Anya's eyes, already wide with fear, grew large as dinner plates.

Travix stood on the bowsprit, the broad blade in her hand. The island women formed a half-ring before her. The one she had disarmed lay on the deck, groaning and retching from the punch that had felled her. Travix could not escape; she knew that; she knew the ship was taken. One boat had got away; the captain had not taken her.

In the centre of the ring, above the woman on the floor, stood the Prince of Lidir, ashen-faced, with Niri under his arm. Behind him, the remaining pirates were being herded to the deck by his lieutenant and his men. The ones in the rigging were being allowed to come down to be spread-eagled on the deck and tied. Cautiously, the Prince put Niri down. 'Keep back,' warned Travix. 'Put down your sword.' She crouched above the tethered Princess. The Prince had little choice; he obeyed. 'Now back away.' His eyes had narrowed down to slits. 'Niri . . .' whispered Travix, and Niri's dark eyes widened momentarily before she looked away. Travix smiled. And when the Prince looked down at Niri, Travix saw the scratches furrowed in his cheek. That gave her cause for satisfaction too. She saw the blonde girl in the background, struggling with a native woman of great beauty, but greater strength. The woman carried a whip. Travix smiled again; she found the match appropriate. She looked again at the one who must be the Prince. He had bearing, it was true, but no strength. She despised him for that. He was fighting back the tears; his heart was thumping, Travix knew, but hers was steady – though she faced this horde of weaklings who surely wished her dead.

'I should have finished you long ago,' she said to him, 'but I will finish you now.' She kissed the blade. 'I salute you, in your weakness, Sire. And this fitting gift to a frail heart, I bequeath.' And the blade flashed down and cut the rope that tethered Anya's feet to the spar. Her body dropped like a stone and swung. The Prince screamed, 'No!' ran forwards, then stopped, for Travix had moved quickly. She was balanced out above Anya with the blade poised to cut through the one remaining rope. Each time he made a move, the blade threatened to slide across it.

'I can cut this before you reach me,' said Travix. 'If you do not think so, try it.'

'Yield,' cried he in desperation. 'You cannot get away. Yield to me now and you will be spared. I promise.'

Travix laughed. She twisted the dangling body round, so the Prince and Princess were face to face and Travix could see the Princess's terror reflected in his eyes. Then she pronounced sentence. 'You are weak – a coward. A stronger man would have taken her back by now; a stronger man would not have let her go.' And then her expression changed: it seemed that some terrible haunting vision was written on her face. Her head lifted defiantly against it. But her next words were distant and spoken slowly, as if by someone else. 'Perhaps I can yield to you this one service – with this cut, perhaps I can teach you strength.' And she turned her cheek – the scarred, disfigured cheek – and smiled again, even as the blade chopped down. A single strand remained. 'And now, my lord, I fear it is too late.'

The cry came – a terrible cry – and it momentarily stayed her hand, for it was not the cry she had expected.

From behind the Prince, a small man carrying a large wicker box appeared through the hatch, pursued by several women. He tripped; the box burst open and chickens spilled and sprawled and skittered across the deck. In the turmoil, Travix moved to make the fatal cut. Before the blade had touched the strand, the Prince had dropped; his sword was flung. It should have passed straight through her heart; but instead, it was deflected by an airborne chicken, which plummeted into the sea. Travix jumped up, laughing. There was a swish. She looked down to see the whipcord wrapped around her ankle, then looked up to see the beautiful woman, and there was nothing she could do. Ikahiti tugged; when she was sure the woman's balance was broken, she threw the handle of the whip after her, then watched her disappear, watched the water fleetingly churn, then still.

The Prince ran out on to the spar; when he reached for his Princess, the strand broke, her hands slipped through his fingers and a hammer blow smashed through his heart. She dropped like a spear through the air and into the water. The screams

224

of the islanders, he ignored. He did not hear them. He hardly even saw the canoes. All he saw were the dark shapes in the water, and he dived.

He could not reach her; she kept slipping smoothly, endlessly down. He had to fight against the buoyancy the giant gulp of breath had given him. Then he was hit by a shark. Its head lifted as a dozen spears struck into its back and it knocked the breath from his body; for a second he floated in velvet blackness.

He opened his eyes to find himself in the large canoe, surrounded by the women. 'Where is she? Where!' he cried. But she was not there. They held him back, held him down. '*Nika, shiru,*' they said gently, but he could see it in their eyes. The women around him were wet; the water droplets were gathered on their skin. How long had he been unconscious? A woman surfaced beside the canoe; another woman dived. He screamed, knocked his comforters away and dragged himself to the side. The water was black; there was a black impenetrability there. He looked at the women; the expressions in their eyes – the way they looked at him – spoke a terrible sadness. A haunting quiet had fallen. He counted the seconds; he listened; he looked into the black. How could she live? Her hands and feet were tied. The diver surfaced, shook her head. And he was in the water again, diving into blackness, reaching out, shouting under water, then choking, surfacing and banging his head against the boat. The arms reached out to grab him and he fought them, screamed. Then everybody suddenly stopped. He wiped the water from his face and turned. She was there; but she was dead; no life was in that body being hauled into the canoe opposite.

He swam across but he had not the strength to climb aboard and nobody would help him. When the gag was removed, her head lolled back. Her lifeless body was thumped and slapped and turned and pummelled. Then there was total silence as they listened; there came more thumps, followed by agitated chatter. The women crowded closer; there were several quick slaps in succession, then excited cries, then hush. One of the women was kissing her. And in that hush and amid those kisses, he heard her choke and it was the sweetest sound he had ever heard. In a second he was aboard and beside her. And he was afraid – he was a coward; his eyes filled up with tears and he was too frightened to touch her for fear that that frail gift of life should even now be taken away – for fear that she should be snatched away from him forever.

She lay in the broad bottom of the boat. Her eyes were closed, but she was breathing. Her nose was streaming. Beside her lay a stunned and sodden chicken that blinked in mild bewilderment and clucked with faint concern.

[15]

Firebrands of Passion

No bodies were given up by the sea. The boat in which the captain had escaped was washed ashore, capsized next day and its occupants were never found. That night, Anya and her Prince stayed aboard the ship, though the islanders had wanted them ashore. The pirates had been taken in ropes and chains and their slaves had been freed; some of them had gone with the island men. The blonde girl had remained with Ikahiti; she had hardly left her side since the fatal incident on deck. Anya had interceded on Ratchitt's behalf. In the end, he had been freed and Miriri had taken him under her wing. Anya saw them several days later; they made a handsome pair. The Prince's crew had survived the wreck and the journey overland and were now distributed equally between the island and the ship, with plans afoot for stocking her for the long voyage home. Anya had mixed feelings about this trip; there were people here who had shown her great kindness and consideration. She felt a warmth for many of them – Miriri, Ikahiti, the younger girls and, it had to be admitted, even one of the men.

There was a strange irony in the fact that she slept that night in Travix's cabin. The terrible events of that day – the whippings, harsh pleasures, pain and ultimately the deaths – were dissolved in the warm security that she felt in her Prince's arms. He had followed her relentlessly across the ocean in a ship stripped bare of provisions, then he had battled through the jungle, across the mountains, and he had dived to almost certain death to try to save her. She would never forget his expression when the cord had snapped and she had fallen; and when she had opened her eyes again he was there beside her in the boat. She snuggled up against him now. He had not

227

tried to take her, though she could feel his strength of hardness pressed against her back. She took his hand and held it to her belly and his other hand and held it to her breast. She tensed when his fingertips moved down. With butterflies in her belly, she opened her legs and directed his fingers to the ring; she allowed him to explore it. The feeling was strange and frightening. She listened to his breathing: how would he react? When he turned her to examine her, Anya closed her eyes.

He could see the marks of the strap upon her body; she had been thrashed with a leather belt. He touched her very gently and she murmured – and he saw that her sweet full lips had been bitten in a cruel kiss; the upper lip was swollen and at the corner was a spot of blood. Her breasts showed broad criss-cross bands; when he touched them, he felt the raised contusions there – even her breasts had been punished. He showered them with gentle kisses; he sucked the hard distended nipples, then he looked down at her belly. It formed a perfect rounded swell of pink, punctured by the deep dark oval navel. Faint lines of deeper pink traversed it; they became deeper, darker, more crowded, angrier yet across her lower belly; they were dense across the front of her upper thighs, then they weakened lower down. She had been smacked only in those places that deserved nothing but gentle kisses. What manner of mind would execute such wicked tortures upon a creature of perfect beauty such as this? She murmured again when he opened her thighs, but the Prince gasped, not at the ring, but at the fine lines – whip marks – lashed into her tender skin and the wicked dark oval stains imbued into the sides of her sex. Her flesh looked as though it had been gripped between iron tongues and squeezed until it was bruised. She whimpered softly when his fingertips touched that very tender skin, and the small gold ring stirred. He knew what that tiny movement meant, but he also knew that he must show his lover tenderness and concern.

And so it was that the Prince of Lidir slept not at all that night but knelt or sat beside his lover, watching over her while she slept intermittently and he caressed her back, her belly, her breasts and legs and lips, stroking the wiry curls about her sex until they turned to silk, stroking the fine down upon her bottom, continually tickling her skin until her expression had softened, until even in her sleep she smiled. For the Prince, a task such as this was both sweet and taxing, for every time he even touched her skin, his cockstem stood up hard. This was the effect she had upon him. Even in sleep, her body exuded a continuous sensuality – in the way she moved, even in the way she breathed, the way she would place her breasts against the sheets whenever her body turned, the way her thighs would gradually open when his fingertips approached, the way she would become aroused then, half awake, would direct his fingertips into her and push herself against him. And in the middle of the night, the long slow liquid pleasuring would begin.

Her slim thighs would be spread deliciously wide, so wide that her mound would form a perfect bulge, which would be moving as her belly moved, as her bottom lifted and slid across the sheets. His fingers would be sliding against the warm soapy wetness, pressing against the inside of the front of her sex, which felt like the curve of a soft nose. And when she gasped, the feeling would well inside him, his head would buzz and he would hold her there, his fingers lifted against her, curving inside and he would draw the hood back, expose the ring and suck it. He would rub his tongue-tip round and through it until her belly trembled, then he would take his fingers out of her and, with the hood still held fully back, would gently suck her nipples. Then the hood would be released and the slow wet rub inside her would begin at the back wall, then move to the front. It would be followed by the lifting back of the hood, the suck upon the ring and then the nipples. The rubbing inside her would then be delivered with the legs closed, then open, the hood would now be pinched back harder and the upstanding ring would be licked. She would be turned on to her side with her legs tucked up and squeezed together while her sex was not touched, but the entrance to her bottom was explored with a fingertip and then a tongue. Then the whole process would begin again – the turning on to her back, the opening of her legs, the gliding of her bottom over the sheets, the fingers rubbing inside her sex, the pulling back of the hood, the sucking of a nubbin that was bone hard, the sucking of the nipples and, when she pleaded with him that she could take no more, the placing of a pillow underneath her bottom to lift her hips and open them yet more, and the holding of the hood back while he watched the nubbin moving the ring almost imperceptibly as the tip of his middle finger rubbed inside her. And when he made her curl her head down, lift her breast and suck upon her own left nipple, her pleasure came.

To the Prince, witnessing his lover take her pleasure was as sweet as pleasure itself, and that very forfeit of his own pleasure helped to stave off the guilt that haunted him. For while his lover was being abused and whipped, the Prince, seeking solace after his long journey, had lain in another's arms, and even now, though he looked upon the only woman that he loved, the memories of those strange pleasures inveigled his guilt-ridden mind.

Anya slept soundly, dreaming they were lying on the sun-drenched sand. In the early morning, her thoughts began to drift. She sat up and glanced around the cabin, at the large circular mirror, the stool beside it, the sheepskin draped across the floor, and the whips and a pale blue suit which hung behind the door. She crept across to the dressing-table and looked at herself in the mirror, then she covered her breasts to hide the marks. On the table were a cushion and a brush. She picked up the brush and began to brush her hair. Then she saw that the drawer was partly open. Nervously, she opened it fully; inside was a blue silk sleeve and a soft brushed velvet cloth. When her fingertips touched the cloth, her eyes closed and she shivered. She could feel her pulsebeat thumping in her throat.

Anya quietly closed the drawer and returned to the bed. She looked upon her Prince's sleeping face and the scratch-marks on his cheek; they reminded her of something else – a scar. She touched the single earring, then kissed the lobe and again she shivered. She had wanted to bite it, to draw blood, and that feeling frightened her.

She began to wonder again what fate had befallen him when he had arrived in the village – what the women had done to him and his men as strangers. He had not spoken of their arrival. She examined his body minutely, then gasped. There was a fine red line about his cockstem at the base. He murmured when she touched it. He was tender. What had they done to him? Anya turned him on his side; she placed a pillow beside his belly for her head. Then she kissed his cock and took it in her mouth. She kept it in; she protected it. At intervals she sucked it. She took it slowly, but she brought him on fully; she made him kneel astride the pillow where she lay. She controlled him with her hands cupped about him, pressing up against his belly, pressing gently, while her head lifted and her wet lips pushed – not sucked – but pushed, slow wet pushes which came warmer, wetter, slicker, as his pleasure yielded to her will.

On deck that afternoon, Anya asked about the rescue.

'The young woman – Ikahiti – saw the footprints on the beach, then she found my signet in the sand. She cares for you a great deal. She was a friend?'

'Yes,' said Anya and glanced away. Her hand came to rest on the gilded ropework armband she still wore.

'But she was crying, as if it were her fault.'

Anya bit her lip. 'I must see her – to thank her. We must go ashore.' But the Prince seemed very reluctant. 'What is it?' said Anya.

'I must stay with the ship. I will not lose another.'

'But the ship is safe now. Your men are here.' He stayed silent, so she asked about the wreck.

'We managed to make rafts,' he said. 'We ferried the men and what little we could salvage from the reef to shore. Then we trekked through the mountains.'

'How did you know which way to go?'

'The pirates seemed to be sailing round the island – they never approached the shore. We guessed and headed north. Eventually we came to a river, followed it and the women found us. We were picked off in twos and threes.'

'They . . . they took you to the Princess?'

He would not look at her. 'Kalisha – yes,' he whispered. But she could imagine the rest – the cruel punishments in the clearing, the torturing of his flesh; and she had seen the signs upon his body. But how had he been freed and allowed to lead the rescue?

'They knew we understood ships. None of them had been inside one; they had no knowledge of the layout; no woman who had been taken to a ship had ever come back and I think they were afraid.' As he spoke, there was an intensity in his gaze which surprised her. And there was a hurriedness in his words. The words were spilling out. 'The one you call Niri – that word means something else – she is Aka-lisha; she is the sister to Kalisha. She was taken on another ship. They had given up all hope of seeing her again.' Anya stared at him; he seemed to realise and turned away. She wondered how so much had been communicated when none of the women spoke Lidiran. She should have asked him, but she didn't; something in his expression prevented her.

Late in the afternoon, they went ashore. A boat came for them and it was paddled by two of the painted women, the Princess's guards. Anya was a little anxious; she was still afraid of these women and of the Princess, to whom they were clearly being taken.

But her fears were dispelled when they entered the cave. A large throng had gathered there; there was dancing, singing and feasting; drums and long instruments resembling heavy flutes were being played. There were men – the shackled slaves and also the Prince's men, who were mixing freely with the women, but there were none of the island men. The Princess sat majestically in a great chair before a fire. Tied to the leg of the chair was her slave. She smiled at the Prince while she stroked her slave like a dog. To one side was a smaller chair containing the cat-woman; behind her stood more of the painted women. But to the Princess's right was a woman of great beauty, whom Anya did not recognise until she stood directly opposite her. It was Niri, but gone was the cowering Niri that Anya remembered. Her movements were graceful. She seemed taller. She was dressed in a pure white costume embroidered with shell and gold; her arms bore bangles of fine twisted gold inlaid with sparkling jewels; her hair was polished, tied and pinned. The eyes were the same – wide and very dark – but sedate, no longer frightened. They were looking with admiration at the Prince, who kept glancing at her as if he too did not recognise her.

The Princess stood and there was silence; the dancing stopped while she made a long speech interspersed with many smiles at the Prince, references to Aka-lisha and gestures with her hands – they kept coming to rest against the Prince's arm and then his hands until she finally took his fingers in her own while a wreath of large bright flowers was brought and placed around his neck. Anya watched the smooth pale bronze fingers that were closed about his and she waited for the contact to be broken. She glanced at the Princess, then at Aka-lisha, their faces full of rapture. She felt very uneasy. At last the Prince withdrew his hand and, by gesture, introduced Anya. The Princess smiled at her briefly. Extra chairs were brought; she was placed to the Princess's left and the Prince was placed on the other side, between the Princess and Aka-lisha. Anya was upset to be separated from her Prince and he too seemed unhappy and rather nervous whenever Kalisha addressed him.

Anya had hoped very much to see Ikahiti, but she never appeared and that seemed odd. Then something even more odd happened. She was staring at the fire when something dropped into her lap – a bracelet. She heard a giggle and turned, but could see no one who might have thrown it. When she examined it more closely, she saw it was made of plaited twine. She stared around again, but nobody seemed to have noticed. She toyed with it for a minute, then slipped it over her wrist. She suspected where it might have come from, but she spent a long time wondering what it meant.

When the feasting was done, the Princess offered them the freedom of her quarters and Anya was very relieved when they were able to take their leave. She was still afraid of the Princess; she did not like the way she looked at the Prince or the way she had touched his hand and she believed that the Prince too was afraid. She could see the uncertainty on his face, the reluctance to enter this place, though it was very beautifully decorated. She thought of Kalisha's slave and of the marks she had seen on the Prince and she wished they were aboard the ship. When they had bathed, Anya stretched out on the bed beside her Prince. He was looking at the ceiling.

'What are you thinking, Sire?' she asked. It was a very large bed and Anya had to stretch across it to offer her hand. He took it but did not reply, though when she kissed him, he smiled. 'Is it about the Princess?' Anya asked. The smile faded and the Prince turned away and remembered.

When he closed his eyes, he saw her – her sweet golden body, not decked in royal finery, but naked – so very naked, so very sweetly nude. All that she wore was the small jewelled sword on its chain around her neck, the sword that matched the image on his signet ring. How she had come upon this amulet, he knew not, for he had seen its counterpart only in the Castle of Lidir, yet it was clear that she cherished it deeply. She had kissed it, then she had kissed the seal upon his ring. And on this very bed he had taken her in his arms and touched her nudity, so smooth and bronze and inked with precisely curling patterns. Those perfect lips between her legs had seemed swollen with desire and between them was a curious attachment slipped beneath the hood, a tapering segmented snake fashioned from burnished gold. It was about as long as his little finger and it had slunk with a heavy liquidity each time her body moved. He had held it in his palm as it moved like a living thing; he had felt her naked sex lips touching his skin, brushing the hairs on the back of his hand, while he held this heavy slippy golden thing that flowed with living quickness in his palm and her belly had tightened, sunk, then slowly bulged as her fingertips squeezed her nipples. When he had slipped the flesh sheathing back, he had seen that the snake was fastened by a fine gold wire in such a way that the tiny gold teeth lining its mouth appeared to grip the distending nubbin. He had turned the snake's tail round and used it to tickle this point of attachment till the belly writhed. Then he had opened the lips and fitted the body of the snake between them. He had held her, kissed her and touched those bulging lips until her body had turned to stone and she had shuddered – her lips had trembled against his nipple; the small distended bud in the mouth of the snake had seemed to burst and his fingertips had been covered in warm wetness.

Then he had laid her down and opened her and kissed her, licked the snake, sucked the point of its attachment; he had

234

drunk her warm emissions; then he had lifted the snake and draped it over her naked belly. Her sex had formed an open small soft rubber ring which felt too tight to take him when he entered, yet her legs had opened wide. Her fingertips had slipped between them to coax and tease the head of the snake. Then her legs had wrapped around him to fix his buttocks open. The painted women had approached. He had murmured his faint protest. He had not seen, yet he had felt something firm and round being pushed inside him – like a plug it felt, though it was not. It was a broad gold ring that kept him open – open though he tried to close; open when the Princess squeezed him, pushed her small warm tongue into his mouth, then pinched his nipples; open when her urgent fingers wrapped the cord around him; open when the women slipped the heavy cold sliding flexible thing up through the ring. And when it weighed against him deep inside, then it was twisted, so the weight moved and the coldness touched again, his pleasure came, though with the cord fastened and now nipped tight, the pleasure could not escape and he felt that deep inside him, he had burst. Yet the Princess kept moving, kept him open with her legs around his and her sex softly sucking upon his stem while her small tongue continued to explore his gasping lips and her neat round breasts and precisely pointed nipples gently rubbed against his chest. Then later, when he had felt the pleasure coming the second time, she had held him down and pinched his nose between her heels while she had dangled the snake attached to her sex inside his open mouth. She had bound the cord around him again and kissed his cockhead slowly and wetly and the pleasure had seemed to burst behind his eyes.

But how had he allowed himself to do it? To come so far to seek one woman, only to end up in another's arms? And afterwards, he had not had the courage to face the woman he was supposed to have loved – he had sent the ring with Ikahiti – and he had almost lost Anya for good. She had nearly died.

He felt her fingertips stroking his shoulders now. And from her words, it seemed to him she sensed his anguish.

'My lord. Think not of her – of the cruel things she did – think only of me,' Anya whispered. He turned and kissed her

235

full warm lips; he tasted there the warmth of a forgiveness that he needed. He felt the stirrings of desire. And very soon his desire would burn, for though neither knew it, his atonement was at hand.

Ikahiti and the blonde girl swooped into the bedchamber; the attack was planned, the execution was smooth. Before he knew what had befallen, his wrists were tied above his head, the rope was fastened down and he was gagged. Anya recognised the posture; she saw the glint in the blonde girl's eye. Ikahiti put her finger to Anya's lips, then kissed them. Anya, not knowing what to do, glanced across to the Prince, then back. Her heart was thumping. Ikahiti touched the knotted rope round Anya's arm, smiled, then kissed her again. She began kissing down her body. Her nipples were gently sucked. Then she felt her ankles being drawn down the bed. It was too late now; Anya had succumbed. She would not need to give her thanks to Ikahiti – Ikahiti would take those thanks in kind. Anya's thumbs were tied together; small leather cuffs were slipped about each big toe; the cords were tightened; the feeling was sweet. Her nipples were sucked again, then pinched; tiny cuffs were slipped about them too. Cords were fastened around each leg at the top. The ends were fastened loosely to the ring between her legs and the feeling now was awful; the loose loops brushed her sex lips when she moved. She was aware of each constriction – her toes, her nipples, the tops of her legs and the ring that seemed to nip her swelling nubbin. Her arms were lifted to form an arch above her head. Her underarms were kissed simultaneously; two pairs of lips explored her, one pair warmer, thicker, softer, brown, the other more tickling, pink. Then her underarms were wetted with saliva, bathed until they dripped, until the hair slicked down in deep red shining swirls.

And the Prince, tied and gagged, was forced to watch his lover being pleasured at his side. He was forced to watch her body caressed by eyes which were wide and deep with love, and her flesh being teased by lips and tongues and fingers that were ruthless. Her lips were kissed – deep sucking kisses which she returned – while her legs were held open, the cords between were readjusted, traced by two pale fingers, then her upper thighs were tickled. When the cuffs about her nipples were tightened, the sides of her sex – the places that were bruised – were wetted with the point of a small pink tongue. Her feet were lifted in the air; then the sides of her sex were tongue-washed until the strands of hair were plastered down in narrow lines and the sex looked almost bare. Then the cords of the cuffs about her big toes were tied together. She was left thus, her hands above her head, her legs tucked up, the wetness evaporating slowly from her underarms and the tender bare flesh at the sides of her sex, while her lover was taken in hand and spanked – a task which fell to the blonde girl, who blamed him for many things not entirely of his doing, whilst giving him insufficient credit for having introduced her to Ikahiti.

Before she spanked, she touched the scratchmarks she had yesterday ingrained into his cheeks, knowing there would be marks ingrained elsewhere ere long. Then she removed the gag and placed loosely over his mouth and nose a soft brushed-velvet cloth, one of several mementos recovered that evening in a secret pillage of the ship. His legs were free: he could have struggled, not then perhaps, when the touch was tender, but later when the pleasure and pain were one. But his legs and belly remained still, acquiescent to her will. Perhaps he conceded it as part of his atonement. Perhaps there was simply a peculiar pleasure for a Prince in such a situation; perhaps he had never been used in quite this way before. Perhaps pleasure was not the right word, for the way that she smacked was cruel. She had had a good instructress.

She knelt astride him so his upstanding sex rested against her lower belly and, from behind, he could see her buttocks moving, but he could not see what she was doing. She wetted the underside of his stem with spittle at the place where it joined the bag. She concentrated the rubbing around the soft thick tube within. Then she held the sex up against her belly, so the cap was poised below the hollow of her navel. Her caresses were deceptive. She lifted up the bag and pressed his legs together. Then she moved back. Her bare and faintly bristled sex brushed over his belly and the cock slipped down, but not completely, for it was hard. He saw her buttocks open, the small eye peep, then the hands lift to remove a leather choker that was fastened at her neck. She used it as a strap. At the first smack, he tried to lift, but could not, for Ikahiti held his feet. At the second, he tried to cry out, but the girl reached back and stretched the velvet over his open mouth. All that he could smell was female heat; the cloth was steeped in it; his burning breath released it. At the third smack, the buttocks above him moved back and deliberately opened wider. The bare sex felt as hot as fire against his chest. He could feel her wetted fingertips caressing the tip of his cock, rubbing smoothly, slipping, pleasuring him slowly; then suddenly, the next smack came and his belly tried to throw her in the air. His head jerked, the velvet fell away and as he gulped for air, he could smell her.

But it was as if a burning brand was placed across him where his cockstem joined his bag; and now she kept smacking in that one place as her bottom edged closer towards his bare lips, as her fingertips smoothed his cockhead – small soft fingers rubbing gentle wet circles around the underside of the plum, then lifting the bag, spreading it, holding his tip in place for the smacking, then touching the burning tubes inside him – numb at first, then prickling with heat – then rubbing the inch-wide band of bright red skin that formed a half collar round the base. And all this time, the skin of his bag softened, yielded and spread until the shapes of the bumps inside were clear and could be tested individually while the head of his cock was sucked, the small pink eye of the buttocks nudged against his chin and her scent came even stronger in his nostrils.

Then the smacking was repeated with his legs open, his ballocks lifted and Ikahiti taking over the leather band. She used it as a whip upon the place where the seam of skin extended down into the groove between his buttocks, while the blonde girl sat and opened herself upon his lips and kissed them with her bottom. She bathed his cheeks and lips and nose with her heat – not the heat of her sex, but the heat of her bottom – while she kept the tip of the cock collared with her thumb and finger, wetted to make them slip, and Ikahiti smacked the hard smooth flesh below the bag until that flesh was taut and red, as if below the skin was a curved iron bar that stiffened their victim from his cocktip to his bottom. Then the leather band was passed back to the blonde girl. Ikahiti's fingers pushed inside the Prince and lifted, kept the pressure up against that sensitive place, while the blonde girl held the end of his cock in a lightly closed palm, with her thumb rubbing gently back and forth upon the undersurface, and the thin leather band whipped down – at the base again, falling sometimes on the tube within and causing it to pulse, falling sometimes on the cords inside that fed into his ballocks and, when his bag was gathered in Ikahiti's free hand and held, falling sometimes to the sides. And curiously, it was the smacking of the sides – between his legs, next to his ballocks, close to the creases – that almost brought him on, while Ikahiti's fingertips maintained that upward pressure inside as a gentle urging against the root zone of his stem. When they were satisfied that his excitement was aroused to the brink of coming, they collared his cockstem at the base and at the plum with two soft leather cuffs and tied his legs together at the ankles and the knees, then gagged him with the velvet but turned him that he might see his true love's face when her pleasure was delivered.

Anya's thumbs were untied; the cuffs about her nipples and toes were released, the cords about her thighs were freed and every place that had been constricted was sucked – her toes alternately, and her thumbs, then her nipples and, in stages, the complete circumference of the tops of her thighs. Then with Ikahiti positioned at her front and the blonde girl at her back, she was touched inside; the fingers entered gently; her inner wet was bathed about her sex and belly. It was tasted, it was smeared about her bottom, then she was sucked at the back and at the front. The tongues slipped into her alternately. When she began coming on, the suction at the front was stopped. Her leg was lifted that her man might see her belly tremble while the small tongue continued slipping into her from behind. Her nipples were worked with fingers previously wetted inside her sex; her belly was rubbed then licked, then her sex was sucked again until the trembles came once more. And so her pleasure continued; the women changed places; the lips and tongues were replaced by fingers when the pleasure came too strongly and her inner wet was gradually distributed

239

over her upper thighs, into the groove of her bottom and over her belly until the animal smell of heat and the sour sweet smell of spittle hung upon the air and her pleasure was at last delivered with her toes curling up so tightly that they cramped. And that pleasure was delivered by the lightest touch of Ikahiti's tongue, licking the base of the ring. It was the last time that Ikahiti ever touched her. The blonde girl slipped a plaited cord about her belly and the women left.

Anya reached to untie her Prince, then hesitated: the women had left several things on the bed. She recognised two of them straight away – a thin leather bandage and a small round pebble. The other two items were new to her – one was an ornament, a very heavy gold snake, and the other was a large gold ring. When she touched the snake, it moved; it was segmented. She shuddered. It reminded her of the creatures in the pool. She looked at the Prince – he was turned on his side. Then she saw the velvet gag and realised what it was. When she touched it, a buzzing came in her ears and a churning in her belly.

Anya stroked her Prince, then untied his legs and took the collars from his stem. She picked up the snake; its body thickened only slightly at its head, which was about as wide as the ring. She examined the ring itself; it was more like a collar which flared out at each end. Suddenly, Anya knew and again she experienced the feeling that had come upon her that morning when she had seen her Prince defencelessly asleep and she had wanted to bite his earlobe until it bled. But now that feeling did not frighten her. She felt warm in her belly and excited. She snuggled up to him, wetted the ring and held his hot bare cockstem in her hand. When she pushed him over on to his belly and he watched her wet the ring again, she heard him murmur. But again she felt the warmth inside.

The entrance was tight. 'Shh . . .' she whispered, 'Shhh . . .' to reassure him. But she worked the short gold tube into him until it stayed in place, holding the muscle open, however much he might subsequently tighten, and tighten he surely did when the thick gold flexible snake was slipped inside the entrance, through the ring. She made him kneel with his head down and his bottom in the air, in the way she had seen Ikahiti do with her slave. 'To make you more accessible to this pleasure,' said she, for she meant to take her time. She collared the tube and slid the outer skin to draw it tight. His ballocks hung down; the bag was loose from the warmth of his exertions; the fingertips of her other hand could support the bag and sink into the softness of its skin and she could feel the bumps moving inside him. They felt so vulnerable when she squeezed them. And every so often, the heavy gold snake could be fed a little deeper, drawn by gravity and the contractions deep within him which the slow milking of his cockstem would induce. Anya held the bag and kept sliding the tube of skin until the thick droplet of milt appeared. As always, she tried to control this droplet, extending the stimulation to his belly and his nipples, brushing the soft hairs of the backs of her hands and forearms gently across his skin, then taking the ballocks in her mouth and sucking, then rubbing the bridging flesh below the ring, then when the droplet had thickened and welled to the point of detachment, initiating that detachment by edging his thighs wider yet apart, tickling the tip of his spine and taking the tail of the snake – the only part now visible – and gently twisting, then watching the powerful painful contraction against the unmoving metal ring as the droplet began to sink down smoothly on a thread of crystal silk. She caught it on her fingertip, lifted the gossamer thread back up and spun it round the plum. Then she tasted the seepage on her finger. On this occasion, she would not allow herself to taste the fullness of the final pulse. She would draw it but it would not be permitted to emerge. That trapping of his fluid deep inside would surely hurt him. It caused a shiver in her belly – that this kind of pleasure would hurt him. It was a wrongful thing to do to him, she knew. But on this occasion, she would do it anyway.

She rubbed him gently up to dripping point again, then took the stone and pressed it very firmly to the base of the stem, in the way she had seen the women do to their captives, closing the tube then sealing it with the leather bandage. Then she sucked the silky liquid that remained within the stem. She removed his gag, placing it carefully aside, then slipped under him, between his legs and let him suck her. In fact she forced him to suck her, holding his head against her. And she pushed the cockstem with her lips, kept pushing the wet cup of her lips against it until the welling tension came and she felt his body start to tremble. Then she pressed her hand against his belly and slid the snake out, completely out, though very slowly, so the pleasure would not erupt inside, and she pushed her lips against his cocktip at intervals to keep the feeling keen. She slipped her middle finger through the ring and into him and touched him from inside, kept stroking him, then tapping against that hard front wall as her mouth slipped slowly down to engulf the remainder of stem until his thick plum filled her throat and she could not breathe. When she felt him shudder, she kept her mouth very still while the pad of her middle finger rubbed, or rather rolled, like a small ball of pressure inside him, rocking against him, causing everything to explode, causing the pressure of the milt inside him to force a pain that was exquisite while the cruel sweet lips stayed tightly closed around the leather band, sealing him completely. And throughout these long and harsh contractions, the warm sweet body below him kept brushing against his naked skin and her warm wet sex kept kissing its soft thick lips into his open mouth. Here was a woman he could surely die for; in fact he almost had — he felt as if he had burst completely open, deep inside.

Anya slithered out from under him. She was satisfied, for the present. She removed the instruments of torture and lay beside him, kissing his face and neck and nipples. She kissed the earlobe with the ring and nipped it with her teeth and sucked it until she tasted blood. She untied his hands, then lay behind him with her breasts and belly pressed against his back and took his stem in the soft brushed velvet cloth and gently held it in her hand. When he fell asleep, she drew the covers over them, but continued to touch him while he slumbered.

A short time later, a strange incident befell. The Princess came quietly into the room and she crept up to the bed. Anya pretended to be asleep but saw Kalisha stroke the Prince's skin, then slip her fingers under his chin and whisper something. Though he did not hear her, Anya did.

'Sweetdream-sire,' said Kalisha, then she left. The words, though broken, were quite distinct. How had the Princess picked the words up – especially these words? Then Anya saw that the gold snake had been taken. She looked at the Prince, who still slept, and her eyes grew wide – around his neck now was Kalisha's gold necklace bearing the jewelled sword. She knew then that it was time for them to leave.

She turned him, smoothed her hands upon his chest, then touched his sex, rubbing it gently. When it was fully awake, she whispered softly: 'Did I hurt you more than she did, Sire?'

'More than who did?' he replied.

'The Princess. Your Kalisha.' Anya lifted the jewelled sword hanging round his neck and the Prince's colour drained. 'She did this?' said Anya. She touched the score marks still visible below the shallower red bands in his skin. He did not answer. 'When you spent the night with her?' she ventured. And the Prince of Lidir looked away, from shame. Anya gave him one last chance:

'Did she take you to the clearing?' she nipped the scored flesh gently.

'The clearing? What is that?'

'You do not know, Sire?' The force of the nipping gradually increased.

'No.'

Anya set her chin. 'Then I shall arrange it that my lord finds out.'

The Prince pursed his lips; he glanced down again at the necklet, then took it off and placed it well away from him at the far side of the bed. Anya smiled. She made him sit back on his heels. She gathered the burgeoning weight of his flesh into the soft brushed velvet cloth. Two fingers pushed into her mouth and came out thickly wetted. 'Lift, Sire. There . . .' And when he murmured, Anya whispered: 'No, do not close your eyes, Sire. Look at me.' He gasped; he looked into her olive eyes. 'Keep your eyes fixed only upon mine.' He groaned; her hands moved gently. 'Shhh . . . Keep it close; keep it near,' she whispered cruelly. Her tongue stretched out, licked upon his upper lip and lifted it. She bit; her sweet lips sucked; her fingertips sought the pulsing vein inside him and his pleasure yielded to the velvet.

That final hour before departure, they spent upon the sun-warmed sand. Anya sifted it through her fingers, making patterns – spires of soft dream castles. Then she painted the shapes that made her name, the ones her Prince had taught her long ago. It set her thinking.

'My lord?'

'My love?'

'When we are married, Sire . . .'

'Yes, my darling?' He took her hand in his.

'When we are married, my lord . . .' But she faltered.

'Anya – what is it? You know that you can ask me anything.'

Her fingertip stirred the sand. Then Anya looked straight at him. 'My Prince, when we are married – will you tell me, then, your name?'

He dived for her and missed. Anya jumped up, kicked the sand and ran. He dived again; his hand snaked out and caught her ankle, and he did not let her go. For in her face was the tenderness of abiding love and, upon her cheeks, the warmth of shy desire. But when she looked up – in the split second before she kicked him – he saw the firebrands of passion that were burning in her eyes.

HELP US TO PLAN THE FUTURE OF EROTIC FICTION –

– and no stamp required!

The Nexus Library is Britain's largest and fastest-growing collection of erotic fiction. We'd like your help to make it even bigger and better.

Like many of our books, the questionnaire below is completely anonymous, so don't feel shy about telling us what you really think. We want to know what kind of people our readers are – we want to know what you like about Nexus books, what you dislike, and what changes you'd like to see.

Just answer the questions on the following pages in the spaces provided; if more than one person would like to take part, please feel free to photocopy the questionnaire. Then tear the pages from the book and send them in an envelope to the address at the end of the questionnaire. No stamp is required.

THE NEXUS QUESTIONNAIRE

SECTION ONE: ABOUT YOU

1.1 Sex *(yes, of course, but try to be serious for just a moment)*
Male ☐ Female ☐

1.2 Age
under 21 ☐ 21 – 30 ☐
31 – 40 ☐ 41 – 50 ☐
51 – 60 ☐ over 60 ☐

1.3 At what age did you leave full-time education?
still in education ☐ 16 or younger ☐
17 – 19 ☐ 20 or older ☐

1.4 Occupation _____

1.5 Annual household income
under £10,000 ☐ £10–£20,000 ☐
£20–£30,000 ☐ £30–£40,000 ☐
over £40,000 ☐

1.6   Where do you live?
       Please write in the county in which you live (for example
       Hampshire), or the city if you live in a large metropolitan
       area (for example Manchester) _____

SECTION TWO : ABOUT BUYING NEXUS BOOKS

2.1   How did you acquire this book?
              I bought it myself   ☐   My partner bought it ☐
              I borrowed it/found it ☐

2.2   If this book was bought ...
              ... in which town or city?   _____
              ... in what sort of shop: High Street bookshop ☐
                                              local newsagent   ☐
                                              at a railway station ☐
                                              at an airport   ☐
                                              at motorway services ☐
                                  other: _____

2.3   Have you ever had difficulty finding Nexus books on sale?
              Yes   ☐   No   ☐
       If you have had difficulty in buying Nexus books, where
       would you like to be able to buy them?
              ... in which town or city   _____
              ... in what sort of shop from
                  list in previous question _____

2.4   Have you ever been reluctant to buy a Nexus book because
       of the sexual nature of the cover picture?
              Yes   ☐   No   ☐

2.5   Please tick which of the following statements you agree with:
              I find some Nexus cover pictures offensive/
                  too blatant   ☐

              I would be less embarassed about buying Nexus
                  books if the cover pictures were less blatant   ☐

              I think that in general the pictures on Nexus books
                  are about right   ☐

              I think Nexus cover pictures should be as sexy
                  as possible   ☐